The Story of Charlie Mullins

The Man in the Middle

by

Jim Wygand

CCB Publishing
British Columbia, Canada

The Story of Charlie Mullins: The Man in the Middle

Copyright ©2010 by Jim Wygand
ISBN-13 978-1-926585-97-0
First Edition

Library and Archives Canada Cataloguing in Publication

Wygand, Jim, 1942-
The story of Charlie Mullins : the man in the middle /
written by Jim Wygand – 1st ed.
ISBN 978-1-926585-97-0
I. Title.
PS3623.Y43S86 2010   813'.6   C2010-904141-0

Original cover art design by Jinger Heaston: www.jingraphix.org

Publisher: CCB Publishing
             British Columbia, Canada
             www.ccbpublishing.com

To my granddaughters Rachael and Antonia,
my sons and their wives, and my step-children,
and especially to my own "Gina" (you know who you are!)

I love you all, deeply.

I

"Mullins! Don't forget, I want those financial reports by Thursday!" Fred Perkins always barked his orders and everybody at the Shaw Corporation except Charlie Mullins lived in mortal fear of the terrible-tempered vice-president and treasurer.

"They're already finished, Fred. You want 'em now or shall I send them to your office?"

"I'll send Laura around. I've got a meeting now." Perkins snapped.

"OK Fred. As you wish."

Perkins stalked off, his mood now even fouler than before. Charlie Mullins got him ruffled. He was the only one who dared to call Perkins by his first name. Everyone else at Shaw called him Mister Perkins and did so with trepidation. Every time Charlie used his first name, Perkins felt an adrenaline rush and he could almost feel the sharp rise in his stomach acid level. It was Perkins' habit to always refer to subordinates by their last name and he always barked it. Charlie always seemed to be ready for him and his demands and always with what Perkins thought was a slight tone of mockery in his voice. He felt like every time he dealt with Charlie his power suffered an imperceptible reduction.

Fred Perkins was the quintessential sycophant. The irascible vice-president recognized only two kinds of people in the world – those below him and those above him. The former he bullied with his tirades and foul humor. The latter he treated with servile deference. Employees lived in mortal fear of Perkins' tirades. He would berate, insult, humiliate, and reduce the unfortunate object of his wrath to a quivering mass. But Charlie Mullins never rattled. Because Charlie was not intimidated by Perkins the latter was always reluctant to bully him and that drove Perkins nuts. The minute Perkins would raise his voice, Charlie would simply say, "I can hear you Fred." and Perkins would lower his voice to his normal bark.

Charlie leaned back in his chair and watched Perkins stomp away in the direction of his own office, even though he said he was going to a meeting. He smiled inwardly. He knew that he ruffled Perkins' feathers and he enjoyed it but he knew that it was not Perkins who would pay the consequences. The bastard would take his anger out on his longsuffering personal assistant, Laura.

Charlie let Laura enter his thoughts for a moment. He liked and felt sorry for her. She was divorced and had a son in college. She couldn't afford to leave the Shaw Corporation because there just were not that many jobs in South Jersey where she could earn the same salary. She did her best to placate Perkins but it seemed that the harder she tried, the nastier he got.

Charlie snapped out of his short daydream to see several of his colleagues and subordinates staring at him. They all marveled at the way he handled Perkins.

As Charlie looked around at his fellow workers they immediately started lowering their heads into their work. Later they would comment to each other about how, once again, Charlie Mullins had moved Fred Perkins one step closer to a stroke.

Charlie spun his chair to face the window and looked out across the Delaware River to Shoreville, his home town. If he squinted his eyes, he could see the outline of the houses where many of the workers of the Shaw Corporation lived. In spite of his executive job, Charlie still lived in Shoreville. He never moved across the river to Wilmington where most of the company's management lived. He had been born in Shoreville, went to school there, and most of his friends lived there.

"Charlie?" his reverie was broken by Laura Metzer, Perkins' personal assistant. When he spun around he noticed that her eyes were red and puffy. She was trying hard to hold back the tears.

"Hey Laura. You OK?"

"I'm fine Charlie. He's a terror today. He just jumped down my throat because I had some pencils spread out on my desk. He told me I was sloppy and my desk looked like hell. Well, you know the routine."

"Aw hell, I'm sorry Laura. I probably set him off by calling him 'Fred' again."

Laura managed a wry smile. "He *hates* that, you know. He'll never admit it, but he really hates it. You're the only person in this whole department who doesn't bow and scrape to him and it almost kills him. What's your secret Charlie? If anybody else did what you do they'd be out of here before Personnel even had time to fill out a pink slip."

Charlie smiled, more to himself than to Laura, "I dunno Laura. I guess it's just because I have been with the company for 10 years and my father worked here for over 30. A lot of senior people here knew my father and liked him. Maybe Fred thinks I have some sort of leverage with someone above him. Then again, maybe I just have a sixth sense for knowing what he wants before he wants it."

"Well whatever it is, Charlie Mullins, you sure keep him off balance. And I'm the one who pays for it." She shrugged and then added, "Well, I guess it is just worth it to know that someone can stand up to him. He's just so nasty to people."

Charlie smiled again, this time at Laura. "I'm sorry for that, Laura. I really am. You know, in spite of his attitude and the way he treats people, he *is* a pretty good professional."

"Yeah, I know" Laura answered, "I just wish he could control himself a little more. Anyway, I guess you know I am here to pick up the financial reports."

"Right here, Laura." Charlie handed her the papers.

"Well, thanks for listening Charlie. I guess I better get back before he comes looking for me."

"No sweat, Laura. Keep cool. By the way, how's your son?"

"A mother's pride Charlie! Straight A's. He's a good kid!"

"You don't have to tell me that. He's got a good mother. Hang in there Laura. Don't let Fred grind you down."

"Thanks, Charlie and thanks for asking about Billy."

As Laura Metzer headed back down the hall to her desk Charlie thought to himself that Fred Perkins would probably love to fire him if only he could find a cause. Charlie was methodical and organized. He was always a step ahead of Perkins and it amused him that others thought he had some sort of sixth sense about what Perkins would demand next.

But Charlie knew that people like Perkins were not hard to figure out. They were bullies. He'd seen them in the Army, in college, and in corporations. The minute they thought you were intimidated they puffed up and started bellowing even louder. The more you quaked, the more they bullied. All you really had to do was relax and look them straight in the eye. When you did that, they usually lowered their voice and backed off.

Charlie remembered the one and only time that Perkins had lit into him. It had been shortly after Charlie had joined the company and the incident involved Perkins' demand for some report. When Perkins began his tirade, Charlie relaxed his body and stared directly into Perkins' eyes with a glare that told Perkins that there might be something cold and steely behind it, and that it might not be wise to try to find out. He said, "I can hear you, Fred." By the time Perkins got his third word out of his mouth, he was speaking in his normal "bark". Charlie gave Perkins a friendly smile which said "That's better, Fred" and he replied in a calm and steady voice, "I'll have that report for you by the end of the day, Fred."

Perkins was perplexed. Charlie had not challenged his authority, just his authoritarianism. He acquiesced with his dignity intact and Perkins was not sure what to do, so he did nothing. But after that incident, he never again tried to bully Charlie and Charlie never gave him the opportunity to do so. It was a standoff. And Perkins *hated* standoffs. There was no room in his psyche for equals. His world was populated only by superiors and subordinates, the latter being treated with sadistic cruelty. Charlie was not his superior and he refused to accept the treatment Perkins reserved for subordinates. It made Perkins furious.

Charlie leaned into his work. He had a lot to do and he planned to go up to Philly over the weekend. He was not going to let his work back up and move into his personal time.

II

_____

The only thing people in Shoreville thought strange about Charlie Mullins was that they never saw him around town on weekends except for a few hours on Saturday when he went to softball practice with his friends. It was a small town and everybody there either worked for the Shaw Corporation or one of its suppliers. A few people worked in the small chemical factories and oil refineries in the area, but Shaw was by far the largest employer in the small South Jersey town.

Charlie knew practically everyone in Shoreville and because he was a first assistant treasurer at Shaw and had lived there all his life, everyone knew him. The fact that he stayed in Shoreville after ascending the corporate ladder endeared him to the locals. And, of course, everyone had known his parents.

The Shaw Corporation sponsored bowling leagues, softball teams, theater groups, concerts and other cultural activities in Shoreville and during the week Charlie could be seen at most company-sponsored events. He bowled with his old high school buddies and played softball with company employees in the warm summer evenings. But, on weekends, Charlie Mullins was nowhere to be seen.

A lot of people in Shoreville thought it was the divorce. When Charlie came back from his tour in the Army, he resumed dating and then married his high-school sweetheart, Mary Jo Mannix. Like most marriages in Shoreville, it was what was expected: local boy returns, resumes romance with his old sweetheart, marries her. They eventually have kids, join the Little League, PTA, and so it goes.

However, Mary Jo had ambitions which she one day concluded she would not satisfy in her marriage to Charlie. She wanted to live in a high-mortgage neighborhood in Wilmington, not in Shoreville. Charlie was perfectly content to stay where he was comfortable and did not like the idea of living in some expensive digs around a bunch of people he did not know and really did not care about.

Early on in the marriage Mary Jo tried to get Charlie's career on what she thought was the "right track". She would tell Charlie that he was far too complacent and that he should be more concerned about his future at Shaw. She suggested that they consider selling their house and moving to a "better neighborhood". She would point across the river to Wilmington and say, "*There* is where we have to live, Charlie. You'll be around people who can help your career. We can get involved in community affairs and mix with the 'right people'."

Charlie endured her entreaties with patience but told her clearly, "Mary Jo, those people *live* the company day in and day out. I don't want to live that way. I'm perfectly content right here in Shoreville where we are around friends. I don't want to be going out for drinks, dinner, and theater with someone just because they can get me promoted."

But Mary Jo was relentless and in the second year of their marriage she left Charlie to marry a lawyer in Wilmington. She crossed the Delaware to conquer her space with the "right people". There were no children and Charlie was left with the mortgage.

Charlie was both surprised and not surprised. He was surprised and hurt that Mary Jo would have treated him that way and subjected him to public humiliation but he was not surprised that she left. Her ambition was just too great. Charlie always suspected that she would be vulnerable to some smooth character who would promise the world to Mary Jo. Her ambition would cloud her reason, and she would fall. She had no patience with Charlie's calm approach to life. He was sure that she was in for a lot of disappointment in life but could not convince her. When Mary Jo got pregnant by her second husband, he left her high and dry. The last Charlie had heard of Mary Jo, she had moved somewhere "out west".

Charlie endured the initial outpourings of sympathy from those in Shoreville who were indignant at Mary Jo's behavior. He tolerated the avalanche of "serves-her-right" comments that surfaced when the word got out that Mary Jo had been left by her second husband. He was no longer angry at Mary Jo. In fact, he felt sorry for her. But he just shrugged his shoulders and smiled when others blasted away at her.

Then, stoically, he put up with all the attempts to get him married again. He took to leaving town on weekends to escape the numerous dinner invitations to meet the lone female guest that had been invited for his sake.

What began as weekend escapes soon turned into weekend forays as Charlie reaped the advantages of a social life outside Shoreville. He looked up some of his old friends from La Salle College in Philly. Sometimes he would head down to the casinos in Atlantic City, or spend a quiet weekend in Cape May. In all the places he went, he could relax and be away from people that he saw all week, at work, at the grocery store, at company-sponsored events, at church and so on. His professional life was public knowledge as was everyone else's in Shoreville, but unlike his neighbors, his private life was absolutely private. He intended to keep it that way.

Charlie Mullins liked beautiful women. He liked intelligent women. And he certainly liked the creature comforts that money bought. But most of all Charlie Mullins liked power. And power to Charlie Mullins meant being in charge of your own life. His very private social life was a form of power in tiny Shoreville.

He once commented to a friend, "You know, the first loss of power comes when you lose your privacy. When you join the Army, what's the first thing they do to keep you under control? They take away your privacy. They put you in a barracks with 40 other guys. You have open closets and only a footlocker which an officer will open every week. Prisoners have no privacy so they have no power. Look at college students – put 'em in a dorm, no privacy. Makes it easier to handle them. The same thing happens in companies. Take those office partitions for example. They never go all the way to the ceiling. No private office, no power. No private conversations, no power. Got it? Take my word for it, the first step in acquiring power is to make sure you have privacy." Charlie never abandoned that view.

Consistent with his view regarding privacy and power, Charlie tried to make sure that folks in Shoreville knew nothing of his ambitions, personal views, and personal life. Even as a child he had always been known as a bit of a "loner". He was a quiet, observant kid who took in everything around him. But if you asked anyone what Charlie Mullins thought, they would probably begin their answer by saying, "Well, I don't really know, but I would guess that….."

As to his "lost weekends", a lot of people in Shoreville were quick to attribute them to grief, anger, and embarrassment over the divorce. More than one resident had been known to comment, "Poor Charlie Mullins, ever since that bitch left him he's just disappeared. Guy's got no social life at all. He shows up alone at company functions and goes home alone when they're over. Damned shame is what it is!"

Charlie paid more attention to what was said about him than the residents of Shoreville suspected. Although many accepted Charlie's strange-for-Shoreville lifestyle and chalked it off to idiosyncrasy and hurt feelings, some were intrigued by *any* form of behavior that deviated from the Shoreville norm and took to watching Charlie and commenting about him.

This latter group concerned him. They were busybodies who would eventually try to invade his privacy if only to certify that he was "normal" by Shoreville's standards. Charlie didn't want people prying into his life.

He showed up at company-sponsored functions so he could hear from friends and associates what was being said about him.

III

Every year the Shaw Corporation sponsored an Easter Party at a local national park in Shoreville. The park was a former World War II military installation along the shores of the Delaware River. It had been converted to a national park after the war. There were picnic tables in abundance and lots of room for the kids to run. The party was for the community of Shoreville, not just Shaw employees. There were Easter egg hunts and games for the kids. Everyone in Shoreville who worked for Shaw and a great many of those who didn't, always showed up for the event. That and the Christmas party were the two big social events that the company sponsored that everyone truly enjoyed.

Even though he had no children and both parties were always scheduled for a Saturday, Charlie never missed the events. He liked to watch the kids play and he could talk to the adults in a relaxed atmosphere.

One of the first persons he saw at the Easter Party was Ben Hopkins, a marketing manager at Shaw. Hopkins came striding straight toward Charlie, "Chaarlie! How ya been, buddy?"

"Fine Ben, how 'bout yourself?"

"Doin' all right Charlie, all right. Haven't seen you around in a while Charlie."

."C'mon Ben, you saw me in the cafeteria in Wilmington just yesterday."

"Oh yeah, the marketing meeting. No, but what I mean Charlie is I haven't seen you around town. You know."

"You're looking at me right now, Ben and we are, as you say, 'around town', aren't we?"

"Of course, Charlie but you know what I mean. C'mon we went to school together ever since third grade. I mean, well, you know, I haven't seen you at the Royal Bar, Jimmy Balsamo's joint, dating any of the available broads, you know, that kind of 'around town'. Jeez Charlie you were always a popular guy with the ladies in school and bein' single and all, I just figured...."

"I know what you figured, Ben" Charlie replied amiably, "I'm still a popular guy with the ladies, don't worry. But you know as well as I do that every woman in this town knows every other woman and all of them knew Mary Jo. Why in the hell would I want to go out with somebody who is going to sit there all night telling me what a bitch Mary Jo was for leaving me? Shoreville is already small enough. It's even smaller for a bachelor. What if I went to bed with one of the local women, Ben? We both know that the next day the whole damned town would know it. They'd be hearing wedding bells. 'Charlie's finally found somebody!' You know it's true."

"I guess you're right Charlie. I hadn't thought about that side of it. I'm not trying to pry, you understand. It's just that, well, folks around like you Charlie. They like being with you."

"Right!" thought Charlie, *"that's why you must have called me at least twice in the past ten years!"*

"No problem, Ben. It was good to run into you. Who knows, maybe I will show up at your house one of these weekends to join you and Sally for dinner?'

"Oh, ah, uh, yeah, good idea Charlie. Oh, I gotta go, Sally is calling for me. But, ah, Charlie, make sure you call. You know how fussy Sally is. If you showed up and she didn't have the very best on the table she'd be embarrassed."

Charlie noticed that Sally had her back turned to him and Ben. She would have found it difficult to call to him from that position. He smiled inwardly at Ben's discomfort. He imagined himself showing up at the Hopkins' door, "Hi, Ben. I thought I would take up your offer and show up for some overdue socializing." He let a small smile begin as he watched Ben fidgeting.

"Well, Charlie. Gotta be goin'. Sally's calling me. Wouldn't want her thinking we're hatching up some bachelor party now, would I?"

"God forbid, Ben. You better get going. Nice to see you again and say 'hi' to Sally for me."

"See ya, Charlie. Show up one of these days, OK?"

Ben took off in the direction of his wife who still had her back turned and was talking to one of her friends.

A few minutes later Charlie saw Ben talking animatedly to a group of people. He was telling them what he had just learned from Charlie. He was gesticulating and most certainly telling the group how he almost had to invite Charlie to dinner, how it appears that Charlie has girlfriends in other places, how Charlie wants to avoid getting hooked to just one local girl so he leaves them all alone, and so on. He knew he was the subject of the conversation because every once in a while someone in the group would glance at him as Ben was talking.

Charlie watched Ben and made a mental note of every person that he had been talking to in case he should come across them or Ben again soon.

After the Easter Party a small group of "Charlie Watchers" began to develop among some of the people Ben Hopkins had talked to. They started looking for Charlie whenever they went anywhere. Charlie noticed their attention during the week when he would show up at the bowling alley or at softball games. They would stare at him when he walked into the Royal Bar or into Jimmy Balsamo's restaurant. They would then start talking animatedly and every once in a while one or the other would glance over at Charlie. You didn't have to be a rocket scientist to figure that he was the topic of the conversation at the table.

At first, Charlie found the local surveillance amusing. He was going to the same places he had always gone during the week. The only thing that was unusual was the increased interest of others. However, he was concerned for that kind of curiosity with regard to his weekend behavior. That was his private time away from Shoreville and he did not want that time invaded and subject to the scrutiny of Shoreville's busybodies.

Some of the housewives in the "Charlie Watchers" group even looked for Charlie during weekday shopping trips to Wilmington at 11-o-clock in the morning when it was obvious that at that time of day he was in his office at the Shaw Corporation.

The group picked up on every "Charlie Sighting" report. Bill Gallagher thought he saw Charlie coming out of Bookbinder's Restaurant in Philly. Diane Simms said that a friend of hers told her in absolute confidence that she had seen Charlie Mullins on a Saturday night coming out of the chic Positano restaurant with a really attractive girl on his arm. "So help me God," Diane said, "she told me the girl did not look a day over 18!"

It wouldn't be long before people started swapping "Charlie Stories" and women would be trading information and speculations at the local beauty parlor.

Some of the rumors started making their way back to Charlie and he made it a practice to remember the name of the source whenever he could get it. Charlie wanted to make sure that he knew who was trying to invade his privacy and, even more important, to be sure that he really had *not* been seen where someone said they saw him. After all, he *had* been at the Positano and he had not been alone. He pretended to be amused by the surveillance, but he was not.

On at least two occasions, Charlie noticed what he was sure were Shoreville residents following him on the Interstate to Philly. Both times he got off the Interstate and did some evasive driving around the port city of Chester, and then headed back to the highway. He managed to shake his followers but not before noting the license plate of the car. If necessary he could check the plates with a friend in Philly who had contacts in the New Jersey DMV. But he didn't have to bother because on Monday morning he saw the car pulling out of the YMCA where a lot of Shoreville wives went to aerobic classes. He recognized Diane Simms in the passenger seat and Sharon Gallagher at the wheel.

"Jesus Christ!" he thought, *"two horny, nosy broads with nothing to do on a Saturday morning decide to follow me around. Shit! What a pain in the ass!"*

Charlie noticed that the rumors were getting back to him with increasing frequency, implying that more people were claiming to have seen him. The thing was snowballing. The small community of Shoreville had found something more interesting to talk about than bond issues for the school, property taxes, and who was screwing whose wife. The town had a mysterious bachelor. Imaginations ran rampant. It was said that Charlie secretly frequented porn shops in Philly. He was supposed to have been seen on weekend binges in bars in Chester. Someone said they had seen him in a gay bar in Philly. Just about anything and everything that someone could imagine a bachelor doing on a weekend was attributed to Charlie.

To many bachelors this kind of attention might even be welcome. Mystery adds to romance. An enterprising bachelor could play that kind of curiosity for all it was worth. Charlie Mullins was not the least bit amused. This was more than a minor irritation – it was a big damned problem.

Sooner or later it had to happen. Somebody who claimed to have seen Charlie really did see him. Someone had told Tony Mazza that they saw Charlie coming out of the Ritz-Carlton on Penn Square. The snitch told Tony that Charlie was with a beautiful brunette with "legs up to her neck!"

When Charlie showed up at the bowling alley one Wednesday night, Tony confronted him with the news. "Hey Charlie, you old dog! I heard you were seen around Philly with a real looker. You holdin' out on your old pals?

"What are you talking about, Tony?"

"C'mon, Charlie, somebody here in town saw you comin' out of the Ritz-Carlton Saturday night. He said you had a dame with you that would make Sharon Stone run for cover. That wasn't no local girl, no sir. They don't make 'em like that in Shoreville! You holdin' somethin' out on your old high-school buddies Charlie?"

"Who said it was me, Tony? What the hell would I be doin' with some broad who looked better than Sharon Stone, huh? Jesus, Tony, where would I meet somebody like that?"

"I don't know where you might meet someone like that, but somebody swears it was you. Maybe you could tell me where *I* could meet somebody like that!"

"Tony, I've been hearing a lot of rumors about people claiming they saw me in one place or another and sometimes two places at the same damned time. It's all bullshit, Tony. I don't even know how all this stuff got started. It's crazy! Who told you it was me, huh?"

"Oh hell, Charlie, it was Tommy Peterson. He said he was sure it was you and that he would never forget the woman you were with. C'mon Charlie, level with your old buddy. You got a new love in your life?"

Charlie wondered whether to try to brazen this one out or simply confess. Tommy Peterson had been his next-door neighbor when they were kids. He definitely knew what Charlie looked like and would not have mistaken someone else for him. Besides, he had been at the Ritz-Carlton on Saturday and he had been there with Gina. And Gina was everything that Tommy said she was. He decided that it was too risky to try to deny. Tommy probably did see him. He decided to take the hit.

"OK, Tony, you got me. Yeah, I was at the Ritz-Carlton Saturday. I was with a friend of mine."

"Yeah? Well based on what Tommy said that was some friend. He said nobody in this town ever saw anything like that except on a movie screen. Has she got a sister?"

"Tony, you know Tommy. He probably exaggerated. I mean it was a good-looking girl I was with, but Tommy's description sounds a bit over the top."

"Yeah, maybe so, but he did say that if he ever saw her again he would sure as hell know it was her. He said you don't forget a woman like that! C'mon Charlie, what's the score?"

"No score, Tony. I was just out with a nice looking lady. Is that a sin?"

"Hell no, Charlie, not for a good-lookin' bachelor like you. It's just that, well hell Charlie, you have become a kind of a game in this town."

Charlie felt a sudden discomfort. "Game, Tony? What kind of game have I become in this town? What's going on, Tony?"

"Aw hell, Charlie, you know. This town's so goddamned boring that when you got divorced everybody figured after a couple of years you'd be married to some other local girl. Well, it never happened. Then you started disappearin' on weekends. Everybody figures you're pissed or embarrassed, right? Goes on for another year. Now all of a sudden nobody sees you around in Shoreville on weekends, right? You go to softball practice on Saturday morning and then you disappear. Soooo, all the wives get to talking. 'Charlie's never gonna get married again.', 'Didn't Charlie like Evelyn Patterson? He never called her back after the Durkens invited them both to dinner.' You know what I'm talking about, Charlie. You know the kind of trash people talk around here. All of a sudden the thing got blown out of proportion. People started betting…"

"Betting?" Charlie almost shouted it. "Betting on what, Tony? Wait a minute. Let's go down to Jimmy Balsamo's place and have a drink. This sounds like a long and complicated story."

They walked down Broad Street to Jimmy Balsamo's bar and restaurant and got a booth. Tony started his story.

"It's like this Charlie, you're kind of a celebrity in Shoreville. At least people made you one. Hell, the last time anything exciting happened here was when Frankie Phillips tried to shoot off Tommy Porter's prick because Tommy was screwing his wife. People talked about that for years."

"Yeah, I remember, but keep going, Tony. How did all this get started?"

"It's like I told you. Folks thought you would get married after a while. When you didn't they tried to fix you up. When that didn't work everybody kind of forgot about it for a while. You started disappearing on weekends and most people figured you had a gal stashed away. But then you still didn't get married. Fact is, for a while people even forgot about you. But then one day, aw, I forget who it was, said they saw you coming out of an Italian restaurant in South Philly. They said you were with some really great looking broad. That started people talking again. Then there's all those company affairs, art shows, concerts, you know, and you still show up alone and go home alone. You take off on weekends, and you still don't show up with a woman."

"Well, so what, Tony? I mean it's not like I *have* to, right? I mean, hell, everybody knows I'm normal. Everybody knows I'm not gay. What's the big deal?"

"If you lived in a bigger town, Charlie, it wouldn't be a big deal at all. But this is Shoreville. You aren't the most eligible, mature, good-looking bachelor in this town. You're the *only* eligible, mature, good-looking bachelor in this town. See what I mean, Charlie? Every divorced woman, every unhappily married woman, and every woman with hot pants is talking about you. The thing just kind of snowballed. Hell, it even got to the point that Sharon Gallagher said she was going to follow you to Philly one of these days. I heard that she did but lost you around Chester. In fact, I think that's how the drinking rumor got started."

"DRINKING rumor?! Tony, what the hell are you talking about?"

"Well, I think it started with Sharon. When she lost you in Chester she figured you were doing something in Chester. What do you do in a town with nothing but docks and cheap bars? You drink, I guess. I guess Sharon just figured that was what you were doing there and you know how it is. Something starts along the chain as speculation and ends up as fact."

"Jeez, Tony, did you buy that story? How long have you known me?"

"No, Charlie, I didn't believe it and I even said so to people who asked me about it. I've known you since grammar school and drinking alone in sleazy bars is not your style. In fact, I don't think you even drink much at all to be honest. But who the hell goes to Chester on a Saturday morning, Charlie?"

"Who the hell *cares*, Tony?"

"Yeah, I know, but don't take it out on me, Charlie. I didn't do anything, so help me. Like I said, you just started being a hot topic around town and then people started guessing about your life. It didn't take much for gossip to become fact when some people started saying they saw you with a gal who looked like a movie star. I mean, that's how peoples' minds work in a town like this. People start living other people's lives and building fantasies. You know that. Hell, you make good money, you live modestly so you probably have a big stash, you're free, and you're young and good-looking. Jeez, Charlie, are you surprised that you would be the subject of a lot of crap?"

"Nah, I guess not, Tony, but please do me a favor."

"Yeah, what's that?"

"Next time you hear that kind of nonsense, just tell people that my life is none of their damned business. Will you do that for me, Tony? I don't need this kind of stuff. There is nothing going on in my life that is worth all that conversation and speculation. I'm just a single guy, who was seen dating a good-looking woman in Philly. I'm not breaking any laws, not putting the make on anybody's wife. I mean when you think about it, I am not doing anything at all unusual or weird, right? I'm just not discussing or showing off my private life to Shoreville! There's no big secret out there, Tony."

"I've done that already, Charlie. But I'll be glad to continue doing it. You're right. Those women would do far better to just take care of their own business and not worry about yours. And some of the guys are no better. But you know that this town has no secrets and when people think you have some kind of secret life, they start getting nosey and stupid. It's even worse when you are a well-to-do eligible bachelor in a small town."

"Yeah, OK Tony, I know what you mean. Just do what you can to try to put a stop to this shit, OK? It's inconvenient as hell and it's my private life that when you analyze it is nothing terribly special. So, if you hear anything else just ask whoever is talking to you why they give a damn about Charlie Mullins' personal life. Just tell 'em you're my friend and you are sure I don't like it."

"Will do, Charlie, how about one for the road?"

"Fine Tony, and thanks!"

They ordered another round, reminisced about old times and eventually laughed about the whole silly affair. But Charlie Mullins was not amused. He walked back to his car and drove slowly home.

IV

"Shit! I wasn't ready for this" Charlie thought as he drove home *"talk about nuts! The whole damned town betting on and talking about my life and I don't have the slightest idea how to stop it!"* That wasn't the kind of power Charlie wanted. He didn't want a whole town talking about him and whether he had a girlfriend or not. He imagined people talking about him at the Rotary Club, and Lion's Club meetings and in beauty shops. This was a mess and Charlie Mullins was worried.

The next morning Charlie had a meeting at the auditing firm of Wexler and Santori in Camden. The firm had been the external auditors of the Shaw Corporation ever since the company had been founded. It grew with the Shaw Corporation as it mushroomed from a small equipment repair shop to its current status as a major multinational. A few times it had been suggested to Phillip Shaw II, the son of Shaw's founder, that the company use a more prestigious auditing firm – one of the big ones. "Junior" as Phillip was called by the older employees at Shaw, said he had no objection to hiring one of the big auditing firms if someone could give him a good reason for doing so. He said he saw no reason for dropping Wexler and Santori simply because they were a local firm. Besides, they knew the company inside and out in a way that no new auditing firm possibly could and he saw no reason to pay higher fees just because the new auditors were "prestigious". Since no one was ever able to offer a good reason to change, Wexler and Santori continued to audit Shaw's books, file its tax returns, and provide support to Charlie's department.

Charlie knew all of the auditors at Wexler and Santori on a first name basis. Many had been at the firm for as long as Charlie had been at Shaw.

Shaw Corporation was a closely held family-owned company. It was professionally managed and only one family member, Phillip II, worked for the company. There were no outside shareholders, the company had no debt and was flush with cash so preparing the audit report was more an internal affair than a public matter. The annual report was sent only to family members, the local banks, some local and a couple of national newspapers, and was, of course, available to the tax authorities should they wish to inspect. Shaw was the darling and the target of the banking community. Every bank in the country wanted to loan money to the cash-rich company. Every investment bank salivated at the prospect of underwriting a public stock issue by Shaw. Initial public offerings, IPOs, offered enormous opportunities for helping "friends" of the bankers. If you do it right, the regulatory authorities are none the wiser and everybody makes out. To the chagrin of the bankers, Phillip Shaw and the members of his family were not interested in going public – at least not at this time. Phillip was still young and while probably the last Shaw who would run the company, the family could wait until he retired before considering a public offering. That might be a good twenty years from now.

Charlie left home earlier than usual to allow himself time to evade any surveillance from what he now referred to as "The Crazy Ladies of Shoreville". If necessary he would double back on his route to see if anyone was following him. He cursed under his breath at the inconvenience this was causing but he had to protect his privacy and "The Crazy Ladies of Shoreville" had made it necessary for him to be more vigilant. Charlie decided to take the New Jersey Turnpike to Camden. There were two service areas along the route where he could stop to see if he was being followed and anyone from Shoreville trying to pick him up en route would probably expect him to use Interstate 95 as he usually did.

The usual 30 minute ride to Camden took almost an hour as Charlie stopped along his route and then took a few evasive maneuvers when he got off at exit #4 and headed toward Camden. He was satisfied that he was not being followed. He pulled into Wexler & Santori's lot and entered the building.

Phyllis Collins, the receptionist, was at her usual post. "Hello, Mr. Mullins, it's good to see you. You're here to see Mr. Cummins, right?"

"Yes, thanks Phyllis. How's the family? Boys OK?"

"Oh yeah, Mr. Mullins. They're doing just fine. Thanks. Just a second and I'll buzz Mr. Cummins."

Phyllis told Bill Cummins that Charlie had arrived and was on the way up to his office. Charlie walked to the elevator, "Thanks, Phyllis, see ya on the way out!"

Bill Cummins was a senior partner in the Wexler & Santori firm and was Charlie's principal liaison. Charlie liked Bill – he was competent and steady.

Cummins' secretary was waiting and showed him into his office. "Charlie, good to see you. How was the traffic on the way up?"

"Same as usual, Bill, how are you doing?"

"Fine, thanks. Have a seat. I received the reports the other day. Fred Perkins sent them over."

"He signed off on them?"

"Yeah, Charlie, I know it must kill him to not find any errors or things to question. He initialed everything, as usual. Sometimes I think he should just initial with a swastika – everybody would know it was him anyway."

Charlie let a wry smile cross his face but he said nothing. He did not like to encourage comments about others in the company, even among friends.

"OK, Bill, let's go through the documents and see if you have any questions or changes you think should be made."

In spite of the fact that Perkins had signed off on all of the reports, Charlie liked to follow up to make sure nothing had been missed. Perkins would like nothing better than to let some error slip through that he could later blame on Charlie to make him look bad with senior management. He would give Charlie one of those "what-are-you-trying to-do-to me?" lectures. Charlie had seen those lectures with other employees. Fred would accuse the object of his wrath of trying to embarrass him with senior management by purposely overlooking an error in the report. He would rant that the employee was bucking for promotion at his expense and then go into his "who-do-you-think-you-are-anyway?" spiel, finishing with a scathing comment about how presumptuous and stupid the employee must be.

So, Charlie would make sure that once Fred Perkins had signed off, he would double check with Bill Cummins to make sure all was in order.

"Let's go through the reports. You want some coffee?"

"Sure Bill, coffee's fine."

Cummins pushed the intercom button on his desk, "Myrna, would you be good enough to order some coffee for me and Mr. Mullins, please?"

"Yes sir, Mr. Cummins." In a couple of minutes a white-jacketed kitchen employee entered the office with a hot pot of coffee and two porcelain china cups, matching sugar bowl and creamer with real cream. He served Charlie and Cummins and then departed as discreetly as he had entered. This was the service reserved for long-standing and well-regarded clients at Wexler & Santori. Those dealing with the junior auditors got their coffee from the Mr. Coffee coffee makers that were scattered around the labyrinth of small offices on the second floor. They drank it in Styrofoam cups and used powdered creamer.

Cummins went to his large and expensive walnut desk and picked up a file folder marked "SHAW-2nd QTR CURRENT YEAR".

"Here we are, Charlie. Everything is in order. I did make a couple of adjustments on the taxes payable calculation because you had a carry-forward from last quarter. It was nothing major, but why give the government more than it deserves, right?"

"OK, Bill, let me see the adjustments." Charlie went through the changes in the report making sure to initial the changes he saw. "It looks good, Bill. Go ahead and consolidate and send me the statements."

"Done, Charlie, by the way, Phil Shaw was in here last week. Seems some more investment bankers were after him to go public. Any news in that area?"

"Nah. You know those guys, always looking for a deal. Phillip Shaw is not about to give up family control of this company until he is good and ready. He's got no reason to. The company is flush with cash. Profits are good. If he went public now, some sharks would smell blood and try a takeover just to get their hands on that money. I'll bet that before he does anything he will take a couple of poison pills first. He'll pay out some dividends, take out some loans, and only then go public. He won't want to see the company dismembered for its cash. Shaw is one of the few companies left that still has a reputation for being loyal to its employees and won't see them put out of their jobs by some Wall Street sharks!"

"Yeah, it's not like he needs the money either!" Cummins laughed.

"That's for damned sure. Old man Shaw worked damned hard to build this company and he's now got the assets to prove it!"

"Hey Charlie, did you ever think about getting up close to one of the available Shaw sisters? They're not bad looking and Cecilia Shaw is divorced and they say she is looking around! You're a good looking bachelor guy. Why not make a pitch?"

"You gotta be kidding, Bill! You know the saying; 'When you marry for money you *really* earn it'? I can't run with that crowd! Weekends in Bermuda, polo ponies, soirees in Washington and New York, private jets and all that. That's way out of my league Bill. Besides, I suspect that the crowd she runs with would be more than just a bit boring for me. Not my type. I can handle a softball game in Shoreville, but I don't think I could handle a polo match in the Hamptons!"

"Yeah, I guess you're right Charlie. That is a fast crowd. Listen, you want to stay for lunch? I can have the kitchen fix something up if you want to stay around for a while."

"No, thanks anyway Bill, I've got some stuff I have to do before I go back to the office. I'd better get going. Will you send me the copies of the changed reports for my files?"

"Sure, Charlie. They'll go out in the afternoon pouch. You'll have them by end-of-business today. Good to see you again. Drive carefully."

Charlie took his leave and headed out to the parking lot. He looked around to see if any of "The Crazy Ladies of Shoreville" were parked nearby. When he was certain that he was not being watched or followed, he got into his car and left the Wexler & Santori parking lot and headed for the Ben Franklin bridge and into Philly. He would stop by Gina's place before going to the office.

V

Gina Ferrelli and Charlie first met after his divorce. He had looked up some of his old college-day friends in Philly and one evening while he and Joey Esposito were having dinner in a small South Philly *trattoria* that neither had been to before, Gina walked in with a group of friends. One of Gina's friends worked with Joey and the group joined Joey and Charlie at the table.

Charlie and Gina hit it off immediately. She had an easy laugh and a relaxed way about her that Charlie found captivating. She was beautiful and sexy as hell but she did not flaunt it. She seemed almost unaware of or perhaps didn't care about her effect on men – which was considerable to say the least. She possessed the kind of beauty and bearing that causes a restaurant to suddenly get quiet when she walks in as the patrons wonder what movie they had seen her in. She carried herself like the model she could easily have been if she wanted, and her smile was quick and natural. She was a beautiful woman who was comfortable with herself.

When the evening ended, Charlie asked if she came often to the *trattoria* and she said it was one of her favorite places and she and her friends often stopped in for a glass of wine. Reluctant to ask for her phone number after just meeting her, Charlie said "Great, I'd never been here before. It's really a great place and I hope I see you here again."

To his surprise, Gina said "Why don't you stop by this Saturday night? My friends and I will probably be dropping in about 9-o-clock."

Charlie could hardly wait until Saturday night to go back to the *trattoria* and hope that Gina would show up. She did. It was just a little before 9:15 when Gina walked in with a couple and a female friend. She saw Charlie and waved him over to her table. It was all he could do to keep from running to the table.

"Hello, Charlie, why don't you join us? It's nice to see you here again."

"Thank you, Gina. Since you said you would be here tonight, I thought I would stop by. I really did enjoy meeting you last week."

"Why, thank you Charlie. That's nice and quite charming. It's also nice to know you would drive up from Jersey just to see me again."

"Is she nuts or just toying with me?" Charlie thought, *"I'd drive from Alaska in a blizzard just to get a glance at her. God knows what I would do to be with her for an hour or two!"*

For the first time in his life Charlie was flustered. He could think of nothing to say but, "Well, I enjoyed myself so much last week that I thought I would treat myself to a repeat."

Charlie noticed that as soon as Gina had suggested he join her table a waiter was immediately standing nearby with a chair. He mused to himself that beautiful women must always get that kind of attention. Waiters, doormen, taxi drivers, traffic cops, department store clerks, hell, any male of the species will go out of his way to be helpful to a beautiful woman. He couldn't decide if he thought such deference would be welcome or discomfiting to someone like Gina. Charlie noticed that she thanked the waiter by his first name and did not take such deference for granted.

The evening was a pleasant one. Gina's friends were interesting and conversational and not at all part of the "fast crowd" that Mary Jo had wanted to run with. The lone female was a psychologist with a small clinical practice in Philly and the couple was part of Philly's growing artist community that lived in the area known as "So-So" at the far end of South Philly.

Once again Charlie had one of the most relaxing and enjoyable evenings he could remember. The conversation flowed. There was no posturing or phoniness. Nobody was trying to prove anything to anybody else. Charlie could hardly wait for another evening like this one.

However, he was still reluctant to ask Gina for a date or for her telephone number. He was sure that a woman as beautiful as she was constantly being hit on and he did not want her to think he was just one more of the many that probably had tried to get her into bed. Not that Charlie thought that would not be an interesting proposition. He just found her so captivating and fun that he was reluctant to risk seeming to come on too strong. When the evening ended, Charlie once again asked Gina if she would be showing up at the *trattoria* again the following week. She smiled and said, "Well, if you are going to be here, I'll make it a point to show up."

"Deal!" said Charlie, not believing what he had just heard, "See you then, about the same time?"

"OK" said Gina "drive carefully back to Jersey."

Charlie's week seemed to drag by. He went bowling on league night with some of the guys from Shoreville, but his mind was in Philly. "Hey Charlie, snap out of it! We need a strike on this one!" Tony Mazza yelled, "Let's go, you're up."

Charlie managed to force himself to concentrate and rolled the requisite strike for his team to win the evening. Later, over beer Tony Mazza asked him, "You're not takin' your work home are ya, Charlie? You look like you're up in the clouds somewhere. No company is worth messing up your bowling average!"

Charlie laughed. "You're right, Tony I was just daydreaming a little. But, we won, right? Let's have another beer to celebrate. Hey Mildred, bring us another round, willya?" Charlie yelled to the waitress.

"That all you want is a beer, Charlie?" Mildred yelled back. Tony and Charlie both laughed. Mildred didn't hide her needs. "Yeah, Millie, that's all for today at least!"

Charlie poured himself into his work for the rest of the week and he took off again for Philly on Saturday.

He was back in the *trattoria* at 9-o-clock that night when Gina walked in. She was alone this time. Charlie waved to her from his table and as she started over to the table he noticed that she was wearing a simple black dress and a string of pearls. She was absolutely stunning and he had to work to keep his jaw from falling. Charlie got up to greet her and pull her chair but the waiter was already there holding it for Gina. "Thank you, Johnny." Gina said. Charlie stood there for a minute before realizing he had to sit down again.

"Hi, Gina, how was your week?"

"Hi to you too, Charlie, it was fine. Nice and calm, the way I like it."

The idea that Gina would like a calm week and could actually have one was something Charlie could not quite grasp. He imagined her having to run from guys following her around the entire time.

"Where are your friends tonight?" Charlie asked. "You look like you just came from dinner at some nice place. That's a nice dress." Charlie thought, *"Mullins, you are sounding so damned stupid!"*

"No, I'm not coming from a dinner. I'm going to one. I thought maybe you might be a bit tired of this *trattoria*, so I thought you and I might go out for dinner. I hope I am not being too forward. I mean we can stay here if you want, but I thought you might want to vary the routine a little. Is that okay?"

Charlie's heart was almost in his mouth. He had not expected to be invited to dinner by this marvelous creature sitting across from him. "Why no, I mean, yes. I mean yes it's okay and no, you are not being forward. Yeah, let's go to dinner."

Suddenly Charlie wondered where he should take Gina. Her outfit was appropriate for any nice restaurant but her looks justified only the best. He had no idea what she might be used to. This was not the kind of woman you would take out for a Philly cheese steak sandwich! On the other hand, he did not want to seem to be showing off or seeming to be trying to impress her. After only a couple of meetings, he knew that Gina Ferrelli was not easily impressed and would not be bowled over by the most expensive place in town. He thought, *"Where the hell can I take her to dinner that we can eat well and have the right atmosphere without seeming to want to impress?"*

He suddenly remembered a very nice restaurant on S. 17th Street. "He asked Gina if she knew the place. She did and liked it.

"I know it, and it's just fine Charlie. I would just like a quiet evening, a good meal, and some interesting conversation with a gentleman. That OK, Charlie?"

"I can't imagine a better suggestion." said Charlie.

Johnny, the waiter, suggested that they take a cab to the restaurant, leaving Charlie's car in the parking garage across the street from the *trattoria*. He went outside and flagged down a cab for them. He told them not to worry about a reservation. He had a friend who worked at the restaurant and he would make sure they got a table.

Over dinner Gina asked Charlie about himself. He told her that he was a financial executive at the Shaw Corporation and that both his parents had died while he was in the Army. His father had been a technical representative – a kind of troubleshooter with customers and his mother a housewife. His father died of a heart attack during a visit to a client company and his mother died about a year later of cancer. He was sure that his father's death just sapped his mother's will to live. They had been close and were exceptionally dedicated to each other. Living alone for either would have been a death sentence. He told Gina about his days at La Salle and his friend Joey Esposito. He mentioned his marriage and divorce and what now seemed to be a rather boring life in Shoreville. Gina listened attentively. Charlie had never felt so comfortable around anyone and he told her everything about his life. He was surprised at his own openness given his almost obsessive concern with privacy.

He suddenly realized that he had practically monopolized the entire evening talking about himself. Gina, however, appeared interested. He was not boring her, or at least it appeared that way.

25

He stopped, "Jeez, Gina, I've spent almost the entire evening talking about myself. I'm sorry. Tell me something about you."

Gina told him that her parents had died in an automobile accident when she was a toddler. She was raised by her uncle to whom she was totally dedicated. She went to Catholic grammar and high school and went to college at Bryn Mawr where she majored in Literature. Her uncle was a wealthy businessman and did not want her to work so he paid her a hefty allowance and put her up in an upscale apartment in a building in which he was a partner. To keep herself busy and not feel like a parasite on her uncle's largess, Gina was involved in numerous local charities and did volunteer work at the Catholic grammar school where she had studied.

Charlie had a bit of difficulty getting his mind around the idea of not having to work for a living. He was from a working class environment. His father literally worked himself to death for the Shaw Corporation and his mother managed the house, saving every available cent to send Charlie to college. Charlie had worked his entire life starting as a bag boy at Joey Wilson's father's grocery store. He had held part-time jobs in high-school for spending money and to help finance his college education. He had worked part-time in the library at La Salle for spending cash. He could not even imagine a life without work. He wondered why Gina was so unpretentious given her circumstances. She obviously had the money and the poise to be running around with Philly's "hoity-toity" crowd. But she was a down-to-earth person who appeared to be unconcerned for those people. The only people he had known who did not have to work were the daughters of Old Man Shaw and they were the most pretentious, self-centered people he had ever seen. If Gina had not told him about her circumstances, he would have thought of her as a young career woman maybe working for a publishing company.

By the end of the evening, Charlie was totally taken by Gina and he wondered what sort of chance he would have with someone like her. Having shared their respective pasts and mellowed by the good Tuscan wine that accompanied their dinner, Charlie said, "Gina, I really enjoy being with you. You didn't mention any guys in your life and I wonder if we could see each other more often. I have to confess that I have never been around someone like you, but I really enjoy your company. Could we do this again?"

Gina laughed easily. "Charlie, do you think I had nothing to do this evening? My friends called me and wanted to go out. I said 'no' because I wanted to have dinner with you. Just the two of us. I wanted to get to know you because I like being around you too. As for any men in my life, no, I am not in a relationship. I am well aware that I am attractive to men and my financial situation makes me even more so, but I am totally bored by the guys I have met. They are all so bent on impressing me that they come across as totally phony and so damned self-centered that they have no time for me as a person. I'm not anyone's trophy."

Charlie was ecstatic and he was down for the count. Gina had him totally wrapped up and he had not the slightest concern about it. He had opened himself up as never before with a woman he had known for only a couple of weeks and he did not feel vulnerable. His privacy had not been invaded – he had opened the floodgates himself.

They finished their dinner, had some espresso and then called for a cab to take them back to Charlie's car. The *trattoria* was still open when they got back to the parking garage. Gina turned to Charlie and said, "Don't worry about taking me home, Charlie. I'll stay in the cab and you can go get your car."

"You sure, Gina? I don't mind dropping you off." Actually, Charlie wanted to spend as many minutes as possible with Gina.

"No, I don't live far from here. I'll just stay in the taxi. Thanks for a wonderful evening. I've really enjoyed it and I hope we can do it again. Shall we meet here next Saturday?"

"Yeah", said Charlie a bit too quickly, he thought. "Same time next week?" He wanted to ask Gina for her telephone number but since she had not offered it, he decided not to. The *trattoria* would serve as a meeting place for the time being.

Gina gave Charlie a light kiss on the cheek and said good night. Charlie stepped from the taxi and offered to pay the driver when Gina said, "That's OK Charlie, the dinner was my idea, I'll handle the cab."

"No, Gina, let me get this. You're not supposed to pay your own way. I'm still a bit old-fashioned. I'll get it."

"No Charlie, I'm a liberated woman and one of independent financial means. I can handle a cab fare." She laughed gently and Charlie realized that he was not going to pay the cab no matter how much he insisted.

"OK, Gina but next time I pay, OK?"

"Fine Charlie, see you next week."

Charlie walked over to the parking garage. He saw Johnny the waiter standing at the door of the *trattoria* until he got inside the garage and Gina's cab pulled away.

* * * * *

The next day Charlie went early to his parents' gravesite. He sat down on the grass facing their grave markers and "talked" to them as he had done since they died. "Mom, Dad, I still miss you guys a lot. I always want you to know how much I appreciate the sacrifices you made for me. The job at Shaw is going along well. A couple of weeks ago Joey Esposito, you remember him from my days at La Salle, introduced me to a really wonderful gal. She's the first person I've met since my divorce that has really impressed me. You'd like her. There's a little bit of a glitch because apparently she is very rich. Her uncle is a businessman in Philly and she gave me the impression that he has a lot of money. She went to Bryn Mawr and doesn't have to work. Her uncle gives her an allowance. She might be too rich for my kind of upbringing but she is a real down-to-earth person. I feel good around her and I guess she feels good around me too. She's hardly the Shoreville type and I have to admit that I feel a little intimidated around her. But she is so unpretentious that you would never know she is rich. I wish you were here so I could hear what you think. I like her but I don't want to seem to be after her money, you know? I don't want to ruin the first easy relationship I have ever had. She is so unlike Mary Jo that I hardly know how to act around her. So, as you have said before, Dad, I just relax and try to be me. Well, that's the news for this week. God keep both of you." Charlie said a silent prayer for his parents and then went back to his car and drove home.

When he got home he called Joey Esposito. "Joey? Charlie here, you in the mood for a cheese steak sandwich? I gotta talk to you."

"Sure Charlie, c'mon by. I was gonna watch the Eagles game but a cheese steak and a beer sounds like a better idea."

"Be there in about an hour, Joey. Bye." Charlie rang off and walked to his car. He needed to talk to Tony about Gina.

He pulled up to Joey's apartment building in Philly. Joey was in his usual weekend attire of sweat pants and a cut-off sweat shirt. "Hey Charlie, what's up? Want a beer?" Before Charlie could even answer, Joey tossed him a can of beer. Charlie popped open the can and sat down. "What do you think of the Eagles' lineup this year, Charlie? They goin' to the Super Bowl?"

"Who knows, Joey? They always surprise me. Some years you think they have a shitty team and they go to the finals. Other years they have a five-star lineup and they tank. Just have to wait and see, I guess. But I need to talk to you about something else, Tony. You remember Gina, the gal you introduced me to a few weeks ago?"

"Everybody remembers Gina, Charlie. You don't forget a gal like that. Yeah, you guys seemed to hit it off pretty good that night. What about her?"

"Well, Joey, I am really impressed by her. I mean, really! I barely know her but last night she showed up at the *trattoria* looking like a million bucks and alone. She suggested that instead of sitting around over a couple glasses of wine, we go out for dinner. Joey, I swear to God, I never had such a pleasant evening in my life. She is a terrific person. And I think she likes being around me, too."

"OK, I see nothing special about Gina looking like a million bucks. She'd look that way dressed in rags, Charlie. As for going out to dinner, so what? I mean she does eat, you know. And she probably likes being around you. There are so many phony guys that hit on her that you are probably somebody she can relate to easily. What's the beef?"

"I don't know, Joey. She told me that she doesn't have to work for a living because her uncle, the guy who raised her, is a wealthy businessman who doesn't want her to have to work. Joey, I've worked all my life and she has never worked. Know what I mean? Would we hit if off?"

"C'mon, Charlie. You've only known her for a couple of weeks. You're hitting it off so far. Why not just relax and enjoy her company? She seems to like you and you like her. Just relax my friend. It's a little early to be in love, isn't it?"

"Oh yeah, I'm not talking about being in love. In fact, I don't know what I am talking about. I guess it's just that I have never met a woman like Gina. I think about her all the time. I can't wait to see her at the *trattoria*. The other day the guys in the bowling league thought I was daydreaming, and I was! I was thinking about meeting Gina at the *trattoria* on Saturday."

"Holy shit! Charlie my Sicilian grandfather would say you were hit by the 'thunderbolt'. You're about to fall in love, Charlie! Let's go have that cheese steak sandwich – I want to hear this story! The most eligible bachelor in Shoreville, New Jersey meets the most beautiful girl in Philadelphia, what a story!"

"C'mon Joey, I'm serious. This is not some movie. I'm really confused."

"I don't doubt that one bit, Charlie. Let's go. We'll talk about it at my favorite greasy spoon."

They took the elevator to the street and walked to Joey's favorite sandwich shop where they ordered a couple of beers and a superb Philly Cheesesteak – the trademark sandwich of the city. When they were served, Joey said, "OK Charlie, start talkin'. I'm all ears!"

Charlie told him about meeting Gina at the *trattoria* the week after they met. He talked about how easy it was to be with her, about her friends that showed up with her, and about their dinner. "Joey, I hardly know this woman but it feels like I've known her forever. I mean besides being a real class act, she is just so composed and relaxed anywhere. I don't want to push her but I love being around her. Know what I mean?"

"Look Charlie, I've known Gina for a while. I was never close to her but we went to the same grammar school. She was a class act even when she was 9 years old. I also know a lot of her friends, so I know exactly what you mean. You have to understand only that she is a very special person, Charlie. She detests phonies and those 'fast track' attorneys and bankers that cross her path. She is as comfortable going out for a meatball sandwich as she is at some hoity-toity joint. Her uncle is very rich and very discreet. He is protective of her and loves her even more than a father probably could. He is a widower and never had any kids, so Gina is his only child."

"What about this guy, Joey? Gina only told me that he is a wealthy businessman."

"Why don't you just let Gina tell you herself? You don't like gossip and second-hand information and neither do I. She'll tell you when she is ready. There are no secrets so just relax. If you like her and she likes you, I wouldn't go any further. Things will either develop or they won't. Gina is cool and believe it or not really works hard in her volunteer work. She probably works harder than she would if she had a regular job like the rest of us working stiffs. She loves the kids at the grammar school and she is always involved in community stuff. Like I said, she has been chased by every phony asshole in this city. You're a genuine guy, Charlie, and probably someone she can be comfortable with. You're not somebody who has to have the latest BMW, a thousand-dollar fountain pen, a fat salary, and maxed out credit cards to impress people. I've always known you as a genuinely nice guy and maybe that's the way Gina sees you too. If it doesn't turn into romance, it will be an easy friendship so just relax. Frankly, I'm betting it turns into romance, but what do I know?"

"Yeah, I guess you're right Joey. I've got nothing else to do anyway, so why not go out with an intelligent, beautiful woman?" Charlie laughed. "Gina is smart, fun, and easy to know. I'll take your advice and just take it easy. It's just that she blew me away, you know?"

"Yep, the 'thunderbolt' Charlie. My grandfather was an ignorant peasant but he wasn't dumb. He knew people and a lot about life. He died sitting in his rocking chair after busting his ass in construction work all his life. Tough guy!"

Charlie and Joey finished their meal and then made small talk about old times, the outlook for the Eagles this season, what a boring place Shoreville was for a bachelor, and a little about work. Joey was a loan officer at a large bank and he and Charlie were both on ascending career paths. Both were a little bored with corporate life and they shared a few laughs about some of their colleagues who were trying to be "movers and shakers". They walked back to Joey's place where Charlie had parked his car.

"You want another beer, Charlie?"

"Naw, thanks Joey. I'm going back to Shoreville. Gotta put the house in order and do some yard work. It keeps my mind busy. Not a helluva lot to do in Shoreville on a Sunday so I keep busy with the house."

"Boy, it is a good thing you met Gina, Charlie. That's a real exciting life you got over there!" They both laughed and Charlie headed home.

* * * * *

Gina, too, was talking about her feelings that Sunday. She went over to her uncle's place for Sunday brunch and to tell him about Charlie.

"Uncle Carlo, I met a guy a couple of weeks ago." she started.

"Nothing new about that, Gina. You got guys chasing you all over this town."

"But this guy is different, Uncle Carlo. He is really a nice guy. He lives over in Jersey and we met through some mutual friends a couple of weeks ago. He's different than all those other guys I've met. He listens. He is nice. He doesn't treat me like a china doll and he doesn't try to impress me with who he knows and how important he is."

"Sounds to me like he did impress you, Gina. You say he is different and that you like him. That's the first time I've heard that from you about a guy you met."

"Yeah, I even asked him to take me to dinner last night. I'd never done that before."

"You invited him, Gina?" Carlo laughed, "That's a new twist. Usually you're turning down dinner invitations."

"I know. We met at the *trattoria* that I always go to with my friends and got together there again a week later. He seemed a bit shy about asking me out, so I thought I would take the initiative. I showed up alone and dressed for an evening out. He is such a gentleman and so different that I thought it would be nice to get to know him one-on-one, you know?"

"Well, he might be timid, but you sure aren't Gina. You've always known your own mind. I'm not surprised. Tell me something about this guy."

31

Gina told her uncle everything that Charlie had told her over dinner. Her uncle listened attentively and when she was finished he said, "Mullins? Irish? Jeez Gina, you never did anything by half measures!" Carlo laughed and continued "You gonna teach him to dance the *tarantella*? Couldn't find a nice Italian boy?"

Gina laughed. "No Uncle Carlo, I couldn't care less about that kind of stuff. You know that. He's just a nice guy. I mean we're not talking marriage or anything like that. It's just so hard for me to find genuine male friends. He doesn't seem to care about my money. In fact, he seemed to be a little bit uncomfortable when I told him that I didn't work at a regular job."

"Well, that's a good sign, I guess. If you like the guy, I don't see any harm in going out with him. I care about you, Gina and I just want you to be happy. You are my only child, my sister's beautiful daughter, and I have been your father as best as I know how. I trust your judgment and if someone makes you happy, what the hell! If it winds up getting serious, I'm sure you will tell me."

Gina kissed her uncle. "Thanks, Uncle Carlo. You know I would never disappoint you. You have been more than a father to me. You have been a friend and a counselor. You brought me up to always do the right thing and to be faithful to my principles. You can be sure I will tell you if this becomes more than friendship."

"I'm not worried Gina. I know your life has been lonely sometimes. You're a beautiful young woman and a great catch for a guy. You're the only heir of a rich uncle and you are right to be cautious about guys who approach you. You're demanding about the kind of guy you want to meet. Not many can measure up to your standards and that is tough for you. You've suffered a lot of disappointments as a result. If this guy makes you feel good, then go with the flow, as your generation puts it, and see what happens. I get the impression from what you told me that he is not pushing, so if you are happy around him, enjoy! If this guy gives you a hard time, just let me know."

"It doesn't bother you that his family is Irish, Uncle Carlo? He does like Italian food." Gina said innocently.

"Everybody likes Italian food, Gina. Besides, the Irish flag has a green stripe and a white stripe in it, just like the Italian flag so what the hell, he's two-thirds Italian. If you get serious about this guy, bring him around."

"Thank you, Uncle Carlo. We're still a long way from that. So far it's just a nice easy relationship that makes me comfortable. But, yes, if it were to develop, I would certainly bring him around to meet you. You're my father, right?"

"You bet, sweetheart. Now, forget about this for a while and enjoy your meal, OK?"

They finished their brunch while Gina told her uncle about her volunteer work and they made small talk. She felt good that she had told her uncle about Charlie and even better that he seemed to approve of their friendship. He was a doting uncle and protective of her but he always gave her the freedom she needed to be independent. He trusted her and the upbringing he had given her. She never gave him a reason to mistrust her and she did not want to hide her relationship with Charlie from him. If he found out from anyone else but her, he would have been disappointed.

After their brunch, Gina went home, relieved and anxious to see Charlie again. She too, was confused by her feelings. The word "love" had not entered her thoughts but she had to admit to herself that Charlie was a special person and that she wanted to see him again, and soon.

VI

Exceptionally light traffic allowed Charlie to arrive early to his office Monday morning. He bought a cup of coffee from a street vendor and made his way to his office. Since no one was around, he put his feet up on his desk, allowed himself a few moments of reverie and thought about his career at Shaw and his life before meeting Gina.

When he joined the Shaw Corporation immediately after mustering out of the Army, Fred Perkins was Charlie's first boss. One day, after Charlie had been in the company for about a month, Perkins started on him about a financial report that had not been folded properly. He told Charlie that the spreadsheets were not folded the way they were supposed to be in the Treasurer's Department of the Shaw Corporation. Taken aback at first Charlie just stood there while Fred appeared to be ready to start foaming at the mouth. However, unlike the other employees who would tense up and get stiff as a board when Fred Perkins started into them, Charlie relaxed his body and looked Perkins straight in the eye. Perkins was suddenly shaken by Charlie's reaction. Here was a guy who would not be bullied. Perkins did not know how to react and his voice immediately began to lower. Charlie said, "Sorry, Fred. I'm new to the company. If you just give me the report I will fold the spreadsheets properly and get it right back to you. It won't happen again and I thank you for calling my attention to my mistake."

A number of other employees were watching the incident and they were amazed at Charlie's cool. No one had ever dealt with Perkins that way. Everybody else just lowered their eyes and took the verbal beating.

Perkins shoved the report at Charlie who took it gently and stood there until Perkins said "Get it back to me quick. I need that report in a hurry!" Charlie knew that was bullshit, but Perkins needed a closing statement. As soon as Perkins did an about face and stormed off to his office, Charlie went into his cubicle, folded the spreadsheets the way Perkins wanted them folded, and almost followed Perkins to his office. Perkins was knocking back a couple of Maalox pills when Charlie knocked on his door. "Here's the report,

Fred. I think you will find it appropriately folded. And, thanks again for the constructive criticism."

Perkins wasn't sure if Charlie was mocking him or if he really did consider the criticism as constructive. Providing constructive criticism, of course, was not Perkins' intent. He wanted the new employee terrified of him and that didn't happen. Perkins would try again in the future, but Charlie never caved in. Moreover, Charlie made a special effort to make sure that Perkins never again had a legitimate reason to jump down his throat.

It wasn't long before the word got out that Charlie Mullins had stood his ground against the irascible, terrible Fred Perkins. Perkins' reputation as an unpleasant person was legion in the company. Operating department heads who had to go through budget reviews and project approval with Perkins hated the experience. Perkins always thought it his obligation to say no to every initiative. It was his authoritarian personality and not his zeal for the Shaw Corporation that marked his encounters. He wanted to make sure that everyone was afraid of him. Everyone agreed that Perkins' nitpicking often pointed to problems or risks that made their budgets or projects better, but they despised Perkins for the way he went about voicing his criticisms. More than one department head had come back from a meeting with Perkins to say, "God that man is unpleasant! I wonder if he beats his kids! Jeez what a bastard!"

It wasn't long before those who lived in mortal fear of Perkins started informally consulting Charlie before submitting their work to Perkins for approval. Charlie seemed to always be able to figure out where Perkins would find fault and he helped the operating guys prepare arguments to get their projects approved. Perkins suspected that Charlie was helping the operating guys but he never had an opportunity to catch Charlie at what he considered a usurpation of his power. Charlie was not really going over his head to senior management, but he was, in Perkins' narrow view of things, reducing Perkins' power. He watched Charlie like a hawk but was never able to catch him. Charlie knew from the operating guys that Perkins was suspicious of him. They would tell him that Perkins would fume when they came back with strong financial reasons for backing their budgets and projects and how he would reluctantly give in while cursing and muttering. They would laugh to themselves every time Perkins popped another antacid pill just before signing off on their proposals.

Charlie's colleagues were also impressed. Many wanted to know his "secret" and tried to imitate him when dealing with Perkins. But Perkins had the sadist's sixth sense for weakness and he would bellow and berate the employee until the poor guy finally gave in. Charlie would tell his colleagues that he did not have a "secret". He told them of his father's advice to always just do your job as best you could and be able to defend your views. That was it as far as he was concerned. Charlie said, "You know, most people start out on an assignment worrying about Fred's reaction. I don't do that. I just research my work and make sure that it is well-documented. I say no when I think I should say no and yes when I think I should say yes. When you think about the reaction instead of the job, you will always miss something and that's where Fred catches you. You lose your focus and Fred is a smart professional. He will pick up even on a misplaced comma if you are not careful. When you try to compensate for his attitude, you risk making mistakes. It's a lot like playing ball. If you take your eyes off the ball when going out for a pass and you are watching for the guy who is going to hit you, you won't catch the pass. Get your hands firmly on the ball first, and then worry about the hit. And don't start running for the goal line before you have a firm grip on the ball."

But Charlie's colleagues never got over their fear of Fred Perkins and over time Charlie's work drew the attention of senior management. While that irritated Perkins' stomach lining even more, he was not about to tell his superiors that Charlie had failings. Fred Perkins was little more than a groveling quivering mass of jelly when dealing with his superiors. He was the typical court sycophant and if someone higher up praised Charlie, he would too – even if it meant more antacid pills. He made sure that his performance evaluations of Charlie were a study in "sucking up". He would try to be as neutral as possible and praise Charlie only to the extent that he thought would satisfy senior management and Charlie's performance would seem to be the result of his excellent leadership. Consequently, Charlie's star was rising in the Shaw Corporation.

He let his mind wander to his ruined marriage and eventual divorce. A few months after joining Shaw, Charlie married Mary Jo. He had a job and now he wanted a family. The small Shoreville church was packed with well-wishers and friends and more than a few senior people at Shaw who had come from Wilmington for the wedding. Mary Jo was impressed and was sure than she had made an excellent "catch". This was not your average Shoreville wedding. Charlie had attracted a lot of important corporate people from Shaw. After a short honeymoon in the Poconos, Charlie went back to work and Mary Jo settled in to managing his career. It wasn't long before she was telling Charlie that his chances for promotion would improve if they moved to Wilmington and, who knows, maybe joined a country club. In the beginning Charlie just laughed it off. "C'mon, Mary Jo, you really wouldn't like those people outside the office. They're never really outside the office. They're always manipulating and looking for an angle. It's boring."

"Charlie, how can you say that? You know you have to play politics in a corporation. You can't just wait for things to happen. You have to blow your own horn."

"Look Mary Jo, Dad died of a heart attack because he lived his job. I'm not gonna do that. I am well thought of in the company. I have plenty of power and I like my job. You saw who came to the wedding. I'll be moving up, don't worry about it."

"But that's what I am talking about Charlie!" Mary Jo's voice would turn to a whine, "those people from Shaw who came to the wedding can help your career. You need to court them, Charlie. You need to be around them socially, not just in the office. You need to go out to dinner and the theater with them. Play tennis with them on weekends. See them at church."

"Jesus, Mary Jo, I see those people all day, five days a week. Most of them are good professionals and I like them, but God Almighty, getting into their personal lives really doesn't interest me. Why should I pretend to be interested in someone in whom I am not interested? Pretty soon you'll tell me to start playing golf instead of softball."

"God yes, Charlie! Golf is an executive game. Softball isn't. And bowling – jeez, Charlie, executives don't go bowling except when they take their kids out!"

"Mary Jo, I hate golf. I thoroughly despise the game. I tried it in college and I thought it was the dumbest game I ever played. It's certainly not a sport and it sure as hell was not recreational for me. I wasn't even that bad at it – I just hated it."

"Charlie" Mary Jo whined, "You don't have to like golf to play it. It's a chance to be around the 'right people'. A lot of business gets done on a golf......"

Charlie interrupted her, "I know Mary Jo, but let's just drop it. I am not going to play something I hate and waste a Saturday or Sunday doing it. Change the channel. I am not going to do it and I have no interest in living in Wilmington either. My friends and my life are here. I play softball to be with my friends. I go bowling to be with my friends. I like those people, Mary Jo, and I don't want to leave Shoreville, at least not now. So, let's just drop it, OK?"

"Well, Charlie Mullins, if this is all you want from life, I guess I don't have much choice do I?" her tone was unpleasant so Charlie just ignored her comment.

But Mary Jo never let up on her pressure. Her protestations became more frequent and more aggressive. Charlie tried to persuade her that his career was right on track, thank you, but Mary Jo simply did not see it that way.

After a year, Charlie had simply given up on talking to Mary Jo about his career and lifestyle. He was disappointed and thought that as a local girl, Mary Jo would have been content to be around her friends. He was wrong. Mary Jo started talking to her friends and anyone who would listen about how important Charlie was at Shaw. She made herself unpopular with her bragging. When Charlie got a couple of promotions she would tell the whole town and say that someday she would be moving away to a "better neighborhood". That did not settle well with Shoreville's residents. Charlie was a popular guy and people felt bad that his wife was such an ambitious shrew. Mary Jo took to spending money as fast as Charlie made it to try to impress others. She succeeded only in making herself the object of derision. People starting avoiding her. At community events sponsored by the Shaw Corporation she would ignore her neighbors and try to cozy up to any Shaw executives who were present. She was not helping Charlie's career and she might eventually hurt it with her unbridled ambition. Charlie dealt with it stoically. He was not a confrontational person and he would simply tell Mary Jo that she was not helping herself or him with her attitudes. Mary Jo would go off like a firecracker and start complaining that Charlie had no ambition, that his friends were boring and ignorant, that Shoreville was no place to live, and on and on. One day Charlie had finally had enough. He looked at her and said, "Enough, dammit! Look Mary Jo, why in the hell did you marry me? You have known me since high-school. You knew my parents. You know all these people in Shoreville just like I do. You must have known I had no intention to leave this place just to suck up to a bunch of people I don't know. If I had a good reason to move to Wilmington, I would do it. But I don't think being around what you call the 'right people' is a good reason for moving and I can tell you right now that I am not, read my lips, not going to do it. So quit the nagging. I've tried to understand your ambition. I'm ambitious too, but I have limits. You don't Mary Jo. You want to use people to satisfy some sick need to lord over others. That is not my bag now and it never has been and you, of all people, should know it." He calmed down and continued, "Look Mary Jo, I'm doing just fine at Shaw. I've been promoted twice. I'm perfectly satisfied with the pace of my career. Nobody is telling me I should 'show up' more and change my lifestyle. You're making enemies for yourself, Mary Jo, and unnecessarily. We're not competing with anyone here. Relax." Charlie was being as accommodating as he felt like being and his patience had worn thin.

Mary Jo responded to Charlie by simply saying "Humph" and stomping off to bed. Charlie stayed up and watched TV for a while and when he got to bed, Mary Jo was either sound asleep or pretending to be.

After that evening, Mary Jo started going over to Wilmington to go shopping as often as she could. She ran up credit card bills that after pleading with her to "cool it" Charlie would pay with reluctant chagrin. She took bridge lessons and joined a woman's bridge club in Wilmington. She joined a gym in Wilmington and started hanging around with some of the wives who went there. She was trying to advance Charlie's career in spite of him and she was not succeeding. The corporate wives she met were more interested in their own husbands' careers. They sniped at Mary Jo behind her back and began to avoid her.

The inevitable happened when Mary Jo met a recently divorced attorney at a Wilmington restaurant. It was just what she thought she wanted – an ambitious successful husband and she started an affair. The lawyer, none too smart, fell for Mary Jo's ambitious plans for her life. She went home one evening and told Charlie she wanted a divorce. Charlie was shocked and asked her if she had found somebody else. She denied it but Charlie thought otherwise. He said they could talk about it the next evening after she had a chance to think it through. He never got the chance. While he was at work the next day, Mary Jo packed up and left. The divorce papers arrived the next day. He didn't have to pay alimony because Mary Jo thought she had found financial security with her new victim. She wanted out as quickly as possible so Charlie gave her the divorce and started a new life in Shoreville as the community's newest bachelor.

Charlie stoically endured the outpouring of sympathy, both genuine and feigned. He refrained from speaking ill of Mary Jo in spite of his anger and disappointment. In retrospect, he knew the marriage was over even before it had really got started when Mary Jo had begun to voice her ambition. He had tried to placate her more from a sense of obligation than from agreement. But he saw the clouds on the horizon and knew that the storm would eventually hit. The rest of Shoreville, however, would have liked to have crucified Mary Jo.

As Charlie refused to attack Mary Jo and feed the gossip mill, people eventually stopped talking to him about her perfidy. But the wives of

Shoreville started trying to get Charlie married again. He was suddenly deluged with dinner invitations and at each dinner there was some single or divorced woman who had been invited for Charlie's "inspection". Since everyone in Shoreville knew Mary Jo, he was not comfortable dating her old friends and neighbors. At one of the regular softball games he appealed to his male friends, "Hey guys, how 'bout talking to your wives and telling them that I am not interested in getting married again right now? I appreciate the concern, but I am OK, really. I know the ladies in this town and if I want a date I can arrange it myself. I know your wives mean well but I really am not interested in another marriage right now. I'm fine just the way I am for the time being. Know what I mean?"

"Yeah Charlie" said Bob Simms, "I'll tell Diane to lay off the cupid stuff. She's been trying to get you married ever since Mary Jo left. She talks about it all the time at home. I'm getting a bit tired of it myself."

"Thanks, Bob, I appreciate the concern, I really do, but I'd kind of like to chill out a bit, you know?"

Charlie's buddies agreed that they would talk to their wives. The dinner invitations didn't stop, but they slowed a good bit. To make sure he was not around on weekends when he would be invited to meet Shoreville's "availables" he started going up to Philly to see some of his old college friends. That's when he had looked up Joey Esposito and went to the *trattoria* where Joey had introduced him to Gina.

Charlie smiled to himself. Meeting Gina had been a stroke of luck that Charlie had not planned on. *Maybe my "chilling out" days are over,* he thought. He acknowledged to himself that he had grown tired of the "singles scene", weekends in Atlantic City or Cape May (if he wanted some peace and quiet) and wondered if he had not let himself get caught in a rut.

His reverie was interrupted by the arrival of his subordinates, so he sat up in his chair, directed his attention to the papers on his desk and got back to work. But he was sure that somehow his life was about to change.

VII

Charlie's week dragged by even more slowly than usual. He was anxious to see Gina again, especially after his conversation with Joey Esposito. He figured Joey was right about simply taking it easy and appreciating his relationship with Gina for what it was – a pleasant and relaxing experience that might or might not turn into something.

Fred Perkins had been his usual irascible self the entire week but Charlie barely paid attention.

Saturday morning he went to softball practice with his team. They were headed for the finals and everybody wanted to get in some practice. Twice Charlie had let a good pitch slip by. Tony Mazza launched a friendly barb, "Hey Charlie, that was a double you just missed there! You could have knocked that one way out in the middle of center field. Ya dreamin' or what?" Charlie had been concentrating on Gina and his plans for the evening and the pitch had gone by without so much as Charlie even seeing it.

"Sorry Tony, I read the pitch wrong" Charlie yelled back. He hit the next pitch well into left field just to prove he could still hit and that he wasn't dreaming. But he was, in fact, daydreaming. When practice was over, the team went out for pizza and beer. Charlie said he would catch up later but he had some stuff to do immediately. That was not Charlie's usual habit and the team commented later. "What's buggin' Charlie?" Art Samuels asked. "He usually hangs around after practice. Today he's got somethin' to do? What the hell is there to do in Shoreville on a Saturday afternoon? Anybody know what's goin' on?"

Bill Gallagher was the first to chime in, "I think it was just the divorce, guys. Sharon says he needs to get married again. Maybe she's right. She sure talks about it enough. Let the poor guy work it out. He's our buddy and maybe he just needs to be by himself for a while."

The team all agreed and the matter was closed over a few pitchers of beer and some pizza.

When he got home Charlie took a shower and then wandered around the house trying to find something to do before heading off to Philly. He reorganized his book shelves, moved pictures from one side of a credenza to another, tried to read a magazine. He tried to read a book then watched some TV, but his mind was already in Philly and the evening awaiting him. He went back into the bathroom and shaved. He checked his closet for what he was going to wear. He hadn't done that in years. *"Mullins, you're acting like a fool you know"* he thought *"this isn't the first time you've been on a date. Snap out of it!"* He smiled to himself and decided to take a short nap. That, too, didn't work and he just laid there, half awake until it was time to get ready to go to Philly.

He dressed. He put on a blue blazer with a light blue Oxford cloth shirt, moccasins, and khaki pants. He looked in the mirror and said to himself, *"Ivy League as hell! Well, it's standard fare and it can't offend anyone or make me look silly. Besides, it's my style. Esposito was right, just be myself!"*

The only thing different Charlie did this time was to splash on a little cologne. He had purchased a bottle of an expensive Armani cologne. That was way beyond his usual behavior. He was usually content to buy the Aqua Velva at Rexall's. If he really wanted to put on a smell, he would buy some Old Spice, his father's favorite. He didn't know if Gina would even notice, but he just thought that he should use something a little more sophisticated and expensive than the usual fare. *"Jeez, I hope I don't smell like a French whore!"* He thought. He also secretly hoped that he had not purchased a scent that was designed for the homosexual market. He didn't know much about men's perfumes or colognes and the sales girl had told him that women liked this fragrance. He felt like a high school kid who had purchased his first bottle of English Leather.

So, with the fragrance of Armani on his face, Charlie drove to Philly. He pulled up to the parking garage instead of leaving his car on the street and walked into the *trattoria*. It was almost 9 on the dot and he was surprised to see Gina already there with a few friends. She saw Charlie coming through the door and waved to him to join her table. Charlie was elated to see her again but a bit disappointed that she was with a crowd. He walked over to her table and she got up and gave him a kiss on the cheek. He wasn't ready for that and he turned crimson. "Hmmm, don't you smell good! I hope that's for me!" He turned even a brighter red for just a moment.

"Charlie, let me introduce my friends. This is Bob and his wife Emily. Bob is an architect and is working on a project for the municipal housing authority. They want a higher quality housing unit for the projects and Bob has some interesting designs. Emily is a painter still waiting for her first big exposition. But I like her style. The guy sitting across from you is Frankie.

He's a banker but he coaches one of the CYO league teams at the school where I volunteer, so, don't hold it against him that he works for a bank." Charlie laughed, "Nice to meet all of you. I look forward to our evening."

"Whoa, Charlie" Gina said, "You better talk to everybody fast because you and I are going out for dinner – alone, unless you would rather sit here and talk."

"Jeez, you put me in a tight spot Gina. I have to choose? Your friends look like great people but how can I refuse to go out with you alone?"

"Nice going, Charlie" Gina said "You got through that one OK." She laughed. She turned to Emily, "Emily, I have to powder my nose before I leave, let's hit the powder room." Gina and Emily got up and headed for the ladies' room.

"So you are the guy Gina has been telling us about, huh?" Bob said. "You wiggled out of that dilemma pretty well. You an attorney?"

"No, I work in finance for the Shaw Corporation. But thanks anyway. Gina gave me a real Hobson's choice there."

"Well I thought you handled it pretty well. Gina said a lot of nice things about you. She's a very special person you know. I don't think she has a mean bone in her body. I've never seen anyone who does volunteer work do as much as she does. You'd think she was getting paid for it!"

"Well, maybe she is." said Charlie. "Money is not the only way we get paid in life. Sometimes knowing that we helped someone is a form of payment."

"Well said" added Frankie, "I think Gina is that kind of person. Besides, the one thing she doesn't need is money."

Bob shot Frankie a quick glance that said "Shut up, Frankie." Charlie saw it but did not react. He wouldn't have followed up on the comment anyway, but Bob could not have known that. He was impressed by Bob's loyalty to Gina.

Frankie quickly changed the subject and said, "Yeah, Gina spoke well of you. She thinks you are a nice guy – which is pretty important in Gina's lexicon."

Charlie was flattered. He had not expected Gina to be talking about him to her friends but then he remembered that he had talked about Gina to Joey Esposito. "Thanks, Frankie. I will try to keep it that way."

"Good idea" said Bob and then laughed.

Emily and Gina returned from the ladies' room. It didn't look like either had powdered her nose and Charlie figured there was some girl talk going on. When Charlie stood to pull Gina's chair she said, "OK, Charlie Mullins, you had your chance to hold a conversation. Now you belong to me. Let's have some dinner!"

Charlie did not want to seem rude so he said, much against his real feelings, "Why don't you guys join us? You're Gina's friends and it will be a nice evening." He stood there hoping that no one would accept the invitation. To his relief Emily said, "Thanks Charlie, that's generous of you, but we have already made plans. We were only here to have a quick cocktail with Gina. We're on our way now, so you guys enjoy yourselves! Nice to meet you, Charlie."

Relieved that he would have Gina to himself for the evening, Charlie responded, "Same here, have a good evening." as he and Gina headed for the door to flag a cab.

* * * * *

Over dinner Gina and Charlie continued the "getting-to-know-you" phase of their relationship. Gina talked about her volunteer work and Charlie about his job. They were now beyond the preliminary stuff and were learning about what each believes to be important. They discussed values, attitudes, things they liked, things they didn't like, people they thought were interesting, people they thought were boring. Gina laughed easily at Charlie's stories about Fred Perkins. "Poor man," she said, "he must be really frustrated and angry, not to mention insecure." She complimented Charlie on how he handled Fred and laughed at the incidents he described. She told Charlie about the children she worked with and the community projects she was putting together. Charlie was amazed at her tremendous energy and drive. She was planning an exhibition for Emily and was waiting only for her to have enough paintings to put on display. Next week she was promoting a book signing for a photographer who had put together an anthology of photos of Philadelphia landmarks. "Why don't you come to the signing, Charlie? You'll enjoy the people who will be there. The photographer, Jerry, is really talented and has an encyclopedic knowledge of Philly." The evening passed far more quickly than Charlie wished. They were the last couple to leave the restaurant and the waiters stood patiently by while they finished their espressos. Charlie noticed that none of the waiters started clearing off tables as they tended to do when they wanted to tell you it was time to leave. Gina appeared to have an almost hypnotic effect on people and as long as she was around, no one wanted her to leave, so the waiters just stood there until Charlie finally settled the bill and they left the restaurant.

"That was a great evening, Gina. You are really a wonderful person to be around" Charlie said.

"Thank you, Charlie. The feeling is mutual. Why not come up for the book signing next Saturday? We can go out for cocktails before and dinner after. Jerry is a very talented guy and you will like the group that will be there."

"Of course," said Charlie, "you have a fantastic group of friends – at least those I have met so far. I'll be there." Charlie felt emboldened by Gina's invitation and asked, "Gina, sometimes I feel like giving you a call just to see how you are doing and talk a little. Would you give me your telephone number?"

"Why don't you give me your number, Charlie? I'll call you and we can talk to your heart's content."

That caught Charlie by surprise until he remembered that he had told Gina he was divorced. *"I'll bet a lot of married guys tell her they are divorced just to try to get her into bed."* he thought. *"She's right to protect her privacy until she can verify the things I have told her."*

"OK," said Charlie as he pulled out a leather-bound pocket notebook and wrote down his number. "I'm almost always at home by about 7 pm except Wednesdays when I bowl with the guys starting at 8-o-clock.

"What do I do if a woman answers at your home phone, Charlie?" Gina laughed.

"Call the cops, somebody has broken into my house!" he laughed back.

"You can bet I will, Charlie!" He was sure she meant it.

They left the restaurant to go through the usual departure ritual – back to the *trattoria* where Charlie had left the car and Gina continuing home in the taxi. When they got back to the *trattoria*, Charlie noticed that Johnny the waiter was standing outside near the alley next to the *trattoria*, smoking a cigarette. He waved to Johnny who waved back. He felt like he almost knew the guy. Gina smiled and said, "Good night, Charlie. You'll be here Saturday, right?"

"Wouldn't miss it for the world" said Charlie. Gina moved to kiss him on the cheek as she had done last week and Charlie leaned toward her. She surprised him with a quick kiss on the lips. "See you next week, Charlie Mullins. You're a great guy and a lot of fun!"

"Good night, Gina. Until Saturday. It was a great evening!"

Charlie walked to his car and noticed that Johnny was still standing in the entrance to the alley as he entered the parking garage.

"I think I like that cologne" Charlie thought as he exited the parking garage *"I hadn't expected that kiss on the lips!"* It occurred to Charlie that up to now he had been considering Gina as an interesting, beautiful, and unattainable woman. He relished being with her the same way one would be like being around a work of art – admiring from a respectful distance and in the abstract. Now he realized that he desired Gina. He imagined her naked on a bed. He wondered what it would be like to make love to her. He imagined her long legs wrapped around him and the two of them panting and reaching climax together. He imagined her raking her long nails down his back in a fit of pleasure. He did not just feel deep friendship for this woman. He wanted her. He felt passion. *"Oh man"* he thought *"I'm getting hooked on this woman. Take it easy, Mullins, you've only known her a few weeks. Don't go messing around with her. She's not the kind you come on strong with."*

* * * * *

Sunday morning Charlie slept in until around 10, showered, dressed and went grocery shopping. When he returned from the supermarket he spent some time organizing the house, doing his laundry, and then went out for lunch. He ran into Tony Mazza at the sandwich shop. "Hey Charlie, what happened to you last night. You said you would catch up to the group and just disappeared. You fall asleep or what?"

"No, Tony, I just went out for a while. I drove around and wound up going up to Philly."

"You got something going in Philly, Charlie? You hittin' the discos looking for snatch or somethin'?"

Charlie laughed "C'mon Tony, get your mind out of the gutter. I was just in the mood to drive around. You know I can't deal with that singles hustle. You see some available broad and the first thing she says is 'What's your sign?' Jesus! The next day you are in a motel with her and she wants to go for breakfast and says she wants to see you again. She asks 'Was it good for you?' and you have to say yes, even it was the worst you ever had! No, Tony, I was not doing the singles scene. Just relaxing, that's all."

"Jesus – first guy I ever saw drive up to Philly to relax! You're a real trip Charlie." They both laughed.

After lunch with Tony, Charlie drove out to the cemetery to visit his parents' gravesite. As usual, he sat on the grass and talked to the headstones. "Mom, Dad, the woman I met is really a wonderful person. We had dinner again last night. She is really a beautiful, warm person. I think I am getting serious about her." Charlie sat at the gravesite in silent meditation. He said a prayer for his parents and just sat there for a while thinking about his youth, his parents at home, the day his father died, his mother's illness and her sadness after his father passed away. Every time he came home on furlough he could see that she had wasted away further and it hurt him to see her alone. She would never have thought of marrying again. Her life with her husband had filled her completely and no one would be able to occupy that space.

Charlie's mother had not been terribly fond of Mary Jo. She commented once that she thought Mary Jo a bit too ambitious and demanding for her own good. But she was Charlie's wife and that meant she would respect Charlie's choice and say no more. Charlie would either handle Mary Jo or he would not. Charlie said another prayer and got up to return to his car and drive home.

When he got home he changed into a pair of shorts, gym shoes, and a cut-off sweat shirt. He got a basketball from the closet and walked down to the park on his street to shoot some baskets. His mind was on Gina and last night's kiss and he didn't want to sit around the house. He got into a short pick-up game with some other guys on the court and that temporarily took his mind off Gina. He worked up a good sweat.

After the game which ended as the sun was going down, he walked back home, showered, and then fixed some dinner. Since getting divorced Charlie decided to learn to cook, at least some rudimentary stuff. He quickly grew tired of going out to local restaurants where the locals would look at him with a mix of pity and anger at Mary Jo. He didn't need that. Besides, constantly eating in restaurants and sandwich shops was both expensive and hard on the waistline. He found that he was having to work out more often and harder to keep from loosening his belt a notch or two. He had purchased a mini-oven and he could fix up a roast chicken breast wrapped in aluminum foil that left him with no pots or pans to clean. He cooked up the chicken breast with a pat of butter and a bay leaf. It came out tasty and healthy. He would fix a side dish of rice in a microwaveable package and he had a dinner. No fuss, no mess – just the way a bachelor likes it.

As he ate, his mind wandered again back to Gina. He had not realized before meeting her just how alone he had been since Mary Jo left. His softball games and bowling league activities always ended with him going home alone while the rest of the guys went back to wives and kids. The guys thought he had the perfect life. "Ain't you the lucky guy, Charlie. I gotta go home to hear the wife complain that I am never home and to bitch about how dirty my uniform is and that she will have to wash it. You're free, man. You can do whatever you damned well please – throw your socks around the room, drop your pants wherever you feel like, open a beer, belch, fart, do whatever you want!"

Charlie laughed at their comments. "You think I live in a pigpen, guys? At least you have someone to wash your uniform. I have to wash my own or take it to the laundry. There's no one at home to even complain about me. And I don't toss my socks around the room either! I don't think belching and farting is much compensation for coming home to an empty house!"

The group would go silent when Charlie reminded them that the life of a bachelor in a small town full of married couples was a bit empty.

One of them would try to break the silence by saying, "Yeah, but what about the broads, Charlie? You can go out every night with a different one. We have to look at the same old face."

"I got into that singles thing after Mary Jo left, but I can tell you that it's not what you guys fantasize it to be. You go to some bar, meet somebody else on the make, go to a motel, wake up with a hangover, and look at some stranger who doesn't look anything like she did the night before. Then there is this silence as you try to figure out what to do next. She's gotta leave and so do you. Maybe you drive her back to her car. Then you don't know if you are supposed to kiss her goodbye or pay her! She feels obliged to say she'd like to see you again, even if she can no longer stand even looking at you. Most of the time you don't even remember if you enjoyed the sex or not. It's mostly mechanical – human hydraulics. You pump her, she pumps you. You fall asleep and wake up with bad breath and a stranger. A bachelor's life ain't what it's cracked up to be guys."

"Well, why don't you hook up with a local broad, Charlie?"

"That's easy enough to answer. What do you guys think would happen if I shacked up with a local woman? The next day the whole town would know about it. I don't want to date some woman who is going to be telling me what a nasty break I got from Mary Jo. I don't want to be sharing my feelings with the whole town and you know that's what would happen."

Charlie broke out of his reverie, finished his dinner which he washed down with a glass of wine, and put his plate and silverware in the dishwasher. He picked up his sweaty gym clothes and tossed them in the washing machine. He was ready for another week of work and Saturday night with Gina.

After watching some news on CNN, he switched off the TV and went to bed.

* * * * *

Like Charlie, Gina, too, had followed her regular Sunday routine, going to her uncle's home for brunch. She kissed her uncle hello and relaxed in a large leather easy chair while she told him about her week and again about Charlie Mullins.

"Uncle Carlo, I think I am getting serious about Charlie – the guy I told you about last week."

"You mean the 'mick' from Jersey?" Carlo laughed.

"The same" said Gina, "he really is a very nice guy and I think I have some pretty strong feelings toward him."

"Ah, love is wonderful, even if it is with an 'Irish'" said Carlo.

"C'mon, uncle Carlo. Don't get hung up on that Irish stuff. I know you are just kidding."

"Yeah. I'm kidding. Do you really like this guy?"

"Well, I sure feel something different. When I am around him I feel relaxed. He's not pushy, and he seems to be pretty sure of himself. I mean he is quick and witty, comfortable with who he is, and most of all respectful of my space. You know most of the guys I date wind up with eight hands and I have to fight them off and put them in their place. It's no fun. They're such idiots! But Charlie is different. He listens to me. He respects my views on things and even asks me what I think. He doesn't seem to be in any hurry in the relationship and we enjoy each other's company."

"That's where relationships get built, my beautiful niece. When friendship precedes passion and lust, the relationship will last. You want me to check this guy out? You know, see if he is telling you the truth about his life and his divorce, all that?"

"Not yet, Uncle Carlo. I want to wait a while. I can tell if something is not quite right. So far, he has been above board on everything. Let's see how it goes. I'm not in a hurry."

"Ah, but I might be in a hurry, my dear Gina. I'm not such a young guy and I'd like to see a few *bambini* running around before too long."

"Uncle Carlo! Here I am telling you that I think I might really like this guy and you are talking about *bambini*." She laughed.

"Gina, you are a beautiful woman and you will have beautiful kids. Everyone likes beautiful babies and I'm no exception. Anyway, I'm just daydreaming. You know it's your happiness I want."

Gina kissed him. "Thanks, Uncle Carlo, I know. I just think that for the first time I have found a guy who can make me happy."

"Just one question, sweetheart. Am I gonna have redheaded grandchildren with freckles? Imagine a redheaded Italian with freckles – *má ché*."

Gina laughed heartily. "No, Uncle Carlo, Charlie is what they call "Black Irish". He looks more Italian than I do. He has black hair, black eyebrows, and could really be Italian for all I know. And like I said, it's early to talk about grandchildren."

"Well, so when do I meet this Mr. Irish Wonderful of yours?"

"I'll let you know, Uncle Carlo. Maybe in a couple of weeks, maybe never. It will depend on how things move forward. But I am really fine with the relationship for the first time in my adult life. And try not to keep calling him 'Irish', Uncle Carlo. His name is Charlie!"

"OK, *bambina mia*, let's have something to eat. You're not losing weight are you? You look thin."

"I *am* thin, Uncle Carlo, and I intend to stay that way. You've been looking at too many of those 'mamas' in the neighborhood. God forbid I ever get like that!"

They enjoyed their brunch, made small talk, and Gina kissed her uncle and went off to meet her friends to discuss some of her projects for next week.

VIII

After yet another uneventful week at his desk at Shaw, Charlie dressed for his date with Gina. As usual he had been to softball practice and again, skipped out before the regular pizza and beer.

Bill Gallagher commented to the group, "Hey, Charlie skipped again. You think he's home?"

"What if he is and what if he isn't Bill?" said Tony Mazza. "Does he have to have pizza and beer every Saturday? He's not like us – we're married. We can afford to get a gut. Charlie's single. He has to look trim, right? C'mon Bill, give him a break."

Charlie had to get the house in order earlier today. The book signing was at 7-o-clock so he would have to leave a couple hours earlier than usual.

As promised, Gina had called him during the week. She first called on Thursday afternoon and left a message on his answering machine. She said, "Well, I guess you're not married Charlie. And if you are, this message should really mess things up!" She laughed and rang off. Charlie laughed when he heard the message when he got home. She called again at 8-o-clock. "Well, Charlie Mullins, if you were married this morning, you are in trouble tonight! I presume you got my message?"

"Satisfied now, Gina? But what if a guy had answered, would you have thought I was gay?"

"You're glib, Charlie," she laughed, "I know you're not gay. I have a few gay friends and they told me that you are definitely, really definitely not gay! They claim they can tell. I don't know how, but they say they can! But to answer your question, yes I'm satisfied. You'd be in deep trouble after that phone call and you would not have answered this one if you were married. Anyway, I'm calling just to hear your voice and to tell you that the book signing on Saturday is scheduled for 7. Can you make it?"

"I'll be there Gina. Where is the signing?"

"Meet me at the *trattoria* like before. Six-thirty OK? We'll go from there by taxi."

"OK. You know, I'm beginning to feel like a spy meeting you at the *trattoria* every time. Wouldn't you rather I picked you up somewhere?"

"I like the *trattoria*, Charlie. It's my special place now because it's where we first met."

"OK, Gina, *trattoria* it is. I'll be there at six-thirty. And, by the way, I'm glad you called."

"Good to hear that, Charlie. It means you're not in trouble." She laughed again.

Charlie laughed to himself about the phone call while he showered and shaved. He applied the expensive Armani cologne and thought, *"The last time I used this stuff she kissed me. Whether it was luck or fragrance, I'm not taking any chances. Do your stuff Mr. Armani!"*

Charlie left for Philly at a quarter-to-six and pulled up to the *trattoria* just a little before six-thirty. Gina had not arrived yet so he went in and sat at a table. Johnny the waiter was there and he said "Good evening Mr. Mullins. Nice to see you again."

Charlie was impressed. *"The guy knows my name already. It must really be nice to be a beautiful woman. Even her dates get noticed!"*

"Hi Johnny, I'm waiting for Gina. Could I get a glass of the house red?"

"Sure thing, Mr. Mullins."

While Charlie was drinking his wine, Gina came through the door. She had an entourage of about half-a-dozen friends. "Charlie! Hi!" She came over and kissed him on the cheek. Charlie thought, *"I could get used to this!"*

"You want to finish your wine? We can wait."

"No, that's OK, Gina. I'm ready to go."

"OK, these are a bunch of my friends. Friends, meet Charlie, Charlie meet my friends. I'll introduce all of you properly at the book signing."

Gina was dressed in an expensive navy blue linen business suit with white trim. She was wearing blue stockings and a pair of expensive navy blue high heels. Under the jacket she wore a cream colored silk blouse and a thin gold chain around an exquisite neck. Charlie thought she looked like a million bucks – as usual.

Charlie left the payment for the wine on the table and the group split up to drive or take taxis to the book signing. Charlie and Gina went alone.

In the cab Charlie turned to Gina and said, "You look terrific! Are you always this beautiful?"

"No way I can answer that one, Charlie. If I say yes I will sound like I think I am beautiful and if I say no, you might wonder what I look like when I'm ugly!" and laughed.

"Gina, I really find it hard to believe that you could be ugly. Not even if you tried!"

"Why, thank you Charlie Mullins! I'll remember that when I look in the mirror covered with face cream and curlers in my hair!"

They arrived to the hotel where the book signing was to take place. The room where the signing was to occur was packed. Gina moved through the room like a diva. She would stop at some group, introduce Charlie, kiss a few people on the cheek and move further through the crowd until she reached the table where Jerry would be signing the books that were piled up nearby the table. Waiters were circulating with trays loaded with flute glasses of ice-cold champagne. Jerry's book was one of those big coffee-table jobs of photographs. He had assembled a collection of the old and the new in Philly. Some of the pictures were in color and some were black-and-white. There were some pictures of the Irish and Italian immigrants that had populated South Philly and some shots of the old townhouses that had been renovated in the 70s by young couples who moved into the center city. It was a very nice piece of work and Jerry's photos were captivating. He had captured well the energy of Philly in his shots.

Charlie purchased one of the books and Jerry signed it: "Charlie Mullins, to the guy who has brought happiness to Gina." Charlie was at least confused. *"What power that woman has over people! I'm known as the guy who makes her happy. They are all so protective of her,"* he thought.

Charlie watched as Gina worked the room. She seemed to know everyone and everyone knew her. He sipped at his champagne while he watched her flit from one group to another like a butterfly gathering nectar. As she moved closer to where Charlie was standing, she signaled for him to join her. She introduced him to several people and he saw plainly that when Gina introduced him it meant immediate acceptance. This was not just a book signing, it was a collection of friends and Charlie felt comfortable to be among them. No one seemed to be posturing. Gina was supporting actress to Jerry's work and she was superb in the role.

As the crowd began to thin, Gina again moved from group to group to say goodbye and thank people for coming to the signing. Jerry looked satisfied and pleased. She took Charlie along with her and introduced him to each group as they left. Charlie had the impression that everyone left knowing who he was, not because he was Charlie Mullins of Shaw Corporation but because he was there with Gina.

She had introduced him to the friends that were with her when she showed up at the *trattoria* and they all seemed to know about Charlie. Clearly, she had talked to them about him.

"OK, Charlie, we can go now. Are you ready for dinner or have you had too many canapés?"

"No, I'm fine, Gina. I took it easy and I'm hungry. In fact, what I would really like is a good steak. How about you?"

"I can do with a steak, Charlie. It's been a long day."

Over dinner Charlie told Gina how much he enjoyed the evening and how he was impressed with the way she seemed to make everything work. "Gina, you must know everybody in this town. And, I'm sure that everyone sure knows you. You were like an orchestra conductor at the signing. It was absolutely seamless. I am truly impressed – really."

"Maybe it's easy when they are your friends, Charlie. I like Jerry a lot. He is a very talented photographer and he was ready for a show. He looked happy, didn't he?"

"You know what he wrote on my copy, Gina? Look!" he opened the book to the page with the autograph. Gina blushed. "Jerry is so nice. He thinks he needs to protect me and he wants to see me happy. Don't take it the wrong way."

"Oh no, that's not it, Gina. I mean I get the feeling that while you manage and organize these events, everyone there is also protecting you. I don't know how to describe it. Maybe it's like you are a plant with deep strong roots but a very delicate flower. I mean it's obvious you are a strong person. You are sure of yourself and have enormous poise. But somehow you are vulnerable. I don't know. It's strange and exciting in a way."

"Exciting, Charlie?"

"Yeah, it's not every day a man meets someone like you. There is enormous depth to you, Gina. I sense character and integrity. You love your friends and you do things to help them. You don't seem to need them but they seek to protect you. It makes you sort of mysterious." He stopped. "Am I sounding silly? Do you know what I am trying to say?"

"I do, Charlie and it's very nice. I do think my friends are protective of me. Especially in the area of emotions and romance. I know I am attractive to men and I am financially independent. That scares a lot of guys, you know? They figure they can't control me, you know. I don't depend on them. I've been hurt a lot by that. I'll meet a guy and when he gets to know me, he disappears. Maybe I am a delicate flower, Charlie, but a lot of guys have thought I was also poison. That's my vulnerability, Charlie. And my friends try to protect me and watch over me. Jerry was being sincere and grateful when he said you are the guy who makes me happy."

"Look, Gina, I've never met anyone quite like you. I would be lying if I said I was not impressed by your beauty. I'm not concerned about your money and I am certainly not interested in controlling you. My parents had a close and very interesting relationship. I never heard them argue about money. I never even knew what my father's salary was. We weren't rich by any means, but money was just never a concern in our family. Mom and Dad had a partnership. It wouldn't have mattered if either or both had been rich. What held them together was first of all respect and second, love. Money was just what you needed to pay your bills. It did not enter the relationship. I would feel terrible if I thought I had to control you. I would want you to support me in what I do because you respect me and love me."

"Charlie, I sometimes think you are too good to be true. I get scared that I might just be wrong and that you will back away from me like others did."

"I don't think so, Gina. That's not my style. I learned that I should never stand in awe of someone as long as he puts his pants on one leg at a time. The only person you have to consider as possibly better than you is the one who can put their pants on by simply jumping into them with both legs. Since I've never met anyone who can do that, I don't figure I have to stand in awe of anyone. Now, maybe you don't wear pants, but I bet you put your pantyhose on one leg at a time, right?"

Gina started to giggle. "That's funny Charlie. I actually had a vision of someone standing up and trying to put on a pair of pants without doing it one leg at a time!"

"Yeah, it's ridiculous to imagine." Charlie continued, "So I make you happy, do I? That's really nice to know because I have never been so comfortable around a person in my life. I live in the town where I was born and raised. I know just about everybody in it. All the guys I went to school with are there and we play softball and go bowling together and I feel more comfortable around you than around people I have known my entire life."

"Thank you, Charlie. I feel that way too. I only have my uncle and he sheltered me all my life while he taught me my own style of independence. But he was always there when I needed him. I barely remember my parents. He was all I had and I suspect that I was all he had. He loves me and doesn't want to ever see me hurt. Anyone who makes me happy has his heart too. My friends are my other pillar of support. I love them all dearly and they love me. They are all just regular people with tremendous talents in their respective areas or a dedication to the well-being of others. I never ran with the 'fast crowd', never wanted a coming out at some debutante ball, and I don't hang around country clubs. My life is with my friends and my volunteer work and I like it that way."

"OK, so let's lighten up. I make you happy and you make me happy. Where do we go from here?"

"Charlie, I feel very strongly about you and I want to continue seeing you. I want to see if our relationship will grow. I want to go slow because we have to get to know each other very, very well. I want to be sure. And I'm sure you probably feel the same way. After all, you suffered an enormous deception. You had known your wife all your life, right? And look how little you really knew about her after all. I'm not afraid of risk, Charlie, but I do believe in looking before I leap."

"That's fine, Gina. I agree with you. But I have to confess that I have already begun to miss you during the week. I think about you a lot and I can hardly wait to see you on the weekend."

Charlie ordered espressos and Gina looked at him tenderly and said, "Charlie, why don't you come back up to Philly tomorrow? We can do something simple. Maybe go to a park, walk around, feed the ducks, and have some lunch."

"You're on, Gina. I'll be back up here at noon. *Trattoria* again?"

"For the time being, yes. Is that OK Charlie?"

"Sure, I think my car can get there on automatic pilot by now!"

Gina laughed.

They left the restaurant, flagged down a cab, and went as usual back to where Charlie's car was parked. "Well, here we are again, Gina. I hate to have to leave, but I'll be back tomorrow at noon – same time, same station." Gina's eyes were misty and when he turned to kiss her good night, she grabbed him and kissed him with passion. Charlie responded and when they separated both were breathing hard. "You're wonderful Charlie, I just hope I am not dreaming. I really do think you are wonderful."

"Don't worry, Gina. I won't do anything to hurt you and I certainly do not want to leave you." He smiled and added, "and you don't intimidate me either."

She smiled back. "See you tomorrow, Charlie"

IX

Thus began Charlie's weekend sojourns to Philly. Charlie accompanied Gina to art shows, book signings, theater, concerts, and sometimes they just had dinner together. He would go up on Saturdays and again on Sundays. They would go for Sunday brunch at one of the hotels and then walk around Olde Towne or one of the city's parks.

This was when Shoreville started noticing Charlie's absences. He would miss the occasional softball practice on Saturday. To have his house in order, and no longer able to organize on weekends he took to organizing during the week. He missed a couple of league nights at the bowling alley.

While grocery shopping after work one evening he ran into Tony Mazza. "Charlie, you missed softball practice on Saturday. I called your house but there was no answer. I didn't bother to leave a message on the machine. You OK?"

"Yeah, Tony, I'm fine. I went up to Philly for an art show. I needed to get out of town. I've been too much of a shut-in since the divorce and I just wanted to do something different."

"But you can't miss practice, Charlie. Jeez, we might take the league trophy this year. The guys missed you."

"I know, I'm sorry Tony, but I just had to get out. I'd been using my weekends just to straighten out the house, do laundry, go shopping, and all that kind of stuff. You guys have your kids and your wives. I just got tired of the routine and being shut in the house."

"Bill Gallagher said he bet you found some gal."

"Oh, Bill is full of shit, Tony. He sits around listening to Sharon talking about how I need a wife and a life. It's none of his damned business if I found a girlfriend or not. For your information, I haven't but don't tell Bill. Just let him run his mouth and don't tell him anything. He passes everything on to Sharon and she's the biggest gossip in town. If he asks you anything, just tell him you don't know."

"You missed bowling night last Wednesday too, Charlie. Philly?"

"No, Tony, just extra work from the office and accumulated stuff around the house. I wanted to go, but I just had too much to do. I got promoted at Shaw and for the first time I had to take some stuff home," Charlie lied "it couldn't be helped."

"I thought you swore you'd never take the office home with you."

"I did, but the new job required that I make some changes in my routine and I got kind of backed up a little. No sweat, Tony, I won't be doing that kind of stuff on a regular basis. I just need to get a new rhythm going. Know what I mean?"

"Yeah, I guess. Just try not to abandon your buddies. OK?"

"Right, Tony. I'll see ya' around." Charlie and Tony each continued his shopping. Tony had a long list from his wife and couldn't be standing around talking. Charlie wondered if he had given Tony a plausible story. He was not ready to talk about Gina to folks in Shoreville. The whole town would know about it in a matter of hours and his privacy would go to hell. He needed the privacy and the space to develop his relationship with Gina. He would tell the town when he was good and ready. Besides, what if it didn't work out with Gina? Then he would have to put up with another wave of sympathy and renewed dinner invitations. He didn't need it. Tony Mazza was an old friend. He would probably chalk off Charlie's absence to his bachelor's life and think nothing more of it. Bill Gallagher was another matter. He was a busybody and told Sharon everything. Charlie finished his grocery shopping, checked out and went home to put away his purchases.

Unlike Charlie, Gina did not have to and did not want to keep her friendship with Charlie such a secret. Her tight circle of friends knew about Charlie and was supportive. She told her uncle that their regular Sunday brunch might suffer and that she would stop by after Sunday Mass instead of having a leisurely late morning brunch. Her uncle was supportive but appropriately concerned. However, he trusted and deferred to Gina's judgment and agreed to stay in the background for a while. He told her that she should decide when to bring Charlie by to meet him. He added that if she had any problems with her "Irish" she had only to tell him.

Gina would call Charlie a couple of times a week. They would talk about their respective activities. Charlie would tell her his Fred Perkins stories and Gina would both laugh and commiserate. "How do you stand that guy, Charlie? He's a real piece of work and most unpleasant."

Charlie would laugh. "He just thinks he's tough, Gina. He is really a pretty good professional and doesn't need the unpleasant façade. But, it's just his nature. He has probably always been a bully and he doesn't know any other way to relate to people. Sometimes I feel bad for the guy, but that doesn't mean I give him any space. If you stay ahead of him, he can't get to you. The guys I work with just get terrified even before he opens his mouth and that's all he needs."

"Why don't you just leave Shaw, Charlie? Maybe you could move to Philly…"

"I'm not ready for that, Gina. My Dad worked at Shaw for 30 years. It killed him and I have something to prove to both his memory and to myself. But, when the conditions are right, I might think about getting out of there. Besides, I still have my friends in Shoreville and until I met you, they were an important factor in my life. They stood by me after the divorce. I know their wives and their kids. They kept me busy when my marriage collapsed. They were good friends. I have to admit though that now that we have met, I have a fuller life and my need for their support is no longer so great. You've filled a big void, Gina."

"I know what you are talking about Charlie. I feel the same way. We do have fun together, don't we?"

They talked a little more and Charlie said he could hardly wait for the weekend. Gina said she was anxious to see him too, and said "Kisses, Charlie. I'll see you Saturday," and rang off.

Charlie didn't know it, but Sharon Gallagher was already talking to people about Charlie's "lost weekends". She and Diane Simms would get together and try to figure out what Charlie was doing. Her husband Bill had remarked that it was not like Charlie to miss softball practice and that he had even missed a bowling night. Sharon immediately said, "He's got a girlfriend, Bill. I just know it. He's found some gal in Philly and he's keeping it a secret! I'm going to find out."

"Stay out of it, Sharon. It's Charlie's business and it's his life. Leave the guy alone."

"No way, Bill. There's not much that goes on here that I don't know about. Besides, what harm can it do just to know what Charlie is up to? In fact, it's fascinating! He's the most eligible guy in this town and a lot of my friends who are divorced and some of the ones still looking around would love to catch him. I probably owe it to my friends to find out if he is no longer available."

"Sharon, I'm telling you it would be best to leave it. Charlie Mullins has always been a private guy. No one even knew he was having marital problems until Mary Jo left him. He keeps things to himself and you are going to piss him off. Just leave it be."

"Oh Bill, you are such a silly. You know women like a good mystery and some hot gossip. Charlie is a bit of an icon in this town, especially among the women. He's good looking, a helluva nice guy, and most of all available. I'm not going to pry; I'm just going to satisfy my curiosity."

"OK, Sharon. But don't you get Charlie pissed off. I know he won't say anything, but he will be a lot cooler to me and I like him. Don't get aggressive and once you have satisfied your curiosity, as you call it, then lay off. OK?"

"I promise, Bill." But Bill Gallagher knew his wife would be relentless and she and Diane Simms would eventually do something stupid. Charlie *would* be pissed if he found out and Bill was right that he wouldn't say anything, but he would cool off with Bill. He might lose a friend.

Charlie took to driving up to Philly on weeknights after work. He would pick up I-95 and drive straight up to Philly from Wilmington. He would head straight for the *trattoria* and meet Gina and her friends, now becoming his friends, for happy hour. Gina would call him at home and they would agree to meet and Charlie enthusiastically made his way up the highway at every opportunity. The change in Charlie was visible to everyone. He was more relaxed at work, and even more unflappable with Perkins.

The change was not wasted on his friends and their wives in Shoreville either. As usual, Bill Gallagher was the first to mention it. One night when the guys on the softball team were having their weekly pizza and beer he commented, "Old Charlie seems distracted these days. Think he's got a broad somewhere?"

"Christ, Bill," Tony Mazza said, "why can't you just leave it? Jesus, you sound like a woman. Charlie was practically housebound after his divorce. He's a young guy. So fucking what if he's found somebody? C'mon Bill, give the guy a damned break."

"Aw, I was just speculating. Hell, Charlie's one of us. He's a buddy. What's the beef, Tony?"

"The beef is, Bill, if Charlie's got a broad or not is none of our fucking business. It there was anything to be concerned about as Charlie's friends it would be that he did not go out, not that he is seeing somebody! I think it would be a good idea for you to tell Sharon to soft-pedal it too. My wife told me she has been talking about following Charlie to Philly some day to see where he goes. Shit, Bill! That's a bit much, no?"

"Hell, you know Sharon, Tony. She gets a wild hair and it's hard as hell to control her."

"Yeah, well I think it would be a good idea if we all, and I mean all, left Charlie alone. Maybe he's finally got a life for himself. We should be glad that he's getting a social life."

"Well, no need to get upset, Tony. I was just commenting. I agree."

"Good, let's drop it and finish our beer."

X

When Charlie met Gina during the week, he told her that he had missed softball practice the previous Saturday and he would have to show up on the field this Saturday so he might arrive a little later to the *trattoria*. Gina said it was OK but she was worried about Charlie missing practice. "Charlie, I don't want you abandoning your friends in Shoreville. Get here when you can. If I have to leave, I'll tell Johnny where I am going and he can put you in a cab."

"Thanks, Gina, I hoped you would understand. I have not told anyone in Shoreville about us yet. You know it's a small town and within minutes everybody would be discussing my private life. I told you how the wives tried to get me married. I just don't want the hassle."

"Not to worry, Charlie. I wouldn't think you are ashamed of me," she laughed.

"Gina, if I could I would have you on my arm everywhere I went. The problem is really my status in Shoreville and the fact that it is such a small place. People would start poking around your life too, trying to figure out who you are, who introduced us, and so on."

"Oh, I know that Charlie. I was just kidding. I know you value your privacy and I value mine as well. We don't need a bunch of busybodies down our throats. You're a handsome guy Charlie and I am sure there will be a lot of disappointed women in Shoreville if you start telling people you're dating."

"I wish I could disappoint *all* of them Gina. Then maybe they would leave me alone and find something else to think about."

"Yeah, Charlie, they would start thinking about me and trying to find fault. They don't want you marrying outside the circle. They'd be calling me the Philadelphia hussy or worse. Don't worry, Charlie, just get here when you can. I miss you."

"Me, too Gina. I'll probably get to the *trattoria* around 8, 9 at the most."

Charlie worked his way through the rest of the week. He went to the bowling alley on Wednesday night and showed up for softball practice on Saturday morning. On Thursday he went to Philly after work and to the *trattoria* for a glass of wine. Johnny the waiter was there but Gina wasn't. He ordered a glass of the house red, hoping that while he drank it Gina might show up. "Sorry, Mr. Mullins, Miss Gina hasn't been in yet. She doesn't always come here, you know. But if she shows later and you're not here, I'll tell her you came by."

"Thanks, Johnny. This place seems empty without her around."

"Yeah, Mr. Mullins, Miss Gina tends to light up a place. She is a very special lady. Everybody likes her."

"Have you known her long, Johnny?"

"Well, yes and no. My kids study at the Catholic School and Miss Gina helps them with math. You know, sort of tutoring, I guess. I was always dumb as a rock in math so she helps them with what I can't. The kids love her and so does the missus. So I guess you could say I know her. Of course, she also comes here with her friends often, so yeah, I guess I know her. But if you mean do I know her family, the answer is no."

Charlie decided it would be best to leave this line of questioning. He didn't want Gina thinking he was checking up on her. If Johnny said anything, she might not be flattered and indeed might think that Charlie was spying.

Johnny went off to take an order from another table, and Charlie nursed his glass of wine. It was the first time since meeting Gina that he had been in the *trattoria* without her. Gina seemed to give the place a different kind of life and Charlie felt alone and even a bit out of place without Gina present.

After about an hour and one more glass of wine, Charlie asked Johnny to tell Gina he had stopped by on a whim and in the hope that she would be there. He had not set anything up so Gina was probably off working on some project. He paid Johnny for his wine and walked slowly back to his car. He hoped that in the brief trip to the car, Gina might show up, but if he walked any slower people would think he was ill. Resigned, he sighed and got into his car and drove home.

Gina called before he left for work the next morning. "Charlie, I am so sorry I missed you. If I'd known you were going to drive up, I would have met you at the *trattoria*. I stopped in for a glass of wine about an hour after you left. Johnny told me you had been there. I was so disappointed to have missed you. I didn't stay long even though I was with friends because the *trattoria* isn't the same without you there."

"That's exactly how I felt without *you* there," exclaimed Charlie, "it's amazing how people can make a place!"

"Not people, Charlie, <u>you</u>. You make that place special for me now. When I go there alone now, I feel your absence."

"Well, Gina, I can tell you that it was the lousiest glass of wine I have had in a long time." Gina laughed.

"But we're still on for Saturday, right? I mean you don't have some sort of night game or anything, right?

Charlie laughed, "No Gina, no night game. I just want to make sure I practice with the guys to keep them from poking into my life and so they will tell their damned wives that I was there and I was normal."

Gina laughed out loud, "Charlie, you don't know much about women, do you? Believe me the wives of Shoreville – that coven of witches – know that you are normal. Take my word for it. That's their problem, in fact. You *are* normal. I'd bet half of them have erotic fantasies about you."

"Oh Gina, I don't know about …."

"Take my word for it, Charlie Mullins, there are some pretty horny women in your town. I listened to your stories. Watch your step! In fact, get yourself up here as quickly as possible before one of them tosses a net over you." Gina laughed heartily.

* * * * *

Saturday morning Charlie showed up for softball practice. He was not distracted and hit well. The guys were doing all their infield chatter and having a hell of a good time throwing the ball around and bonding. After practice he even joined them for some beer but begged off the pizza. "What? No pizza Charlie? You tryin' to keep your silhouette or what?" Bob Simms asked. "Yeah Charlie, afraid the ladies won't like you if you get a gut?" asked Art Samuels.

"C'mon guys, give me a break!" Charlie laughed, "I'm just trying to stay in shape. I've had a lot of work to do and I haven't worked out as much as I should. I'm watching the intake, OK?"

Art Samuels stood up and made an obscene pumping gesture with his hips, "Yeah, we know what kind of workout you been doin' Charlie." The guys at the table broke out laughing.

"All right, who wants some more beer?" Charlie asked as he reached for the pitcher. He filled a few of the glasses and then proposed a toast to the league championship. Everybody forgot Art's comment and gesture and raised their glasses, "Here here!" they all cheered. Charlie hung around a little while longer to let the beer dull his teammates' attention then took his leave. "OK guys, I'm heading for the shower. See you tomorrow!"

"Bye Charlie, don't do anything I wouldn't do – or maybe that I *can't* do!" yelled someone from the group. They all broke out laughing and Charlie went out to his car and drove home. He showered, shaved, and then splashed on a discreet amount of his Armani cologne. *"I'm beginning to like you, Mr. Armani. You seem to be bringing me luck! Keep up the good work and I'll buy some more of you!"*

He dressed his standard fare, blazer (a black one this time), a light grey oxford cloth shirt with requisite button down collar, charcoal-grey pants, black socks and pair of black Gucci loafers. He checked himself out in the mirror and thought he might be able to leave the first button of the shirt open. He did. Then he closed it again. Then he thought he looked too buttoned up so he opened it again. He would open and close the button another 4 times. Finally he decided to leave it buttoned.

Charlie usually went up to Philly by taking the bridge over to Wilmington and then driving straight up I-95. It was the most direct and in his view the fastest way to Philly. As he was approaching the connecting road to the bridge he saw a car parked along the side of the road. The car pulled out and fell behind him as he passed. The two cars crossed the bridge and entered I-95 together. Charlie noticed that the car stayed behind him. He accelerated slightly and so did the following car. He slowed down to let the car pass and the car slowed down too. He looked more closely into the rear view mirror. He could see two women in the car. Then he remembered that someone said that Sharon Gallagher had said that she would follow Charlie "one of these days". *"Shit!"* he thought *"just what I needed, somebody tailing me!"*

He made a mental note of the license plate and the make and model of the car. When he came close to Chester he suddenly exited and then quickly went through some back streets. Then he headed toward Philly on the Chester Pike all the way to Wannamaker Avenue until he was sure he had shook the tail. He stopped along the way to write down the license number of the car, and then got back on the Interstate off Wannamaker. He got to the *trattoria* at 8:45. Gina was waiting for him and nursing a glass of red wine. Gina noticed the apprehension on his face. "Hi Charlie," she said, "giving him a light kiss on the cheek, "what's the matter you look upset."

"Jeez, Gina, would you believe somebody followed me from Shoreville? I picked up the tail when I got on I-95. It looked like there were two women in the car. I'm sure it was some of those busybodies from Shoreville. Christ!

I mean if I were Bruce Willis or something, but Jesus, following me to Philly on a Saturday evening?!"

"Take it easy, Charlie. Here, sit down and have a glass of wine. Don't worry about it. Did they manage to follow you here?"

"No, I got off in Chester and then drove around a bit. Then I went up for a while on the Chester Pike. I'm sure I lost them along the way. Then I got back on I-95 and here I am."

"OK, so your privacy is intact, Charlie. Here, drink a little wine and chill out. I told you there were some horny, nosy women in Shoreville. Had to be. Tell you what, tomorrow take a different route. Come up on I-295 and get off at Camden. If they're watching for you to cross the bridge to Wilmington, they'll roast in the car all day waiting for you.

"Yeah, I guess I'll do that. I could just stop and confront them too."

"Don't bother Charlie. That will just whet their curiosity. They probably think you are running around some place in Chester right now and they lost you. Don't let them rattle you. Do you think they knew you saw them?"

"Aw, I don' know Gina. I was so damned mad I didn't think about whether they knew I had picked them up. I just got off the interstate and drove around until they got caught by a traffic light and I got well ahead of them. Then I just turned down a few streets while I guess they tried to catch up. Anyway, I don't know if they thought I was on to them or not. Doesn't matter much I guess."

"Well, I don't think they will stop at this attempt, Charlie. They're not going to rest until they find out where you go. That's for sure."

"I guess you're right, Gina. I don't know what to do."

"Just be unpredictable, that's all. I suppose they have families and husbands so they can't be watching you all the time, Charlie. They have things to do so if you keep them off balance, they won't know how to monitor you. If they follow you, just do like you did today. I've had guys stalk me in the past and it's not too hard to keep them off balance once you get the hang of it."

"Well, let's just forget it. What do you want to do tonight?"

"Do you like jazz, Charlie? There's a great little jazz place and a bistro nearby. We could have dinner and then listen to some jazz if that's OK."

"Wow, terrific! I love jazz. I didn't know you were a fan. Yeah, that sounds like a fantastic program."

As usual, Johnny hailed a cab for them and they left the *trattoria* for the bistro. Charlie noticed that Johnny waited again by the door until the cab pulled away. "Johnny must really like you, Gina. He makes sure you leave safely every time. I see him watching until the cab pulls away and he is even hanging around when we come back."

"Well, I told you, Charlie. I tutor his kids and I've known him for some time. I guess he feels protective, just like all my friends do."

"Yeah, if there is one thing I've noticed about your friends it's that to the last one they try to protect you."

"They love me, Charlie. Most of them have known me since I was a young girl. Many went to grammar school and high school with me. They know that I lost my parents when I was a child and I guess they all see me as a bit vulnerable emotionally. I guess in some ways I am, but I am also strong in ways they don't really understand. I am what you might call resilient, Charlie. I can bounce back pretty quick and I have learned over the years to deal with disappointment and not to idealize people. But my friends protect me anyway, and I love them for their concern."

"Well, so far every one of them that I have met has been a really nice, unpretentious and open person. You pick your friends well, Gina."

"I think so, and I'm glad you like them. They have all said they like you."

After dinner at the bistro where they swapped stories about their respective weeks, they left for the jazz cellar. It was a typical jazz place. You walked down a flight of stairs where tables were bunched up around a makeshift stage area. A single spotlight in the ceiling illuminated a trio. A piano, an acoustic bass, and a drum set played sets of old jazz standards. It was the kind of melodic jazz that Charlie liked. Moreover, it was romantic. The dark cellar and easy listening jazz was about as good as it gets when you are with a beautiful woman. The waiter showed them to a quiet table where they were a little separated from the other patrons and away from the trio so they were able to talk without talking over the music. It looked to Charlie like the best table in the house.

Again, Charlie was amazed at how beautiful women always seem to get the best without even having to ask. They ordered drinks – scotch on the rocks for Charlie and a manhattan with two cherries for Gina. When the drinks arrived Gina said, "They make a wicked manhattan here, Charlie, have a taste." Charlie sipped the manhattan and it was perfect – not too sweet, not too dry. "I really don't like manhattans that much, Charlie, I'm crazy about cherries," Gina laughed.

They clinked their glasses together and before Charlie could say anything Gina said, "To the horny wives of Shoreville – they sure as hell know what they're missing!" She broke out into a laugh.

Charlie laughed with her and said, "Gina, that's the first time I've heard a profane word from you since I've known you."

"Surprised Charlie Mullins? I'm not Little-Bo-Peep you know. I can hold my own with the best of them. I'm a Philly broad, remember?" and she laughed again.

She reached over and unbuttoned his first button on his shirt, "Look at you, all buttoned up like an executive! Let's open that shirt and relax a bit." That solved Charlie's problem about whether to button or unbutton the first one. He thought he would blow up when Gina unbuttoned his shirt and the temptation just to rip it completely off seized him.

Gina was in a really light mood and Charlie had never seen her so relaxed. She was completely at ease with him and he felt like he owned the entire world. The trio did a jazz rendition of "Stairway to the Stars" followed by "Stardust", two of Charlie's favorites and he noticed that Gina would close her eyes for a few seconds and savor the music. She was in a romantic mood and so was Charlie.

"It's nice here, no Charlie? So relaxed."

"You bet. I love this kind of music and the place. Not many places like this in Shoreville and I enjoy jazz trios. I remember when I was a kid and we would go to Atlantic City – before the casinos. There were always some guys on the beach or the boardwalk playing music. They'd have a set of conga drums and an acoustic guitar. Once in a while there would be a singer there too. I used to love to just stand there and listen."

Gina reached across the table and squeezed Charlie's hand. "I think you're a great guy Charlie Mullins." She didn't remove her hand and Charlie covered hers with his other hand.

They sat in silence for a few minutes and Charlie, emboldened by her gesture and the romantic environment, said, "Gina, I think all the time about you. I can't wait to get up here to see you. If I could I would be around you all the time. I feel like a kid when we are together. Even if our relationship never goes beyond friendship, I want you to know that I would never, ever do anything that I thought would hurt you. You're special to me, Gina, more special than you are even to your wonderful friends."

"I'm sure our relationship is going to take us beyond friendship, Charlie. I haven't known you long, but I think I am a pretty good judge of people. I trust you Charlie. I think I know what you value and what you don't. You really believe the things you say and you live them. I admire that and I have looked for it in the people I have met and generally found it lacking. In a word I guess I am saying you have character, Charlie. And character to me is more important than money, than advancing in this world, even more than my friends. I drop anyone from my circle of friends who does not have character. I would never be able to love someone who did not have character. And I don't believe character means following a bunch of rules imposed by society. Character arises from loyalty. Loyalty first to one's family, to friends, and most of all to oneself. A person with character keeps his word. I grew up in South Philly around a lot of poor people. Many, like my uncle, were Sicilian immigrants who spoke practically no English. I went to school with their kids. Some of them stole to feed their families. They cheated the bosses that hired them at sub-human wages. Some of them ran numbers. Some were enforcers for the Black Hand. They had to survive and they did so the best way they could. I would never judge them."

"I know what you mean, Gina. My great-grandparents came from Western Ireland. Their land was taken over by Irish landlords to raise horses. The family was part of a deliberate effort by the Irish elite to "export" their own people. They called it 'landlord assisted emigration'. You were assisted by the local sheriff who tore down your cottage and the goons of the landlord who marched you down to a boat at the point of a shotgun. At the dock you signed on to work in America. The company hiring you covered the cost of passage which they would deduct from your meager wages once over here. It was a lot cheaper than having to feed the people when the potato famine struck. Some people were so starved they even ate the same grass the landlord's horses grazed on. I guess the landlords didn't want to share even that grass. Those that couldn't leave were put into forced labor and allowed to die. The English helped, of course, but they were largely content to let the Irish landlords kill their own. That's the English way."

"I never knew much about the Irish, Charlie. That's a horrible story."

"You should see the newspaper articles from the 'London Times' during the potato famine! One article was about a man on a works project. He was seen leaning on his shovel instead of digging up the field as he had been ordered. The reporter had cited him as an example of the lazy, good-for-nothing Irish. When someone went out to see why the man wasn't working they discovered that he was dead! Dead, Gina! The guy died propped up on a shovel. Another article informed the world that the Irish were little more than primitive cannibals because a bunch of starving people attacked and ate parts of the corpse of a man who had drowned and his body washed up on shore. And every St. Patrick's Day, the descendents of those unfortunate wretches go out and parade, yell 'Erin Go Bragh', and wear green in honor of their Irish 'heritage'. They give money to the IRA in the ridiculous belief that they are somehow supporting the noble cause of Irish independence. The only thing Irish about me is my name, Gina. How can anyone proudly claim a cultural inheritance from a country that tried to kill them?"

"Wow, Charlie. Ireland sounds like it suffered even more than Sicily that was invaded over and over by outsiders."

"Well, I don't know much about the history of Sicily but I'm not sure one can compare levels of suffering. Suffering is personal. It's like pain. Everyone has a certain threshold. One man's suffering is another man's absolute grief. There's no way to put a number or a value on horror and suffering."

"I agree," Gina said, "my grandparents came over from Sicily as displaced persons. They arrived here with about twenty-five dollars and everything else they owned in a small suitcase that each was allowed to bring along. My uncle was five years old when his parents brought him over from a war-ravaged Sicily. He spoke only Sicilian dialect and for years spoke with a heavy accent. Kids in school gave him a hard time. A Sicilian priest, Father Pesce, who was assigned to the local parish took him under his wing and helped him learn English. Life was tough for him and he worked damned hard to advance. He was a tough kid. I guess that's where I get my resilience. He made it in a hostile world and he owes nobody any favors, except perhaps that kindly priest. To me he is a study in personal character."

"My grandfather was like that. He was orphaned at the age of nine. There were eight other kids in the family. His father was killed by a train one night as he was coming home from work in the Pennsylvania anthracite mines. He'd been drinking with a few friends. He couldn't hear the train. Did you know that if the wind is blowing the wrong way, you can't hear a train coming up behind you? My great-uncle told me that. They brought his body home in two pieces. His wife died a year later from what they called blood poisoning. She cooked for the miners and sewed for their wives after her husband died, and one day she cut herself while preparing something or other. She developed an infection that eventually spread through her body and killed her. The older girls in the family went to work as servants of local families while the older boys went to work in the mines. Only one, the youngest, who was seven years old when his mother died, was not able to work. He stayed with one of the sisters. My grandfather worked on what they called the "breaker". His job was to break pieces of shale off the hard coal. Shale has a lot of sulfur in it and it had to be removed so it would not accumulate in the chimneys of the steel mills and other industries that burned anthracite or when they converted the coal to coke, I don't really know.

When he didn't work fast enough, the supervisors would throw small stones at his back as he sat on the breaker. Nine years old, Gina! Yet, I never heard him complain about the life he led. He worked all his life, enjoyed life to the full, and held down two jobs during the Depression to keep his family alive. When he died, poor of course, my aunt found an envelope in his dresser with some money in it. On the envelope in his scrawled handwriting was 'For my funeral'. He used to say that every man should be able to at least pay for his own funeral rather than burden his family. Until the day he died he sent every grandchild and great-grandchild one dollar on their birthday. I was working and making good money and he would still send me a dollar on my birthday. It was the most precious dollar I had ever received. He had character, real character."

"Well, Charlie, it looks like we come from pretty solid stock. Your grandfather and my uncle would probably have hit it off pretty well even if your grandfather was Irish!" Gina laughed.

"No doubt about it," replied Charlie, "but I'm more interested in how you and I hit it off, Gina. I mean if you want us to just be close friends or you are not interested in a relationship, I understand. But I have to raise the question. I at least want to be on the same sheet of music as you are."

"Charlie Mullins, how corporate! Same sheet of music!" Charlie turned crimson, "Of course we are, as you say 'on the same sheet of music'! And, I must say you blush handsomely!" Charlie turned even redder. "I hope this works Charlie because I really do want it to. I want our relationship to be much, much more than just a friendship." Gina leaned close to him and gave him a long, tender kiss on the mouth. When she pulled away, Charlie could only stare into her eyes. He was speechless for the first time in his life.

"I'm going to have to tell my uncle about this, Charlie. He knows about you and knows I care for you, but I want him to know how really important you are to me."

"Fine, Gina. We have time. I don't know how much more we have to learn about each other because I'm sure it's a lot and I'm equally sure that nothing I could learn would change my mind about you. I respect your need to talk to your uncle. I talk to my parents about you too, at their gravesite, but obviously I don't get much feedback!"

Gina smiled tenderly, "That's nice Charlie. It's nice that you continue to honor your parents in memory. They must have been wonderful people."

"Well, Gina, where do we go from here? I hadn't really planned this conversation, it just kind of happened."

"Kind of happened, Charlie? I was hoping that this jazz cellar and the romantic environment might draw you out a bit. I confess that I was curious about how you really felt. When you showed up with your shirt buttoned up to one button shy of the collar I thought 'Gina, you gotta make this guy relax'"

"What a schemer! You set me up, Gina," Charlie laughed.

"A woman's wiles, Charlie Mullins. You men think you are the only ones who make plans? I have a life too Charlie and I want to know where it's going."

"You know now, pretty lady?"

"Yep, and once I talk to my uncle I am going to put the pedal to the metal, mister. You're going to have to meet him, you know."

"Is that so terrible?" Charlie asked. "How bad can he be if he is *your* uncle?"

"Well, like I said, he is protective and might even be just a bit jealous."

"I suppose all fathers are like that with their daughters." Charlie replied.

"Charlie, you've made me very happy tonight – happier than I thought I might ever be. This thing of ours will grow Charlie. We are going to be happy, I just know it!"

"Like I said, Gina, I will never do anything to hurt you. Maybe I will disappoint you on occasion, but I will never hurt you."

Charlie looked around and the jazz cellar had practically emptied. The musicians were packing up to head off to some after-hours jam session with their friends and the waiters were standing around waiting for the last patrons to leave so they could clear the tables. One of them was courteous (or perhaps foolish) enough to ask Charlie if he and the "missus" would like one more round. He was obviously hoping neither would want another drink. Charlie thanked him and asked for the check. The waiter appeared relieved and rushed back with the requisite leather folder with the bill inside. Charlie paid and he and Gina climbed the stairs to flag down a taxi.

The night air was cool and Gina said, "Why don't we walk a couple of blocks before we get a cab, Charlie? It's a beautiful evening."

They walked holding hands for about 3 blocks until a cab appeared and Charlie flagged it down. He gave the driver the address of the *trattoria*. "Come back up tomorrow, Charlie, will you? We can take a walk in the park and celebrate this evening. I'll talk to my uncle in the morning and then we can set a date for you to meet him. OK?"

"Oh yeah!" Charlie exclaimed, "You can bet I'll be back. I don't even want to go back to Shoreville!"

"One day you won't Charlie," Gina said softly, "one day you won't. I promise you."

When they got to the *trattoria*, Johnny the waiter was holding what seemed to be his constant vigil. Gina kissed Charlie passionately and melted into him." Charlie thought he was going to explode. They pulled apart slowly. "Gina, tomorrow can't come soon enough. Call me when you finish talking to your uncle and I'll be up here in a flash. Your bodyguard is on duty again, I see."

"Oh yeah, Johnny. He's a dear. Be careful driving home, Charlie and I'll see you tomorrow. I'll call."

Charlie got out of the cab and waved to Johnny. Johnny nodded back and watched to make sure Charlie got into the parking garage safely and then watched the cab pull away.

XI

After eight-o-clock Mass on Sunday Gina drove over to her uncle's house. She pressed the control device to open the gate to the property, pulled into the long driveway and drove around to the back of the house. She entered through the back door into the kitchen. Her Uncle Carlo was sitting at the kitchen table sipping an espresso. She walked over and kissed him on the cheek. "Hey, Uncle Carlo, how was your week?"

"Same as always, Gina, it was calm, thanks. How 'bout yours?"

"Actually pretty busy, Uncle Carlo. Charlie and I went out a couple of times and again last night. I want to talk to you about us."

"Eh, *ma ché, bambina mia*, this sounds serious!"

"It is serious, Uncle Carlo. I really do want this guy in my life. He makes me truly happy and I told him so. This is going to grow into something, Uncle Carlo, something very serious and very beautiful."

"Well, I know he hits a mean softball, Gina...."

"Uncle Carlo, have you been spying?" Gina said, surprised.

"Ah, *bambina*, you are so excitable. Maybe you could call it spying. But I was just checking on him. Nothing invasive, just a kind of overview. You know how important you are to me."

"Yeah, I know Uncle Carlo, but I'm willing to bet you came up with nothing bad, right?"

"Right, my little niece. And you were right about his looking 'Italian'. Nice lookin fellow, your 'Irish'."

"Well, you don't need to spy anymore. I want you to meet him!"

"Well!" Carlo replied, "It sounds like you got something really going with this guy. Are you sure you know where you're going with this?"

"I'm positive, Uncle Carlo, I've thought it through over and over. I'm sure he's not perfect, but he's perfect for *me*. He can hold his own with me. He's neither intimidated nor mesmerized by my financial situation. He's a gentleman at all times. My friends love him. He's from a nice solid family. He's loyal. He's...."

"*Managia*," interrupted her uncle, "you make this guy sound like Saint Anthony!"

"God, I hope not!" laughed Gina, "I'm not looking for a saint. I'm looking for a man in my life."

Carlo laughed out loud. "Ah, that's my *bambina*. You always did know what you want. I'm sure that even if I said I didn't like the guy, you would see him anyway."

"No, Uncle Carlo, I wouldn't see him that way. I am just sure that you will like him so I don't think that is going to be an issue."

"Gina, my little baby, you know how to wrap me around your finger so easily. It scares me sometimes. Here I am a tough businessman and I'm like soft clay around you. You know I trust you, I brought you up so I know how your devious mind works when you want something and nobody, I mean nobody, can resist."

"Well, Uncle Carlo, will you meet him or not?"

"How could I say no? Of course I'll meet your 'Irish'. I have to travel up to New York next week, but the week after, I'll be home. The guy works, right? I figure you will want to bring him by on a Saturday or Sunday. Why don't you bring him by for lunch on the Sunday after next?"

"Oh, Uncle Carlo, thank you. I just know you'll like him! I just know it!"

"How like a little girl you are sometimes, Gina. If this 'Irish' meets with your approval and he makes you as happy as you look right now, you know I will approve. I think the meeting will be more for him than for me."

."You're not going to call him 'Irish' are you Uncle Carlo?"

"Oh, I don't know. Maybe I will, maybe I won't. It will depend on his sense of humor."

"Uncle Carlo! Be serious, please! This could be the man of my life!"

"Not to worry. I'll be on my best behavior, I promise."

"That's what I was afraid of," Gina laughed.

Carlo laughed with his niece.

Gina joined her uncle in another espresso before going home to get ready to meet Charlie.

Charlie made a trip to the cemetery that Sunday morning. He made his way to his parents' gravesite as he had done so often since his parents had both died. "Hello Mom, Dad. He crossed himself as he approached the pair of headstones, "I've got some things to tell you. The girl I've been dating could easily become my wife. We went out last night and we decided that we really care a lot about each other. I mean in a really serious way. I've never felt this way about anybody. I'm almost certain this is going to work out. I hope you can bless me and pray for me up there in Heaven. Dad, the job is going really well. Fred Perkins is his usual pain-in-the-ass self, but I've got him under control. The guys in the department say I drive him nuts. I know you never had much contact with Fred but I also know that you didn't think much of him. Sometimes I feel sorry for the poor bastard, but the operational word here is not 'poor', it's 'bastard'. He really can be nasty. I remember that you once told me that when you left the company parking lot you would keep your windows shut and wave to the 'big shots' and say, 'Good night' and then whisper 'asshole!' I feel that way sometimes when I leave the company. I work around some nice people, but I'm not too big on the corporate scene. There are a hell of a lot of phonies looking to screw their buddies for a promotion. It can be pretty nasty sometimes. Mom, I don't know what to do about some of the women in this town. A couple of them followed me up to Philly yesterday. It was the weirdest thing I ever experienced. I mean what the hell do they care about my life, you know? Well, there's nothing I can do about it, I guess. I'll just have to wear them down. Well, that's the news for the week. I hope you and Dad are together in some place beautiful. I love you both." Charlie said a brief prayer and went back to his car.

He drove home and took a shower and changed before heading off to Philly to see Gina. While he was toweling off after his shower Gina called. "Charlie?" her voice was excited.

"Hey, Gina. I'm getting ready to drive up there. *Trattoria* again?"

"Yes. Can you be here by about one-o-clock?"

"Sure," answered Charlie.

"Charlie, I can't wait until you get here to tell you that I have set up for you to meet my uncle. He agreed and I'm so excited. I'm sure you two will hit it off! I'll tell you everything when you get here. Kisses! See you in a little while! Bye!" Before Charlie could say anything, Gina rang off.

Charlie laughed to himself. Gina sounded really happy and like a little kid. He was sure that her uncle's approval would determine whether they got together or not. It was clear that he had a lot of influence, if not control, over Gina.

After dressing in jeans and a rust-colored sport shirt, and putting on a pair of sport moccasins, he walked out to his car to drive to Philly. He looked up and down his street and saw what he thought was the same car that had followed him on Saturday. He could see what looked like two women in the car. The car was parked some distance away so he decided to drive right by it. When he got fairly close, the two heads disappeared below the dashboard.

He made a mental note of the license plate and without even checking what he had written down before, he was sure it was the same as the one on the car that followed him yesterday. He pretended not to look into the parked vehicle as he drove by. His peripheral vision allowed him to see into the passenger seat and he could see what he was sure was a woman hunched down. He couldn't see her face.

Because he was going the other way and the street was practically deserted on a Sunday, the other car did not give chase. Charlie chuckled to himself. *"Too bad ladies,"* he said to himself, *by the time you get turned around I will have lost you! Why don't you go home and fix lunch, do the laundry, or something?"*

Charlie went straight up I-95 again because he was sure he had eluded the two women who were watching him. They couldn't get their car turned around until he had traveled down the street a good distance and by that time he had taken some evasive maneuvers and then gone down to the entrance to the bridge to Wilmington to connect to I-95.

He checked along the way just to be sure the two women had not caught up to him on the interstate. *"Coast clear,"* thought Charlie, *'maybe I'd make a good spy!"*

When he got to the *trattoria* Gina was waiting for him. She was fantastic in a pair of jeans, a cream-colored silk blouse, and a pair of cross trainers that didn't look like she ran in them very much. "Don't you look great!" said Charlie, "I've never seen you in jeans. You're a knock out!"

"Well, aren't you the gallant one, Mr. Mullins? I'm not always dressed to the nines you know!"

"Anyway, Wow!"

"Charlie, you know what I would like today before going to the park?"

"Your every wish is a command," said Charlie.

"I'd love to go for a Philly cheese steak sandwich with lots of pepper and onions! Got a problem with that?"

"Not in the least! You got a favorite place?" Charlie knew that there were Philly cheese steaks and Philly cheese steaks. Philadelphians knew the really good places. The others were for tourists. The first thing you noticed about an authentic Philly cheese steak place was the Tasty-cake display. Every place that had good cheese steak sandwiches always had a generous display of the famous (and regional) Tasty-cakes. They were standard fare in Charlie's lunch box for years. Charlie remembered the butterscotch krimpets, the chocolate cupcakes, Tandy-cakes and the pies that the Tasty Baking Company made in Philly and sold only in the Delmarva Peninsula and Philly.

You couldn't find them beyond the area for years. They were always fresh, and above all delicious.

Gina said "I sure do!" and it was the place where he and Joey Esposito had gone to talk about Gina. When they sat down Charlie laughed and said, "Gina, I've known this place for years and Joey Esposito and I had lunch here no more than a few weeks ago when I told him about you – and us."

"Charlie, Joey knows and so do I. This is the *only* place in Philly for a cheese steak sandwich."

Charlie ordered two sandwiches, "all the way". "Drink, Gina?"

"Beer of course, Charlie! You can't eat a Philly cheese steak without a beer!"

When their meal was served, Charlie watched Gina delicately, but with resolve, devour her sandwich. "Gina, I swear, you are the only woman I ever saw eat a Philly cheese steak sandwich with class. I'm truly impressed."

"Practice, Charlie, practice!" she laughed.

"So, Gina, tell me about your uncle. He said he wanted to meet me?"

"Of course, Charlie. He's my uncle, my father, and a friend. Why wouldn't he want to meet you?"

"So what's his name, Gina? I'll have to call him something."

"His name is Carlo – a common Italian name. I'll tell you more before you meet him. But for now, just know him as Carlo."

"Wow, what a mystery!" Charlie said, "Is there some reason why I can't know his last name?"

"No, but as I told you, he is a wealthy businessman. You'll know his name when your hear it. Be patient, Charlie Mullins. Go with the flow. C'mon, Mullins, let's walk off the calories in the park."

Charlie and Gina left the sandwich shop and headed for the park. It was about a six-block walk and Gina grabbed his hand as they left the shop. "Fantastic day, isn't it Charlie? Light breeze, sun shining, and the two of us together. You want any more in life?"

"Well, right now I can't think of anything, Gina. I'm working on it."

Gina squeezed his hand. "Don't work too hard, Charlie. I don't want you thinking of alternatives. Who knows, you might decide you want one of those Shoreville ladies!"

"Speaking of Shoreville ladies, Gina, I think a couple of them planned to follow me here again today. I saw a car on my street and when I drove in the direction of the car, I saw what looked like two women ducked below the dashboard. I couldn't tell who it was but why would they hide unless they intended to follow me? It was the same car that followed me yesterday."

"Didn't I tell you, Charlie? They are not going to let up until they figure out what you are doing. You sure neither of them has the hots for you Charlie?"

"I don't think so, Gina. I don't even know who they are. I'm going to have a friend check out the license plate to see who owns the car. When I do..."

"You're gonna do what, Charlie Mullins? Punch 'em out? C'mon, there's nothing to do. They'll keep following you until they get tired of it or until something else occupies their tiny minds. Based on what you told me about Shoreville, you'll know soon enough anyway."

"Yeah, I guess you're right sweets." Charlie turned to look at Gina and could not resist kissing her.

"Hey Mr. Mullins! I might get used to that!"

"I sure as hell hope so, Miss Ferrelli. It's something I enjoy a lot. Gotta keep Charlie happy, you know."

"Chauvinist pig!" Gina laughed, "Only you have to be happy, huh?"

"Well, I didn't want to presume. I figured I would only worry about what pleased me on the assumption that you might not be inconvenienced."

"Oh yeah?" Gina turned and gave Charlie a kiss. Her body melted into his and he felt desire like he had never felt before. "Happy now, Mullins?" Gina laughed lightly.

They sat on the grass for a while and Charlie laid back with his head in Gina's lap. "You know, Gina. I had never thought about my job at Shaw before and how dull it is. I was content just to show up and do my work but now, it seems so sterile and so dry. I think if I were around you every day, things wouldn't be so bad or so boring. But now, when I go home to my house, it seems very, very empty."

"Same here, Charlie. I was always busy with my promotions, charity, and volunteer work. I find myself wanting to talk to you about things at the end of the day. You're not there and the apartment seems terribly empty."

"OK, Gina then when do I meet Uncle Carlo – the guy with no last name?"

"Two weeks from today, Charlie. We are going to have lunch with him."

"Lunch, huh? Am I going to need to wear a suit?"

"Oh, jeez, Charlie! This is my uncle you're talking about. Of course you won't need a suit. Just wear your usual casual business stuff – that blazer, khakis, those Guccis, and a shirt. I wouldn't suggest anything very weird like sandals and Bermudas, but you don't wear that stuff anyway. Just be your usual buttoned down self."

"Gina! You make me sound like some sort of corporate weasel!"

"Not at all, Charlie. My uncle is not going to look at what you wear unless it is weird. He's going to look at *you* – and quite well I should add. Like I said, just stay away from the 'California look' and you'll be OK. If you wear a suit, he will be equally formal. Relax, Charlie. Like you say, he puts his pants on one leg at a time, just like you."

Charlie broke out in a laugh. "Boy do you pay attention, girl!"

"I hang on your every word, Mullins, or haven't you noticed?"

They kissed again.

It was time for Charlie to head back to Shoreville so they reluctantly got up and left the park. They walked back to the *trattoria* which was a reasonable distance. They didn't talk – each savoring the presence of the other. When they got back to the *trattoria*, Charlie noticed that Johnny was once again in the alley, smoking.

"Gina, how does Johnny know to be outside when we arrive?"

"Oh, c'mon Charlie. He's just having a smoke."

"He's always having a smoke or standing around when we arrive, Gina."

"I told you already, Charlie. He's known me for years. I tutor his kids. He is as protective of me as my friends."

"Well, he protects me too. I noticed that he always waits until I get inside the parking garage before leaving what looks like his 'post'."

"It's just Johnny, Charlie. He's no different than many of the others around me. He thinks I have to be protected. It's harmless."

"If you say so, baby. You gonna call me during the week?"

"As always, Mr. Mullins – I cannot resist your sexy voice!"

"That's the first time anybody ever said that to me, Gina!"

"Good – see how original I can be?" I'll call you Charlie. "See if you can dream about me. And get back here as soon as possible, OK?"

"You bet, see ya' later Gina."

"You're forgetting something, Mullins. Give me a kiss!"

Charlie gave her a passionate and long kiss. When they parted he was flushed. "Whew – Gina you are tooooo much." He walked toward the parking garage, waved goodbye to Johnny, who nodded as before. He got his car and drove south to Shoreville as he had done for the past few weeks.

XII

Monday morning Charlie Mullins headed for the bridge to Wilmington and to his office at Shaw. He had to drive by the YMCA on the way and he saw the car that had followed him twice pulling out of the parking lot. At the wheel was Sharon Gallagher and in the passenger seat was Diane Simms. They were coming from their morning aerobics class. *"Son of a bitch,"* Charlie thought, *"so it was Sharon's car that followed me. Bill's gonna hear about this!"*

Wednesday night was bowling league night and Bill Gallagher was there. Not wanting to say anything in front of the others, Charlie asked Bill to join him at the bar for a beer. "What's up, Charlie? Everything OK? You're really hot tonight, be careful you don't break the pins.!"

"I've got a problem, Bill and I need your help and advice."

"Well, that's a new wrinkle. Charlie Mullins with a problem that he wants to talk about? You're always so reserved Charlie, nobody thinks you ever have a problem. Why even when your marriage was...."

"OK, Bill. I gotcha. My problem involves Sharon." Bill Gallagher felt a sudden pang in the pit of his stomach.

"Oh hell, Charlie, is Sharon pestering you again to get married? I told her to lay off that shit!"

"No, Bill, actually it's a little more serious. Sharon and someone else followed me last Saturday morning as I was driving to Philly. I got off the interstate at Chester and managed to lose them. I didn't want to talk to you about this, but I've known you and Sharon both for years, so I figured I would bring it up. Could you talk to her and tell her that I really don't appreciate being followed around? I'm asking you as a friend, Bill."

"Oh, Christ, Charlie! I'm sorry. Jeez. I'll talk to her as soon as I get home. She told me she was going shopping in Wilmington with Diane Simms on Saturday. I had no damned idea..." Bill lied. He knew that Sharon would one day follow Charlie to Philly. She had said so to him herself.

"Thanks, Bill. I appreciate it. I don't want problems with my friends and neighbors. I just want my privacy. Sharon crossed the line."

"Yeah, I know, I know. Sharon can be a real pain in the ass sometimes and it's worse when she gets around Diane. They both think you have to get married to one of their friends here in Shoreville."

"Whatever, Bill. I'd just appreciate it if you would take care of it."

* * * * *

Bill Gallagher arrived home hopping mad. "Sharon! goddammit Sharon, I want to talk to you!"

Sharon stepped into the living room, "Calm down Bill, I can hear you. What's so damned important that you have to yell?"

"I was just talking to Charlie Mullins. He told me that you and someone else – most certainly Diane Simms – followed him up I-95 toward Philly last Saturday. Godammit, Sharon, didn't I tell you to leave him alone and to butt out?"

"Who said it was me, Bill? How did Charlie know it was me who was following him? Hell, it could have been anybody and maybe nobody was even following him!"

"Knock it off, Sharon! He wrote down the license plate number and he saw you driving out of the YMCA on Monday. It was you, Sharon – you! And he said somebody else was with you. I'm willing to bet it was Diane, wasn't it?"

Sharon knew she had been caught and it would do no good to deny. "OK, Bill it was me and Diane was with me, but so what? We were only satisfying feminine curiosity. If he wasn't doing something wrong it shouldn't make any difference!"

"Sharon, I'm gonna say it again – it's none of your fucking business nor any business of Diane Simms if Charlie is doing something wrong, something weird, or whatever. Leave him alone, dammit! Besides, you remember what Charlie's job is at Shaw? He could probably have me fired with the connections he's got. I could be shoveling shit and you could be waiting tables at Jimmy Balsamo's. You want that?"

"Bill, Charlie is your friend. He wouldn't do something like that and you know it."

"Bull shit, Sharon! Charlie is my friend and friends don't go poking around into personal matters of other friends. And that goes for friends' wives as well. I want to keep him my friend, so just take your feminine curiosity, as you call it, and stifle it! You hear me? You stifle it, you understand?"

"All right, Bill. You're overreacting and being silly about this, but all right. I won't follow him ever again." Sharon lied.

"And you tell Diane to lay off too, you hear? I'm damned sure Charlie is going to tell Bob the same thing he told me. I don't need this shit and Bob doesn't either!"

"Jesus Bill, next thing you know Charlie will be firing everybody at Shaw! It's not that serious! But I already gave you my word so let's just drop it."

"Good idea, Sharon – damned good idea. Drop it. Just drop it – completely."

Bill Gallagher was right. Charlie did talk to Bob Simms too. He told him the same thing that he had told Bill but added that he wasn't sure it was Diane with Sharon. Bob said that Diane said she was going to go shopping with Sharon that Saturday morning so it might have been. He said he would look into it and if it was true, he was sorry and that he would make sure it didn't happen again. When he got home he had basically the same conversation with Diane that Bill had with Sharon. He reminded his wife that Charlie was a "big shot" at Shaw and if he got pissed enough he might just get revenge. Not having talked to Sharon, Diane denied involvement in the chase. Bob simply said, "Don't deny and don't confirm. Just listen to me good. Don't bother Charlie Mullins. Stay out of his life and leave him alone. If you weren't with Sharon, no big deal. But if you were, don't do it again. Ever!"

"Maybe Charlie is just paranoid, Bob. Who's to say he was being followed?"

Bob Simms lost his temper. "*Charlie* is to say if he is being followed. I don't care if he imagined it or not. If you and Sharon were behind him, and got off behind him at Chester like he said you did, it's my view that you were following him. So, I will say it again, read my lips: Leave Charlie Mullins alone!"

"All right, all right! You don't need to yell. I got your message."

"Good!"

Thursday morning Bill Gallagher called Bob Simms at work and asked him to meet him for a beer after work. Bob asked, "This is about the girls, right? Charlie talked to me and told me he had talked to you too. Shit! What a drag."

"Yeah, well, we have to put at stop to it, Bob. Let's meet tonight and talk this over. Besides the fact that Charlie is a friend, I don't want him so mad that he gets on my ass at work. He does have a lot of friends in management and I like my job!"

"Yeah, I know what you mean, Bill. See you tonight."

Gina called Charlie Thursday night. "Hey Mullins, where have you been?! I've missed you."

"Sorry Gina, I had to go to bowling league last night in part just to show up and also to talk to the guys whose wives I presume were the ones who followed me. I was sure about one, but the other I couldn't see, but I'm pretty sure I know who it was."

"Wow – and I missed that! So what happened, Charlie?"

"Oh, I don't know, Gina but I am fairly sure that there is some domestic discord in Shoreville tonight! Neither guy seemed terribly happy. They both work for Shaw and I figure they probably thought I might do them some damage on their jobs."

"Would you do that, Charlie?"

"Of course not, Gina, I am not into that kind of corporate stuff. I certainly would not mix business with my personal life just to get even. Besides, they didn't do anything; it was their wives who did."

"You're a nice guy, Mullins. My uncle probably would have kicked their butts."

"Well, I felt like kicking the butts of their wives, that's for sure. But those poor guys are just married to a couple of wackos. I can't blame them – at least not until they talk to their wives. I suspect the talks won't be exactly pleasant either."

"Well, Charlie, I guess I only see you Saturday, right?"

"Yeah, Gina, I'm sorry but I have a lot of stuff to do around the house before I take off. Is that OK? I'd love to see you, but I can't let things slip here."

"Charlie Mullins, you need a woman in your life!"

"I thought I had one, did you change your mind?"

"Oh no, I just thought I would bring it up to remind you!" Gina laughed.

"That's better, not that I need reminding. You'll call me tomorrow night?"

"You bet. If I can't see you, at least I can hear you. My senses need you, Charlie."

"Careful, young lady, that kind of talk could lead somewhere."

"I hope so. Talk to you tomorrow. Kisses!" Gina rang off.

* * * * *

Bill Gallagher and Bob Simms met after work at Jimmy Balsamo's bar. They got a booth and ordered beers. "Jesus, Bob, what a pain in the ass. Why the hell can't they leave Charlie alone, huh?"

"That's easy enough to figure out Bill. Diane and Sharon figure they owe it to their divorced or single friends to fix them up with Charlie. And that's in addition to the fact that both of them are nosy as hell. They just love some 'secret' that they need to figure out and talk about and off they go."

"Yeah, well Charlie is a buddy and I sure don't want him pissed at me because of Sharon's nonsense."

"Same here, I read the riot act to Diane even though Charlie said he could not be sure she was with Sharon."

"I did the same with Sharon. You think they'll stop?"

"Want the truth? Probably not, but they will cool off for a while. I scared the shit out of Diane saying that it might cost me my job."

Bill laughed, "Me too, I told Sharon she might wind up having to wait tables here at Jimmy's while I got a job shoveling shit. I think that cooled her down a lot."

They both laughed. "OK", said Bob, "I think we have at least stopped the nonsense for the time being. Next time Diane says she is going out shopping with Sharon, I'll call you. If they try that shit again, maybe we can stop 'em!"

Bill Gallagher lifted his beer mug, "Bob, here's to the days when the broads chased *us*," and laughed.

"I'll drink to that, Bill. Those were the days. Here's to what it was tryin' to get laid!"

They clinked their beer mugs together, laughed again, and then ordered another beer before going home to a pair of sullen wives still smarting from yesterday's lectures from their respective husbands.

XIII

Gina called Charlie on Friday night. "Hello Mr. Mystery Man of Shoreville. This is Gina calling."

"I kind of figured that much out, young lady. Should I identify myself?"

"No, I know by the voice I am talking to the same Irishman I talked to yesterday," Gina continued, "are you in the mood for an art exhibit tomorrow night Charlie? A friend of mine has a showing and I thought we could go before having dinner."

"*Trattoria* again?" asked Charlie.

"Why not?" said Gina, "What about six-thirty? Is that too early?"

"No, I can leave at about quarter to six and be there on time. No problem."

"It's a date, Mullins. Now tell me about your week and how it has been since yesterday," Gina laughed.

"Well, you know Fridays in corporations, Gina. Casual day. Everybody goes to enormous pains to look really casual but not *too* casual. You have to look sort of casually uptight." Gina laughed.

"Sounds truly stressful, all that casualness!"

"It's really stupid," Charlie replied, "it means you have to have a special casual wardrobe in addition to a collection of suits. I mean you can't show up in a sweat suit and sneakers, you know? So a lot of guys run around buying those men's fashion magazines to see what is considered studiously casual. Casual but not too casual. It's like the bullshit about calling people by their first names to imply a sort of family relationship among colleagues. You know, like 'Say Bob, I just tried to fuck you at that last meeting. Is that OK, Bob? Good to see you again, Bob. Have a nice day, Bob. And, by the way, Bob, you are a real asshole, Bob!"

Gina broke out laughing, "You've got the corporate scene down pat, Charlie! Sounds a bit cynical though. I get the impression you don't buy into it."

86

"You got that impression, huh? No, Gina, I don't think much of the screw-your-buddy approach to life. My Dad used to tell me to treat people well on the way up the ladder because you might pass them again on your way down."

"That's a wise man, Charlie. I used to hear a lot of the hot-shots I met bragging about how they knocked down one guy or another only to find out that somebody had knocked them down a little later."

They talked for a little while longer and then rang off. Charlie set about getting his laundry done, running the vacuum cleaner, and putting dishes in the dishwasher. He watched some TV and then went to bed. He felt good.

XIV

On Saturday morning Charlie went to softball practice as usual. Both Bill Gallagher and Bob Simms were there. Each approached him separately and told him they had talked to their wives and he should have no more problems with their trying to follow him. Charlie thanked them for their understanding and said, "OK guys, let's get some practice." Both Bill and Bob were relieved.

After practice it was the usual pizza and beer. Charlie begged off claiming work at home. After he had left, Bill Gallagher and Bob Simms sat together. "Charlie talked to me, Bill, and thanked me for talking to Diane."

"Yeah, he did the same with me," Bill said, "I guess he's not pissed."

"Well not yet, anyway. But if it happens again he is not going to be so nice about it."

"Yeah, I know. Have a slice of pizza!"

Tony Mazza said in a loud voice, "Anybody seen Charlie? I know he's Irish, but pizza is good for you with all that tomato sauce and fiber. I'm worried about his health."

"Stifle it, Tony!" Bill Gallagher yelled back, "he's got work to do."

"Yeah, I know what kind of work!" Art Samuels chimed in and then repeated his obscene hip pumping gesture.

The group laughed and then further reference to Charlie was drowned in pitchers of beer and smothered in slices of pizza.

Charlie went back to his house and finished up the cleaning he had started Friday night. He did some more laundry and put his softball uniform to soak. He fixed a light lunch of tuna salad on whole wheat bread and washed it down with a beer. He relaxed for a while by watching a movie on cable TV and then showered and shaved, splashed on the Armani that he was now using on a regular basis.

He dressed, this time in a dark blue suit. He thought about putting on a collarless shirt to look like what he figured might be the way Bruce Willis would dress but all he had were cotton T-shirts. *"Nope!"* he thought *"I'm gonna have to wear a tie."* He put on a light blue oxford cloth shirt and then chose a patterned tie to reduce the severity of the dark suit. He also put on a pair of black tassle loafers instead of a pair of lace ups so he would look like what he thought was "less corporate".

At a quarter-to-six he left the house on the way to Philly. He checked the street to make sure his warnings to Bill and Bob had the desired effect. As he approached the bridge to cross over to Wilmington he checked again. No car parked nearby. He picked up the entrance to the bridge and when he hit the entrance to I-95 he checked again. *"Thanks guys,"* he thought.

He arrived to the *trattoria* a few minutes early. Gina had not yet arrived. When she did, Charlie was thunderstruck. Gina was wearing a black silk dress. The bodice was two pieces of silk that tied behind her neck. She was showing just enough cleavage to cause Charlie to wonder if he would not be salivating all night. She was not wearing a bra.

Charlie got up to greet her and noticed the ubiquitous Johnny already with a chair for Gina. "Hey handsome, she said. Don't you look the success!"

"Thanks, Gina, but next to you I feel like I'm dressed like a busboy."

Gina laughed, "This old thing?" and then laughed again. She *knew* she looked good.

"Yeah, that old thing," said Charlie "I guess you bought it at Goodwill, right?"

"There 'good will' in it, Charlie but, no, it's definitely not Goodwill!" Gina continued, "Charlie, you know what I would like to do tonight?"

"Go to an art exhibition?"

"Smart ass! Yes, go to an art exhibition then go out for dinner at a place where we can dance. Can you dance, Charlie?"

"A real Fred Astaire my dear. To your Ginger, of course! Yeah, I think I can hold my own on a dance floor."

"All right!" Gina gave Charlie a "high five" to which he responded a bit shyly.

"Never been high-fived, Charlie?"

"Not by a beautiful woman, no. You surprised me."

"I have a lot of surprises in store for you Mr. Mullins, but let's get going. We have an art show to go to."

Johnny hailed a cab for them and they headed for the exhibition. Charlie dutifully looked at all the paintings. He shook hands with Gina's friends, some of whom he had not yet met others he knew from previous events. However, Charlie's mind was on the prospect of holding Gina close and dancing with her. After wandering around with Gina and saying hello to a lot of people, Gina whispered into his ear, "Let's blow this joint, Mullins, I wanna dance."

Charlie could not stifle a laugh. "Blow this joint, Gina? Where'd you get that kind of talk?"

"I told ya, Mullins, I'm a Philly broad! Let's go."

"Took the words out of my mouth, lady. Take my arm, we're on the way!"

They stepped outside and Gina kissed Charlie firmly on the mouth. When he recovered he noticed an approaching cab and flagged it down. Gina gave the driver an address where they could have dinner and dance. On the way to the restaurant, she kissed him again. "Boy did I miss you this week, Charles! I really did."

"Well, at least we have that in common, Gina," Charlie laughed.

When they arrived to the restaurant Charlie was already climbing the walls. Gina had him almost hypnotized and he was loving every moment.

Again, they were given superb seating. The restaurant was crowded and Charlie noticed that when they walked in every eye was on Gina. He thought to himself, *"The world is a tuxedo and I'm a pair of brown shoes!"* She followed the headwaiter to their table with Charlie close behind and it looked to Charlie like there was a spotlight on her. The whole place took in her exquisite beauty and it was clear from the table they got that she must have been somebody important. Again, Charlie marveled at the power that beauty provided. When Gina had seated herself with the help of a waiter who could not help looking at her cleavage, Charlie settled into his chair. He noticed that no one was holding his chair for him.

They ordered dinner and a fine Chilean wine – Don Melchor. Gina seemed pleased that Charlie seemed to know his wines. A man like that was romantic she thought, especially when it seemed to be natural and not something he had read in the most recent edition of *Esquire*.

A small orchestra was playing some nice slow dance music and Gina said "Why don't we have a dance before the wine and the dinner arrive?"

"I thought you would never ask!" replied Charlie.

They moved to the dance floor and Charlie wondered how he was going to dance with Gina without melting into the floor. He reached for her lightly and she pressed into him delicately. She planted her cheek firmly to his and they danced. "I'm impressed, Mr. Mullins, you are a regular twinkle toes."

"Not bad, I guess, Gina. Maybe it's just easy to dance with you."

"Oooohhh, isn't that gallant? I accept the compliment willingly."

After the music stopped they worked their way back to the table. Charlie wondered if he might be panting and, if so, if Gina could hear it. He had always been impressed by Gina's self-composure but she seemed even more so tonight. She was quick, witty, and seemed to be enjoying herself immensely.

They enjoyed their dinner and Charlie ordered another bottle of wine. "That's really a delicious wine, Charlie. A wonderful choice." Gina was just a little giddy from the wine. He was giddy from holding her close all night and smelling her perfume. He thought it was "Opium" but what the hell did he know?

They danced until the last patrons were being informed that it was "last call" which meant, "get the hell out, we're tired of watching you dance!"

Gina looked at Charlie and said, "Charlie, I don't think you are going to be able to drive home."

"Nonsense, Gina. I'm fine."

"I don't know, Charlie. We've had two bottles of wine – that averages out to a bottle each and that will put you over the alcohol in your blood limit in Pennsylvania, Delaware, and New Jersey combined!" Gina giggled.

She looked at Charlie intently and added, "Why don't you stay at my place tonight? We'll take the cab from here and you can leave your car in the parking garage at the *trattoria*."

Charlie was dumbfounded. "Ah, well, I don't want to impose, Gina. I mean I guess I could sleep on your couch."

"Won't that be crowded, Charlie? I mean it's not a big couch and one of us might fall off."

"Holy shit!" thought Charlie, *"I've died and gone to heaven. Did I hear her right?"*

"Say that again, Gina! You want me to sleep with you at your place?"

"Would you rather I sent you an engraved invitation, Mr. Mullins? I think you understood what I said. Or no? Are you being reluctant, Charlie?"

"She means it! Oh my God. Mullins, you are the luckiest guy in the world!"

"Ah, oh, no, Gina. I'm not being reluctant. In fact, let's get the hell out of here!"

"Thought you'd never ask!" she said.

Charlie paid the check and then flagged a cab in front of the restaurant. Gina gave the driver the address.

Gina's apartment was as beautifully appointed as Gina. It was feminine and organized as only Gina could make it. It was also clearly expensive. She lived well. Gina looked at Charlie and said, "Welcome, Charlie. This is my space." Then she moved closer to Charlie and kissed him. They stood there kissing for several moments. She melted into him and could feel his excitement. He returned her kiss with equal passion. His hands automatically moved to her breasts and she gasped and pushed closer. When they pulled apart, he said "God, Gina, I'm crazy about you! I want you."

"Me too, Charlie, now kiss me again while I undo your shirt." She kissed him fiercely and began to unbutton his shirt while his hand reached back to the knot at the base of her neck. He untied it and the two parts of the dress fell downward to reveal her beautiful breasts. Charlie looked at her for a moment and then began kissing each breast. He thought he would explode. They both yanked off the rest of their clothes and Gina led him to the bedroom.

What Gina lacked in experience she made up for in enthusiasm. She was a passionate and wild lover. Charlie did not remember a more beautiful moment in his life. Tony Mazza once commented to him that the best thing in the world was to make love to a woman you really loved. Tony had that kind of relationship with his wife, Marie. Charlie now knew what Tony meant.

When they had recovered from their lovemaking, Charlie looked over at Gina and said, "You are the most beautiful creature in the world, Gina. I'm in love with you. I want you for me for the rest of my life."

"Nice of you to say that Mullins after I just finished seducing you." She laughed heartily, "I love you too if you didn't notice."

"Oh, I noticed all right," said Charlie "I won't be able to take my shirt off in the locker room for a couple of weeks, I think."

"Ohhhh, did I do that?" Gina teased as she looked at the red furrows down Charlie's back. She bent over and kissed his back tenderly, "well maybe if the horny wives of Shoreville see those welts they might think twice about messing around with you. I could scratch their eyes out!"

"I don't doubt it, Gina. You certainly are passionate."

"You do that, Charlie. It's you."

They made love twice more then fell asleep in each other's arms. Gina dozed off first and Charlie looked at her beautiful face and body until he also fell asleep. He felt like the happiest man in the world and slept like he had not slept in years.

XV

Charlie woke up Sunday morning to the smell of strong coffee. He was starting to sit up in bed when Gina entered the bedroom with a cup of coffee. "Good morning, Mr. Mullins. Did you sleep well? Would you like some coffee?"

Charlie took the mug in his hands and looked at Gina. She was wearing a short silk baby doll and a semi-transparent floor length negligee. Her beautiful feet were in a pair of silk bedroom slippers. "Do you have some sort of fairy godmother that makes you beautiful in the morning?" Charlie asked.

"No fairy godmother, Charlie, love. Love blinds you and that makes me look beautiful," she laughed.

"Whatever," said Charlie, "I'm not gonna question what works!"

"So, how was your evening, Charlie?" Gina had a sly look on her face.

"Oh, so-so, said Charlie. I only made love to a beautiful woman and fell asleep in her bed. Could have been better I suppose." Charlie laughed.

"Really?" Gina slipped into the bed, "think you could do it again?"

Charlie was already aroused when Gina touched him. "I guess you can!" she exclaimed and pulled him to her.

Charlie fell back out of breath when they had finished. "I've died and gone to heaven!" he exclaimed.

"Well, what do you say we catch a cloud and get some brunch?" Gina said.

"Yeah, I think I am pretty hungry," said Charlie "it must have been the exercise."

"OK, Mullins, get your ass out of that bed and shower up."

"Oh hell, Gina. I only have the same clothes I wore last night."

"Bad planning Charlie. Just goes to show that you didn't start out thinking you would get me into bed. I'm pleased."

"Yeah, maybe you're pleased" said Charlie but I have to wear the clothes I wore last night. Can you stand being around me?"

"Tell you what, Charlie, why don't I just send out for something and we'll eat here. That better?"

"Have you got a razor here, Gina?" Charlie asked.

"Nope, how about some hot wax for your beard?"

"Oh my God! He exclaimed, "I think not. It sounds painful."

"It is, baby. It's the price of beauty. If we women can take it, why not you?"

"I'll forgo the pleasure, thanks," said Charlie.

"Take your shower, Charlie and I'll order some breakfast for us. Take your time, it'll be about half an hour before the stuff arrives."

Charlie walked to the bathroom, closed the door and turned on the shower. The warm water felt good but stung his back. When he stepped out of the shower he turned to see his back in the mirror. He was pretty well scratched as far as he could see. *"It was worth it,"* he thought *"I hope it stings all week so I can remember last night!"*

The bathroom was a woman's bathroom. Perfumes, creams, several hair brushes, a hair dryer. Not a masculine thing in the whole place. He looked around for an extra toothbrush and there was none. "Gina!" he yelled, "have you got an extra toothbrush I can use?"

"God, Charlie, after all we did last night and all that kissy face, I think you can use mine, no? Are you fussy?"

"Nope, OK with me. Thanks." He brushed his teeth, wrapped himself in a towel and looked around for his clothes that were strewn all over the place. He put on his shorts, pants, and shirt. The breakfast arrived in a few minutes while he had another cup of strong coffee. Gina had ordered their breakfast from a bakery nearby. It was delicious and Charlie was famished.

"Charlie?" Gina asked, "Do you have a credit card or some cash with you?"

"Yeah, I have both, Gina. Why?"

"Well, since you are going to be here all day, why don't we go to the mall and get you some clothes and some shaving stuff? You can leave it here for when you come back."

"This is too damned good to be true!"

"OK, Gina. Are you sure about this? I mean…."

"You mean what, Charlie. You mean you would rather walk around in the clothes you wore yesterday than have some clothes hanging in my closet?"

"God no Gina, I mean I don't want to intrude on your space…."

94

"Oh, I see. You make love to me 4 times in the last 24 hours and you are worried about hanging some clothes in my closet! Charlie Mullins, you are really, really weird!"

"Oh hell, I don't know what I mean, Gina. I love you. I respect you. I want you to be mine. I just don't want to feel like I am forcing something on you..."

"There you go again. As I recall, it was I who seduced you last night. You think I am going to mind if you hang your pants in my closet? Yesterday they were on my floor! Let's go Mullins, we have to do some shopping!"

"Charlie and Gina went down to the garage in the basement of her building. She walked purposefully to a black Mercedes. C'mon Charlie, let's rush out to save. We'll find us some nice stuff on sale. The more we spend the more we save, right?"

Charlie got in on the passenger side and noticed that the windows were tinted – perhaps more so than the law allowed. Anyone outside the car would have a hard time seeing inside. The cops didn't like that but then again, maybe a beautiful woman can convince them that the dark film is necessary to her safety. *"Who knows?"* he thought.

Gina drove to a local shopping center. Charlie accompanied her to a men's store where she sat down and let him choose whatever he felt like buying. After he had chosen a couple pairs of pants and about 3 shirts she interrupted him, "I want you to buy silk boxer shorts, Charlie." Charlie asked her, "What, Gina? Did you say silk boxer shorts?"

"That's what I said, Charlie. They're sexy and I imagine myself pulling them down. Got it?"

"Silk boxers it is!" replied Charlie.

"I'm going to step out for a minute while you try all this stuff on. I want to run by another store for a minute. OK?"

"Sure, Gina, go ahead. I'll be here for a few minutes anyway."

Gina left and came back in about 15 minutes with a small package. "Here, Charlie. Put this with your purchases."

"What's this Gina?"

"It's a bottle of Armani cologne. You think I didn't recognize the fragrance when you switched from that awful drug store stuff you had been using?"

Charlie laughed out loud. "You're too smart for me, girl. I'm in your hands. Take me!"

"Right, Charlie. The pants fit OK?"

"Yeah, they're fine. Don't even need to alter them. Just right."

"You got some shirts, socks, and…."

"Yeah, I got silk boxer shorts, Gina. Navy blue OK?"

"Oh my God, Charlie, navy blue sets me off like a roman candle!" Gina feigned a fainting spell.

Charlie paid for his purchases with his credit card and they headed for a local drug store in the mall to buy some toiletries. Charlie got some shaving gel, a pack of disposable razors, deodorant, a tooth brush and looked for a moment at the cologne display.

"Don't even think about it, Mullins!" Gina said, "Never again. You've got your sexy cologne now."

Charlie laughed, "OK, beautiful. From now on you pick the smell."

"You can bet on it, Mr. Drugstore Cologne. I'll take over in that department if you don't mind!"

When they had finished the purchases Gina said, "Hey Charles, you gonna starve me to death? I'd love some lunch. What do you say?"

"God yes, Gina, I'm sorry, I forgot. So much has happened in the last several hours I'm still a bit dizzy."

"I think you're dizzy from hunger, Charlie. I know I am. Let's go."

They found a Ruby Tuesday's in the mall and served themselves from the salad bar. When they finished, Charlie paid the bill and they drove back to Gina's place. When they got there and entered the apartment, Gina took on a serious look. "Charlie, let's talk. I need to tell you something. I don't want to surprise you and I don't want to be surprised either. Sit down and I'll fix us an espresso."

Gina went to a small espresso machine and fixed two cups of the strong coffee. "Charlie, don't ruin this with sweetener, right? This is real Italian espresso and it would break my heart to see you fill it with a list of chemicals that reads like the side of a detergent box."

Charlie laughed, "Gotcha, Gina. Sugar it is."

"Charlie, next week you meet my uncle, my father, and one of my best friends all in the same person. I want to talk to you about that meeting."

"I've been waiting for this Gina. At least now maybe I will know the last name of the guy I'm going to meet." He laughed.

Gina remained serious. "It's Rizzo, Charlie. His last name is Rizzo." She looked at him apprehensively.

The name did not register with Charlie at first. "OK, first name Carlo, last name Rizzo. Carlo Rizzo….Carlo Rizzo?"

Suddenly Charlie realized that he was saying the name of the most famous Italian in Philly. Carlo Rizzo, chief capo of the Philly mafia.

"Excuse me, Gina, did you say Carlo Rizzo?"

"No, Charlie, I said 'Rizzo'. YOU said *Carlo* Rizzo."

"You mean Carlo Rizzo, the guy who is supposed to be...." Charlie pulled himself up short.

"The head of the Philadelphia mob, Charlie? Yes, *that* Carlo Rizzo. That's the man who is my uncle." For the first time Gina had fear in her eyes. She was waiting for Charlie's reaction and she hoped it would not be the same as so many of the others she had known. When she told other guys what her uncle's name was, they paled. Most of them found a reason to take off and never called her again. She didn't want this to happen with Charlie but it would not be possible to keep her uncle's name a secret.

"I, ah, never, I mean, who would have, that is...."

"C'mon Charlie. Out with it, Carlo Rizzo, reputed mafia don of Philadelphia is my uncle. He is my father. He raised me from almost infancy. He kissed me goodnight when I was a child. He gave me aspirin when I had a fever. Yeah, that Carlo Rizzo is my uncle. He's the guy you're gonna meet. Now what?"

"Gina, give me a minute to digest this. I never suspected that you were Carlo Rizzo's daughter. I mean you are the same girl you were an hour ago, but you are Carlo Rizzo's daughter, niece, whatever. Having spent the most wonderful night of my life with you last night and then hearing you tell me you are Carlo Rizzo's daughter, niece, I mean wow, that's some 24 hours, and it's not even 24 hours yet!"

"Charlie, you've got a week to think about this. If you want to call off the meeting, you can. I know what you might be thinking. I've been through this before so I am not surprised. I told you I am resilient. Let me just say that I do love you, Charlie. But if my uncle's reputation creates a problem for us, for you, I will understand."

"No, Gina, I love you. Your uncle is not a problem for me – at least I don't think so. The fact that he is....ah, Carlo Rizzo...doesn't bother me. I mean, I had not expected this particular information. I don't know why not, because you could be anybody's niece, right? It just happens to be Carlo Rizzo. Why not? Why would I think that Carlo Rizzo would not have relatives, huh? I mean he puts his pants on one leg at a time, just like me, right? He most certainly had a mother and a father. He has a beautiful niece. Why should Carlo Rizzo be any different than any other human being?"

"I'll tell you why, Charlie. Because he is powerful, that's why. People are afraid of him the way they are afraid of other powerful people."

"Gina, look, I don't want to discuss your uncle. I want his approval of our relationship and our love. He is the person who raised you and it is not up to me to judge him. I want *you*. All I want from your uncle is his blessing and approval."

Gina broke into tears. "Oh, Charlie. Oh my God, Charlie," she was sobbing "I am so happy that you said that. You can't know what I have been through. I love you so much and I was so afraid to lose you but there was no way I could hide you from my uncle or him from you. I had to do this."

Charlie pulled him to her and hugged her. He kissed her forehead and her tears. He lifted her face to his and said, "Gina, I have never felt about anyone the way I feel about you. I loved you the first time I saw you. I confess to being surprised at your uncle's name and fame, but so help me God, I cannot love you less and I can't leave you. I don't want to and I won't!'

Through her sobs Gina smiled and said, "You got balls, Mullins. Man do you have balls!" then, still sobbing, she let out a laugh. "You're going to meet the most feared man in Philly. Do you know that? I know him as an uncle, everybody else knows him as a terrible man. No one ever refers to him as 'mister' in the press. They call him The Don, or Don Carlo! How stupid! A poor peasant kid from Sicily who made it as best he could and they can't call him Mr. Rizzo." She looked up at Charlie, "Are you sure, Charlie, I mean really sure?"

"Gina, my father taught me that life is short and it can be tough. He also taught me never to stand in judgment of anyone else. This man is your uncle and I will consider him as such. I want you. I have never wanted anyone more in my life. I love you, more than I ever thought I could love someone. I'm not going to lose that because you've got an uncle with a reputation."

"You know, of course there are some implications for you because you are my guy, Charlie. A lot of people will avoid you and a lot will try to get close to you because of my uncle...."

"So how is that different from the corporate world I inhabit, Gina? A lot of people avoid me because of my contacts in the company and a lot try to suck up because of my contacts. Doesn't strike me as a whole lot different."

"Charlie!" Gina was still sobbing, "God how I love you. You are the most wonderful man I have ever met. I was right when I said you had character. You are a man's man Charlie and you are a woman's man. You are what I want in my life. But you have to listen to me. Being the boyfriend or fiancé, or whatever, of Carlo Rizzo's niece is a bit special Charlie. People will look at you differently. The press will bother you. They don't do that in your job. You might find yourself being harassed by the FBI. There are a lot of things 'special' about my uncle."

"Gina, let me be clear. If not having to deal with any of that would mean not being with you, I don't give a shit. I mean it! If I have to put up with idiots and harassment, I'll do it. What I *don't* want is to be without you in my life. OK?"

"Oh, God, yes, Charlie. OK, OK, OK! I love you," Gina broke out in tears again. She was crying for years of frustration and disappointment. She was crying out of sheer relief that this time she was free. She had found a man who was not intimidated, fearful of losing his job, or trying to get "mobbed up". She had found a man who simply loved her. It was what she had looked for all her life.

Gina sat down, still sobbing and trying to control her tears. "Charlie, would you pour me a drink? Just a little scotch. I need to come down. I'm a wreck."

"Charlie got the bottle of scotch and poured a couple of fingers worth into a glass. Here Gina, relax. When you are more composed we can talk."

Gina took the glass, took a sip, shuddered and took another small sip. "Thanks, Charlie. Give me a minute and I'll be OK."

"It's Sunday, Gina. I'm not going anywhere. Relax. I've got all day and hopefully the rest of my life to talk to you. No rush."

"Thanks, Charlie," Gina replied between sobs, "you brought years of frustration to an end and I guess I just let it all out. I feel exhausted."

Charlie embraced her and she fell into him. She felt emptied. She felt as if an enormous weight had been removed from her back. She felt light and dizzy. Charlie continued to hold her, rocking steadily and stroking her hair. "It's OK, Gina. I'm here and I always will be for you. I'm here. I love you and I'm here for you. Relax, baby. It's over now. We have each other. We can deal with it and worse if necessary. Shhhh!"

Charlie felt her sobs diminish in intensity and frequency. She was coming down. A lot of pent up emotion had spilled out of Gina Ferrelli. She had inherited a new life this day. Everything about her past that haunted her was eliminated in one fell swoop. She was free and overwhelmed by her freedom.

The enormity of the decision Charlie had taken was yet to be understood. He was concerned for Gina. He was comfortable with his decision. He wanted her and would do anything to keep her. But he sensed that trouble lay ahead. He would have to deal with some tough issues and he had no idea at this time what they might be. It was his woman who was upset and had been scared out of her wits. Charlie knew now how much Gina loved him and he was overcome with emotion himself.

"Charlie?" Gina said weakly, "can we lie down for a while? I feel exhausted."

"Sure, baby. C'mon, let's go into the bedroom. He led Gina to the bedroom, took off her shoes, and laid her down. He laid down next to her and she immediately fell into his arms. "I love you, Charlie", and then she fell sound asleep. Charlie held her in his arms and dozed off lightly himself.

Two hours later, Gina woke up. She was refreshed but still seemed a bit dazed. "You OK?" asked Charlie, "You slept like a log. You even had me worried for a while!"

"I'm OK, Charlie. I feel like a huge weight has been lifted off me, or like a festering infection had been lanceted. It was like everything just came out all at once."

"Can we talk a bit now, Gina? While you were sleeping I started thinking about a lot of things that happened since we met."

"Like what, Charlie?"

"Well, for example, let's start with Johnny the waiter at the *trattoria*. Does he know you're Carlo Rizzo's daughter? Is that why he hangs around whenever we go out. He waits until we leave and he is always there when we come back. Is he kind of watching over you?"

"Yes to all, Charlie. Johnny knows my uncle. My uncle once helped him out of a difficult scrape. He was on welfare. His kids were always sick. His wife couldn't find a job. My uncle got him the job at the *trattoria* and enrolled his kids in the Catholic School – the school is expensive you know. Johnny has always been grateful for my uncle's help. My uncle still pays the tuition for the kids and I tutor them for free. Johnny loves my uncle and he would do anything for him. He sees it as his job to make sure I'm safe whenever I am at the *trattoria*. I remember one night some obnoxious yuppie type started giving me a hard time. He tried to grab me. Before he even knew what was happening, Johnny had him by the throat. He literally carried him out the door by his throat and was about to really work him over when I ran out and asked Johnny to stop. He did, but not before giving the guy a punch in the ribs. I think he must have broken three of them. Johnny put him in an ambulance and told the driver to take him to the nearest hospital. Somebody told me the guy had moved to Seattle when he got out of the hospital. Johnny must have whispered something to him before he put him in the ambulance."

"Sounds like I better not argue with you at the *trattoria*," Charlie joked.

"Not funny, Charlie. Johnny really hurt that guy. I felt awful."

"Well, God knows what I might have done if I'd been there. Maybe Johnny let him off easy." Charlie continued, "So that's why Johnny was always there with a chair, always watching and protecting. And here I thought it was only because you are so beautiful. Was it because of Johnny's relationship with your uncle that we got such good seats at restaurants and never had to have a reservation?"

"I'm sure it was, Charlie. Johnny's an important person in the restaurant workers' union. He knows practically all of the waiters in Philly. If you ever need a good table in a hurry without a reservation, Johnny can arrange it with a phone call."

"Wow! Again I was sure it was the fact that you are beautiful."

"Why don't you keep thinking that way, Charlie? It's a lot more flattering than knowing that people are scared, ah, shitless, excuse my French, of my uncle."

"OK, Gina. Maybe I will be able to think it's because I am Charlie Mullins, too." He laughed.

Finally, Gina laughed back. She was coming out of her shock and getting back to her normal self.

Emboldened by the change in her attitude, Charlie said "I mean it Gina. What you told me changes nothing. I love you and that's that."

"I believe you Charlie, especially about loving me. But don't say it changes nothing. It will change everything in your life. Think about it. Just spend next week thinking. You will see how it will change everything. People will never be the same around you. You might even have to leave your job. You might be persecuted, investigated, your privacy invaded, and I know how important that is to you."

"Gina, no matter what you can say, nothing changes the fact that I love you. I want the rest of my life with you. If that means I leave the Shaw Corporation that's fine with me. I'm not letting you go and that's that."

"Oh Charlie, I am so happy. Let's stay in tonight and just be together. I really don't want to go out."

"Neither do I." said Charlie, "I'll have to get back to Shoreville to get ready for work tomorrow. I can leave late, but I will have to get back, Gina."

"No problem, I'm okay now Charlie, just a bit shook from the emotional flood but otherwise, I am just fine. In fact, I don't know when I have ever been finer."

"What do you want to do then, Gina. You want to send out for Irish Stew?"

"Send out for *what*, Charlie? What is Irish Stew?"

"Actually, I don't know Gina. I never had it but I did read the recipe for it once and it's got mutton in it. I *hate* mutton. I would hate it more boiled like it is in Irish stew. Listen, Gina, the one thing the Irish learned from the English is how to cook – badly. No flavoring. Just take a piece of meat, cover it with water and boil the hell out of it. I used to hate lunch time when I was in school with all the Italian kids. They all had these lunches that smelled of tomato sauce and oregano. I always had an apple jelly sandwich. You ever had an apple jelly sandwich, Gina? It's a grade above cardboard! It was a treat when I got some peanut butter with it."

"Poor boy," Gina laughed, "I'll fix you good Italian fare every day."

"So, Gina, what I meant to say after that little story was, let's send out for a pizza. OK?"

"Marvelous, Charlie, I'll call."

Gina ordered the pizza and a couple of beers and they both moved to the living room where they sat together on the sofa. Gina kissed Charlie gently. "Charlie, I want you to think about all this during the week. Your life is going to change. I know now that you love me but we now have to think about what our love means for your life. Mine is already cast. I'm Carlo Rizzo's niece and that's that. Those who know who I am understand and accept me when they are friends and ignore me when they are not. Those who don't know I leave to their ignorance because it is easier for all concerned. My uncle is a wealthy man, but you won't see him on the society page of the newspaper. Bankers seek him out in private but he is never invited to their soirees or cocktail parties. The only time he is photographed is when he is being hauled in by the FBI. Then he is photographed in handcuffs. When people learn that you and I are together and that you are an important executive, you'll see what I mean. I want you to be ready to deal with that Charlie. It won't be easy, believe me."

"Let's deal with that when it becomes an issue, Gina. We've been out a number of times and nobody has printed our picture in the papers or made any offhand comments."

"That's because you've only been around my friends, Charlie. Remember all those events we went to. No press, right?"

"Yeah, you're right. There were no press people there now that you mention it."

"That's because they weren't invited Charlie. And some of them wouldn't go if they were invited. Why should the niece of an accused mafia don show up on the society page with the cream of Philadelphia society?"

"I guess you're right, I hadn't thought about that. Well, what the hell, I'm in for the duration. You're mine and that's all there is to it. As Martin Luther King used to say, 'ain't nothin' gonna turn me 'round'. So, I will think about it and I will adapt, and we, you and me, will overcome. OK?"

'OK, Charlie. I love you so much. Oh, before I forget. Here, I want you to have this." Gina pressed a key into his hand.

"What's this for?" Charlie asked.

"It's the key to this place, Charlie. We don't have to meet at the *trattoria* any more. If you want to, you can bring some clothes up here. Maybe you want to leave a couple of suits, some ties, and dress shirts so you can leave here for work. Bring up whatever you want. I don't lack for closet space as you can see."

"Are you sure, Gina? This is your home. I don't want to invade your space."

"Oh, that's just great, Mullins. You take me to bed. You hear me out. You tell me you love me and then you don't want to invade my space? Charlie, you've already invaded my space more than anyone ever could and you are welcome in it. Bring up some clothes if you want. I think you'll find it more comfortable."

"OK, baby. I'll bring up some stuff during the week and some more over the weekend."

"That's better, Charlie Mullins, and enough of that 'invasion' nonsense. You invaded my heart and my body and I love it."

Charlie looked at his watch. It was eleven-o-clock. "Gina, I'm going to have to go back to Shoreville. Are you sure you will be all right? I can call in sick tomorrow at the company…"

"No, Charlie. No need for that. I'm fine now. You get yourself home and get a good night's sleep." Gina took out a pad and wrote down her telephone number. "You can call me now. Give me a call tomorrow morning. I'm ready to pass out now so I won't call to see if you arrived OK and if you call, you'll just get my answering machine. I'm exhausted."

"OK, Gina, I love you and don't forget it."

"No way I could, Charlie, good night."

Charlie took the elevator down from Gina's apartment, flagged down a cab, and went to the *trattoria* to pick up his car. The *trattoria* was closed but Johnny was still standing there in the alley, pretending to smoke a cigarette. Charlie waved to him and flashed a big smile. Johnny waved back and offered what Charlie thought might be a grin. He got in his car and drove back to Shoreville. It was the happiest night of his life.

XVI

Charlie woke up at his usual 6:30. He showered quickly and had some breakfast. After putting the breakfast dishes in the dishwasher, he got dressed for work. Before he left for Wilmington, he called Gina's number.

Gina was still asleep and her voice told Charlie that he had awakened her. "Gina, did I wake you? I'm sorry…"

"No, Charlie, I had to answer the phone anyway", she giggled.

"Aw, jeez, I'm sorry Gina. I was just going to leave for work and I wanted to tell you again how much I love you."

"I love you too, Charlie and because I do I want you to think very carefully about what everything I told you yesterday will mean to you and your life."

"I promise, Gina. But my life is already changed anyway because you are in it. Everything in life has a price and if the price of loving Carlo Rizzo's niece is a major change in my life, so be it. I can't imagine a life without you, so I guess I have to think about what it will be like *with* you."

"Just remember, Charlie, I love you. If you were to be unhappy with me, I couldn't stand it. So, please, I mean it really. Please think this all through very carefully."

"OK, Gina. Let's drop it for now. I promise I will think it through."

Charlie was careful to make sure that his conversations with Bob Simms and Bill Gallagher were still having the desired effect. He looked up and down his street and watched his rear view mirror carefully on the way to the bridge to Wilmington. The coast was clear.

While driving to work he thought about his conversation with Gina. He was beginning to appreciate the enormity of the changes that would occur in his life. Would he be able to remain as a financial executive at the Shaw Corporation when it became known that he was engaged and eventually married to the daughter of the capo of the Philadelphia mafia?

Shaw had government contracts, a number of which were with the Defense Department. Certain employees, Charlie included, had to have security clearances and that meant FBI investigations. The clearances were updated annually, although sometimes they went beyond a year before renewal. If it were known in the meantime that he was engaged to Gina, he most certainly would not get his clearance renewed. Without a security clearance, he would have a lot less responsibility. The fact that a clearance was not renewed would also raise the eyebrows of senior management. His career might grind to a halt and he would most certainly be fired. He did not like the idea of being drummed out of the company. Fred Perkins would most certainly volunteer to dismiss Charlie and would try to do it with as much humiliation to Charlie as possible.

His life in Shoreville would change too. He tried to imagine how the local gossip mill would handle the news that he was engaged to a "mafia princess". If he lost his job at Shaw there would be no more softball league to play in. He could still play with his buddies, but it would be different. There'd be no more bowling league. He'd still have his friends but he was not sure how anxious they would be to associate with him because of his new "connections". They had their own careers to worry about and Charlie might wind up being a poison pill for his own friends.

Gina was right. He was going to have to think this through. His life would change not just in terms of a new routine because of a wife. He would be taking on a whole new life.

But he was determined that he would not lose Gina. He would make any sacrifice necessary to have her in his life. End of story.

He pulled into the Shaw parking lot. The security guard gave him a mock salute and he said "Good morning, Mr. Mullins." Charlie wondered if that same security guard would escort him out of the office, scrape the parking sticker off his window, and tell him he should not return if it turned out that he would be fired. He'd seen it happen to others in the company. One day the guy would be wielding his power, saluted by the security guard on his way into the parking lot, served hot coffee when he arrived as his personal assistant put his schedule on his desk. That same afternoon he would be escorted to the parking lot, carrying his own cardboard box of private "stuff" – pictures of his wife and kids, maybe a few personal files that had been closely inspected by the security guard – the same guard who saluted him in the morning – his corporate credit card would be chopped up and the pieces still on his desk. A bunch of papers – non-compete contracts, waivers of any right to seek legal redress, a promise to not recruit any company employees, and so on would have been shoved in front of his face for signature. He would watch forlornly as the security guard scraped his parking sticker off the windshield of his car. He would then be watched as he drove out the gate.

In his rear view mirror he would see the security guard telling the gatekeeper that the man was not to be allowed back on the company premises unless otherwise advised by the personnel department. The fact that the guy had 5, 10, 20 or thirty years of service with the company would mean nothing. As far as the company was concerned, the guy was dead. The only thing that was missing was somebody yelling "Dead man walking!" as the poor guy carried his cardboard box down the hall to the elevator.

Some of the guys Charlie had seen let go had been fired by Fred Perkins. Fred was particularly sadistic. He considered anyone who was being fired as someone who had been disloyal to the company and, therefore, deserved to be dismissed with as much cruelty as possible. The humiliation should be as public as possible in Perkins' mind. Charlie would not give Fred Perkins that satisfaction.

He walked to his building and took the elevator to the 9th floor where his office was located. He walked past Laura Metzer who was dutifully organizing her desk in expectation of Fred Perkins' complaints. He felt bad that Laura might not have a friendly ear if he left. She was a nice person and Perkins certainly did not deserve such a longsuffering, dedicated personal assistant.

He saw his office perhaps now for the first time. It wasn't his. It belonged to the Shaw Corporation. His job was little more than a box on the company's organization chart. He had never lived his job like a lot of the other executives at Shaw, but he was always honest and forthright in fulfilling his responsibilities. He realized that this could all be simply taken away because of the girl he wanted to marry. He chuckled to himself at the irony and phoniness of it. He would be suspect not because he had changed. He was the same Charlie Mullins but he would be judged because he fell in love with the "wrong" woman.

Gina was right, people would come to fear him, not because of his position in the company and his authority but because his wife was the daughter of the head of the Philly mob. The company would fear that he could or would bring in organized crime. The government would take away his security clearance for fear that he would pass secrets on to the mafia, even though he had never before told anyone about Shaw's government contracts. And it would all be because Gina had been born to the "wrong" parents and had the wrong uncle.

Charlie entered his office, sat down to his desk and immersed himself in his work. The operating departments had sent in the drafts of their quarterly budget revisions and he had to go over them in detail before they came back as finals and Perkins would tear them apart over the slightest error in logic or even grammar.

Charlie Mullins was a hard worker but his staff had never seen him as absorbed in his work as he was on this Monday. Charlie barely looked up from his papers throughout the entire day. He went out to lunch and came back in almost virtual silence.

Billy Johnson, one of the junior financial analysts in the company commented to one of his co-workers, "Boy, Charlie is really deep in his work today! You think we are about to get hit with a wave of work?"

"No more than usual, Billy, Charlie is not that kind of boss. He's just probably got something on his mind. We're coming up on the first round of budget review drafts so he's probably concentrating. He's a good professional and he doesn't miss much because he pays attention. It's probably no more than that."

But it *was* much more. Charlie was questioning his life for the first time. He had been born, raised, educated, and married in Shoreville. He went to work for the same company his father had worked for. It was not because he had no options, he just never questioned his life. He was comfortable in it. Don't mess with a winning team was his philosophy. When Mary Jo left him he was grateful for his friends, at least the male ones, for being around and keeping him occupied with softball and bowling, pizza and beer, and the occasional happy hour at Jimmy Balsamo's. Mary Jo was the one who left Shoreville; why should he? His career at Shaw was moving along satis-factorily and he was making good money. So, it just never occurred to him to question the way he lived. Now, however, with Gina in his life he had to seriously ask himself if what he had was what he really wanted.

Gina's life was a busy one. She had an enormous array of exhibitions, events, tutoring and a collection of interesting and talented friends to occupy her. Charlie had to admit that he rather enjoyed going out when it was with Gina and her friends. He assumed (correctly) that Gina's friends knew who her uncle was and they accepted her in spite of it. He liked them for their loyalty to her as well as their down-to-earth way. They were good people, interested in bringing beauty to life. His close friends in Shoreville were like that in some ways, but they were not sophisticated. They were just good, hard-working and hard-playing people. But he knew that his life with them was largely confined to playing ball and bowling because they all went home to wives and families. They didn't know of his loneliness at the end of each day. They didn't know that his routines lacked meaning because there was no one there to share them. They liked him but they didn't really know him.

He admitted to himself that it was partly his own doing that his friends didn't know him better. He was not one to share emotions and he kept his life private. It wasn't his friends' fault. He did shut them out of at least one important compartment of his self.

When the Shaw clock on his desk showed 5 pm, Charlie put his papers in his desk, stretched, and said good night to his colleagues, "See you tomorrow folks, quitting time." He walked down the hall as he had done for years, took the elevator down to the lobby and walked to the parking lot. He saw other Shaw executives heading for their cars as well and he had to laugh inwardly at what his father had told him years ago. He thought of his father in his old Studebaker with no air conditioning driving out of the parking lot with the windows rolled up so no one could hear as he said "assholes" while waving goodnight. Today, Charlie Mullins' life seemed to him extraordinarily ordinary.

He drove back over the bridge. When he got home he called Gina. She was still at home and getting ready to go out with some friends. "Gina? Hey! Just thought I would try to catch you at home. Would it be all right if I drove up tomorrow night after work with some clothes? I'm taking you at your word."

"You don't even have to ask, Mr. Mullins. I'll be here. Shall I keep my hat on, as the song goes?"

"Oh, Jesus, Gina, don't do that to me! I might never recover in time to get back to work on Wednesday." Charlie laughed, albeit a bit uneasily. The image of Gina waiting for him in nothing but a hat rushed through his mind and he was excited.

"Well, I'll be here. I'll leave it to your imagination to figure out how I might be dressed – or undressed. Just get your Irish butt up here, OK?"

"Right!"

"Charlie," Gina said, "have you been thinking about what I told you yesterday? Are you sure about all this?"

"Never more sure about anything in my life, Gina. I'll talk to you about it tomorrow. I want to look into your beautiful and mysterious eyes while we talk. But, yeah, I've given it a lot of thought today and I'll be going over it again and again tomorrow, and for the rest of the week. I'm sure though that I love you and nothin's gonna turn me around!"

"That's one day down and six to go, Mullins. Keep up the good work. Just remember, Charlie, no matter what you decide, I will love you always. You've made me happier than anyone ever has and if it all ended tomorrow, I would not have regretted a moment I spent with you."

"I hope you will say that ten years from now, Gina. Now, I'm going to fix some dinner and pick out some suits, ties, socks, and so on, to take up to Philly."

"Don't bother picking any undershorts, Charlie. We can get some more navy blue silk boxer shorts up here," Gina laughed.

"OK, no undershorts. Got it! Gina, I love you and I'll see you tomorrow. Good night, baby."

"Good night Charlie. Sleep well and dream about me."

Charlie rang off and went about his chores. He was floating. He was no longer alone. He wondered to himself if it would always be this way. So many of his friends seemed to have fallen into ruts in their marriages and their lives. But he remembered Tony Mazza telling him, "Charlie, I've been around a good bit and I was a real womanizer before I met Marie. You know something? There is no sex better than making love to a woman you truly love. It's different and you never get tired of it. You want her pleasure and she wants yours. Nothing like it!"

Charlie thought to himself, *"Well, if it's good enough for Tony, I guess it's good enough for me. It sure seemed he was right when I made love to Gina last weekend. Maybe there won't be any ruts!"*

Charlie separated a couple of suits, half-a-dozen ties, a blue blazer, 7 pairs of socks, and about 6 dress shirts – two blue and four white. When he looked at his underwear drawer he laughed out loud. He looked at his closet and was, for the first time, surprised to see that he had a lot of business attire and an equally large selection of athletic clothing – sweat pants, cross training athletic shoes, sweat socks, and cut off shirts. He had little sportswear in the form of casual shirts and pants. He had only a couple of casual shirts for those formally casual Fridays and two pairs of khaki pants to wear with a black or blue blazer. *"Well,"* he thought, *"I now have some stuff at Gina's place. But I guess I should improve my casual wardrobe now that I have a woman in my life. I can't take her out wearing my sweat pants, and a suit at the trattoria would be a bit much!"*

He put his clothes into a travel bag and laid the bag carefully in the trunk of his car. He didn't want anybody seeing a bag hanging from a hook in the back. Although Charlie traveled often on business he was now doubly careful to have anyone know that he had packed a bag. Someone like Sharon Gallagher or Diane Simms might just be especially curious about where he was going. Tomorrow would look just like he was leaving for the office like he did every other day.

Again, Charlie checked the street before getting into his car to drive to his office. Again, there was no sign of anyone ready to follow him. As before he drove to the entrance to the bridge to Wilmington and checked as he drove for anybody following him. The coast continued clear and Charlie thought that Bill Gallagher and Bob Simms must have really told their wives a thing or two. He would find out tomorrow night at the bowling alley.

He pulled in to the Shaw Corporation parking lot and returned the salute of the security guard. He could no longer look at the guard without thinking that he, too, might be one of those whose parking sticker was scraped off his windshield by the otherwise affable man. *"Man's inhumanity to man"*, Charlie mused, remembering the phrase from a literature course he had taken in college. It was amazing how otherwise decent human beings could so easily turn into incredibly cruel people in defense of what is not theirs. He saw it in the Army but at least there you were being trained to kill in warfare. He figured however, that the principle was the same. Love of country and love of company probably arose from the same psychological roots somewhere in the recesses of the human mind. People needed to *belong* and maybe they would do anything asked of them to assert their belonging. He wondered if that was what kept Gina's uncle in power too.

His thoughts switched to what he was going to say to Gina's uncle. He pulled himself up short and thought, *"Whoa, Mullins. Remember that this guy puts his pants on one leg at a time. Don't forget that. Regardless of what he does for his living, he is Gina's uncle. It was luck of the draw, an accident of birth. Gina didn't go off looking for an uncle and pick him. I'm going to talk to him as Gina's uncle – not as Carlo Rizzo alleged mafia don."* He was surprised that he thought "alleged". Was he rationalizing? Why didn't he just think "mafia don" instead of "alleged mafia don"? *"Maybe I don't want to believe that he is really the head of the mob in Philly."*

* * * * *

Charlie entered his building and took the elevator to the 9th floor. Fred Perkins was in the same elevator and Charlie could not help but notice that the passengers gave Fred wide berth. It was as if they did not even want to get close to him for fear he might bite them or scream at them for crowding, whatever. "Morning, Fred." He said to the fearsome Treasurer. Since everyone else had said "Good morning, Mr. Perkins," they all waited with bated breath to see how Perkins would react. "Morning, Mullins", Perkins grunted. They rode to the 9th floor in silence. When Charlie and Perkins got off on their floor, the elevator literally buzzed with comment, "Did you see the look on Perkins' face when Mullins used his first name? I thought I would burst out laughing."

"Good thing you didn't. He wouldn't have done anything to Mullins, but I bet he would have discovered your name and department and had you whacked!" The passengers laughed uneasily and each got off at his respective destination.

As they walked to their offices, Perkins asked Charlie, "Mullins, you've been quiet these days, are you working on those budget reviews?"

"Yeah, Fred, they'll be ready before the weekend and that will give the departments another week to make their adjustments and come back with their revised figures. Do you want to see the reports before I send them back?"

"No need!" Perkins growled, "I can wait for the final figures."

Charlie knew that Fred Perkins would not give any advance signs of his concerns. He would wait for the final revisions and set his traps for each department head so he could catch them by surprise. He liked to "sucker punch" people. He had no room for dialog. He would catch one minor error of logic or arithmetic, or even a grammatical error, and then mercilessly drill into his interlocutor who would have to sheepishly return to his office to re-do his work.

Charlie wondered what would be Perkins' reaction if he just walked into his office one day and said, "I quit." For sure, Perkins would probably be speechless for the first time in his life. Charlie said good morning to Laura Metzer as he passed her desk and entered his own office.

Again, he worked with incredible concentration until lunch time. He went out to lunch, stayed out the requisite hour and walked around downtown Wilmington before going back into his building. Four hours later he was on his way to the parking lot to drive to Philly.

* * * * *

When he reached Gina's apartment he rang the doorbell. Gina opened the door and asked, "Have you lost your key already, Charlie?"

"Oh, God, I completely forgot I had the key!" Charlie said, "Sorry Gina."

"Oh Charlie, don't apologize. Just remember that this is now your place as much as it is mine. Don't be so formal."

"Sorry, Gina, it's just lack of practice." He reached in his pocket and pulled out his key ring, "See? I have my key. Just silly of me, I guess." He stepped into the apartment and moved to kiss her. She melted into him and for a moment he forgot that his suit bag was still in his car. "Oh, jeez. I left my bag in the car, Gina. You get me so confused…"

"Well, you are not going to go back down to the garage now, mister", and Gina pushed Charlie toward the bedroom. He fell onto the bed and she quickly jumped on top of him. "Got time for a quickie, Mullins?"

Charlie started tearing at his clothes while Gina removed hers and in a matter of seconds they were both naked on the bed. He made love to her as passionately as before and she responded in equal measure. When they were both satiated, Gina climbed off him and laid down next to him. "Thanks, I needed that!" she kidded. "That was quite a reception," Charlie panted, "will that be standard practice in our home?"

"Any reason why it shouldn't be my dear?" Gina laughed.

They rested in the bed for about half-an-hour and Charlie said, "Well, I guess I can go back down and get my bag now."

"Now there's an idea, Mr. Mullins. C'mon, start moving in. I want to hear the pitter patter of big feet in my house."

Charlie pulled on his pants, put on his shirt, and slipped into his moccasins without putting on his socks. He went downstairs to the guest parking slot in the garage of Gina's building, removed his bag from the trunk and carried it to the elevator. When he got back to the apartment, Gina was dressed again and she showed him where to put his clothes. "Want me to put your name on the closet door, Charlie?" she kidded.

"I think I can remember, Gina, but thanks anyway. This isn't summer camp. I'm here to stay until further notice. Please note that I didn't sew on any labels with my name on them either."

"What would you like for dinner, Charlie? I prepared lasagna. Is that OK with you? There's some wine in a rack in the kitchen. You can pick one and open it to let it breathe a bit."

"My God, she can cook too!" Charlie exclaimed, "a beautiful woman who can cook. Who woulda thought it?"

"All right Mullins, that's quite enough. Of course I can cook! I'm Italian, right? How many Italian women do you know that can't cook?"

"None, Gina but they all *look* like they can cook, know what I mean?"

Gina broke out laughing, "You mean 'mamas' Charlie?"

"Well, yeah. Some of them are not so big yet, but you can see it happening. They get married looking like models. A year of so later they look like they're ready to pose for a Renaissance painting. After a couple more years they look like Santa's wife. Most of the women I know in

Shoreville are in the transition phase from Renaissance model to Santa's wife."

"*All* of them, Charlie?"

"Well, no. Tony Mazza's wife has kept her figure pretty well. But I think it's because Tony is always grabbing at her. He's nuts about her and she makes it a point to look good for him."

"See what love can do, Charlie? Keep loving me and I promise I will never be a 'mama', deal?"

"Deal? No! It's a contract. I'll take it as a promise. And don't worry I'll stick to my end of the contract too."

"I'll remember that every time I look at a plate of manicotti, Charlie. Make sure you continue to work out so you don't get that big belly that Italian men call 'prosperity'."

Charlie finished putting his clothes in the closet and went to the kitchen to open a bottle of wine. Gina followed closely behind to heat the lasagna in the oven. While the meal was heating up, she set a table for two on a small circular table in the kitchen. "You mind eating here, Charlie? I don't feel like carting this stuff into the dining room and back. Is that all right or do you want me to serve you in the dining room like a good Italian 'mama'?"

"Well, since you put it that way, far be it from me to have you serving me. You might change your mind and look like a 'mama'. Then what would I do?"

"I just knew you would see it my way", Gina kidded.

The lasagna was delicious and Charlie remarked on how good it tasted. "It was a recipe I found in my mother's stuff. Uncle Carlo said she was a terrific cook. The important thing is not to overcook the pasta. There is nothing worse to an Italian than overcooked pasta. It's like…ah…what, Charlie? What tastes awful to an Irishman?"

"Absolutely NOTHING, Gina! Maybe bad mashed potatoes, I don't know." Gina broke out in a belly laugh. "Is it that bad, Charlie?"

"Look, Gina, my mother would never have gone down in history as a gourmet cook. She was the 'here, eat it if you want to' type. She had some favorite recipes that she picked up from those TV programs that teach you how to make a Christmas tree table centerpiece with a pineapple. You know what I mean?"

Gina laughed again. "How did you manage to acquire a taste for good food, Charlie?"

Charlie laughed, "First it was the Army. It was an improvement over Mom's cooking. I figured if the Army could cook better than Mom, there must be more out there worthy of taste. When I came back from the service and joined Shaw, I went out to some nice restaurants and cultivated a taste for good food. Unfortunately, Mary Jo thought pots and pans were kitchen decorations. She couldn't boil water without burning it!"

"Poor Charlie, gastronomically challenged! Never more my darling. If you promise not to get fat, I will feed you the food of Roman gods! OK?"

"Word of honor!"

Charlie was at a bit of a loss for what to do next. He was so used to going out with Gina that he wondered if she expected it. "Gina, you want to go out somewhere?"

"Why, Charlie? Aren't you settled in yet? Would you feel better if we went out? I'm perfectly content to watch a movie on TV or just sit and talk with you. But if you want to go somewhere we can."

"No, actually I kind of wondered if you expected to go out. We always did."

"That was before you had a key to this place and had your clothes in the closet. I'm more than happy just to curl up on the couch with your arm around me and watch a movie. You're the first man to enter this apartment and I'd like to know what's it's like to sit with my man and just watch the tube."

"OK, let me show you", Charlie said.

Neither saw very much television as Charlie told Gina about his week and what conclusions he had reached. "You were right about my life changing, Gina. As soon as everyone knows that you are mine, I am certain that people will relate to me differently. I'm sure that some things like losing a government security clearance is a distinct possibility. That would put a ceiling above me in terms of my moving up in the company. More likely, it would cost my job."

"I was sure of that, Charlie. I've seen what my uncle went through. Are you really prepared for all of that?"

"Gina, for the first time in my life, I had to ask myself 'what did I really want from life?' For the first time I looked around me and saw just how sterile my life had become. Bowling on Wednesday, softball practice or games on Saturday, work around a psychotic boss who would fire me in an instant if he could – regardless of how well I do my work. I asked myself if the company would fire me if you and I got together or I lost my security clearance and I figured I probably would get the ax. It wouldn't be fair but it would be likely. I work for a corporation, not a bunch of friends. The company would drop me in a flash if it thought its interests were at risk. My father's service wouldn't matter. My years of honest service wouldn't either. I was just used to going to work, doing my job as well as I could, and not looking around me. I also took a close look at my friends. I love them all dearly, but they all have wives and children to go home to. They have things to talk about and someone to talk to. I don't. I didn't think about it much until I met you. But I miss talking to you, being around you, and coming home to someone."

"I didn't want to say anything that would seem like I was trying to influence your decision. I knew your life was sterile. I saw how you enjoyed yourself with my friends and at the events we went to together. It was pretty clear that you were starved for interesting company and things to do. You had just isolated yourself. But I could not in good conscience talk to you about any of that without thinking that I was manipulating you into what you might regret later."

"I love you for that, Gina. I arrived at my conclusions on my own steam. I am as certain as I was before about us. If I have to find a job somewhere else I'll do it. If we have to move to Seattle to have peace, I'll move. I might have a problem with a place like Ohio, but even if we have to go there, I'm game. I was only hanging around the Shaw Corporation because it was a comfortable niche. It was better than working in a strange environment and having to claw my way to the top. At Shaw it was easy for me because a lot of people knew my father. Maybe even some of them felt guilty because he died on the job. He lived for the company and he busted his butt to help build it, at least insofar as he was able. I never had any reason to question what I was doing until we met. Gina, the truth of the matter is, I don't give a shit what I have to do to be with you. I'll do it! I have to admit that I don't have the slightest idea how to talk to your uncle, but I'll figure it out by the end of the week. I keep telling myself that he puts his pants on, one leg at a time. I know he does and at the right time I will be ready."

"Charlie, I'm speechless. I think you are fantastic. You know what you want and you sure as hell know how to go about getting it. You'll do just fine with my uncle."

They watched television for a while longer and then went to bed. Charlie made love to her again and they fell asleep in each other's arms.

Wednesday morning Charlie woke up at the usual 6:30. He wandered sleepily into the bathroom, almost losing his way in the new environment. While he was brushing his teeth, Gina got up and started making coffee. Gina's coffee was European style – strong. Charlie liked it. He thought to ask Gina for the name of the brand she purchased, but he remembered that he could have it every day if he simply came back to the apartment at night. Then he remembered that he would not be able to stay at Gina's place every night. He would have to first talk to her uncle and then work out his strategy for being with Gina. He couldn't just leave Shoreville and move in with Gina. He couldn't announce a new love in his life – not yet. He needed to think about what to do because he was not going to lose his job and depend on Gina and her uncle to support the house. Charlie would not live that way no matter how much money Gina had. He was proud and he would be the man of the house and the provider.

He showered and dressed and made his way to the kitchen. Gina had fresh fruit, cereal, and her strong coffee with fresh cream. Charlie was used to a couple of pieces of toast and instant coffee swallowed quickly as he went out to his car. He sat down to the table and Gina came over and kissed him. "Good morning, Mr. Mullins. You look nice and buttoned up this morning. You're so handsome in your executive costume." Gina smiled at him.

"Costume it is, Gina. It's a uniform. We're part of the army of corporate bureaucrats – 'corpocrats' is the word I have heard before."

"Well, you're handsome in your armor, Charlie."

"Thanks, baby." Charlie finished his breakfast, kissed Gina tenderly and said, "Gina, look, I'm going to have to go to Shoreville tonight. It's Wednesday and league night at the bowling alley. I don't want to start that stuff about following me around again."

"I know, Charlie, I understand. Once we have talked to my Uncle Carlo and he has given us his blessing, we will figure out what to do. Now go off to work and have a nice day thinking about me."

"I'll call you from home tonight. I love you." He kissed Gina and went to the elevator to get his car in the garage.

XVII

Charlie continued his work on the operating department draft budget revisions. He would have them ready for submission to the department heads by Friday. He worked through lunch, picking up a sandwich and a soft drink from a vending machine. He left at the usual 5-o-clock and went home. The traffic was heavy as usual at that time. He got home an hour later and got out his bowling gear. He quickly fixed a microwave frozen meal. He always bought a few frozen meals for when he just didn't feel like cooking something, and today he did not feel like cooking. At 7:30 he got into his car and headed for the bowling alley.

All the guys in the league were there. Art Samuels yelled to him, "Hey Mullins! How ya doin'. We gonna win tonight?"

"You bet, Artie! I'm ready to rock and roll!" Charlie yelled back.

"Hey, Charlie," Tony Mazza said, "you up for it tonight?"

"Couldn't be better, Tony. Let's kick butt!"

He saw Bill Gallagher and Bob Simms and waved to them. He was in a good mood and after seeing that he was not being followed any more he was no longer upset with Bill and Bob. It wasn't their fault anyway. "Hey guys," Charlie said.

"Charlie," Bill Gallagher approached him, "I thought you might not make it tonight."

"Why is that, Bill? I almost always show, don't I?"

"Well, Sharon said she thought you might be sick or something."

"Why would she think that, Bill? I'm just fine, as you can see."

"Well, she said you didn't even turn on your lights at home last night."

"Oh shit!" thought Charlie, *"are we back to that crap again?"*

"Sharon was watching my house, Bill?"

"Oh no, Charlie, she just said she drove by your place on the way back from the supermarket and it was dark as a tomb."

Charlie's house was not on the way to the Gallagher's from the supermarket. "Bill, is Sharon getting antsy about my life again?"

"God no! I put her in her place after you and I talked. No, she just made a comment. I think she was just worried that you might be sick, that's all. You know, flu going around and all that."

"OK, Bill. Well just tell her you saw me and I'm fine and not to worry about me. OK?"

"Will do, Charlie, will do."

"A fat lot of good your talk did, Bill!" Charlie said to himself, *"She didn't have to go by my house last night. She's still got her nosy ass in a fit. I'm going to have to keep watching."*

They bowled and lost that night. When the evening was over, they all went for pizza and beer and to talk about what they did wrong. Tony Mazza looked at Art Samuels, "Shit, Artie, what happened tonight? If you had just bowled two more strikes we would have taken those guys!"

"Ah, hell Tony, I guess I'm just in a slump. To tell the truth, I was thinkin' that I have to start painting the house this weekend. I hate that shit! Just thinking about it drives me nuts."

Tony laughed, "Wow, that's the first time I ever heard that a guy would bowl a lousy game because he has to paint his house!"

"Aw, c'mon, Tony, it wasn't a lousy game, I was just a little off, that's all. Old Charlie here had a damned good night, though."

Charlie smiled and took a sip of his beer. "Yeah I guess I was on my game tonight."

"Hey Charlie!" It was Mildred calling from the bar, "you need anything tonight?"

"Thanks anyway, Mildred. Would you respect me in the morning?"

"God, I hope not!" and she laughed heartily.

The group broke out laughing. Tony Mazza leaned over to Charlie and said, "Charlie, that broad is so horny, she must be the best piece of ass in town."

"Thanks Tony, but I don't need problems and Mildred would be one."

Tony laughed, "Boy, you got that right. Three husbands! Must be some kind of hysteria surrounding her!"

"Yeah, and you want to throw me into it? Thanks, Tony!" They both laughed.

Charlie was light throughout the evening but observant, particularly of Bill Gallagher and Bob Simms. He was sure that their wives would once again start invading his privacy. They were like guerrilla fighters who would go to ground when necessary only to surface later and catch the "enemy" by surprise.

* * * * *

Thursday morning Charlie left the house half-an-hour earlier than usual in case his "spotters" might be waiting for him. He was apprehensive again after Bill Gallagher's comment at the bowling alley. He was only going to work, but he did not want the aggravation of being followed around. He drove to the bridge and over to Wilmington without incident. This night he would drive up to Philly and stay with Gina.

Charlie poured himself into the draft budget revisions and got them finished by the end of the day – one day sooner than necessary. On Friday he would make sure there were no omissions or errors and have them all delivered to the operating department heads. If they needed the time, they would have the weekend as well as all of next week to prepare for their meetings with Fred Perkins. He called Gina's apartment and left a message on her answering machine that he would be going to the apartment after work.

He left the office punctually at 5 pm and watched carefully for Sharon Gallagher's car as he walked to the parking lot. The coast was clear so he headed toward I-95 and Philly. When he checked his rear view mirror he again saw a car following him but it was not Sharon's. Two women were in the vehicle. He slowed and the car behind him slowed. He passed a truck and the car behind him did the same. He was being followed again. As before, he got off in Chester and did evasive maneuvers. The car exited behind him. Again, he noted the license number. He thought he recognized the car, but he was not sure.

He lost his surveillance again in Chester and this time, instead of picking up the Chester Pike, he went back on I-95 by doubling back on his route. The trailing car was nowhere in sight and he headed to Philly. When he arrived to Gina's building he entered the basement parking garage. Gina was already home and this time he let himself in with his key.

"Gina!" he called.

"In the kitchen, Charlie, I'm fixing dinner."

He walked into the kitchen and kissed Gina. "Hello, beautiful. I've missed you if even for just a day. How are ya?"

Gina turned away from the pot she was stirring and kissed him back. "Doin' fine. I'm making some minestrone. I figured you might not want pasta every day so you could keep your dashing figure and avoid accumulating too much 'prosperity'. Is that OK? I also got some good Italian bread from the bakery. Why don't you open a bottle of wine while you're standing there watching me. I hate to see a man idle!"

"Gotcha! Share the work, right?"

"You got it, Mullins. No kitchen slaves in this place."

Charlie picked a bottle of Tuscan wine, pulled the cork to let it breathe and then said, "Gina, you were right about those women. Someone followed me again. I got off in Chester, drove around and then doubled back. I lost 'em, but what a damned aggravation. Don't they have anything better to do?"

"Probably, but they are not going to do it when they can be prying into someone else's business my dear man. They are not going to quit as easily as you thought and their husbands are not going to make them. Take my female word for it. Now, the soup is ready. Let's sit down and have a glass of wine and then we'll eat. Forget those broads for now."

Charlie was amazed that Gina could seem so feminine at one point and then refer to two women as "broads" the next. "Gina, I wouldn't have expected you to call them 'broads'..."

"Listen Charlie, there are women and there are 'broads', the one's following you are best described in the latter category. Sorry for the French, but that's what they are."

Charlie laughed and served up two glasses of wine. "OK sweets, let's have some wine."

Gina turned down the flame on the gas stove and they moved to the living room. Charlie raised his glass slightly and said, "To the most beautiful woman I have ever met."

"May you always see me that way", replied Gina and tapped her glass to his.

"Gina, is there anything special I have to know about meeting your uncle on Sunday?"

"I'm glad you asked, Charlie. Yes, we will have to be careful when arriving to his house. You probably noticed that my car has tinted glass and it's a little darker than what the law calls for. My uncle had it put on the car and told the police so they would leave me alone. It's difficult to see who is in the car. In any case, just to be sure, I want you to disguise yourself a bit by putting on some dark glasses and a cap."

"OK, that sounds kind of weird, but no problem, but why the mystery?"

"Simple, Charlie, the FBI is always photographing people who go in and out of my uncle's place. I don't think you want your picture on file just yet."

"Gina..."

"No, Charlie, don't tell me you don't care. Take my word for it for now. You really don't want to be seen by the feds going into Carlo Rizzo's home. You will have enough aggravation later so let's keep you anonymous for the time being? OK? They always take my picture even though they know damned well who I am and they can't see into the car anyway. It's just to remind my uncle and me that they are watching."

"OK", said Charlie, "I know what you mean. I had a great-uncle who joined the Communist party after working in the coal mines and he had the same kind of problem. He said that two agents owed their jobs to him because they followed him around wherever he went. That was back in the 50's. He used to wave at them whenever he saw them."

"Well, I don't suggest you wave this time, Charlie. Those guys don't have much of a sense of humor and it might not be a good idea to seem to be making fun of them."

"No problem Gina. Shall I put on a fake moustache too?"

"Not funny, Charlie, you'll see soon enough that those guys can be a pain in the neck. If you think the wives of Shoreville are a hassle, wait till you get a taste of the FBI! Until they got it into their thick skulls that I was not a 'courier' for my uncle or involved in any of his business activities, they followed me everywhere – even at Bryn Mawr. I'd be walking around campus and I'd see these guys in suits! Suits, Charlie. I mean how many people on a college campus walk around in suits? Professors wear tweed or cardigans and they always look wrinkled. Here were these guys looking starched up and wearing grey suits and ties. Hard to figure out who they were, you know?" Gina let out a sardonic laugh. "After they realized that I was not a 'moll', they left me alone but they still photograph me whenever I enter my uncle's home. I guess it's a kind of ritual they have established."

"Anything else, Gina?"

"No, once we are inside the house, there are no problems. My uncle makes sure on a regular basis that the house and the phone are not bugged. He likes his privacy too, you know. I told you your life was going to change, Charlie. Are you still sure? I mean this is only the first time. I am sure you will be inconvenienced more as time goes by. I've learned to live with it but you don't have to."

"Gina, I told you, I am going to see your uncle and ask him to give his blessing to our relationship. I'm not going to talk business with him."

"Don't be cavalier, Charlie. If they find out who you are, they will contact your employer, they will visit you at home, they will follow you. They will tell the local authorities in Shoreville about you. They might tell your friends. You will go on a 'watch list'. Believe me, I've been there. Why do you think my uncle doesn't want me to work? One way to harass him is to always cause me to lose a job. They would only leave me and him alone if I were waiting tables in some pizzeria or working as a barmaid, and even then I'm not sure if they really would leave me alone."

"OK, Gina, I understand. I've never done this before so I hope you will excuse me if I say it seems a bit dramatic, but I'll go along."

"Good idea, Charlie Mullins." Gina kissed him, "and just be patient with me. I'm only trying to protect you."

They finished their wine and sat down to minestrone and some delicious Italian bread. When they finished they retired to the living room again to watch some television. Charlie remembered that he had not done that in years. He kicked off his shoes and put his feet up on a coffee table in front of them and put his arm around Gina. She settled into him and put her head on his shoulder. They were happy.

After a couple hours of TV, Charlie said, "Hey, beautiful, you want to go to bed?"

"I thought you would never ask, Mullins!" They walked to the bedroom, shedding their clothes as they went and Charlie made love to Gina before they both fell asleep, again in an embrace.

* * * * *

Charlie woke at the regular time, plodded to the bathroom, brushed his teeth and took a shower. As he was dressing he could hear Gina in the kitchen, singing to herself and he could smell the coffee she was brewing. They had a leisurely breakfast and Charlie headed off to Wilmington. "I'll be back tonight, sweets. Think about what you might want to do. You want to go out for dinner or something?"

"OK, Charlie, you have a good day." Gina kissed him fondly, "boy with a kiss like that I might wind up staying home…"

"Off with you Mullins, somebody in this family has to have a job, you know?" Gina laughed.

"I'm gone", Charlie said, "see you tonight."

When Charlie returned that evening he was greeted by the smell of Italian cooking. Gina had prepared manicotti stuffed with ricotta cheese and covered with a delicious tomato sauce. When he moved to kiss her he noticed that she was perfumed and didn't smell like she had been in the kitchen. "Wow, said Charlie, are we having perfume for dinner? You smell fantastic!"

"You wanted me to smell like garlic, maybe? I've got a man who comes home to dinner now. He deserves to have a wife ready for his arrival!"

The manicotti was exquisite and Charlie told Gina so. "Gina, that was delicious! Where did you learn to make that kind of food?"

"My mom had a whole bunch of recipes that my uncle kept after she died. He gave them to me more as a memento than for actually cooking. I never had anyone to cook for except myself but I did experiment a couple of times just in case I happened to meet Charlie Mullins!" Gina smiled.

After they had eaten, Gina put the dishes in the dishwasher and prepared two cups of espresso and served them with two cordial glasses of black sambuca. The licorice flavor enhanced the delicious flavor of the strong espresso and Charlie thought his life could never be better than this.

"Gina, I thought you might have wanted to go out tonight. You don't have to prepare something every night you know."

"C'mon Charlie, you know how long I have wanted to do nothing but prepare a meal for someone I love? You must have gotten tired of always eating in restaurants or cooking for one, no?"

"Oh, you bet, Gina. Sometimes I would just open a can of beef stew or chili because I did not want to cook something up and didn't feel like going out. You do get tired of that kind of life. And, I have to confess that coming home to a woman as beautiful as you and a meal to boot is more than I ever hoped for."

"Oh, Mullins, you are soooo charming. I'll bet you are going to try to seduce me again tonight, aren't you?"

"Well the thought had crossed my mind," Charlie responded.

"Don't even think about it, Charlie. Tonight I seduce you. How about that? Now excuse me while I slip into something more comfortable."

Gina walked out of the living room and came back in a few minutes later in some skimpy lingerie and a transparent negligee. Charlie was mesmerized. She started a slow strip tease until Charlie started taking off his shirt. She stopped her strip tease and finished undressing him saying, "Boy, I hope you are wearing those navy blue silk boxer shorts. Oooh, there they are!" and she pulled down the shorts with a quick tug. Charlie embraced her and they walked, still embracing, into the bedroom where they fell on the bed and made love. When they were finished Gina said, "Wanna go watch some TV, Charlie?"

"No, Gina, I'm perfectly satisfied just to lie here and hold you close to me. How's that?"

"Sounds good to me," laughed Gina.

As they lay in each others arms, Charlie said, "Gina, I'll be back again tomorrow night, but I am going to have to drive to Shoreville Saturday morning. I can't miss softball practice if I am going to avoid gossip and keep those nosy women from following me around. If what you said about the FBI comes to pass, I could have a whole caravan behind me," he laughed.

"No problem, Charlie. You need to show up and keep them off your back for the time being. When you get back up here, we can go out Saturday night. Maybe we can meet up with some of my friends, or just be together. I'm here and hope I always will be for you. Do what you have to do. I'm a low maintenance Philly broad!"

"Oh yeah, I'm sure, and I'm Brad Pitt!" Charlie laughed.

They talked until they fell asleep.

XVIII

Charlie drove to work from Philly on Friday morning. When he arrived to his office he went through the draft budget reviews and then sent them back to the operating department heads. They would be ready for Perkins' sadistic reviews the week after next.

Friday was "don't-look-*too*-casual-but-look-casual-day" so Charlie had worn his blazer, an oxford cloth light blue shirt open at the neck, a pair of khaki pants, his Gucci moccasins, and navy blue socks. He laughed to himself to think that he was also wearing a pair of navy blue silk boxer shorts.

At lunch time he went out and walked to a hardware store in downtown Wilmington where he purchased a few electric timers to turn his lights on and off in Shoreville. He didn't want the Shoreville busybodies noticing that his house was dark when he was supposed to be there. He would set the timers to match his normal schedule at home so it appeared that he was there. His garage door would be closed and locked so no one would know if his car was there or not. On the way back from lunch he walked out to the parking lot and tossed the timers into the trunk of his car so no one would see him bringing them back to the office.

At 5 pm he drove back to Philly. When he entered the apartment, Gina was dressed in a simple black dress and lightly perfumed. Charlie thought, *"God, this is great! I wish my life had always been like this. She is so beautiful."*

"Hi, there my man!" Gina moved forward to kiss him tenderly, "penny for your thoughts."

"That's all they're worth, Gina?"

"Well, I don't know, wanna start bidding, Charlie?"

"No, I'll tell you. I was just thinking how wonderful it is to come home to someone you love. I was just wishing it would always have been this way."

"Well, if it had been, Charlie, you would not have been divorced nor would you have met me, right? Destiny, Charlie, never question destiny. This is the way it had to be and this is the way it is. Never think about what might have been. It never was, right?"

"That's for sure, Gina. You're too smart for me."

"Glad you recognized that, Charlie", she laughed. "You want me to fix some dinner? This morning you said you wanted to go out."

"Yeah, Gina. Let's just go somewhere, maybe to the *trattoria*, and have a light dinner, a little bit of wine and maybe some conversation with friends. What do you think?"

"Fine, let me call a couple of friends to see what they are going to do tonight. Just one thing, let's not tell anybody you are going to meet my uncle on Sunday. OK? Like you, I don't want the rumor mill started. You know, 'Gina has finally found someone, isn't that wonderful?' We can do without that for a while."

"I agree, Gina. You can never tell when some well-meaning person says something to someone less well-meaning. You've got a point."

"Good, let me call Susan Warner. She's a good friend. She likes the *trattoria* and you haven't met her yet. She's engaged to a really nice guy who's got a small financial consulting company. I think you'll like them." Gina went to the phone and started dialing.

She caught Susan at home and Susan said she would be glad to go out with Gina and Charlie. She asked who was Charlie and he heard Gina say, "He's a very close friend. You'll like him. He works in the finance area too, and I'm sure he and Freddy will have a lot to talk about. It will be just a casual evening, OK?" Gina rang off.

"OK, Charlie, we have some company for the evening. You want to freshen up before we go out?"

"Yeah, I could do with a shower. Gotta wash away the 'corporate casual'" Charlie laughed.

As usual, the evening at the *trattoria* was enjoyable. Charlie and Gina said nothing to Gina's friends about their growing relationship. They were just dating, for all intents and purposes. Charlie suspected that her friends knew better. Gina was lighter and more talkative than usual and the slight sadness that was sometimes noticeable in her eyes had disappeared. Her friends were too close to her to have missed the subtle changes in her demeanor.

Johnny the waiter appeared to know everything. He was smiling and openly deferential to Charlie as much as he was normally to Gina. Whether Gina's friends noticed that, he had no idea.

After a relaxed evening, Charlie and Gina went back to her apartment. They made love and then went to sleep.

* * * * *

The next morning Charlie woke up at the usual six-thirty and started getting ready to drive back to Shoreville. Gina woke up as soon as Charlie climbed out of bed and started to get up to fix some breakfast. "Gina, stay in bed. It's Saturday morning. Don't bother to fix breakfast. I'll just get some toast and make some coffee and be on my way."

"You sure, Charlie? I don't mind, you know. I actually enjoy fixing breakfast for my guy."

"I'm sure, Gina. Just relax. I'll bring you some coffee. Stay in bed."

Gina stretched like a cat and hummed a bit as she did. "Ohhh, Charlie. It's so wonderful to wake up next to you on a Saturday morning. And now, a cup of hot coffee in bed. I could get used to that, you know."

"Well, I hope you do. I intend to stay around for a long time so maybe we agree that on Saturdays and Sundays I will fix breakfast – at least the coffee, I'm not so sure how I would do with something more complicated, but I can learn."

"Mmmmmmm," purred Gina, "that sounds nice."

Charlie went to the kitchen and put the coffee in the coffee maker and while it was running through the filter he took a shower and shaved. Out of a recently formed habit, he put on a little of the cologne Gina had bought for him. He dressed and went back to the kitchen to fill two coffee mugs. He returned to the room and Gina was sitting up in bed. "Thanks, Charlie. It smells good. Seems you have learned how to make coffee the way I like it. Congratulations." She smiled at him.

"Well, it's a lot better than the instant I used to make in Shoreville, that's for sure." Charlie went back to the kitchen to get his toast and came back to the bedroom. He sat on the edge of the bed and munched his toast while admiring Gina. He thought, *"How the hell does she manage to wake up as beautiful as she looked when she went to sleep?"* He wondered if he looked at least presentable when he woke up. He doubted it.

Gina sipped her coffee and enjoyed her first coffee served in her bed. Charlie said, "Penny for your thoughts, beautiful."

"Oh, I was just savoring the moment, Charlie. It's the first time a man ever served me coffee in my bed. I want to experience every second of the occasion." Gina laughed.

"OK, sweets. Now, I'm going to drive down to Shoreville and go to softball practice. I also bought some electric timers Friday and I'm going to put them in the house to turn my lights on and off to match my normal schedule."

"What?" Gina asked, "Why do you have to do that, Charlie?"

"I didn't tell you, but one of the guys at the bowling alley told me that his wife thought I might be sick because the lights in my house were off Tuesday night. She actually drove out of her way to go by my house. Her only purpose was to see what I might be doing or if I was home. I already told you that some women followed me again when I was driving up here."

"Charlie, are you sure you were not a movie star before I met you?" Gina laughed.

"I wish I had been, at least that way I would know why those idiots are following me around. I mean it's ridiculous!"

"Well, Charlie, just get your butt down to softball practice and install your security system to protect you from female stalkers." Gina giggled.

Charlie kissed Gina and said, "I'll be back later, sweets." He went to the parking garage and started his trek back to Shoreville.

When Charlie arrived to his house he thought he saw a familiar car parked down the street. Someone was sitting in the driver's seat but it was too far away for him to tell if it was a man or a woman. He cursed under his breath, pressed the garage control and pulled in. It was still early to go to the park for softball practice so he set about putting the timers in place. He put one in the living room set to turn on at the time he usually arrived home. He put another in the kitchen to suggest that he was preparing dinner. He even put one on the TV to turn it on and off when he normally watched the news broadcasts. He knew that you could tell if someone's TV was on by the way the light coming from the screen increased and decreased with changes in the images. Anybody driving by his house would see that the TV was on and would think he was watching it. Finally, he put one in the bedroom to turn on when he usually went to bed and to turn off a little later, allowing for his normal reading time. *"Now let's see if you are going to quit checking out my house if you see the damned lights going on and off the way they normally do. Maybe you'll quit taking the long way home from the supermarket, bitch!"*

He put on his practice togs, grabbed his glove and drove to the softball practice field where some of the guys were already beginning to assemble. They were tossing a ball around and waiting for the rest of the team to show up. "Hey, Charlie, over here," Tony Mazza called out, "Catch!" He tossed the ball to Charlie who had to catch it with his bare hand because he was still carrying his glove.

"Pretty good, Charlie! You got reflexes! How ya' doin'?"

"Just fine Tony. How 'bout you?" he didn't wait for an answer before asking Tony, "Whose car is that silver one over there, Tony?"

"What? That third one from the left? That's Bob Simms' car. Didn't you recognize it? Bob's over there tossing a ball around with Bill. Why do you ask?"

"Ah, nothing Tony, I just didn't recognize it. I've been thinking about buying another car and maybe I'll ask Bob how that one performs."

"Whatever", said Tony, "let's play some ball. Hey, what's that smell, Charlie. You give up on Aqua Velva?"

Charlie flushed, "Nah, Tony I just decided to change my brand. No big deal!"

"Well, you smell pretty good for softball practice! Hope it won't affect your game." Tony laughed.

Charlie walked over to Bob Simms. "Hey Bob, how ya doin'?"

"Hi Charlie, what's up? You ready for some practice today?"

"As always, Bob. By the way, is that your car over there?" He pointed to the silver sedan that Tony had identified as Bob's.

"Yeah, of course. You've seen it before. It's mine all right. Wanna buy it?" Bob Simms laughed.

"Thanks Bob, but no. Actually that's the car that tried to follow me on I-95 on Thursday. Do you know if Diane had been over to Wilmington this week?"

"Oh, shit!" thought Bob Simms *"Diane has gone and done it again!"*

"I don't really know Charlie, she dropped me off at work and kept the car so she could have gone over to Wilmington. She said she had some errands to run. I came home from work with Bill and Diane had not returned soooo, shit, I guess it could have been her."

"Look, Bob. I told you that I didn't appreciate being followed. It's inconvenient, it's stupid, and it also happens to be against the law. Diane, and Sharon, too, have been stalking me. The last thing I want to do is to have your wife arrested for stalking me. I mean it, Bob. It's damned unpleasant.

I've known you and Diane for years and I don't want to cause you problems but this crap has got to stop!"

"Yeah, I know Charlie. Damn! I don't know what to say. I told her to lay off. I told you you might even have me fired…"

"Oh, come on, Bob! You know better than that! I'm not that kind of a guy and you know damned well I'm not! That's ridiculous. But I want the stalking to stop, OK? I don't care what you have to do, but make it stop. I'm going to talk to Bill about Sharon's behavior too."

"What did Sharon do?" Simms asked.

"I'll talk to Bill about it, but I want both of you to rein in your wives. OK?"

"Jeez, Charlie, I'm really sorry about this. God almighty, I never thought…"

"OK, Bob. I've said my piece. Let's just drop it now. Just handle it, will you?"

"You bet, Charlie."

Charlie walked over to where Bill Gallagher was standing. "Hey Bill, got a minute?"

"Sure Charlie. How ya' doin'?"

"Fine Bill, I just want to make sure you have Sharon, ah, under control with regard to stalking me. I remembered your comment about her saying she thought I might be ill because my lights were off. You know that she does not have to drive by my house on the way home from the Acme supermarket."

"Stalking sounds a bit strong Charlie. Maybe she was just driving around."

"Bill, I hate to make an issue of this, but it is stalking. If she were just driving around she would not have bothered to mention my house in particular. Anyway, this is the second time I am asking you. Rein her in, Bill, I mean it. If she follows me again I will have her picked up by the police and I *will* file a complaint. I don't want to do that, but I will if I have to. I hate to have to say things like this, but it's getting out of hand. There is nothing, nothing about my life that warrants following me around or wondering why my lights were not on. It's crazy Bill and it if continues it is illegal. Please tell her to stop."

"Charlie, I already talked to her and I will do it again. But she had promised to lay off and I don't think she was stalking when she drove by your house, but I'll talk to her anyway."

"I appreciate it, Bill. And I'm sorry to have to bring it up. It's just plain silly but it is inconvenient."

Bill Gallagher was angry, not just at Sharon but also a bit piqued at Charlie. He thought Charlie was making too much of the whole issue. Sharon had always been the biggest busybody in Shoreville and everybody knew it. She commented on everything and everybody and the whole town just ignored it when it turned inconvenient. He wondered why Charlie just could not do the same.

The team went through their usual drills, did the requisite infield "chatter" as they fired the ball around, and then ended practice to go off for some beers and the usual male bonding. Charlie did not bother to go. When they got to the bar Tony Mazza asked, "Hey, where's Charlie?"

Bob Simms was the first to pipe up, "He was a bit uptight today and I think he went home to relax."

"Charlie Mullins uptight? That's a new one!" said Art Samuels, "maybe he's not getting' enough you know what!"

"Aw, drop it Art", Tony Mazza said, "let's just have some beer. I'll talk to Charlie later."

Charlie went back to his house, checked the timers one more time, and then showered and drove back to Philly. He was not in the mood to hang around Shoreville and he was still steaming from his conversations with Bob Simms and Bill Gallagher. He didn't like Bill's defensive posture and thought to himself that if he did catch Sharon following him again, he would tell the police and if possible have her picked up on the spot. At least Bob had been apologetic and promised to check into it. Bill seemed not to believe him.

When Bob Simms got home Diane was getting lunch ready for the kids. "Diane," he began calmly, "Charlie Mullins told me you followed him in our car last Thursday. Is he right?"

"Oh for God's sake, Bob! We already talked about this. Has it occurred to you that Charlie might be imagining things? Maybe the guy is delusional or paranoid. I don't know. But what did you say? Did you say it was me? He accuses your wife of following him, what did you say, Bob? I hope you told him he was full of shit! I really hope you did that."

"Look, Diane, he said that if it happens again he will have whoever is following him arrested for stalking…"

"Stalking?! He accused me of *stalking*, Bob? Come on! I mean it. Why in the hell would I be stalking anybody? I hope you gave him an earful!"

"Diane, if it was you following Charlie and he files a complaint you are going to look damned silly in Shoreville. It will be damned embarrassing and could even be expensive if you get fined. If it was you, Diane, I want it stopped."

"Oh, go to hell, Bob. I'm not going to bow to threats even from Charlie Mullins. I'm not stalking him and you should know it. Why were you such a wimp, Bob? Why didn't you just tell him to go screw himself? Huh?"

"Because I know how you are when you get a bee in your bonnet, Diane. Now, if you were following Charlie, I want it stopped."

"Oh, you're tough at home? Get tough with Charlie, Bob! You tell Charlie Mullins that he is getting delusional. Maybe he just *wishes* someone was stalking him!"

"Diane, if you wind up having to answer to a complaint, you are on your own. I mean it!"

Diane just grunted, "Hmmpf!" and went back to fixing lunch for the kids.

Bob stomped off to the shower, fuming but feeling helpless.

Bill Gallagher was talking to Sharon, "Charlie Mullins said today that you and Diane Simms were stalking him, Sharon. I didn't like the way he put it especially when he threatened to file a suit. Is there anything to what he said?"

"Oh, for Christ's sake, Bill, I'm getting a little tired of Charlie's paranoia..."

"Is it really paranoia, Sharon, or are you and Diane up to your old tricks?"

"What is this, Bill? I gave you my word when we talked about it before..."

"Well, he mentioned your driving by his house on the way home from the Acme. It *is* out of the way..."

"Bill! Drop it! I have to drive where Charlie Mullins thinks I should drive? I can't go out of my way if I want to? Get serious, Bill, Charlie is talking nonsense. He's got a bug up his ass and it's not my problem. Nobody is, as he said, 'stalking' him. That's ridiculous!"

"Well, I told him that I thought he was a bit over the top..."

"Over the top?! He was way out of line, Bill, and if he files any kind of complaint I'll sue his ass. He's taking his accusations too far. Just tell him that next time you see him. I'm not going to change my behavior because of threats from Charlie Mullins. Tell him that!"

"Yeah, OK Sharon, I told him he was exaggerating. Let's just drop it."

"I'll drop it, but you just tell Charlie Mullins to get a wife and get a life. I don't care who he is at Shaw, he's not going to threaten me and that's that!"

"OK, Sharon, don't worry about it."

* * * * *

Charlie pulled into the parking slot at Gina's place and let himself in the apartment with his key. Gina was busy cleaning the apartment. She had her hair up in a kerchief and was wearing jeans and a cut off sweat shirt. "Ah ha! The busy housewife", said Charlie, "and moved to kiss her."

"Hello Mr. Mullins, nice of you to drop by. Why don't you sit down and relax while I get this place in order?"

"Gina, I didn't notice any disorder when I came in. The place is spotless."

"No matter, Charlie, I'm gonna clean it anyway. Got a problem with that?"

"Nope, not at all, want some help?"

"No way, aren't you tired from softball practice?"

"No, but I did have a stressful conversation with the husbands of the two wives who have been harassing me. I told them that I would have their wives arrested for stalking if the nonsense didn't stop."

"Ooooo, that sounds pretty tough, Charlie. What did they say?"

"Well, Bill Gallagher was defensive and said that he thought my use of the word stalking was a bit exaggerated. Bob Simms was apologetic and said he would look into it. But I didn't like Bill's reaction. I don't think either of them have much influence over their wives in this matter."

"I'm sure they don't Charlie. Did you put the timers in place?"

"Yeah, I did. I just hope it works."

"Well, it might, but what if one of them rings your doorbell to ask for a cup of sugar?" Gina laughed.

"C'mon, Gina, you know that's not gonna happen."

"Well, maybe not the sugar part, but I wouldn't be a bit surprised if they got a little bolder, Charlie."

"Hell, I even hooked up the TV and put it on the news channel so they would hear some noise and see the TV's reflection on the curtains."

"Yeah, and you no longer go shopping in the supermarket. You no longer drive around town. You don't go to your regular haunts on weekday nights. You don't think they will notice? Believe me, Charlie, they are not going to quit so soon or so easily. They're nosy. They love talking about others and you are someone worth talking about in Shoreville my dear. I know you are no Boy Scout, but 'Be Prepared'."

"I guess you're right, Gina. I'll watch out. Now let's see the dust fly. Get back to your cleaning. I'll fix some tuna salad sandwiches. You willing to risk it?"

"A man who can fix his own lunch! Imagine! I've hit the jackpot! Sure Charlie, I'd love a sandwich. Go to it!"

Charlie retired to the kitchen to fix up some tuna salad while Gina busied herself cleaning the apartment. He never felt so good and so happy.

They went out later to walk around a shopping mall. Gina bought him a dark baseball cap and a pair of large, very dark sunglasses. "These are for tomorrow, Charlie. I know it might seem silly, but I want you to be unidentifiable when we go to Uncle Carlo's place. With the tinted glass on the car you will be hard to see anyway, and with these on, they will most certainly not be able to identify you."

"Are you sure about this Gina? I mean it's a bit melodramatic, no?

"It might seem that way, Charlie, but believe me and trust me on this. You know the old adage, 'an ounce of prevention....'."

"OK, Gina, I'll do it. Maybe you're right."

"I am, Charlie, I am."

They walked around the mall holding hands and Charlie watched carefully for anyone he might recognize from Shoreville. He saw no one and no one from Shoreville saw him. Everyone was at home cleaning up, fixing dinner, or playing with the kids. They had Little League to keep them busy.

Charlie and Gina went back to the apartment and that night stopped by the *trattoria* for a drink. Johnny was there and greeted them both. Charlie now had a life and hoped soon to have a wife.

XIX

Sunday morning Charlie and Gina slept in until close to ten-o-clock. Charlie was a bit more apprehensive than he thought he would be. He was about to meet the most powerful Italian in Philadelphia. Carlo Rizzo was considered by a lot of people to be a dangerous man. Charlie was more worried about what would happen if Gina's uncle did not like him and did not give his approval to their relationship.

Gina fixed some breakfast while Charlie showered and shaved. She laid out some fresh strawberries, croissants and some ham and cheese and made fresh coffee. When she finished, she went into the shower while Charlie was still shaving. Charlie looked at her body in the mirror and wished he had time to make love to her again. She stepped into the shower and bathed while humming to herself. She was calm while Charlie was nervous. "Got the jitters Charlie? She asked from the shower.

"Does it show, Gina? Yeah, I am a bit apprehensive. I mean I'm about to ask your emotional father if he will let me get engaged to you and marry you."

"Oh, it's not just his blessing for our relationship, Charlie? And you haven't even formally proposed to me!"

"Gina, I know this is not the best place to propose, but will you marry me?"

"Jeez, proposed to in the shower by a man who is shaving. Well, it's *different*. It's more interesting than you getting down on one knee, I guess. Anyway, I'll have to think about it. I mean marriage is serious stuff, Charlie", Gina kidded.

"Gina! I'm a nervous wreck and you're kidding around. Will you marry me?"

"You bet your Irish butt I will! Happy now?"

"OK, Gina. Yes, I'm happy now. Thanks."

"Thanks? You propose to me, I accept and all you can say is 'thanks'? Charlie, when did you get so romantic?" Gina stepped from the shower and pressed her wet body against him. Charlie thought he would explode. She kissed him and said, "Now you'll have to dry off again. Serves you right for being so romantic!" and laughed.

"You're too much for me, woman. God, how I love you."

"Same here, Mullins. You ready for some good Italian food? Uncle Carlo is sure to put on a spread for you."

When it was 12:30 they took the elevator to the garage and walked to Gina's Mercedes. Charlie had his baseball cap and the dark glasses in his blazer pocket. After they had driven for a few minutes, Gina said, "OK, Charlie put on the glasses and the cap. Pull it down low over your forehead and slump down a little in your seat."

"Gina, are you sure…?"

"Trust me, Charlie, just do it, OK?"

Gina hit the automatic gate control button she kept in her purse as they drew close to Carlo Rizzo's driveway as she always did. They could drive straight through without stopping. Charlie saw a guy in a grey business suit with a camera. He was taking pictures as fast as he could. *"The guy is wearing a suit on Sunday. Jesus! How uptight can you get?"* he thought.

Gina pulled into the driveway and drove around to the back entrance where they could not be seen exiting the car. "Keep it on until we get inside, Charlie. You can never tell if they have somebody hanging around back here. They probably can't see anything but I don't want to take any chances."

"OK, Gina but I feel a bit silly entering the house like this."

"Uncle Carlo knows the drill, Charlie. Just keep the cap and the glasses on until we get inside, OK?"

"Gotcha", Charlie was a lot more worried about how he would deal with Gina's uncle than he was about being photographed but he followed Gina's instructions.

A hefty looking bodyguard opened the door as they approached and they stepped inside. Charlie quickly removed the cap and glasses because he thought he looked silly. The bodyguard did not seem to pay any attention to what Charlie thought was weird garb.

"Hi, Frankie!" Gina greeted the bodyguard. "Hello Miss Gina. Your uncle is in the living room waiting for you."

"Thanks, Frankie, how's the family?"

"They're all just fine, Miss Gina, thanks for asking."

Charlie looked at the bodyguard. He looked like the kind of guy that could break an arm like he would snap a twig. And he was talking to Gina like a tender father about his family! *"Well, he's just a person too"* thought Charlie, *"but he is a very BIG person!"*

Frankie led the way to the living room. Carlo Rizzo was leafing through the Sunday newspaper. He closed the paper and rose to meet them.

Charlie looked Carlo over quickly. The man had silver grey hair combed straight back. He was wearing a blue blazer with a cream colored silk shirt and light grey slacks. Like Charlie he was wearing a pair of moccasins that looked even more expensive than Charlie's Gucci's. He was a far cry from the caricature of mafia figures. He looked like what Gina said he was, a successful businessman. Carlo had catlike movements, even at his age. It was clear that he was a wary man. His movements were slow and fluid but one sensed that he could suddenly move very quickly if he had to.

Carlo walked first to his niece, "Ah, *bambina mia*, you look beautiful as always. I'm always so happy to see you." He kissed her on the cheek and then gave her a strong embrace.

Gina backed away after hugging her uncle and said, "Uncle Carlo, this is Charlie. He's the man I told you about."

"Ah, really Gina? I thought you were bringing a total stranger to the house" Carlo said, laughing.

"Aw, c'mon Uncle Carlo, you know what I mean."

Charlie offered his hand to shake and said, "Nice to meet you Mr. Rizzo."

"Nice to meet you too, Charlie. Gina never stops talking about you. She tells me she is going to bring you by the house for lunch today, then arrives here and says 'this is Charlie' like she might have brought somebody else. I just thought that was funny."

"Well, I guess Gina is a bit nervous like I am. I mean you are her father and I, ah, we are here to talk about our relationship…"

"Yes, don't worry", Carlo interrupted, "I know and Gina knows I was just giving her a hard time. I love my little girl. She's all I have in the way of family. So, maybe she is right to be nervous. Anyway, welcome. Have a seat." Carlo pointed to the sofa.

On the coffee table in front of the sofa was an enormous array of antipastos. There was eggplant marinated in olive oil, artichoke hearts in olive oil and oregano, *sardella*, anchovies, salami, olives, and a large parmesan cheese with the center carved out to make a bowl and chunks of the cheese broken up inside. A woman in a maid's uniform came out of the kitchen with a bottle of red wine and a corkscrew. She handed the bottle and the corkscrew to Carlo who deftly popped open the wine, poured a small amount to taste, and after swirling the wine around in his glass and sniffing the bouquet, put a small amount in his mouth and "chewed" the wine to release its flavor and bouquet. "Ahhh, that's a good hearty wine!" he exclaimed with obvious pleasure. He served Gina and Charlie and then himself and they sat down to talk. Carlo was across the coffee table in an easy chair and Gina and Charlie were together on the sofa. "Welcome" said Carlo as he held his glass for a toast.

"Thank you", said Charlie. "Salute" said Gina and they touched their glasses together.

"Gina told me you work for the Shaw Corporation, Charlie." Carlo reached for some antipasto and added, "Come on, eat something. The antipasto is delicious. Paola is a great cook."

Charlie helped himself to some marinated eggplant and placed it on a small piece of Italian bread. He answered Carlo, "Yes sir, I work in the Treasurer's Department. I'm First Assistant Treasurer there."

"Isn't Fred Perkins your boss then? He's Treasurer, no?"

"Yes sir, Fred is my boss. Do you know him?"

"Well, kind of," said Carlo, "I know he's a real prick." He stared at Charlie with a wry smile waiting for a response.

"I can't really answer to that, Mr. Rizzo. I know some people in the company don't like Fred, but I don't have a problem with him. He's my boss and I respect him as a professional." Carlo appeared pleased at the response.

"Nice going, young man" Carlo thought, *"never say anything bad about anybody. Smart guy!"*

"Did you ever know Phillip Shaw? I mean the old man, not his son."

"Not to speak to him, no sir, but I had seen him around the company. My father worked there for over 30 years and I went to a lot of company-sponsored events and Mr. Shaw would often be there."

"I know old Phil. When he was first getting the company started I helped him get some start-up money. Banks don't like to loan to new businesses, you know. They only lend money to people who *don't* need it."

Charlie was surprised that Carlo knew old man Shaw and even more surprised that he had arranged a loan for him. "That's interesting, Mr. Rizzo. I didn't know much about how Mr. Shaw got started except that he worked hard to build the company."

"He worked all right, and damned hard. But you can work your butt off and get nowhere if you can't pay the bills. I was just a young guy, but I introduced him to a friend of mine and he got the money to help him keep going. I liked him. He paid back every dime, thanked me for helping him, and for years sent me a card every Christmas. He would send it by messenger with a basket full of wine, cheese, and other assorted stuff. I liked him. We lost touch over the years, but I was always glad to have helped him through a tight spot. Look at what the company is today!"

"That's really interesting, Mr. Rizzo. I had no idea...."

"Ah, there are a lot people that you have no idea I know." Carlo laughed, as much to himself as to Charlie.

"You and Gina are really serious, huh?"

"Yes, Uncle Carlo" Gina chimed in.

"Ah, *bambina*, I know what *you* told me. I want *Charlie* to tell me."

"Sorry Uncle Carlo", Gina said with exaggerated mock contrition.

"So, you are really serious?"

"Yes sir, Gina is the most wonderful woman I have ever met. With your permission, I intend to marry her."

"You know of course that Gina is like a delicate flower. She has had a very comfortable life but she has been raised in a kind of 'hothouse'. I have been very protective of her. It's not easy being my niece as I gather you saw from the 'photographers' in front of my house. She's tough, you know. She dealt with it over the years. But I know it was tough for her. When she was a little kid the 'suits' would follow her to school. What the hell was a little girl going to do that they had to follow her? She'd be out on the playground and there were two idiots in suits standing around. I tried to protect her from the pressure but I also tried to raise her to be independent and think for herself. So, in some ways she was sheltered. She came to live with me when she was just a little more than two years old. Her parents were killed in an automobile accident. Her mother was my sister. We all came over from Sicily together – I was five at the time – and when my sister died, I became Gina's legal guardian. I made sure she always had the best but she also knew that the best was not easy to come by. I never let her forget her Sicilian parents and how hard they had to work when they came here. So, Gina's got a very unique perspective on life. She's as wealthy as any of the girls she went to school with at Bryn Mawr, but she is a 'real' person who is true to her family origins. She suffered a lot of discrimination from some of the daughters of the 'finer families of Philadelphia', Carlo seemed to almost spit the words, but she held her head high. She got fantastic grades and graduated magna cum laude. She has stuck by me through a lot of stuff."

"That's one of the things I love most about Gina, Mr. Rizzo. She has a wonderful and supportive group of friends who all try to protect her, too. I am aware of her vulnerabilities. We talked a lot about her life. I think you have done a fantastic job of raising her."

"Well, in a lot of ways it was easy. Gina was as beautiful when she was a little girl as she is now. She was and still is captivating – and she knows how to use it too," he laughed, "everybody loved her. It's hard not to love beautiful children, no? She was always well-behaved but she could be a terror if she thought she was wronged. She can be hard-headed as hell, if you want to know."

"Uncle Carlo! Are you trying to help me or scare Charlie to death?!" she cried.

"Oh, you mean you haven't shown Charlie your obstinate side?"

"I never had to and I don't think I ever will have to, Uncle Carlo."

"No problem, Mr. Rizzo, I pretty much sensed that Gina has a very strong will and a mind of her own. I can deal with it."

"Confidence doesn't seem to be your problem, Charlie. That's good. Let me say something, Gina's happiness is everything to me. She has told me that you make her happy and that she is confident that she will always be happy with you. I want my little girl happy and protected. I also want the man she is with to be happy. That might be a bit more difficult in view of Gina's unique family circumstances. We'll talk about that over lunch, but I hope you know what I mean."

"Understood Mr. Rizzo, Gina and I have talked about it a good deal. I want you to know how much I really love her. I will do whatever I have to do to be with her. I've dealt with a lot in my life to get a lot less. I can certainly do whatever is necessary to have the woman I love. I suspect you would do exactly the same."

"That's right, Charlie, I would never walk away from someone or something I wanted because of others. I'm glad to hear you see it that way too. Now let's sit down to some lunch."

They moved to the dining room and Paola set to bringing out the meal. The first course was a delicious penne with prosciutto with a light tomato sauce. It was delicious and light. "I get that pasta from a fellow who makes it here in Philly. It's as good as you can get in Italy."

"It's very light", said Charlie, "not filling at all. It was perfect."

"Ah but wait until you taste the next dish", said Carlo, "it's Paola's specialty and there is nothing like it anywhere in the world!"

Carlo was right. Paola's specialty was veal with black truffle and porcini mushroom sauce. It was done to perfection. Charlie did not know where or when he had ever eaten any better. "Mr. Rizzo, may I suggest you never lose that cook. She is a veritable treasure. I have never had veal that tender and that delicious in my entire life!"

"I'm glad you like it, Charlie. Paola only cooks like that for Gina and now you. During the week she is not nearly so creative!" he laughed.

For dessert they had a lemon *gelato*. It was just what Charlie needed to digest the wonderful meal. They retired to the living room for espresso and black Sambuca liqueur.

Carlo began, "Charlie, all day you have been calling me Mister Rizzo. It would seem that you purposely avoided calling me Don Carlo like they refer to me in the papers and on the street. Why is that?"

"Well, sir, I didn't come here to talk to 'Don' Carlo. I came to talk to Gina's 'Uncle Carlo' whose last name is Rizzo, so I call you Mister Rizzo because it would be ill-mannered of me to call you by your first name."

"I like you, Charlie. You have respect and a lot of guys your age don't any more. You're right. When it comes to Gina, I am 'Uncle Carlo', not that 'Don Carlo' nonsense that started with those stupid movies about Italian gangsters. All they do is walk around and mumble. I don't know any Italians that talk like that. Christ, they said Marlon Brando put cotton in his cheeks to play Don Corleone. No wonder he couldn't talk right. It's like going to the dentist." Carlo laughed.

Charlie thought it genuinely funny that Carlo would make fun of the portrayal of mafia gangsters in the movies. Carlo continued, "You know what we used to call that TV program, you know, ah, 'The Untouchables'? We used to call it 'Cops and Wops'" Don Carlo broke out laughing, "all the bad guys were Italian. No Irish, no Jews, all Italians."

"So, Charlie, let me come right to the point. My reputation doesn't bother you? You want Gina no matter what, is that right?"

"Well, most certainly the answer is 'yes' to the last question. As for your reputation, no it doesn't bother me but maybe that's because I don't have the slightest idea how it affects me."

"Good for you, Charlie. If you said my reputation didn't mean anything, you'd be lying. When your situation with Gina becomes a matter of public knowledge, you are going to think you got hit by a brick, Charlie. You saw those 'suits' out front? They will be all over you like white on snow. That's not something you are used to. I'm sure they would tell the Shaw Corporation about you and Gina and her relationship to me. I know Shaw has defense contracts and they require security clearances. They don't just check for communists, they also ask if anyone has a criminal record or is in any way linked to organized crime. You're not naïve, Charlie, you know what it would mean if you were dating the only daughter of a reputed organized crime figure – a gangster."

"Well, Mr. Rizzo…"

"Let me talk a little further, Charlie. I know what I am accused of. I also know how many politicians come to me for donations to their campaign. They tell me to be discreet. I'll bet they don't tell Phil Shaw to be discreet! I'm supposed to be a crime figure Charlie. Phil Shaw is supposed to be an 'industrialist'. You don't think old Phil Shaw didn't bribe his share of politicians and generals for his defense contracts? You think he didn't use contacts in Europe to sell equipment to both sides during the war? I've bought politicians in my time and I've bought judges. How am I different than Phil Shaw? I don't deal in porn or drugs. Everybody knows that. I keep the drugs under control by handling money for the dealers. If they step out of line, they lose their connection to me and the feds will blow them out of the water. They're going to be here anyway because the cops can't stop them.

"What do I do for a living? I lend money to people the banks won't touch or that they have screwed and now need my help. I run gambling operations in Philly. I'm sure you read the papers. I once was accused of fixing a ball game. Now tell me something, how is that different than rigging a bid on a government contract? Aren't you affecting the outcome? Hell, I would think that building a battleship or a missile is a lot more important to society than a damned basketball game!"

"You know, Charlie, I came from Sicily after the war. I was 5 when I got here. My father smuggled weapons and cigarettes during the war. You know who for? For the Americans! They wanted the Sicilians to engage in smuggling to help get the Germans out of Italy and bring down Mussolini. That was OK, right? When they smuggled cigarettes and guns to make money to feed their families that was 'wrong'. My father didn't give a shit about Hitler or Mussolini. He was a peasant content to raise his olives and oranges. He would smuggle once in a while to make some additional money. The US Army taught him how to be good at it."

"I had a hard time when I started school here. My English was what I learned from other kids and it wasn't good. I had a thick accent and the other kids made fun of me. I got through school thanks to a Sicilian priest in the local parish. He improved my English and helped me with my studies. I got good grades and finished high school. I got a job in construction right out of high school because my family needed money. I was smart enough to figure out the construction companies were padding their costs. I watched for a while and just kept my eyes and ears open. I was quiet and I suppose they thought I didn't understand much English. They certainly thought I was stupid. I got together with some of the other guys and one day we cornered one of the engineers. I told him I knew what was going on and that we wanted the wages they were claiming to pay us. He laughed in my face and told me to shut up or I would lose my job. He started with some stuff about wise-ass guineas and we should be glad we even had jobs at all, being as stupid as we were. One night after work, we caught the guy alone and told him what would happen if he did not pay us what he was claiming. I hit him so hard I broke a couple of ribs and told him that he would remember what I said every time he breathed. The next day he called me into his office. I could see that he was all wrapped up under his shirt. He told me that if I kept my mouth shut I would get full wages. I made sure that his deal included my friends and he agreed. We followed up with his suppliers and found out he was padding on the stuff he bought from them too. So we shook him down for a part of that as well."

"I don't apologize for what I do, Charlie. People might not like it, but all I am really doing is getting a share of what other 'more reputable' guys are doing. When a fourteen dollar toilet seat costs the government one-hundred-fifty dollars, I will go to the supplier and tell him I want fifty. If he doesn't come across, I remind him that I have some judges and politicians on my payroll and that he might find himself under investigation and in a cage for a while."

"I certainly don't hope you think Phil Shaw is a Boy Scout. I wouldn't open too many of his closets if I were you."

"Mr. Rizzo, you don't need to tell me anything. I don't judge you or anybody else. I am love with the woman who happens to be the biological daughter of your sister and the little girl who became your emotional daughter."

"That's admirable, Charlie and I appreciate it. But I'm a businessman that a lot of people talk about. You are going to hear a lot of crap and I want you to know who I am. You're going to hear a lot of stuff, believe me. If any of it is a problem for you, come to me. I'll tell you. You are Gina's choice for happiness. I won't pull any punches. I've played hardball all my life, I know it. So has Phil Shaw and a lot of other guys in this area. They don't apologize for being tough, and neither do I. If you are wearing a uniform and kill somebody for some ideology, you get a medal. If somebody rapes your daughter and you blow his brains out, you get the chair. I'm not here to judge and I'm not here to be judged. I've helped a lot of people and I have hurt some. There are a lot of companies in Philly that wouldn't be here if I hadn't helped them get started. The owners and the presidents strut around and get their pictures on the society page. I'm always on the city page when I can't avoid the press. I don't say it's not fair. It's just the way it is. I was born in Sicily. They were born in Bala Cynwyd or Wilmington. I worked in construction, they went to Harvard or Penn. Different circumstances, different people, same money."

"I'll listen carefully Mr. Rizzo and if I do have questions, I promise to ask. But Gina is the woman I want to marry. If we have to move to Canada or Seattle or Nebraska, I'll do it to be with her. It's that simple."

"Now, Charlie, listen close to me. You and Gina should not make this relationship known to the world when you walk out of here. You are going to need time to make some plans. You don't want to be run out of your job. You should leave on your own terms if that becomes necessary, and it probably will." Gina sat with Charlie and listened.

Carlo continued, "You don't strike me as the kind of guy that would live on his wife's income, Charlie. If your life suddenly goes to hell, you won't find work so easily. Every time you get a job, the feds will show up and talk to your employer. Some of your friends will back away from you and you will be disappointed. My suggestion is that you get things ready for change. I wouldn't want my *bambina* far away, but if she is happy, that's all I care about. I love her Sunday visits, but I would rather know she is happy in Winnipeg than lonely in Philly."

Charlie noticed that Gina's eyes were brimmed with tears. Carlo Rizzo was making the kind of sacrifice he was not accustomed to making. He was dealing from the heart. Charlie knew it must have been difficult for him.

"Mr. Rizzo, I have to say that I have not seen many gestures as unselfish as the one you just made. I promise you, I will think this whole thing through. I will build a plan with Gina and will consult with you as we go. I would not take your daughter from you except to be my wife. I would not deny her the pleasure of visiting you. And I am really not one for letting people tell me how to run my life. But, you're right. We need to think this thing through. I don't want Gina hurt and I don't want to be taking guff from anybody. I have always run my own life and that's not going to change."

"Good", said Carlo, "but don't have any illusions about how different it will be. You don't know Sicily. It's a tough country. It's mean. It's dry. Water is a scarce commodity and people have to pay a lot for it. Politicians exploit water to hold the people down and get themselves elected. It was ravaged by war more than once in its history."

"You're right, Mr. Rizzo, but I do know something about how immigrants were treated in this country. The Irish didn't have it so easy either. I told Gina about my grandfather working in the anthracite mines when he was nine. I told her about his older brother who became a communist while working in the mines and how the feds pestered him all his life."

Carlo smiled and laughed a little, "Yeah, Charlie I know about the Irish. I had a few run-ins with them myself when I was growing up and in business. You guys are tough, that's for sure. And you have the memory of Sicilians for a wrong done to you. The idea that this country is a melting pot is great for school civics classes. The fact is it's a mosaic. It's a bunch of different people trying to hang on to the remnants of the cultures that made them miserable and forced them to leave their homes while having to fight with other people from other countries for the same jobs in America. Like everywhere else, the big shots and the politicians pitted each of us against the other for their own gain. Some of us refused to bow and we fought back. We held on to our pride and refused to fight each other. We banded together like wolves and snarled back. They knew we were desperate so they gave us what we demanded. You know the saying 'never fight an enemy whose back is to the sea'. When there is no way out, Charlie, a man will fight twenty times harder to stay alive."

"Well, Mr. Rizzo, I take it that Gina and I have your blessing?"

"You do, and I'm telling you now that you can count on my help if you need it. I want both of you to be happy and I want some little *bambini* running around in my yard."

Gina smiled through the tears that were spilling from her eyes. "Uncle Carlo, it's a little soon to be talking *bambini* don't you think? I mean from start to finish it's a full nine months for each one. We're still working on letting the world know we're in love! Thank you for your blessing." And the tears rolled down Gina's face.

Carlo laughed. "Yeah, I know, I just want to make sure Charlie understands my priorities."

"How many you want, Mr. Rizzo? I'm glad to oblige."

They all broke out laughing and the mood turned lighter.

The afternoon sun was setting. Carlo Rizzo kissed his daughter on the cheek and hugged her tight. "I love you my little girl. You have my blessing with this good man you've found. He's got guts and brains. Help him to use both! You're both going to need all the resources you can muster. But I am sure it will all be worth it. You are a beautiful couple."

Charlie was dumbstruck. All he could say was "Thank you Mr. Rizzo, thank you."

Carlo Rizzo surprised him with a back slapping hug. "Always take care of my little girl, Charlie. And come by here whenever you feel like it."

Charlie stepped back and offered his hand to Carlo Rizzo. "We shake on it Mr. Rizzo." Charlie could see that Carlo Rizzo was actually holding back tears.

Charlie and Gina said good night to Carlo. Gina gave him a warm hug and started crying again. Charlie looked on and gave a slight nod to Carlo. He thanked Carlo for the lunch and the couple walked to the kitchen. Gina kissed Charlie and then said, "OK, Mullins put on your costume – cap and glasses please. We are going back out into the world now."

Charlie put on the cap and glasses while Frankie stepped outside to look around and then said, "OK, Miss Gina, you can get into your car." He held the driver side door for her.

"Thank you Frankie, say hi to the missus and the kids."

"Thanks, will do, Miss Gina."

As they drove back out of Carlo's property the same suits were there and one of them was dutifully photographing the car again. Charlie was irritated by the intrusion. "Gina, they can't get anything except dark windows. Why do they bother?"

"It's just to remind us they are watching, Charlie. I wouldn't be surprised if they didn't even have any film in the camera. They just do it to keep the pressure on. I've gotten used to it. They leave me alone at home now because they have figured out that I am not involved in my uncle's business affairs. I guess I was more 'dangerous' when I was nine than I am now!"

They drove back to Gina's place and sat down to talk.

"Didn't I tell you, Charlie? I told you Uncle Carlo would like you."

"Gina, he is a fascinating guy. He could easily have been the CEO of some large company. I mean he is nothing like the way the press describes him."

"Don't underestimate him, Charlie. He is tough. He had to be. What do you do if you loan money to some guy or a business that can't get credit from banks and then the guy refuses to pay you? You're not going to discuss the matter in court. What do you do when the guy tells you that he owes you nothing because the deal was not legal? I don't condone some of the things my uncle has done, but I do understand why he did them. Do you have any idea how many otherwise upstanding and outstanding members of society come to him for help? I mean, how would a person with a reputation like my uncle's be able to open a bank account? You think the bankers don't know who he is? They know and they like his money. They just don't want people to know that they deal with him. So, it's hypocritical but that's just the way it is. In some ways my uncle *is* a CEO. He tried and still tries to stay out of the ugly stuff like drugs, prostitution, and porn. But we know it is all out there and would be anyway if my uncle was not around. He at least keeps it under control by making sure he has control over the money. That's what it's all for anyway. He can't get rid of it, the government can't get rid of it. I don't think anybody can get rid of it. I wouldn't say he is a benefactor of society by any means, but I'm not sure who really is in this world."

"I was sure surprised to learn that old Phillip Shaw got started with a loan arranged by your uncle!"

"A Sicilian 'loan arranger'" Gina giggled, "even the pronunciation is right!" and she broke out in a laugh.

"Oh my God, Gina, how bad is that joke?!"

"Charlie Mullins, you would be surprised at the people who have come to my uncle for help! Unfortunately, because of the feds, he doesn't exactly keep open records, you know?"

"Changing the subject, Gina, we are going to have to work out a plan for our life. Everything you and your uncle have told me has registered. Today, with the picture taking I got an initial taste of what things could be like. The minute our situation becomes official I will be out of Shaw in a New York minute. Fred Perkins will do the honors with gusto. I will not let that happen."

"I have to admit", Charlie continued "that my conversation with your uncle certainly messed around with my view of life. I was raised to think in a certain way. Work hard, do the right thing, and you will move ahead in life. My father died on the job. I have to ask myself what he really got for 30 years of hard work. A good conscience? Maybe that's worth something, maybe it's not. Was he happy? I think he probably was. Did he have power and control over his own life? Not really. He was what people would call a 'good man' but he will never see his grandchildren. I wonder how some of the things your uncle has done are markedly different from the things Fred Perkins did. And old Phillip Shaw selling to both sides of a war in which Americans are getting killed! How does that figure into my value system? I'm confused, Gina."

"I had and still have the same kinds of doubts, Charlie. I see a lot of people in my volunteer work who get involved in public projects just to pad the bills and screw the city. They don't care about the work itself. They just see an opportunity to make some money the easy way and get a citation from the city for doing it. They hang the award on the walls of their offices for all to see what great public-minded citizens they are and then go to my uncle to set up off-shore companies to evade taxes. Having been raised by my uncle's 'human side', I always saw him as a man, not as a figure or an icon. He never hit me, even as a child and I don't remember him ever raising his voice to me. He was a loving father. How do I reconcile things? I don't. I just don't judge. Could his life have been different than it was? How do I know? He survived and actually prospered. That's all I am able to say."

"You know, Gina, the Shaw Corporation would let me go without the slightest twinge of conscience. They wouldn't and probably couldn't afford to keep me around if I lost my security clearance. They would lose their government contracts. I would be a grain of sand in their gears and I would have to be removed. It's just the way the game has to be played. I never had thought about it because I never had reason to. I had a nice boring and stable life. I just *thought* I was in control. I bought an illusion that was fed by my 'acceptable behavior' for one of 'my station'. That could all be taken away because I broke the 'rules' and fell in love with someone who has the 'wrong' background."

"Careful, Charlie," Gina whispered to him, "You are angry. Don't walk out on the ice before you know how thick it is. I agree with you about your vulnerability, but we can't defy the system with impunity. You know that."

"You're right, Gina. I want to think this whole thing through. The one thing I am sure of right now is that I love you above everything else. I will not back away from a chance to be happy with a beautiful person."

Gina's eyes brimmed with tears again, "God, I'm a faucet today, Charlie. So much has happened in such a short time. My life has changed too. I never really expected to find someone like you. You are so special to me. What a day!" and she laughed lightly through her tears.

Charlie broke the mood, "Boy that was some lunch your uncle put on. I don't remember ever eating such delicious food and in such quantity. I'm surprised he's not 300 pounds!"

Gina laughed, "He doesn't eat that way every day, Charlie. If he did he *would* be 300 pounds. Today was special for him too. Did you see that he was holding back tears as we were saying goodbye?"

"Yeah, he looked a bit emotional."

"He accomplished the one truly *personal* goal he had worked for all his life, Charlie. He saw his daughter happy and in love. I think everything he ever did was to make that moment possible for me."

Charlie pulled Gina to him and kissed her. She responded with passion and fire. They said nothing and moved toward the bedroom without breaking apart. They fell into bed and made love even more passionately than ever before. Exhausted physically and emotionally, they fell asleep in each others arms.

XX

Charlie awoke Monday morning to hear Gina already moving around in the kitchen. She was preparing breakfast. He padded out to the kitchen in his navy blue silk boxer shorts to see Gina putting coffee into the filter of the coffee maker. He came up behind her and hugged her tight. "Good morning beautiful, what are you doing up so early?"

"I've been up for about an hour, Charlie, I couldn't sleep any more and I sat here thinking for a while. I'm so happy and so worried all at the same time."

"Worried?"

"Of course, Charlie, you've got some tough choices to make and I want to be there for you. You will need my help and my love. I want it all to be sufficient to ease whatever pain you are going to experience."

"Gina, don't worry too much. Like you, I'm resilient. I've been thinking about this since you told me who your uncle really is. I confess that I still don't have a firm plan, but I have prepared myself mentally for any contingency."

"One thing is certain, Charlie you have to make sure that no one in Shoreville is able to find out who I am. That would be the biggest news ever to hit that town. Eligible bachelor links up with mafia princess! That would be the news of the century in that town and it would quickly spread around the Shaw Corporation. You are going to have to make sure those nosy women stay out of our lives. They are probably more dangerous even than the Feds."

"For sure, Gina. They are certainly as aggressive or even more so. And they don't know what they are looking for so if they find something out they will make more noise than a flock of parrots. I'll go by Shoreville after work tonight, drive around a bit and then come back here. I'll try to make sure some people see me. The company has an art show scheduled for next week and I will go to that too. I suppose I will have to try to maintain a semblance of my regular life to keep those broads mollified."

"That's the first priority, Charlie. We can talk about the other alternatives later. Now get yourself dressed, have some breakfast, and be off with you. You've got a lot of work to do!"

Charlie showered and shaved, being careful to avoid his Armani cologne. He didn't want to give off any signals that he had changed in any way or changed any of his habits. *"This is already starting to get complicated!"* he thought as he shaved. Thus began Charlie Mullins' clandestine life.

The first day at the office in Charlie's new life was a busy one. Several department heads called to thank him for his comments on their draft budget proposals and quarterly reviews. Some of them had worked over the weekend and were sending back their revisions for comment. They all wanted to schedule a meeting with Charlie before having to confront Perkins.

XXI

At the end of the business portion of the first day of his new and potentially complicated life, Charlie drove to Shoreville from Wilmington.

He left the office at five as usual and drove over to Shoreville. He saw the familiar crowd of cars driving out of the Shaw laboratory parking lot on the Jersey side and he hoped that some of their drivers would see his car heading for home. He pulled up to his garage, parked his car inside, and entered the house. He had been in the house for only a few minutes when one of the timers turned on his living room lights. He sat down on the sofa and worked out a plan to be seen. He decided to go down to Rexall's and buy himself some Aqua Velva and then pass by the Acme supermarket to pick up some groceries. He would take the groceries to Gina's place in the trunk of his car when he left later. That would take care of Monday night. He would show up at the bowling alley on Wednesday, drive around town after work on Thursday – maybe have a drink at Jimmy Balsamo's place or the Royal Bar, and then sneak out to Philly later while everyone in Shoreville was having dinner. Since he often disappeared on Friday nights anyway, that was not a night he would have to cover. He would come back to the house, turn off the timers, and then set them again on Saturday after softball practice. Charlie figured if he stuck to this routine for a couple of weeks, he would be able to see if it was working as desired. If he got the wrong kind of feedback from any of the guys at the bowling alley or at softball practice, he could compensate accordingly.

He also had to find out when he was due for another security clearance at the company. Ideally it would either be immediately or a year from now. He was sure, however, that it was not the former because he was usually advised of the renewal and he had not heard anything in recent weeks. He would have to check with Laura. He was sure she would not tell Perkins. Fred was paranoid about anyone asking any questions about what happens in his area and he would want to know why Charlie had asked about his clearance. If the clearance was to occur soon, he could count on another year before his connection to Gina would become a "matter of national security". He laughed to himself at the concept of Gina as a threat to national security.

He got back into his car and drove down to the Rexall drug store. He parked on the street where his vehicle could be easily seen and walked into the store. He walked around for a while until the manager saw him and said, "Hi Charlie, how ya' doin'?"

"Fine Bert, and you? I just dropped in to pick up some after shave." Charlie picked up a bottle of Aqua Velva and made his way to the cashier. He paid with a fifty dollar bill so the cashier would have to scrape around for change and would remember that he had been there.

He left the drugstore and drove to the supermarket. He walked around the aisles slowly picking up some purchases. A few people were in the supermarket and one of them was Diane Simms. He made sure he walked by her and said, "Hi, Diane. How's Bob?"

Diane looked a bit flustered remembering Charlie's conversation with her husband at softball practice but quickly recovered and said, "Hi Charlie. Getting some groceries? Bob's fine, thanks. Wish I had time to talk, but I have to run. See ya'." Charlie smiled inwardly at Diane's discomfort. He could not have cared less about talking to her. He was satisfied that if anybody asked about his whereabouts Diane would be glad to say she knew – she saw him at the supermarket.

Satisfied that he had provided enough evidence that he was in town, he moved to the checkout counter. There, he pretended to fumble for his money, not remembering which pocket it was in. The checkout girl had to wait until he exclaimed, "Oh, here it is. I'm sorry. I couldn't remember where I put my cash when I left the drug store." He paid for his groceries and left.

He drove slowly home, again hoping that any busybodies on the street would see him. Shoreville was almost shut down because everyone in the town ate dinner at practically the same time. He would drive home, check the street, pull the car into the garage, and after a few minutes leave for Gina's place.

He decided to use I-295 on the Jersey side just to vary his route. He checked for surveillance along his route. The coast appeared clear so he headed toward Camden and then across to Philly.

He arrived to Gina's building about 45 minutes later, took the elevator up to her apartment and let himself in with the key. He had a couple of bags of groceries with him. Gina was in the kitchen making a salad when he walked in and kissed her. "Mmmmm, that's nice. I hope that's Charlie Mullins behind me."

"Smart aleck!" Charlie replied and smacked her behind lightly.

Gina turned around and saw the bags from the supermarket on the kitchen counter. "What's this Charlie? You bringing your own food into my apartment? Am I not feeding you well?"

Charlie laughed, "No, sweets, this is part of my scheme to outwit the nitwits. I bought some Aqua Velva at the drug store..."

"Oh my God, you've abandoned Armani already?"

"No, Gina. I went into the drug store, picked up a bottle of what I always used to buy and gave the checkout girl a fifty dollar bill. She had to fumble around for change. I spoke to the manager and then left for the supermarket. I was lucky there because I ran into one of the town's most active gossips – one of the women who had followed me. She was embarrassed to see me after I had talked to her husband so she will probably tell somebody that she almost fell through the floor, *et cetera*. I took my time going through the checkout counter, looking around for my money like I had forgotten what pocket it was in. If anybody says they hadn't seen Charlie Mullins on Monday night I have witnesses."

"Gotcha, Charlie", Gina looked into the bags from the supermarket. "Now what do we do with the cans of beef stew and chili? We can use the toilet paper and the napkins," she laughed, "but I'm not big on canned stew and chili. And sin of sins, Charlie, *frozen* lasagna? Frozen lasagna in Gina Ferrelli's place!! My God, who would have thought it?" Gina was laughing almost hysterically. "You certainly created a plausible case for yourself, Charlie. I guess I'll give the canned stuff to the church. The frozen stuff I'm not so sure about. I refuse to throw food away so I will ask Father Molina if he can use it or give it away. He'll probably eat it himself, poor guy."

Charlie broke out laughing, "Well, I had to buy the stuff I normally buy. Can you imagine if Diane Simms had seen my shopping cart with truffles, fancy chocolates, and the like? They're used to seeing me buy Gatorade, hot dogs, and canned or frozen food."

"Gina, I also worked out a schedule for the week that will guarantee that I am seen at my haunts, the bowling alley, and at softball practice. With the timers turning the lights on and off, I can probably keep those nosy women convinced that I'm following my regular routines. Every spy needs to create a legend, you know."

"Spy? Legend? Oh Charlie, where did you ever pick up those ideas?" Gina laughed again.

"Well, I *do* read you know. Before I met you and my life was boring, I read a lot of escapist literature, you know, spy stories and detective novels. I just thought I would use some of the jargon to impress you." Charlie laughed.

"You did", laughed Gina "you're a regular James Bond!"

"Oh no, Gina, not a James Bond, he was a *terrible* spy. Every time he showed up people got killed and everybody knew he was double-o-seven. No, my dear, I want to be George Smiley, the unobtrusive and unlikely spy. The guy who blends into the background, that people would confuse with an accountant or a professor. I know my spy stuff!" he laughed heartily. "For your information, they call it 'tradecraft'."

"Well, aren't you the clever one? I sure hope it works. At least you seem to be up on the terminology." They both laughed and headed for the living room.

"You want to open a bottle of wine? I saw you making a salad so maybe we could just have some salad and a glass of wine. It's late anyway and I'm a little tired from all my spy stuff. That OK?"

"Sure Charlie, but let's go out tomorrow night. I would really love some seafood."

"You're on!"

They had their light dinner, watched a little TV and then went to bed. Both Charlie and Gina were in a light mood and they laughed about Charlie's "tradecraft".

XXII

The following day Charlie left for Wilmington from Gina's apartment. Although he didn't know it, his ruse had worked. Diane Simms and Sharon Gallagher had gone to their aerobics class at the YMCA in Shoreville and Diane was telling Sharon that she saw Charlie at the Acme supermarket. "God, Sharon, I felt like smacking his face after what he said to Bob. Then I thought I was going to fall through the floor from embarrassment. He didn't say anything at all about our having followed him, but I knew he was thinking about it. It was really uncomfortable. I just said 'Hi' and then moved on as quickly as I could. Lucky for me, he was heading for the checkout counter anyway." The two of them talked about Charlie for a couple more minutes then moved on to badmouth some of the other people they knew in Shoreville. Charlie's plan had held up for at least one day.

* * * * *

Charlie had two meetings scheduled for that day. The first was with Bill Miller of the Engineering Department. Bill had worked on his budget review over the weekend and met with Charlie to go over the revisions Charlie suggested. "I really hate having to face that guy, Charlie", Miller had said "he just nitpicks at every goddamned thing. He's a real pain in the butt."

"I know, Bill," Charlie responded, "but you know that's really his job. You guys in the operating departments are always optimistic – you're supposed to be, but Fred's job is to question your assumptions. He doesn't like to waste company money."

"I don't either Charlie. It's not *what* he says. It's how he says it. He just tries to lord it over you and make you look stupid. Nobody here is stupid!"

"Yeah, even Fred knows that. It's just his way. But I think you've got a nice tight budget there. Fred will give you some grief just to make his point but he'll approve this one. Don't worry."

"Well, thanks for your help, Charlie. Without you around here, I think we would all gang up and stab that bastard to death like they whacked Julius Caesar."

Charlie laughed, "No need, Bill. This one's in the bag. Trust me."

Bill Miller left Charlie's office with a lot more confidence than he had when he went in.

Fred Armstrong, head of the steel shot division invited Charlie for lunch. Charlie met him at a local restaurant where they discussed Fred's budget proposal. Steel shot was used by industrial companies to clean big machines. Fred wanted to make sure that he had read the market right. He was afraid that Perkins might question his assumptions and blow his budget to bits. He mimicked Bill Miller's conversation. "Charlie thanks for meeting me here. I really want that s-o-b to stay off my back. You know, we have a service component in our division. We not only supply the steel shot, we will go in and clean machines for our clients. It's tough work. Perkins doesn't appreciate how difficult it is and how much we have to pay people to do that kind of work. He always jumps on the labor costs."

"If you notice, Fred, I worked on your revenue projections a bit by improving your volume. If you can make that volume while holding the line on your costs, Perkins won't have a lot to bitch about. Your bottom line is what counts and you show improvement over last quarter so if he gets on your ass, go immediately to that number. He won't be in a position to discuss volume projections with you. You are the guy who knows the business."

After some coaching by Charlie to reduce Fred Armstrong's anxiety, Fred said, "Thanks, Charlie. I feel better about the numbers now." They paid their bill and left the restaurant.

Back at the office, Charlie had several voice mails of the other department heads. He called each one and scheduled their meetings. By the time he finished setting up all the meetings, it was five-o-clock and he headed out to the parking lot and Gina's place.

Gina was waiting for him in a navy blue wrap around dress that showed a lot of leg when she sat down and crossed her legs. "Wow, don't you look terrific!"

"Charlie, I'll call Johnny at the *trattoria* and ask him to use his juice to make a reservation at Bookbinder's. It's the best seafood in the world and I am really in the mood for fish."

"That's great, sweets. Can we have a drink before we go?"

"Sure, but are you going to drive there?"

"No, let's take a cab. That way we can have a drink here, one there if we want to, and get a bottle of wine."

"OK, sweetheart, you're quite a rummy. Must be your Irish blood!"

"Ah ah, Gina, no ethnic slurs please."

"That's not a slur, Charlie, it's a compliment!" and she laughed.

Charlie went to the liquor cabinet and got out the fixings for a manhattan and a vodka dry martini. He prepared Gina's manhattan first and dropped two cherries into it. He had put his martini glass in the freezer while he was preparing Gina's drink. It was frosted when he took it from the freezer and he fixed his favorite double-dry martini. He grabbed a small serving tray and brought the drinks into the living room. "Here you are my dear, I hope you like it."

"You remembered that I hate manhattans but love cherries, Charlie", Gina laughed, "how nice!" She took a sip of the manhattan and feigned a dramatic fainting spell, "Why this is the most fantastic manhattan I have ever had in my life!" she exclaimed.

"Gina, give me a break. How is it really?"

"It's great, Charlie, really. You're an approved barman."

Charlie clinked his glass against Gina's and said, "To the spy profession and all that it has taught me!"

"Salute", Gina responded.

Gina called first to the *trattoria* and talked to Johnny. "The fix is in, Charlie."

"Gina, where do you get that stuff – 'the fix is in' and asking Johnny to use his 'juice'?"

"Well, the FBI thought I was a moll when I was only nine years old. I had to have learned something, right?" Gina giggled. "Now I'll call a cab and we can go to the restaurant."

That was the night that Bill Gallagher swore he saw Charlie and Gina leaving Bookbinder's.

Charlie and Gina arrived to the restaurant at 8:30 and the headwaiter had an excellent table waiting for them. Charlie noticed that every man in the restaurant was looking at Gina as she entered the restaurant. A number of wives looked like they felt like dumping hot oyster stew into their husbands' laps. He followed Gina to the table watching the gentle sway of her hips while saying to himself, *"Sorry guys, she's mine, all mine!"*

When they sat down and Gina crossed her legs, her wrap-around dress fell away and a lot of very attractive leg was exposed. Charlie thought that any moment some wives were going to push a plate of food in their

158

husbands' faces. Charlie himself was looking longingly at her. "Never seen legs before, Mullins?" Gina teased.

"Like those? No ma'am. Never!" Gina laughed easily.

Charlie asked Gina if she wanted another drink and she said she would prefer some wine. Charlie ordered a California red in spite of the fact that they were going to eat fish. "Do you mind, Gina? Nobody follows that rule about white wine with fish anymore. Besides, Bookbinder's has an excellent selection of California reds."

"I actually prefer red, Charlie. Go for it!"

"Ah what an easy date I have tonight. I can't make a mistake!"

He told the waiter to bring a glass of the house white while the red was allowed to "breathe".

"Gina, would you like to start with some fresh oysters?"

"You sure you can behave yourself after a plate of oysters, Charlie?"

"Not really. Especially with that beautiful leg of yours exposed. If you see me starting to pull the tablecloth off the table, you had better run!"

Gina blushed, "You think the dress is too much or maybe too *little*, Charlie?"

"Oh no, not at all, it gets my hormones flowing and that can't be bad. I'll try to control myself."

Gina laughed, "Are you always going to be this horny, Charlie?"

"As long as you keep provoking, yes."

Charlie ordered Oysters Rockefeller for an appetizer. For the main course Gina decided on the sea-scallops with a carrot sauce and Charlie went light with a grilled filet of sole and a boiled potato. The meal was perfect and they made small talk, looked at each other like a couple in love, and just enjoyed a relaxing evening.

Seven blocks away at the Walnut Street Theater, Bill and Sharon Gallagher were sitting through a musical. When the curtain closed for the last time they went to their car to drive home. "Bill, let's drive through the old city before we go back to I-95. I love to see the old buildings." Bill left the parking lot and drove northward for a few blocks, turned east on Market Street and then South on 2nd Street. He would then turn back up Walnut, circle the block again and drive home. The path would take him by Bookbinder's. As he was turning on Walnut he suddenly saw who he thought was Charlie Mullins coming out of Bookbinder's. "Sharon! Look quick! Is that Charlie Mullins coming out of Bookbinder's? Quick, the guy holding the cab door open, I swear it's Charlie!"

"Damn, Bill, it *is* Charlie! Who's that girl with him? She looks like she could be his daughter! We've *caught* him, Bill, we've caught him!"

"Whoa, Sharon, we're not trying to catch anybody. I just thought I saw Charlie, that's all. Don't start with the curiosity again, please!"

"You didn't *think* you saw Charlie, Bill. You *saw* him. That *was* Charlie. By God, it was him. Wait until I tell Diane about this! Who *is* that girl? I've got to find out. You think Charlie has something going? She looks like she has money. That's an expensive dress she's wearing! You think Charlie bought it for her? Naah, Charlie wouldn't know how to buy a dress."

"Jesus Sharon, cool it! If I thought you were going to go berserk I wouldn't have said anything. Don't start doing something stupid again."

"Oh, stifle it, Bill. I'm not going to do anything," Sharon lied, "but I do feel like a reporter that has just got a 'scoop'."

Charlie had no idea that he had been seen or that the structure of his Shoreville ruse might be knocked down by the accidental 'sighting' by the Gallaghers.

Wednesday morning after Bill had gone to work, Sharon called Diane Simms. "Diane, you are not going to believe this. Last night Bill and I went to Philly to see a play at the Walnut Street Theater. I asked him to drive through the old part of the city on the way out to I-95 and who do you think we saw coming out of Bookbinder's? Charlie Mullins, Diane. It was Charlie and he was with a woman – no, a girl – who looked like she could have been his daughter! She was pretty, but clearly too young for Charlie Mullins!"

Diane listened to Sharon and then said, "I don't think it was Charlie, Sharon. I drove by his place last night and the lights were on. From the reflections on the curtains it looked like he was watching television. You must have seen someone else that looked like him."

"Diane, I know Charlie when I see him. It was Charlie, believe me. I am sure of it and so is Bill. It was him and he had a girl with him. I would swear on it!"

"Sharon, why would the lights be on in his house if he wasn't home? C'mon. It wasn't Charlie. It couldn't have been."

"I'm telling you it was him, Diane. And I'm going to prove it. I'm going to catch him yet and maybe even take a picture to prove it. I'll bet he has been seeing that girl for some time. I think he had his arm around her as he opened the cab door. I'm almost sure of that."

"Be careful with that stuff Sharon, you remember his conversations with Bill and Bob. If you get caught it could be pretty nasty."

"C'mon Diane, you know I won't get caught and I doubt that you will be able to resist coming along with me. This is just too hot to ignore and you know it."

"OK, Sharon but let's just be careful. I don't want Bob down my neck again. He was really ticked off the last time."

The next morning Charlie dressed for work and reminded Gina that he would stay in Shoreville on this evening, his regular bowling night. He would disconnect the timers while he was in Shoreville and then set them up when he left on Thursday morning. "I'll miss you in this bed, Charlie," Gina said. "It's amazing how quickly I got used to your being here. It will be strange without you. Hurry back!"

"I'll be back after work on Thursday, baby," Charlie said, "I'll miss you too, Gina. My house seems so empty nowadays. And I have to confess that I am no longer so excited about my work. Fred Perkins doesn't annoy me anymore, he just *bores* me." He kissed Gina and left for work.

* * * * *

After a busy day at Shaw, Charlie headed back to Shoreville. He pulled up to his garage, pressed the remote control and parked his car. He left the garage door open in case anyone drove by. They would see his car. He didn't see any cars on the street except those that he knew belonged to neighbors. He also did not see Diane Simms hiding behind a tree. She had parked her car around the corner where Charlie would not see it and then waited to see if Charlie would be coming home that evening. She had also been by his house that morning after dropping the kids off at school and waited to see if Charlie left for work. He did not leave but he did come home. She couldn't wait to tell Sharon what she had discovered.

Charlie entered the house and set about disconnecting the timers. When he left for the bowling alley the house would be dark and his whereabouts would be known. He got his bowling gear together, put it into the trunk of his car, and changed into his league uniform. He sat down to watch some TV until it was time to leave.

Bill Gallagher and Bob Simms were talking together at the bowling alley but Charlie thought nothing of it. They were often together so seeing them talking was no big deal. Bill had told Bob about seeing Charlie at Bookbinder's and they both agreed that it would not be smart to even hint at the sighting to Charlie. Bill said he saw Charlie just by accident, but he did not want Charlie thinking he had been spying – not after the last conversation Charlie had with him.

While their men were at the bowling alley, Sharon Gallagher and Diane Simms were busy on the telephone. Diane called to tell Sharon that she had watched to see if Charlie left for work on Wednesday morning and said that she did not see him leave. "But", she said "I did see him arrive tonight. Soooo, it seems to me that he did not sleep at home, right?"

"No other explanation, Diane. He was not home Tuesday night. I told you I saw him at Bookbinder's."

"Why do you suppose his lights were on Tuesday night then?" Diane asked.

"One of two reasons, Diane, he left them on by mistake or he is trying to show people he is at home when he is not. I'm willing to bet he is trying to fool us."

"Why would he do that, Sharon?"

"Because there is something he does not want us to know, that's why. And you know I hate a secret. He's got some secret and he wants everybody to think that he is the same old Charlie. Diane, this could be a lot of fun. Shoreville's most eligible bachelor has a girl friend that he is keeping a secret. Wow! There's got to be some reason why he doesn't bring her around here. He's bowling tonight with the guys. Let's see if he says anything. They're his buddies and maybe he will say something about a girlfriend or something like that. Listen, I gotta go. I have to get the kids ready for school tomorrow. Are we on for later tonight?

"Yeah" said Diane, "I'll pick you up at 9:30."

"Bye." Sharon rang off.

League night ended with the usual pizza and beer and Charlie stayed around with the guys. The conversation was the normal raucous jokes, teasing Mildred about going to bed with her, comparing bowling scores, and softball practice on Saturday. Some of the guys complained about their wives in the usual way. Art Samuels told a few dirty jokes, some of which he had told last week, too. He yelled to Tony Mazza, "Hey Tony, you know why there are no Italian Jehovah Witnesses?"

"No, Artie, tell me why there are no Italian Jehovah Witnesses."

"Because there ain't no such thing as an Italian *witness*!" Art broke out in laughter. The group groaned. "Jesus, Artie," Tony cried back, "my grandfather told me that joke. Get a new routine, will ya?"

"Yeah, but when your grandfather told you, he wasn't joking!" Art yelled back. This time the group laughed.

Tony did an imitation of Marlon Brando playing Don Corleone, "Ya wanna continue breathin'? I'm gonna make you an offer you can't refuse." They all laughed.

Nobody said anything to Charlie about having a girl friend or about not being seen around town, so he relaxed and figured his deception was working. The group broke up and went home and Charlie drove back to his house, pulled into the garage and after letting himself in the house, turned on the late news to watch some TV before going to bed. He was relaxed in the belief that no one was curious about his life now.

He slept well but he missed Gina's warm body next to his and having his leg draped over her hip. Gina, too, was tossing around in her bed reaching for a Charlie that wasn't there.

The next morning he set the timers and left for work. Before heading for the bridge he again checked the street for surveillance. He didn't see the two women crouched behind a tree. Diane and Sharon were watching to see Charlie leave for work. They would come back in the evening to see if he returned. He wouldn't.

Bob Simms had asked Bill Gallagher if he would drop him off at home. "Diane has the car tonight, some Tupperware party, or something."

"Sure Bob, no problem."

Bob Simms came home to only the kids in the house. They were already ready for bed and watching TV. "Hey guys, let's get to bed, huh? You got school tomorrow. Your Mom will probably be home late." The kids turned off the TV and kissed their father good night before heading upstairs to the bedroom.

He went to the refrigerator and got another beer to wait for Diane.

Bill Gallagher also came home to a house empty except for the children. Like Bob, he sent them off to bed with a kiss. He went into the kitchen to get a beer when he saw the note from Sharon. The note said there was meat loaf in the oven if he was hungry and that she had gone out with Diane to a Tupperware party. He walked into the den and turned on the TV to wait for Sharon.

Neither was aware that their wives were parked in a lot behind the high school hatching their plot to unmask Charlie Mullins. "Isn't this exciting, Diane?" Sharon exclaimed, "I feel like a spy."

"Yeah, well you won't find it very exciting if Bill finds out and I sure as hell don't want Bob to know. I'm satisfied with my marriage and I don't want Bob to lose his job either."

"Silly! You don't think I like my marriage too? Don't worry. Nobody's going to find out. Now listen. We have to find out if Charlie is at home when his lights are on. I am willing to bet he won't be. If he's not, then he is deliberately trying to fool us. There would be no reason to do that unless there was some big reason. There is a secret somewhere in all this Diane. We have to find it."

"Sharon, I don't know", Diane was hesitant "maybe Charlie has his reasons. I mean we did try to follow him twice. Maybe he just doesn't want anybody prying."

"Diane, wake up! If he didn't want people to pry, he would bring his girlfriend to Shoreville for dinner or to meet his friends or something like that. He's not ashamed of his friends. He's not like that. Sooo, if he is not introducing his new girlfriend to his buddies, something must be up."

"All right, Sharon, all right. I'll go along but promise me, no nonsense, OK?"

"Of course, Diane, now listen. We have to see if Charlie leaves for work tomorrow morning and then if he comes home at the end of the day. We know he went bowling and I'll try to find out from Bill if Charlie went home after bowling tonight. You ask Bob too, and drive by Charlie's house to see if the lights are on after you drop me off."

They pulled out of the high school parking lot with their headlights off. When they pulled out onto the street Diane turned on the lights and drove Sharon home. "Don't chicken out on me, Diane." Sharon whispered as Diane exited the vehicle.

"No, I won't but just don't do something stupid, and keep me informed so we don't tell different stories to our husbands, OK?"

"Right, Good night, Diane, see you in the morning."

Sharon walked into her house. Bill was sitting in front of the TV, groggy from the beer and pizza and then a beer at home. "How was the Tupperware party, Sharon? How much did you spend?"

"I didn't spend anything, Bill. It was all stuff that we already have. We just spent the night making girl talk."

"OK, Sharon. I'm glad you're home safe, now if you don't mind, I'm gonna hit the sack. I'm bushed. Good night."

"I'll be up in a minute Bill. I'll just check on the kids."

Bill Gallagher padded off to the bedroom in a semi-stupor and Sharon saw to turning off the lights, locking the door, and looking in on the children. She would have an adventurous day tomorrow.

Diane Simms first rode by Charlie's house and noticed that his lights were on as usual, and then she drove home. When she entered the house, Bob was laid back in his lazy-boy chair. Like Bill Gallagher, he was half asleep. "Hey Diane, how was the Tupperware party?"

"Just fine, Bob. I didn't buy anything. But I put my news up to date with the ladies."

"Anything special?"

"No, just the same old gossip and girl talk."

"OK, well glad you're home. We had a good night at the bowling alley."

"Really? Everybody there? Oh yeah, Bill, Artie, Tony, Charlie, you know the whole crowd."

"Did you score well?"

"Oh yeah!" Bob yawned and said, "I'm gonna turn in Diane. Gotta work tomorrow. G'night"

"Night Bob, I'll be right up."

"So, Charlie was there," Diane thought, *"that means he is probably home tonight. Tomorrow we'll know when we see if he leaves the house. He apparently didn't say anything about being followed or Bob would have come in fuming. Good!"* She finished putting a few things in place, adding some dishes to the dishwasher and turning it on. She went off to bed. Bob was already snoring.

, After they had dropped their children off at school, Sharon and Diane met around the corner from Charlie Mullins' house. They stealthily made their way to behind a large tree where they could see Charlie's garage. After a brief wait, the garage door opened and Charlie backed his car out of the garage. Sharon and Diane crouched down low and giggled as they saw Charlie scanning the street for any cars that might start to follow him. He pulled ahead slowly then accelerated up the street. When he was out of sight Sharon high-fived Diane. "OK, we saw him leave. Now tonight we come back to see if he returns home. Make sure you tell Bob you had to go out. I got it; let's tell our husbands that we drove up to Richman's for some ice cream. We just had an urge. We won't be getting home that late anyway and the chances that somebody will be able to prove we are lying will be almost nil."

"Now", Sharon continued "make sure you have some dinner in the oven and you've got the kids stowed away doing their homework or something. Tell *them* you are going out with me for a snack so their story will match yours. I'll pick you up in front of the Acme and we'll come over here to see if Charlie comes home. I'll tell Bill I need the car today and I'll drop him off at the plant."

"Sharon, are you sure....?"

"Of course I'm sure, Diane. Stay cool. Nothing is going to happen. Don't you dare chicken out on me. We're in this together, right? Now let's go. I have to get Bill to work."

Sharon spent the rest of the day singing to herself. Diane was more nervous. Both did as planned. They prepared dinner early. They left notes for their respective husbands saying they had gone to Richman's on a whim to have some ice cream and would be back soon. They'd done this before so neither Bill nor Bob would be the wiser.

At six-o-clock Sharon picked up Diane at the Acme supermarket and they drove around to close to Charlie's house. They sat in the car for a while and then moved to their hiding place behind the tree.

"What if somebody sees us, Sharon? I feel like a fool here."

"Cool it, Diane! Nobody is going to see us. Everybody is busy right now fixing dinner. The kids are all inside waiting for their fathers to get home or doing their homework. Look around you. Do you see anybody on the street?"

"No", said Diane.

"Then cool it!" Sharon said, "It will only be a few minutes. Charlie will either be here by 7-o-clock or he won't be here. He's usually regular as clockwork so don't sweat it."

At seven-o-clock there was no sign of Charlie, but the living room light in Charlie's house turned on as if he had flipped the switch as usual. "Bingo!" said Sharon, "look at that. Charlie did not show up and his living room light went on."

"Maybe we missed him?" volunteered Diane.

"Not a chance", said Sharon, "we saw him leave this morning. If he was coming back home tonight, he would not be able to arrive before now coming from Wilmington. He either came home early, which he has never done, or he has not come home but wants someone to think that he has. This is getting good Diane! Real good! Charlie Mullins is hiding something and we are going to find out what it is."

"Ahhh, I don't know Sharon, I feel a little guilty about this."

"Oh yeah, well do this. Tomorrow come by here in the morning and see if Charlie leaves. If he does, I'll pay for a month's manicures for you."

"Now, I'm going home to tell Bill how delicious that raspberry sherbet at Richman's is and how I just could not resist going up there for some. Let's go."

166

"OK, Sharon. I'm with you, but I'm scared and I don't mind telling you."

"You always were the one to pee her pants first, Diane. Take it easy. We'll take our time and find out Charlie's secret."

They walked back to Sharon's car and she dropped Diane off at home. "Sisters?"

"Yeah, Sharon, sisters. But tomorrow I'm going to check to see if Charlie leaves."

"Do what you want Diane, he's not there. Check if you want to but if you do, let me know."

The following morning, Diane Simms took the kids to school and then went back to the parking spot she and Sharon had used the previous night. She waited for a few minutes and there was no sign of Charlie Mullins. The house was quiet. She had to get back to the house to get the car to Bob, so she couldn't stay too long. But there was no sign at all of Charlie.

In fact, while Diane was watching Charlie's house, Charlie was waking up in Gina's apartment in Philly. They had made love and fallen asleep embraced as usual. Charlie was shaving while Gina fixed breakfast. "Well, Mr. Bond..."

"Mr. *Smiley*, please. I told you Bond was always being discovered. Smiley was the real spy."

"Oh, excuse me, Mr. Smiley. Did you set your timers again?"

"Oh yeah! Timers set!"

"Check" laughed Gina.

"And you went bowling?"

"Bowling done."

"Check" said Gina again.

Gina, as far as I could tell it was 'business as usual' last night. Artie Samuels told his stale off-color jokes, everybody propositioned Mildred, Tony was in a light mood, Bill and Bob kept a respectful distance but were not uptight. It was OK as far I could determine."

"And the wives, Charlie?" Gina asked.

"If they had been up to something I couldn't see it. Besides, Bill or Bob will usually give away whatever is happening because their wives give them questions to ask. Nobody said anything last night."

"Hmmmmmm", murmured Gina, "that could be good news or bad news."

They smiled at each other. "OK, Charlie, finish your breakfast and get off to work. Somebody has to have a job in this house", Gina laughed.

Charlie finished his coffee and rose from the table to grab Gina and kiss her firmly. "I have never been this happy in my life. I just want you to know that. Did you ever hear that country music song, 'Kiss an Angel Good Morning'?"

"No Charlie, I don't think so, why?"

"Ah, because the line goes, 'you got to kiss an angel good morning and love her like the devil when you get back home'. It's a happy tune about a guy who explains the success of his marriage."

"I like the message, but I didn't know you were a country music fan."

"It's a well-kept secret. You know that country and western music sounds a lot like Irish folk music?"

"Interesting fact, Charlie, I'll stick to my jazz if you don't mind. I'm not even big on a *tarantella*."

"I'll use an earphone if I play it, Gina."

"Right! Now off with you before Fred Perkins finds out you are a full-blooded heterosexual!"

Charlie kissed Gina and he took the elevator down to the parking garage. He picked up I-95 and drove down to Wilmington.

XXIII

Charlie's Thursday and Friday at Shaw were taken up by meetings with the various operating department heads to discuss their draft budget reviews. Charlie worked with each of the department heads to tighten up their reviews and go over their numbers. He was satisfied that Fred Perkins would really have to scrutinize each budget to find any fault. He knew, of course, that Fred would find *something*. He almost had to. But, Charlie smiled to himself, he will really have to work for it.

Charlie and Gina were settling into the life of a married couple. However, it was far from a "normal" married couple's life, having decided to keep their relationship a secret until Charlie could work out a plan for the various contingencies that the couple would face once he publicly announced that he and Gina Ferrelli, daughter-niece of Carlo Rizzo were going to be married. He could imagine the tabloid headlines "Mafia Princess to Wed Financial Executive of Shaw Corporation". And there was still the pressure, yet to be felt in its entirety, from the busybody housewives of Shoreville, most especially Sharon Gallagher and Diane Simms. As hard as he tried, Charlie was unable to develop what he considered to be a workable strategy for building his life with Gina. He would lose his job at Shaw for certain. He would find it difficult to find another job with the same responsibilities unless it was with one of Carlo Rizzo's businesses which was not in his plans. He mused to himself. *"Maybe I could open a pizzeria! That's about all they will let me do married to a 'mafia princess'. At best I might open a restaurant."* Charlie didn't think he could be a good restaurateur.

He talked things over with Gina every time they were together and she, too, was at a loss for options.

Friday night he sat with Gina and told her, "Baby, I have to go to softball practice again on Saturday. I'll go early because I want to stop by the cemetery to visit Mom and Dad's gravesite. I'll probably hang around for the pizza and beer after practice just to hear if anyone has been poking around my private life. Don't bother to fix any lunch for me. Let's go out Saturday night for some good Italian food. That OK with you?"

"That's fine, Charlie. Don't worry too much about what's happening at Shoreville. If those women are watching you they still have to link you to me and that won't be so easy. I know it's a pain in the neck, but as long as we can keep them from putting it all together, we're not going to have any problems from that quarter. I'm really more concerned about what will happen on your job."

"Yeah, I know. I talked to Laura today and she told me I am due for my next security clearance review about 9 months from now. A lot could happen in that time so I have to be prepared for the possibility that our situation could become public before then. If it does, there goes the security clearance."

"Charlie, I'm sure we will get this worked out. Maybe we should talk again to my Uncle Carlo. He might have some ideas."

"You're right, Gina. Give me another week to see how things are going and we'll visit your uncle and talk it over with him. As far as I am concerned, the security clearance issue is dead. If it doesn't happen in the next review, it will happen later anyway. I definitely have no future in the Shaw Corporation."

"Are you saddened by that, Charlie?"

"Oh, hell no, Gina, after we met I had a chance to see just how empty my life and my career had become. I had fallen into a rut and was just going through the motions. I was being promoted simply because I had nothing to occupy my thoughts except my work and my activities in Shoreville. But, like I said, I had no one to share all that with. It was a vacuum. You know, people can get used to almost anything and I just got used to being Shoreville's eligible bachelor. I played that role and perhaps even reveled a bit in the backwash of anger at Mary Jo. I became even more popular when she left because my friends wanted to gather round. It was a comfortable niche and I allowed myself to be seduced by the support. Meeting you changed all that and it has been for the better. I'm happy. My life has a direction and a purpose beyond the job and the bowling and softball. I have a person who can share things with me, talk to me when I get home, fix a dinner for us, go out with me and come home with me, a person who doesn't have to leave in the morning from some motel close to the Turnpike."

"So, Charlie Mullins, we have to figure something out soon, right?"

"Right Gina."

* * * * *

Charlie woke up early on Saturday morning. Gina padded to the kitchen to fix breakfast in spite of Charlie's insistence that she stay in bed and let him fix the coffee. "No Charlie, I'm going to get up because I just don't feel like lying in this morning. I want to keep busy. It helps me think."

They had breakfast together and Charlie left for Shoreville and his Saturday softball ritual.

Before going to his house to pick up his gear and change clothes, Charlie drove to the cemetery, parked, and walked out to his parents' gravesite. He said a short prayer and then held his "conversation" with his parents. "Mom, Dad, I missed a trip out here last week. I was in Philly with Gina, the girl I told you about. I'm going to marry her. I really love her and she loves me. She makes your son very happy. We have some problems because Gina is the niece of Carlo Rizzo, the guy who is reported as being the head of the Philly mafia. I've kept our relationship a secret so far, but if we get married, and we will, things are going to change a lot in my life. I will most certainly lose my job at Shaw and I know how proud Dad would have been about my joining the company. Dad, I have to say that my job at Shaw is probably one that a lot of guys would like to have. I make good money, but it doesn't fill the void in my emotional life. I want a wife. Gina's family situation is nothing more than an accident of geography and biology. We don't choose the family we are born into. She is a wonderful woman and I won't lose her and risk my own happiness just because she happened to have the "wrong" uncle. I am pretty sure I am going to have to do some things that might go against what you have taught me over the years. I ask you to understand and forgive me. I am thinking through my options and they are few, at least so far. Maybe things will clear a bit as I think some more. But, I have to concede that much of what you taught me and much of what I believed have been challenged. I won't sacrifice my happiness to convention. I just won't, and that is something you taught me too. I continue to pray for both of you and hope you will pray for me, too." He said a prayer, crossed himself, and walked back to his car and drove home.

At softball practice he did not hear anything that would cause him to think that his ruse had been discovered. Bill Gallagher and Bob Simms were there and in good spirits. Practice went well and everybody went off for pizza and beer as usual. Charlie joined in the joking and planning for the league competitions. Everybody endured Artie Samuels' bad jokes, groaning appropriately when they were really bad. When they had finished the post-practice ritual the group broke up and all went home. Charlie decided to cut his lawn so everyone could see him in the yard. It wouldn't take long because he had a small yard but his neighbors would see him pushing his power mower and that would add to his "legend".

While he was cutting the grass he noticed that Diane Simms drove by. Charlie looked up and Diane waved. He waved back. *"Checking on me, bitch?"* Charlie said to himself. *"Be sure to tell your nosy partner that you saw me!"* Charlie finished cutting the lawn and put the mower in the garage. He went back into the house and checked the timers. He would leave for Philly in a little while, as soon as he thought the word had spread that he was at home and doing his normal chores.

Charlie was right about the news spreading. No sooner had Diane Simms got home than she called Sharon. "Sharon, I just saw Charlie. He was mowing his lawn. He's home."

"Not for long I bet, Diane. He's up to something and we're going to find out what it is. I want to know who that girlfriend of his is. I don't think that was a one-night stand we saw him with. She just didn't look the type. We got time. Thanks for the info. I'll talk to you later." Sharon rang off.

Charlie grabbed a beer from his refrigerator and sat down to think a bit about how he was going to work things out. After finishing his beer, he got up and put his softball uniform in the wash, turned on the machine, and went to the shower. He got ready to drive back to Philly.

Leaving the house he checked again for any possible surveillance. He decided that since he had some time, he would take the Jersey Turnpike up to the Camden exit and cross over to Philly on the Ben Franklin Bridge. He was not being followed as far as he could determine and he arrived to Gina's place without incident. *"Well, so far so good"*, he thought as he pulled into his parking place in the garage. He entered the apartment and kissed Gina. "Hey sweets, I'm back from the ballpark!"

"Hey, big man, you think you might get a job playing for the Phillies?"

"I'm not so sure the Phillies play softball, Gina", Charlie laughed.

"Charlie, I called Johnny and asked him if he could arrange for us to have a table at Positano's tonight. He said not to worry, he'd work it out. Is Positano's OK for dinner?"

"Just right, Gina. Let's get out, have a nice romantic dinner and relax."

They dressed for dinner and called for a cab to take them to the restaurant. Tonight was the night that they would be seen by one of Diane Simms' friends.

Charlie and Gina went to Positano's where they had their Italian meal and relaxed with a good wine. They finished with the requisite espresso and sambuca. When they finished and Charlie had settled the bill they stepped outside to flag a cab on Walnut Street. They were holding hands while Charlie searched the street for an empty cab. They didn't see Diane Simms' friend, Nancy Pagano, watching them. "Hey", she said to her husband, "I think that's Charlie Mullins flagging down that cab."

"So?" said her husband.

"So, Diane Simms said he had some secret girlfriend up here in Philly. I'll bet that's her! Boy, she looks awfully young for Charlie Mullins!"

"What the hell do you care, Nancy? It doesn't look like such a big secret to me. Hell, the guy's holding hands with her. He's sure not making a secret of her that way."

"Exactly! Maybe he thinks no one from Shoreville is around to see him. Boy will Diane be surprised."

"Jeez, Nancy, why don't you stay out of this? Diane is a damned gossip and she is always hanging around with Sharon Gallagher who has the sharpest tongue in Shoreville. Just forget you saw the guy, OK? He's minding his own business and we should too. Let's just go home, for Chrissake!"

"OK, hon." But Nancy Pagano was not going to let this "Charlie sighting" go by. The next day she was on the phone to Diane Simms. "Diane, guess what?"

"What's up Nancy?"

"Donnie and I went up to Philly last night for pizza. I have a favorite place on Second Street and when we were coming out of the pizzeria, who do you think I saw?"

"Are you going to tell me you saw Charlie Mullins?"

"You bet. That's exactly who I saw, and he was with a woman, or maybe a girl. I swear she didn't look a day over 18!"

"Describe her, Nancy, I'll bet it's the same girl Bill and Sharon Gallagher saw him with at Bookbinder's last week."

"Well, besides looking like Charlie's daughter, she was really a pretty girl. She has wavy black hair down to her shoulders. She was wearing a light brown dress that looked expensive. She has a very pretty face and a marvelous figure. She looks like a model or a movie star."

"I'm sure that's her!" Diane exclaimed, "The description matches the one that Bill and Sharon gave me; young, pretty, well dressed. It's her, I know it is! I've got to tell Sharon about this. Bye, Nancy."

Diane immediately called Sharon. "Sharon, you're not going to believe this. Nancy Pagano just called me and she said she saw Charlie last night. He was coming out of Positano's, holding hands with what Nancy said was a *girl* who didn't look a day over 18. She described her and the description matches the one you and Bill gave. I'm sure it's the same girl. We're getting close, Sharon. That's twice now that he has been seen with the same woman or girl, whatever."

"We're getting close, Diane. We can take our time now, Charlie might be getting careless. I noticed that his lights were on again last night and Nancy saw him at Positano's. He can't be in two places at once and I am inclined to believe Nancy's information. Charlie Mullins has a secret! We're gonna catch him! Thanks, Diane. I'll talk to you tomorrow."

* * * * *

Charlie and Gina spent a quiet Sunday at home. They read the Sunday papers and sat on the sofa to watch some TV. Charlie had his arm around Gina and neither cared what was on the TV. He smelled the perfume in her hair and felt her warm body against his. *"How could I want anything else besides this?"* he thought. Gina cuddled against him and dozed off for an hour. Charlie just sat there, happier than he ever remembered being.

At dinner time, they went down to a small bakery on Gina's street and had sandwiches and a soft drink. They walked a little along the street and then went back to the apartment. They went to bed early. Charlie made love to Gina, and they both fell asleep.

Charlie would not have to go back to Shoreville until Wednesday night for bowling league. He was apprehensive about whether the timers were doing their job but he had little choice other than to leave the house dark and that would certainly give away his absence. He had to hope the timers would be sufficient to keep the busybodies at bay. Since no one had said anything at softball practice, he had to assume the ruse was working. It never occurred to him that Sharon Gallagher and Diane Simms would be curious and daring enough to stand watch on his place.

Sharon and Diane met at aerobics class on Monday morning. "Did he leave this morning?" Sharon asked. "I didn't see him leave," Diane answered, "I can't swear that he didn't because I couldn't stand around too long, but while I was there, there was no sign of life in the house and no car pulled out of the garage."

"He wasn't there, Diane. But the lights went on again last night. Let's see if he shows up for league night on Wednesday. I'm going to give Bill the third degree when he gets home."

* * * * *

At the Shaw Corporation, Fred Perkins was poring over the budget reviews of the operating departments. He was almost frantically looking for something in each report that would allow him to browbeat the department heads. He loved the exercise of trying to find mistakes. He couldn't care less if the budgets were accurate or if they advanced the fortunes of the Shaw Corporation. This was his personal moment. It was his opportunity to bully those who were hierarchically his equals on the organization chart but which Perkins considered his subordinates. He was the guy with the money and they all needed him. He didn't need *them*. At least that was how Fred Perkins saw it.

Charlie watched Fred going through the documents and laughed to himself. *"Go at it, you silly bastard. You'll find something I'm sure, but you won't be able to turn any of the projects down. The guys will be ready for you once again."*

Wednesday morning Charlie got up to go to work, had breakfast with Gina, and said, "Bowling night tonight, Gina. I have to go to Shoreville again."

"Ah, bowlers of the world unite, you have nothing to lose but your balls!" Gina laughed.

Charlie laughed with her, "This is really a drag in some ways, Gina. I really don't feel like going bowling tonight. I'll have to go by the house again, check the timers, turn them off while I am there and turn them back on when I leave."

"Something will change, Charlie. I can feel it. Something will change to help us."

"I'd love nothing better than to just sell that house, move over here to Philly, and get on with our life, you know?"

"Me too, Charlie, but nothing stays the same forever, and something will pop up. An opportunity will appear and we can grab it by the neck and move forward. Just be patient and careful. Nothing as beautiful as what we have together can perish. OK?"

"I love you Gina, but how can you be so sure?"

"It's simple, Charlie. Didn't I suffer a tragedy as a child when my parents died? Didn't my mother's brother step in to give me a good life and a good education? Didn't I make good friends in spite of the pressures on me? Didn't you come into my life just when I thought it would never happen? It's not blind optimism, Charlie. Things change and things happen. You just have to be watching. We are watching, and things will change for us. I suspect it won't be long. It's just a hunch I have, maybe woman's intuition, but I can feel it Charlie."

"Well, I'm glad you can. I'm concerned but I guess my little scheme in Shoreville is working. Nobody has said anything and I haven't seen anybody following me or hanging around my street in a car."

"Don't drop your guard, Charlie. I know women and I can promise you those two busybodies are just biding their time. They're probably confused. Maybe they have bought into your scheme, I don't know. But sooner or later they will come back. They've got nothing else to do, remember that!"

"OK, sweets. I'm off. Maybe I will stay in Shoreville tonight. I'll see what happens at the bowling alley. If I have to stay, I'll call."

"Not to worry, Charlie. I'll be home. Oh, by the way. I got a call yesterday from a friend of mine. She's going to have a poetry reading at the Ritz-Carlton Saturday night. She's one of the few girls at Bryn Mawr who would hang around with me. She has come out with a book of her own poetry and has rented a meeting room at the hotel for a reading for a few friends. Can we go? I owe it to her and it might be different."

"Sure, baby, we'll go. We can go out afterward for dinner or drinks or whatever."

"Hmmmm, I like the 'whatever', it's replete with possibilities."

"Hussy!" laughed Charlie, "I'll call you if I have to stay in Shoreville" he kissed Gina and headed off for work in Wilmington to be followed by a night of bowling, pizza and beer, and a chance to hear if there was any gossip about him.

* * * * *

At the end of his work day Charlie trudged back over the bridge to Shoreville. His heart was not really in the evening that lay ahead. He would much rather have been watching TV with Gina, discussing politics, or whatever. He laughed to himself at the "whatever". When he got to Shoreville he merged into the local traffic coming out of the Shaw Corporation's plant in New Jersey. He drove home, waving to a few drivers as always. He went into his house and disconnected the various timers. He had seen no one that appeared to be watching or following him. He got his bowling gear, changed into his league uniform and drove to the bowling alley. He arrived a bit early and only a few of the guys were there. Bill Gallagher and Bob Simms were talking together as always. They clammed up when Charlie approached. "Hey, Charlie, you're early tonight."

"Yeah, nothing on the news so I decided to just make my way down here. I'm going to have a beer. Want to join me?"

"Be there in a sec", said Bill. Charlie walked off to the bar to give Mildred some grief. Bill turned back to Bob and Bob said, "I don't think we should mention that Diane's friend said she saw Charlie at Positano's. What do you think?"

"Hell no", said Bill, "let's leave well enough alone. The wives don't seem to be too curious and I see no reason to tell Charlie he is still being talked about. I'm not in a mood to have to deal with Sharon on this matter and I don't want Charlie down my neck either." Bob Simms agreed and they both wandered over to the bar to join Charlie for a beer. "Hey Mildred, three cold ones over here, OK?"

"Cold ones, huh? I thought you guys always liked hot ones!"

"Not when it's beer, Mildred, and get your mind out of the gutter."

"Nothin' wrong with my mind," Mildred muttered, "here, have a beer!"

The three of them laughed and Mildred gave them all a lascivious smile.

When the rest of the crowd arrived they moved down to the lanes. For the first time, Charlie was bored with bowling and the Wednesday night leagues. He was quiet and decided that the best thing to do was to simply concentrate on his game. He bowled terrifically as a result.

"Boy, you're on your game tonight," Tony Mazza exclaimed, "you been practicing?"

"Nah, Tony, just dumb luck I guess."

Artie Samuels piped in, "I betcha he's getting' some! That's why he's doin' so good."

"Artie," Charlie said, "is that all you ever think about – getting some?"

"What else is there to think about in Shoreville, Charlie?"

Charlie had to admit to himself that Artie was right. There really wasn't a lot to think about in Shoreville.

League night ended as always in the pizza and beer ritual, punctuated by Mildred's sexual innuendoes, Artie's stale jokes, and score comparisons. Charlie was quiet. "You're quiet tonight, Charlie," Bill Gallagher said to him, "what's up?"

177

"Ah, it's nothing special Bill. It's budget review time and I was just thinking about next week when the budget meetings take place. There's a lot on the line for some of the operating guys."

"Yeah, and they all have to deal with that prick, Perkins. Man, I don't envy those poor guys. I hear that Perkins holds them over the fire for as long as he can."

"Fred *is* pretty demanding, Bill. It's pretty damned hard to slip anything by him. I have to help the guys with their drafts just so Fred won't be able to burn them alive." He laughed.

"Well, don't bring your work home, Charlie. Can't let Fred Perkins mess up your bowling average, can you?"

"That's for sure, Bill."

The group broke up and everybody drove back to their homes, including Charlie.

Sharon was waiting for Bill to arrive. She could barely hide her curiosity. "How was league night, Bill?"

"It was good, Sharon, I think we'll take the trophy again this year. Charlie had a great score and the rest of the guys were pretty much on their games too."

"Charlie was there?"

"Of course he was there, Sharon. He's on the team. You know that."

"Well, I thought maybe after we saw him at Bookbinder's he might be up in Philly. I mean it seems he has something or someone to keep him there, no?"

"Oh Christ Sharon, not again!"

"No, not again Bill" Sharon said. *"Still"* she said to herself.

"Charlie was perfectly normal Sharon. He was on his game and relaxed. What's the big deal?"

"Oh, come on Bill, I just asked. Forget it."

Sharon knew that Bill would wind up telling her what she wanted to know. "No, Charlie was just fine," Bill continued, "He was just a little quiet that's all. But he's got a lot on his mind. He's got all those operating department budgets to work on and Fred Perkins, his boss, is a real nitpicker and a bastard when he finds something.'

"You bet he's got a lot on his mind" thought Sharon, *"he's leading a double life and trying to hide it from his friends in Shoreville. But it's not going to work. As soon as the time is right, Diane and I are going to blow the whole story open."*

"Yeah, I guess it's not easy working over there in Wilmington with all the big shots," Sharon said, "I'll bet Charlie sometimes wishes he was working in the lab or down at the plant. Some of those guys over there don't even have a home life. They carry their briefcases full of papers and work at home. It's high pressure, at least I think it probably is."

"Shit, Sharon I think most of them have nothing in those briefcases but their lunch. I sometimes wonder if the company wouldn't be better off if they all just disappeared. What the hell, I'm going to shower up and go to bed. I don't give a damn what they do over there as long as I've got *my* job. You comin' up to bed?"

"Be there in a few minutes, Bill."

Bill Gallagher climbed the stairs to shower and get ready for bed. Sharon sat on the sofa for a few minutes to think about what Bill had told her. *"Lot on his mind, huh? He's got that little girl on his mind! He ought to be ashamed of himself, robbing the cradle. She's probably still in college or something like that. I think it's time to start planning again."*

* * * * *

Charlie Mullins sat in front of a mute TV watching the images while he decided whether he would go to Philly or stay in Shoreville this night. He picked the phone and dialed Gina's apartment. "Hey sweets."

"Hey handsome, you comin' home?"

"No, I don't want to drive after having so many beers, Gina. My blood alcohol level is most certainly over the legal limit and the last thing I need is a DUI charge with all the rest of the issues we're facing."

"You sure Mildred didn't finally win you over, Charles Mullins?" Gina laughed.

"Oh my God Gina, I've faced a lot of temptations in my life, but Mildred was never one of them!" he laughed aloud.

"Well, I know you are not the type to mess around with other men's wives, so I guess I'm safe."

"You're safe, sweetheart, real safe. I only dated women from Shoreville when I needed to fix my carburetor." Charlie laughed.

"Any news from the lanes, Charlie?"

"Nah, all's quiet on the Western Front, Gina. Nobody said a word. I have to admit though that for the first time, I just didn't feel like hanging out with the guys. I would have given anything just to be home with you tonight."

"Me too, Charlie. Relax, we will have our time. Just get a good night's sleep and I'll see you tomorrow night. OK? And don't forget the poetry reading Saturday."

"Good night, baby. I'll see you tomorrow."

"Kisses, Charlie. Good night."

* * * * *

Charlie put the phone back on its cradle and turned on the volume of the TV. He watched the late night news and a talk show and then went to bed.

He left the next morning on schedule. No one was watching. No one had to. The busybodies were biding their time. They were on to Charlie's ruse and were trying to figure out how best to catch him unawares while he was out with Gina.

Charlie spent Thursday and Friday basically watching Fred Perkins prepare his attacks. He would walk by Fred's office and see him bowed over a sheaf of papers. Charlie was impressed that Fred looked almost like a hyena trying to encircle its prey. He wondered if he might wind up like Fred if he stayed around the Shaw Corporation. He wondered what Fred Perkins might have been like in college? Did he go out with his colleagues for a beer or did he stay in the dorm and study? Did he take a beautiful girl to a homecoming game, or did he even go to the ball games? Did he cheer for the team or try to find fault with everything they did? Maybe Fred Perkins had at one time been a perfectly regular guy. Maybe it was the corporate environment that had made him so miserable and mean. After all, the Shaw Corporation was no different than any other large organization. There was a lot of back-stabbing and reputation dashing that went on as guys and women on the executive ladder tried to knock off their competition. Charlie had to admit that he had really been lucky. He had never had to play that game, in part because he had stood his ground with Fred and developed alliances with the operating guys. They were the ones who *made* the money for the company, they and the salesmen. Fred might be able to save it, but he could not *make* it except for some interest rate arbitrage with the company's excess cash. That income paled by comparison to operations. So, maybe Fred was an otherwise nice guy that just got sucked in by the viciousness of the corporate world. Maybe he was not a lot unlike Carlo Rizzo. He just played the game the way he saw it and got trapped by the game itself. On the other hand, maybe Fred really was a prick. Maybe he was even born that way.

Charlie laughed to himself as he tried to imagine a little Fred Perkins, dressed in a tiny suit, and screaming at and berating his kindergarten colleagues. The image was so funny that he almost burst out laughing in his office.

"What the hell" thought Charlie, *"next week Fred will start to dissect his victims. I'll have to sit in on the meetings and I really don't relish the experience. Who knows, maybe this time will be different."*

On Friday, "casual day" again, Charlie dutifully showed up looking, as he put it, "casual but not too casual". He had had a relaxing night with Gina again after having slept Wednesday in Shoreville. Today, he only pretended to work. His thoughts were on Gina and how the two of them were going to make their future. Maybe Gina was right, luck would be on their side and an opportunity would present itself.

Saturday morning Charlie literally dragged himself to softball practice. He would have preferred to sleep in with Gina, have a leisurely breakfast and read the newspaper. He went to his house, picked up his gear and drove down to the practice field. The team members were showing up and tossing balls around while waiting for the rest. Charlie moved into the exchange and started tossing a ball back and forth with Tony Mazza. "What's up, Charlie? You doin' OK?"

"Yeah, I'm fine Tony, how's Marie?"

"Horny as ever, thank God. I can't keep my hands off her."

"Atta boy, Tony, it's good when you have a wife like that, no?"

"You bet your ass, Charlie. You should get one for yourself. Stay away from Marie, though."

Charlie laughed, "Tony, any wife of a friend of mine is a guy!"

"I know that Charlie, if I thought otherwise I wouldn't have said anything", Tony changed his accent to an imitation of Marlon Brando playing Don Corleone, "I'd just make you an offer you couldn't refuse." They both broke out laughing.

When the whole team had finally showed up, they took to the field while each took a turn at hitting some balls into the infield and pop-ups to the outfield. Charlie's mind was elsewhere as he dutifully whacked some pitches when it was his turn at bat. "Atta boy, Charlie, knock one out of the park, Charlie, way to go Charlie." He could hear all the chatter and he was amused because there was no fence around the field so knocking one out of the park was virtually impossible. When practice was over, the group went off for the obligatory pizza and beer again. Charlie went along. He sat near Tony

Mazza. He turned to Tony and said quietly, "Tony, you are really happy with Marie, aren't you?"

"Oh yeah, Charlie, I hit the jackpot and the lottery all at the same time. She's kept her figure in spite of the kids and she drives me nuts. I'm always squeezing her ass or grabbing her tits. She pretends to be bothered by it, but we always fall into bed and have a helluva good time."

"I'd like to have a relationship like that, you know? Mary Jo was a good looking woman but she would nag so much the mood would just disappear. Know what I mean?"

"To tell the truth, no, I just never had that kind of problem with Marie. We dated ever since high school. I tried like hell to knock her up so we would have to get married. She kept telling me to back off, that we would get married anyway and I'd find out what she was like. God, it was fun. You know, Charlie the important thing is not to *love* your wife. That comes after you know how much you *like* her. You have to be *pals* first. Love comes naturally between a man and a woman if they started off liking each other." Tony suddenly broke out in a laugh, "I remember my training sergeant in basic. He used to get right in your face and ask you if you liked him. Of course you would have to say 'yes' because if you said 'no' you'd be doing pushups all day. When you said 'yes' then he would yell in your face, 'Yeah, well likin' leads to lovin' and lovin' leads to kissin' and kissin' leads to fuckin'. I think you're trying to fuck me soldier!" Tony and Charlie both broke out in hearty laughter.

"Charlie", Tony continued, "believe me there is no sex like sex with the woman you love. It's always the best. Both of you are into it. You ain't gotta prove anything. You're not tryin' to impress. You're just living the moment and it's terrific!"

"That's cool Tony, I'm really happy for you. You've been married quite a few years."

"Yeah, and I never get tired of it. I remember your parents too, Charlie. When we were kids I remember that your mom and dad always seemed close to each other. When your Dad died, I was sure your mom would not live long without him. Weird, no?"

"Yeah, Tony, I guess that is what true love is about."

Artie Samuels heard the expression 'true love' and said in a loud voice, "Hey, Tony you know the difference between true love and AIDS?"

"Oh jeez", said Tony, "here he goes again."

"No, tell me Artie."

"AIDS is forever!" and he broke out in laughter. The rest of the group groaned.

"Well, if anything will bring this party to an end, it's one of Artie's jokes" Tony laughed, "I'm outta here."

"Me too." Charlie said.

The group picked up their gear and everybody wandered out to their cars to drive home. "See ya, Charlie" Tony called, "you'll find the right gal, I'm sure of it."

Charlie smiled. He wished he could tell Tony he already had.

Charlie drove back to his house and disconnected the timers. Since he was known to sometimes leave Shoreville on weekends, he did not want to give the impression that his habits had changed. He waited a while and then took off for Philly. He and Gina would go to the poetry reading at the Ritz-Carlton and thought it would be a good idea to stay for dinner there with Gina. He would come back early Sunday and re-set the timers.

Checking the street again for busybodies, he drove toward the bridge to Wilmington. If he found no surveillance he would go up I-95 as usual. He arrived to Gina's building without incident and he felt confident that perhaps the pressure was off. Now he had only to worry about his job. He could forget the busybodies of Shoreville. Or so he thought.

XXIV

Charlie and Gina arrived to the Ritz-Carlton for the poetry reading. Waiters were serving a cold, light white wine and assorted canapés while everyone settled into their chairs. Gina watched Charlie as her former Bryn Mawr colleague read through her work. She laughed to herself as she watched Charlie try to stay awake.

After the reading and a short question and answer period during which the poetess explained her reason for being, Charlie made the rounds with Gina to shake hands with her friends. Some of them had been at other events and Charlie recognized them. Others were new. He thought Gina must have an endless string of friends and admirers.

As he was making small talk to a few of Gina's friends, she came up behind him and whispered in his ear. "You ready to blow this joint, Mullins?"

He stifled a laugh and turned to Gina with a mock serious face and said, "Of course Gina, I guess we will have to leave."

They made their way out of the meeting room and up to the dining room of the hotel. Gina broke out laughing, "Oh, Charlie, I promise never to do that to you again, it was plain to me that a poetry reading from a Bryn Mawr girl is not really your favorite event."

"Well, Gina I have to admit that I have had more exciting evenings in my life."

Gina was laughing heartily, "I was afraid you might start snoring at one point, my dear. I don't know what I would have done if you had fallen fast asleep."

"I tried to stay awake, Gina, so help me I tried. I hope I didn't embarrass you."

Gina laughed again, "God no, Charlie, I thought you held up pretty well. You were too groggy to see the two guys who *did* fall asleep. Their girlfriends almost fell through the floor. I love Stacy to death, but I have to admit that even I was beginning to see visions of the sandman. It *was* a bit much. I thought you held up just fine!"

Charlie laughed, "Well, see what I would go through for you, Gina? I'd even listen to the poetry of a Bryn Mawr girl! Let's get some food. It's not everyday that I play softball and then go to a poetry reading."

The waiter approached their table and Charlie turned to Gina, "Shall I order some wine?"

"What a question to ask an Italian, Charlie. Is the Pope Catholic?"

Charlie ordered a robust Chilean cabernet sauvignon. He asked for the rib-eye and Gina ordered the salmon steak.

Over dinner they laughed about Charlie's reaction to the poetry reading and Charlie told Gina about softball practice. "Gina, you know something? I really felt like I didn't belong there. It was a weird sensation. After practice I joined the guys for pizza and beer and sat with my buddy Tony Mazza. Tony has a fantastic marriage. He says his wife Marie is the horniest woman in the world. Marie says Tony is the horniest guy she has ever known. They really enjoy each other. You know what Tony told me? He said the best sex in the world is when you have it with a woman you really love. He really meant it."

"Ah, Charlie and what do *you* think? I don't think Marie is the horniest woman in the world, I think that title belongs to me. And Tony's got nothing on you, big boy."

"Took the words right out of my mouth", Charlie laughed, "but you know Gina, he's right. I have never experienced the pleasure I have when I am making love to you. It really is different."

"You gonna start clearin' the table, Mullins?" Gina teased.

"Ah, I don't know. The patrons here look a little uptight, wouldn't want to scandalize!" he replied.

"Good idea. Try to restrain yourself at least until we reach the lobby", she laughed in return.

When they reached the lobby, Charlie asked the doorman to flag a cab for them. When the cab arrived, Charlie stepped out of the hotel with Gina on his arm. He gave the doorman a tip and leisurely strolled to the cab with Gina. He didn't see Tommy Peterson approaching Penn Square with his wife Helen.

"Look, Helen, that's Charlie Mullins. Let's see if we can say hi to him. We lived next door to each other for years."

Tommy tried to call to Charlie but he was too far away to be heard over the din of the traffic. Helen stopped him, "Wait Tommy, he is with a date. Don't bother the guy. You see him in Shoreville anyway. Don't bother him."

"Jeez, Helen, how often do you see someone from our neighborhood coming out of the Ritz-Carlton with a woman who looks like a movie star? Maybe she is. We might get an introduction and even an autograph out of this."

"Too late anyway, Tommy, he's already in the cab. Forget it."

"Yeah, I guess you're right. Boy that's too bad, no? She really was a pretty girl, wasn't she?"

"That's for sure, Tommy. She is pretty, without a doubt. But leave Charlie alone, the poor guy has had enough trouble in his life. First there was Mary Jo, then Sharon and Diane trying to fix him up with somebody. All those stupid dinners. Jeez, Tommy, the poor guy deserves to be left alone once in a while, no?"

"Yeah, you're right. Charlie's a nice guy. Let him find his happiness wherever he can."

Tommy and Helen walked to the parking lot where they had left their car and drove back to Shoreville. The next day Tommy ran into Tony Mazza at the drug store. He saw no reason not to tell Tony that he had seen Charlie. He knew that Charlie and Tony were good friends. "Tony, I was in Philly last night with Helen and I swear I saw Charlie coming out of the Ritz-Carlton."

"So?" Tony asked, "What's so special about Charlie being in Philly at the Ritz-Carlton?"

"Well, nothin' really, but you should have seen the gal with him! Wow, what a looker! She looked like she could make Sharon Stone run for cover. What a beautiful broad, Tony. I mean I would never forget that woman if I saw her again. She was just one of those kinds of women that you can't get out of your mind once you've seen them. She had the kind of face you see on the screen down at the Grove movie house, know what I mean?"

"Well good for old Charlie", Tony said, "nice to know he has hit the jackpot after all. You sure it was him, Tommy?"

"C'mon, Tony, I lived next door to Charlie for years. There's no way that I could mistake him. It was Charlie, I'm sure of it."

* * * * *

Charlie and Gina went back to the apartment totally unaware that they had been seen by yet another Shoreville couple.

It was the following Wednesday that Tony Mazza had asked Charlie if he had a girl friend. Charlie felt bad about having to hedge the truth with a friend as good as Tony, but there was too much at stake to risk. He had decided to admit that he had been with a very attractive woman on Saturday night but did not go beyond that admission.

When Tony had raised the issue on Wednesday night Bill Gallagher and Bob Simms had been nearby. They had heard Tony, and Charlie was sure they would comment with their wives.

Charlie and Gina had returned to the apartment that Saturday night and made passionate love once they arrived to the apartment. The next morning their clothes were strewn all over the living room in a path that led to the bedroom. They woke up later than usual and just lay in bed for a while. Charlie got up and went to the kitchen to make some coffee.

When he came back, Gina was sitting up. He handed her a steaming mug of coffee and kissed her. "Good morning beautiful, you look wonderful!"

Gina smiled, kissed Charlie, and took her coffee. Charlie climbed back into the other side of the bed and the couple sipped their coffee. "Well, Charlie, did you learn to appreciate poetry last night?" Gina asked teasingly.

"No, actually I learned to appreciate my woman. That was the best part." They laughed together.

Sunday, Charlie rose at 6 AM, drove over to Shoreville and reset the timers then drove back to Philly and crawled back into bed. Gina barely stirred. He and Gina spent half of their Sunday in bed. They had some more coffee and finally Gina said she was hungry so they dressed and went down to the bakery where they had croissants, coffee, and jam.

XXV

When Charlie arrived to the Shaw Corporation on Monday morning things seemed to be a little different. People were clustered around in groups talking in hushed tones. That was a departure from the usual parade straight to their offices. When he got off at his floor he walked by Laura Metzer's desk. "Did you hear the news, Charlie?"

"What news, Laura?"

"'Junior' Shaw was taken to the hospital last night. The word is that he had a heart attack. Nobody knows how serious it was, but he is in the hospital right now. The Executive Committee is running the company until there is more news or he returns to his job. What do suppose this means for the company, Charlie?"

"Well, it's a little early to try to say, Laura. We'll have to wait for more news. Obviously, the attack was not fatal so we'll just have to wait. Heart attacks don't always stop someone from working, you know. Let's see what comes down the grapevine today. There will probably be some kind of announcement later on."

"He was such a young guy, Charlie. Heart attacks at his age can be serious. I hope he's not in any danger."

"Any heart attack is serious, Laura. But you're right. When it hits a young guy sometimes the damage is greater. But let's be calm. There's no way we can know anything until somebody tells us something. No use speculating and feeding the rumor mill."

"You're right, Charlie. Fred hasn't come in yet. I wonder if he knows already."

"I'll talk to you later, Laura. Just stay calm. I'm sure everything is pretty much under control."

Charlie walked to his office and began his day making a few phone calls to some of the operating department heads to see if they had any information. In the meantime, the Executive Committee sent a bulletin around the company and prepared a press release. The bulletin informed employees that

Phillip Shaw II had a "coronary infarction" and was rushed to the hospital at 2 am Monday morning. The note said that he was recovering and that until further notice the Executive Committee would manage the company. The note expressed hope that "Junior" as he was affectionately known by Shaw's long-term employees would be returning to his responsibilities as Chief Executive as soon as possible.

The press release said basically the same thing but added for the sake of the market that the Shaw Corporation was under capable management and that Phillip Shaw II was expected to return to his job as soon as his physicians determined he would be able to do so.

A couple of operating department heads who were close to the Shaw family indicated to Charlie that they thought the attack might have been pretty serious. But no one had any specific information.

Charlie noticed that Fred Perkins was particularly nervous. It was largely due to Phillip Shaw that Fred stayed in his job. Phillip respected Fred's views while not endorsing his way of dealing with people. He knew that Fred's comments were usually on the mark and that he brought discipline to the financial area and the budgeting process in the company. Fred had to be worrying about his own skin if Phillip stayed out too long. For sure, Fred would not be as gruff as he usually was if he had to report to the Executive Committee. He would be a lot milder than he was when he held private council with "Junior" Shaw. Charlie wondered who might be sharpening their corporate knives now that Phillip was temporarily out. There would be some jockeying for position by the members of the Executive and Finance Committees. Fred was head of the Finance Committee and not everyone in that group felt that he was the right man for the job. He mused that Phillip Shaw might come back to a different company than he had left when he had his heart attack.

However, the note from the Executive Committee meant that everyone was to continue in a "business as usual mode". Charlie dove into his work for the day. He had to prepare for the budget meetings that would start next week. When he walked by Fred Perkins' office to get coffee he saw Fred at his desk apparently in thought rather than poring over the budget review papers. He wondered if Fred might be trying to figure out who might be his allies in a fight for corporate power during "Junior's" absence. Charlie mused to himself, *"He's probably putting together a 'suck-up' list!"*

At the end of the day the Executive Committee sent out another bulletin to inform employees that Phillip Shaw's condition had stabilized. The physicians had said that his life was not in danger and that it now remained to determine the degree of damage to the heart muscle and get Phillip on a recovery path. The note was optimistic and designed to dispel rumors that had been circulating about the eventual health of the Shaw Corporation.

Charlie left the office at 5-o-clock and noticed that Fred Perkins had not yet tidied up his desk and was still staring off into space in deep thought. He said "Good night, Fred" and received only a grunt in response. He wondered if Fred would get another job if he got pushed out. He was a good professional but everybody in the business knew him as a prick.

*   *   *   *   *

When Charlie got to Gina's place she was preparing dinner. He walked to the kitchen and wrapped his arms around her. "Who's that who dares to grab me? My husband will be home any minute, be very upset, and come after you."

"Very funny," Charlie laughed, "you get grabbed often by strangers in your own home?"

"Oh, it's YOU!" Gina said with mock surprise, "Give me a kiss!"

Charlie kissed her and pulled her to him in a strong embrace and she melted into him. "Yeeaaahh!" he growled, "that's the way I like it!"

"Charlie, you up for eggplant lasagna? It's good for you and it's damned delicious, I might add."

"You could make rock soup and I would love it, Gina."

"Yeah and I'm Betty Crocker, right? Why don't you open some wine. It kills bad cholesterol!"

"Speaking of bad cholesterol, Gina, we were informed this morning that 'Junior' Shaw had a heart attack last night and was rushed to the hospital. Word is that he is recovering but nobody really knows anything yet."

"Wow, Charlie, he's not much older than you. Did he have a history of heart trouble?"

"Not that I know of, anyway the Executive Committee will be running the company until he gets back on his feet and returns to his office. Fred Perkins looked nervous as hell."

"I imagine he would. I mean he doesn't exactly win the Mr. Congeniality award at Shaw. He must have at least a few enemies. With the CEO out, I would think a lot of people will be moving for more power. It always happens. And maybe some of those people are the ones who are not too fond of Perkins. What about you, *amore*, will the situation affect you too?"

"Well, somehow it *has* to. I don't have any concern that my job is in immediate danger, I have good relations with the operating guys and I am known as a stable element in Fred's area. But things might change in ways I don't yet know. I've told my people just to sit tight. At least for the time being, it's business as usual. Budget reviews will go on, the company will continue to produce and sell, and we will just have to see how the management thing shakes out. Nobody knows yet how long Phillip will be out so everything now is just speculation."

Gina put their dinner on the table and served Charlie and then herself. Charlie took a forkful of the lasagna. "Oh my God! Gina, please don't ever leave me. I could never go back to canned chili after this. I'll die!"

"Oh, how *romantic*, Charlie, if I ever leave you I'll leave you a copy of my mother's recipes. How's that? Now, before you answer, please remember that the lasagna is *hot*. You wouldn't want in your lap, would you?"

"Uh oh, I guess that's the price of marrying a Latin woman!"

"You got it, Mullins! We are temperamental, hot, and volatile. Don't shake, rattle or roll us!" Gina kissed him.

"Wouldn't think of it!"

"So, Charlie, you think there will be a fight for power in the company while Phil Shaw is out?"

"For sure, Gina, a lot of senior executives thought Phil was a bit too timid as regards expansion. Others wanted to see the company use its excess cash to improve productivity. No CEO enjoys unanimous support for anything. It's not a lot different than politics or the Roman Empire for that matter. Corporations are political animals and when a leader is incapacitated, even for a short time, you know there is going to be some manipulating. There won't be much happening at my level because I am not on either the Finance or Executive Committee. I'm not a challenge to anyone. Fred Perkins is and so are a lot of the Executive VPs in the operating areas. There'll be some blood, I'm sure."

"Sounds like my uncle talking, Charlie."

"Well, every organization no matter what type, has the same problems, Gina. I used to say that when you have one person, you have an entrepreneur – a leader. When you have two you have a team. When you have three, you have *politics*. I suppose the organization survives and prospers because of that process, but I think once politics enters the equation, the ultimate health of the company becomes secondary. It's a power game, that's all."

"Sounds a little depressing, love, want some more lasagna?" Gina laughed.

"You know, Gina, eating is the one physical pleasure a man can indulge in three times a day until the end of his life. Maybe I should have some more to assuage my anxiety."

"Oh no, my dear, you should never eat because you are anxious. You have to eat because it is a pleasure."

"Italians are sooo romantic!" laughed Charlie.

"You ain't seen nothin' yet," replied Gina.

They finished their meal and Charlie helped Gina put the dishes in the dishwasher. "See why I didn't want an Italian husband Charlie? You think an Italian husband would help clean up after dinner? They want their wives pregnant, barefoot, and in the kitchen. Ooooo, how wonderful it is to have an Irishman." Gina readied the espresso machine, embraced Charlie and they moved into the living room to finish their wine before having their espresso.

They watched TV for a while and the news of Phil Shaw's heart attack was on the business segment. The reporter said that the company expected Shaw to return to his normal duties soon. Charlie wondered how true that was. Gina was curled up next to Charlie, with his arm around her. The news could have announced an atomic attack against Philadelphia and she would not have moved.

Charlie did not think that Phil Shaw's situation would affect his personal situation. He was still trying to find a way to resolve the question of his relationship with Gina. He would still be out of a job once the relationship became public knowledge no matter if Phil Shaw came back to work, had died in the emergency room, or never had a heart attack in the first place.

XXVI

On Tuesday morning the Executive Committee sent out another bulletin to the employees of Shaw Corporation. The committee was pleased to report that Phillip Shaw II had been removed from the intensive care unit and was now in a regular room. There were, of course, additional tests to be run, but Phillip's life was no longer in danger.

The news did not appear to mollify Fred Perkins. He knew that regardless of Phil Shaw's medical situation, as long as Phillip was out the power game would be played by both his allies and his enemies, and he had few of the former and many of the latter.

Perkins called Charlie into his office in the usual way by sending Laura Metzer to summon him. Charlie followed Laura back to Fred's office. On the way he asked her, "How is he, Laura?"

"Quiet as a church mouse, Charlie, he's worried that some of his enemies will put his head on the chopping block."

"Well, I think that's unlikely at this point Laura. Cutting Fred's power is one thing, but I don't think anyone is going to be inclined to ask for his head until they know what Phillip's situation is. He would not be happy to come back and find out that Fred had been fired."

"I guess you're right, Charlie."

Charlie knocked on the frame of Fred's door. "You wanted to see me, Fred?"

"Sit down, Mullins," he said in a surprisingly civil tone.

Charlie took a seat in front of Perkins's desk. "I've been going over the budget figures from the operating departments…"

"Oh shit," thought Charlie, *"those poor guys!"*

"And, Fred?" he asked.

"And for the first time since I have been in this company, I think these guys have learned something. They all look pretty good. For the most part, they're financially sound. I'm comfortable with them."

"Oh my God, what a heart attack of the CEO will do!" thought Charlie.

Charlie let a brief smile cross his face. He knew that Fred Perkins was not about to take on the heads of operating departments while Phil Shaw was in the hospital and the Executive Committee was in charge. Those guys had a lot of influence on the committee and some were members. He laughed to himself. *"I hope you have on brown pants today, Fred!"* he thought, *"You can't afford to have anyone know you're crapping in them right now!"*

"Anyway, Mullins, I'd just thought I'd let you know so you can relax a bit before the meetings next week."

"Like you really give a shit about whether I am relaxed or not!" Charlie thought, *"You want me to get on the phone and tell the department heads that you are being cooperative, you bastard."*

"I appreciate that Fred. I'm always concerned that something might have slipped through the cracks."

"Not this time, Mullins. You've done a fine job."

"Jeez, he's even kissing my ass," thought Charlie, *"he must really be scared."*

"Thanks, Fred. That's nice to know. Anything else?"

"Nope, that's it Mullins. You can go."

"Gee, thank you Fred, I didn't know I could go until you released me. 'Dismissed!'" He laughed to himself, remembering his days in basic training

Charlie laughed inwardly all the way back to his office. Fred Perkins was scared shitless and he had decided that it would not be politic to take on the operating heads with Phil Shaw out of the office. He was going to roll over on all the budget figures. He almost broke out laughing out loud when he thought that if he had known Phil Shaw would have had a heart attack he might have suggested doubling the investment levels of each department.

Charlie now knew that the budget review process would be a cakewalk. Next week would be light for everyone except Fred Perkins who would be chomping antacid pills like popcorn.

*   *   *   *   *

He drove back to Gina's place in a light mood. He was concerned for Phillip Shaw's health but he was thankful for the change forced on Fred Perkins. He told Gina about the change that had come over Perkins and she laughed heartily. "What an ass that man is, Charlie. Does he have a spine?"

"Gina, sometimes I think I don't know anything, you know. I asked myself too, how does a man like that live day to day? How does he talk to his kids? What does he think he should teach them? One side of me feels sorry for the guy. The other side despises him for his weakness."

"He's tortured, Charlie. A man like that can never be a real man. Watch out for him, because underneath it all he hates you for being a man. He would just as soon cut your throat as look at you, Charlie. Men like him are dangerous."

"I know, Gina. I've seen them before. Underneath it all they are scared – they're cowards. Their fear makes them unpredictable. They will run or shoot you in the back. I saw them in the Army, in college, and in corporations. I don't think Fred will try to attack me though. He's got more to worry about than me. Fundamentally, he knows I am loyal, not to him, but to my responsibilities. He needs me and as long as he needs me he will be an ally – if that's the right word."

"Things are going to change, Charlie. Maybe this situation will give you what you are looking for, maybe it won't. But for sure things will change. I can feel good news in my bones."

* * * * *

Wednesday's bulletin from the Executive Committee stated that Phillip Shaw II had been removed from the Intensive Care Unit to a regular room and that his condition was listed as "good". It added that Shaw was expected to be released by the weekend to begin his recovery at home.

Charlie went to his regular Wednesday bowling league night after adjusting his timers accordingly. If he stayed for pizza and beer, he would again spend the night in Shoreville. He was finding it increasingly painful to be away from Gina. Gina, likewise, did not relish Charlie's absences but she did not complain.

The main topic of conversation at the bowling alley was not the usual raucous joking and ribbing, punctuated by Artie Samuels' stale jokes. Everyone in the league was worried about their jobs and Charlie was considered to be a good source of information because of his position in the company.

Bill Gallagher was one of the first to raise the issue of Phillip Shaw's heart attack. "Hey Charlie, what do you hear about Phil Shaw? Are those notes from management telling the truth?" Everybody's attention turned to Charlie.

"I can't say for sure Bill, but from what I gather the information is correct. For the foreseeable future things are going to stay as they are and as they have been. The Executive Committee is unlikely to change anything until Phil's situation is stable and the prognosis is known. So far, everyone expects him back on the job following a recovery period. I wouldn't worry about layoffs or job loss. The next quarter is already locked in with the new budgets and they seem to be optimistic and by then we will know something about whether Phil Shaw is on the way back. There is no reason to assume otherwise."

Tony Mazza piped up, "Yeah, I just refinanced my house. I sure as hell can not afford to lose my job now!"

Charlie reinforced his argument, "Don't worry Tony. Everything that I am getting from the operating departments means business as usual. I don't see anybody getting fired. Nobody is talking restructuring or any of those other management 'buzz words' that they like to use in the rarified atmosphere of the board room."

Some of the guys in the group commented on how young Phillip Shaw II was to have a heart attack. Charlie interrupted, "Guys, you have to remember that when Old Man Shaw set up this company it was a small domestic operation. He built it up with a lot of hard work and I'm sure no small amount of anxiety. But what 'Junior' inherited to manage is a global organization of enormous size. I think the kinds of pressures 'Junior' faces are a lot different and more complex than those faced by his father. Maybe the strain was just too much."

"Maybe he ain't the man his father is!" chimed in Artie Samuels.

"Nah, Artie, I think you are comparing oranges and apples. " Charlie continued, "We are talking about two different companies. The first was Old Man Shaw's dream. The second is 'Junior's' nightmare. Old Man Shaw did not have to worry about competition from China. The Executive Committee was a handful of guys he personally picked and most were guys who started out with him. Today you have guys on the Exec Committee that are recommended by other department heads, auditors, outside directors, professionals recruited to run operations, and so on. Phillip's challenges are a lot different. He has to negotiate more, convince more people, consider the effects of his decisions on units abroad as well as in the USA. It's not the job it was even when Old Man Shaw decided to retire."

The conversation about the company and the questions to Charlie continued over the pizza and beer ritual. Charlie stayed around to answer first because these were his friends and they were scared and second because perhaps the fear of job loss would cause Bill Gallagher and Bob Simms to give their wives something else to fret about.

When he got home, Charlie called Gina to tell her he would stay in Shoreville that night and be in Philly after work on Thursday. Gina expressed her disappointment at having to sleep alone in her bed but offered her support for their objective of building a life in private. They reiterated their love for each other and Charlie rang off to do his laundry and organize the house, after which he went to bed.

All of Charlie's pals went home to tell their wives that Charlie said their jobs were secure for the time being and not to worry. Bill Gallagher and Bob Simms both added that this would not be a good time to irritate Charlie Mullins. For once the wives agreed and no one watched Charlie leave for Wilmington the next morning or to see if he came back to his house that night.

* * * * *

Thursday and "casual" Friday were accompanied by the regular notices of Phil Shaw's improving condition. He was scheduled to leave the hospital over the weekend so tensions diminished among the employees. They figured Phillip would be coming back soon.

Charlie and Gina continued in their regular routines and intense lovemaking. They went out to the *trattoria* with some of Gina's friends. They continued to avoid saying anything other than they were simply dating but Gina's friends knew better. However, their loyalty to Gina and her perceived emotional fragility in matters of romance kept them from commenting outside the circle. However, they all noticed a marked change in Gina. She seemed happier and lighter than ever before. The occasional sad look had vanished completely from her eyes. She was clearly happy and all figured the relationship was on a sound footing. They were also sure that Gina's uncle had probably given his approval of the romance.

When Charlie returned to his house for softball practice on Saturday he was surprised to hear a message on his answering machine from an attorney in Wilmington. The message asked only that he call back when convenient and left two Wilmington numbers, one for the attorney's law office and the other for his home.

When Charlie came back from softball practice and before calling Gina, he called the home number of the attorney.

The attorney answered and after Charlie had identified himself and said he was returning the attorney's call, the attorney said, "Thank you for calling, Mr. Mullins. We have never met. I am Phillip Shaw's private attorney and I would like to schedule a meeting with you as soon as possible. Are you available after work on Monday?"

Charlie tried to ascertain what the meeting would be about and the attorney simply said, "I would rather not discuss the matter over the telephone. We should meet in private. Would five-thirty be OK? My offices are not far from the Shaw building. You could even walk there."

Charlie agreed to the meeting and noted the address. When he rang off he thought, *"Shit, somebody has told the company about Gina!"* But he realized that that was improbable if not impossible unless one of Gina's friends had inadvertently commented to someone. No one in Shoreville could have known who was Gina Ferrelli, at least so he thought. He remembered his conversation with Tony Mazza after league night one Wednesday. Tony told him he had been seen a couple of times in Philly. Was it possible that someone from Shoreville knew who Gina was? But Carlo Rizzo had said that he had kept her highly sheltered. Nobody would have thought to check out a Bryn Mawr yearbook. He didn't know if Gina's picture was even in any Bryn Mawr yearbook.

"Well, I'll just have to wait until Monday" he thought.

Charlie called Gina and told her about the strange phone call and the summons to meet the attorney. He voiced his concern that they may have been "found out". Gina however, was not so sure. "Charlie, very few people outside my circle of friends know who I am. Obviously the nuns at school and some of the people involved in my projects know about my uncle. But I don't recall ever having my picture in a newspaper. I didn't have a picture taken for the high school or college yearbooks on my uncle's recommendation. So it would be difficult for anyone to associate my face with my or my uncle's name if they don't know me. I don't rule out the possibility but I think it is very remote."

"Maybe the Feds, Gina? They know who you are. Could they have identified me in those photos they were taking when we visited your uncle?"

"Oh I don't know Charlie. I've tried to take pictures of the inside of the car through the tinted glass and all I ever got were pictures of black windows. I mean maybe they have some way of neutralizing the tinting, but I don't think that's a probability. I could ask my uncle."

"Not yet", said Charlie, "let's wait until the meeting on Monday to see what it's all about. Then, if necessary, I'll talk to your uncle. I don't want to speculate. It's better to find out what the attorney says."

"I agree, Charlie, if it's the worst case scenario the damage is already done anyway and you'll come back from the meeting without a job. If it's not, then it is something else and we will only be able to deal with something else once we know what it is."

Charlie and Gina spent Sunday in the apartment. To keep his mind off the meeting that would take place on Monday he prepared a brunch for him and Gina. They sat on the couch and read the Sunday newspapers. There was some coverage of Phil Shaw's heart attack on the business page.

"Well Charlie, you did a pretty credible job with the brunch. I'm impressed."

"Thanks, Gina. Maybe I have a future as a restaurateur."

"Well, I wouldn't go that far, Charlie. I mean it was good but I think you have to have some more practice before doing it professionally! Besides, I think those hats chefs wear are silly."

"Well, that's another career option shot to hell." Charlie said.

"Chaaarliee, don't wax pessimistic", said Gina "we have no idea what the meeting is all about. You might be in the same job after the meeting that you were in before it. Relax, OK?"

"I'm trying, baby, I'm trying."

"Why don't you let me show you my etchings?" Gina said teasingly, "they're in the bedroom. Wanna see 'em?"

Charlie forgot his problems.

* * * * *

Monday, Charlie drove to Wilmington from Philly. He was now concerned for the meeting at the end of his business day. He sat in on Fred Perkins' first meeting with the head of the division that made machinery for the paper industry. Charlie watched in absolute amazement. Perkins began the meeting by telling the man how pleased he was to see a good tight budget projection. He said that he hoped other department heads were as diligent as he had been. Charlie was dumbstruck. He had never seen Perkins suck up in front of a witness. Perkins was so civil as to be disgusting. When the meeting was over, Charlie could hardly keep a straight face. He returned to his office and sat there stifling a loud laugh. That afternoon, some of the other operating department heads called him to ask if Perkins had gone "around the bend" or was "off his rocker". They had all been informed about the meeting and were asking Charlie if they would sail through just like their colleague.

Charlie laughed and attributed Fred's new personality to the absence of Phil Shaw. They all laughed and said that Phil may have done more for their departments by being out of the office than being in. They didn't wish any bad luck on Phil but asked if Charlie might not be able to get the word to Shaw that he should pretend to have one heart attack every quarter.

Charlie thought to himself, *"If you guys only knew that I am meeting with Phil Shaw's attorney after work today and I might not be here on the job tomorrow!"*

At 5 pm, Charlie arranged his desk, locked away his papers and waited for Fred Perkins to leave. As soon as Fred left for the elevators, Charlie left as well. He saw Fred getting into an elevator car and hung back to make sure he would not be in the same one. Two more cars passed and were completely full. When Charlie finally got into an elevator that was not full, Fred was already reaching his car in the parking lot. By the time Charlie reached street level, Fred was nowhere to be seen. Charlie walked to the attorney's office.

XXVII

Charlie arrived to the attorney's office a little before five thirty. He introduced himself to the receptionist who immediately showed him to a small conference room to wait for Shaw's lawyer.

At precisely five-thirty the door opened and what looked like a very expensive attorney came through it with a file folder in his hand.

"Shit!" Charlie thought, *"This is it, he's got pictures and everything! I wonder if someone is cleaning out my desk while I am here."*

"Mr. Mullins, thank you for coming. My name is Warren Carpenter. I'm Phillip Shaw's personal attorney. Before we begin I would like you to review the documents I have here and if you agree, I want you to sign them."

"Christ!" thought Charlie *"I'm on the street! He's got non-compete documents, confidentiality statements, the works. I'm screwed!"*

The first document was a power of attorney that named Warren Carpenter and his law firm as Charlie's attorneys. It wasn't what Charlie expected and he had to read it twice. "Excuse me, Mr. Carpenter but this is a document that names you as my attorney-in-fact. Let me be frank, I don't even know why I need an attorney and I am sure that I certainly could not afford your fees. What is this all about?"

"Mr. Mullins, the purpose of this document is to ensure attorney-client privilege. What we will discuss cannot be subject to subsequent investigation. Maybe we should look to the next document first. This document," he shoved another paper in front of Charlie, "is a confidentiality agreement that ensures that whatever you and Phillip Shaw shall discuss through me, his attorney-in-fact, will not be revealed."

"The objective is as follows Mr. Mullins, I must speak to you about a matter of utmost confidence and both you and I must be protected by attorney-client privilege and Mr. Shaw and the Shaw Corporation must be protected by a confidentiality agreement. If you are concerned that you are about to be fired, I can assure you such elaborate precautions would not be necessary. You would be given the standard company documents by your supervisor and the whole thing would be done quickly and without a private appointment with me. I am here on behalf of Phillip Shaw, CEO of the Shaw Corporation, not the Personnel Department. Am I being clear, Mr. Mullins? I can't talk to you until you have signed the documents."

"OK, Mr. Carpenter. I don't understand anything as yet, but agreeing to confidentiality should not be a problem. As to your fees to represent me...."

Carpenter laughed gently, "No, Mr. Mullins there is no fee. I won't charge you a red cent. I just need to know that you and I are protected by attorney-client privilege."

"OK", said Charlie, "where do I sign?"

"Right here, Mr. Mullins", and Carpenter pointed to the line under which Charlie's full name was typed.

Once Charlie had signed the documents and Carpenter had returned them to the folder, he began, "Mr. Mullins, before asking me to contact you Mr. Shaw spoke to Wexler & Santori. He asked them who he could talk to with utmost confidence and to whom he could entrust a very serious mission. What I am about to tell you cannot be made known to the public under any circumstances. Wexler & Santori recommended you for this assignment. The partners there said that you were steady, discreet, and qualified."

"Well, it's nice to know I have that reputation." Charlie said.

"You do Mr. Mullins and it is to your credit. I want to start by informing you that Phillip Shaw II will not, I repeat *not*, be returning as CEO of the Shaw Corporation, at least not in any functional way. His medical condition is not so serious that he could not return but he has indicated to me that he does not want the pressure and the risk of shortening his life. He is perfectly content to step down. In fact, we both know he hardly needs to work for a salary."

"That's for sure", Charlie smiled.

"While he does not intend to return to being CEO, Mr. Shaw does not want to name a successor. He feels that could be divisive and even be detrimental to the long term growth of the company."

"OK", said Charlie, "that makes sense, so where do I fit in?"

"Simple, Mr. Mullins, Mr. Shaw wants to make Shaw Corporation a publicly held company."

"Sell his shares?" Charlie asked incredulously.

"That's how it's done, Mr. Mullins, as I am sure you know. Yes, sell his shares and those held by the Shaw family."

"And he needs me for that? Mr. Carpenter, Phillip Shaw can sell his shares whenever he wants to and without my permission or involvement. I don't understand why I am here."

"Mr. Mullins, you and I both know that the Shaw Corporation is cash rich. We both know that interest rates are rising. Consequently, we both know that the cash held by Shaw is increasing in value. Mr. Shaw does not want to see his company bought and then dismembered for its cash value. He believes that the company is worth something as an on-going enterprise. He also respects the effort his father made to build the company virtually from scratch."

"And with a good chunk of scratch arranged by Gina's uncle!" Charlie thought to himself.

"I think I see where you are headed, Mr. Carpenter, but please continue. I want to hear it from you!"

"Bill Cummins said you would understand quickly. He was right. Mr. Mullins, Phillip Shaw wants you to make Shaw attractive as an ongoing enterprise, not as a cash cow. He wants you to work with Wexler and Santori to make acquisitions that will reduce the value of the cash opposite the company's attractiveness as an on-going business."

"You mean a poison pill strategy?"

"Well, not exactly poison, Mr. Mullins, Mr. Shaw does not want to reduce the value of his company. He wants to make it worth more as an on-going business than it would be for its cash value. It requires some sophisticated strategic choices. The market should see the acquisitions as adding value to Shaw's business over a longer term while making it unattractive to anyone who wants to simply buy the company's cash."

"He wants you to develop an acquisition strategy that will pass the muster of financial analysts and discourage sharks. Do you understand?"

"Yes, fully", said Charlie, "but why have I been chosen for this work?"

"It's rather simple, Mr. Mullins, your relationship with Wexler & Santori is the best in the entire company. We will be relying on Wexler & Santori to be constantly evaluating your recommendations and the effect of same on the value of the company. Quite frankly, your direct supervisor, Mr. Perkins, would be most unsuited for working with the auditors in the manner Mr. Shaw desires. This requires teamwork. Moreover, you have been highly praised by the operating department vice presidents. You not only know finance, Mr. Mullins, you also know what motivates the operating departments and what their needs are. Since the acquisitions will essentially be operating companies, your knowledge of operations and your interface with the departments are crucial to making the right kinds of acquisitions. Mr. Perkins is quite talented and excellent in financial acumen, but he lacks the necessary negotiating skills to work in harmony with the operating departments."

"Now that I have told you why you are here, I must emphasize, perhaps unnecessarily, that not a word of this strategy can reach the market or any of the company employees. Mr. Shaw will soon announce that he intends to return after a period of convalescence. He will return and seem to resume his duties. Whatever hesitance he shows with regard to major decisions will be attributed to his heart attack. However, with him present, no one will try to rush things through."

"How long is all this supposed to take, Mr. Carpenter?"

"Probably not less than 3 business quarters, and possibly one year. We can take up one quarter with Mr. Shaw's convalescence and recovery period. During the following two quarters you will be under pressure and will have to be discreet. You will work with Wexler & Santori in absolute secrecy."

"So, Mr. Mullins, only you, Bill Cummins at Wexler, Phillip Shaw, and I know about this. Will you take on this responsibility?"

"Responsibility is the right word, Mr. Carpenter. I would hate for the Shaw family to receive a reduced value for their holdings because of an error on my part."

"That's precisely why you were chosen for the job Mr. Mullins. Mr. Shaw is confident that you will do your best to protect his interests and he does not think that anyone else in the company can do it any better. Wexler & Santori agree."

"Well, I am certainly flattered that I would be given such trust. I'm sure that you can appreciate that this comes as a complete surprise to me."

"Certainly, would you like to think it over before deciding?"

"Well, not exactly before deciding. I mean I am pleased at the offer and I appreciate the challenge. But I would like to take a look at the company's financials in view of this new wrinkle. I had never considered this issue before because it was patently clear that the Shaws did not want to and would not sell their shares and go public. I'd like to do my own analysis and get back to you. I am virtually certain that I will accept the assignment. That's not the problem. I just want to know first what I am accepting."

"I was pretty sure you would not simply say 'yes' and walk out of here, Mr. Mullins. It's prudent of you to want to know where you are going and what limitations you might have to face. Would a week be long enough to conduct your review?"

"Yes, I think that would be enough." Charlie replied.

"OK, let's meet here again on Monday of next week at the same time – five-thirty, is that OK?"

"That's fine Mr. Carpenter. I will come back with my analysis and some observations. Until Monday." Charlie shook hands with Warren Carpenter and walked out his office and to his car almost in a state of shock. He was holding on to what was possibly one of the most valuable pieces of information in the market. What would some investment banker be willing to pay to know that the Shaw Corporation is planning to go public and wants to acquire companies? They could stack the deck anyway they chose, sell the stock to their cronies, make a bundle and then either break up the company or bleed it dry.

He drove home without even bothering to check if he was being followed. He wasn't – fortunately for him. He arrived to Gina's apartment building, parked, and went up to what was rapidly becoming his home. He entered the apartment forgetting that he was over an hour later than he usually was because of his meeting with Warren Carpenter. "Charlie, I was worried about you. You are rarely late and you didn't call. I thought maybe you had to go back to Shoreville or something."

Gina looked at Charlie who still appeared to be dumbfounded. "Charlie, are you OK? You look like you've seen a ghost or something."

"I'm fine Gina", and he moved to kiss her, "I need a drink and then I will tell you everything."

"OK, baby, sit down. I'll bring you a whisky. Scotch neat, all right? You look like you need a jolt!"

"Oh yeah, scotch neat. I do need a jolt."

Gina poured two fingers worth of scotch in a glass and handed it to Charlie. He took a healthy swig before starting to talk. "Gina, I probably have the most valuable piece of information in the stock market at this moment!"

"You'll have to be more specific Charlie. You could take what I know about business, put it in a thimble and it would rattle around like a pea in a barrel. What information is this?"

"Gina, the Shaw Corporation is going to go public."

"Explain that, Charlie, I'm a Lit major, you know."

"It's called an 'initial placement offer', known in the jargon as an IPO. It means they are going to give up family control and sell the company's stock to the public!"

"Ohhh, now I've got it. Is that good or bad for you and the company?"

"If it were done now, it would probably result in the dismemberment of the company for its cash. If it is done after the excess cash is invested, it would be good for the company so long as the investments offered good long term prospects for growth. If not, they would diminish the value of the company."

"Now I get it. So your information that the company plans to go public, as you call it, is worth a lot to someone who might want to buy it."

"Right, sweets, especially if that someone wanted only to acquire the company's cash right now. They would have advance information that would allow them to acquire the company and then break it up and keep the cash."

"Alternatively, an investment bank could set up the placement of the shares in the market and favor its clients through a series of shell companies. It would be a chance to clean up big time."

"The fact is, Gina, there are only four people in the entire world who supposedly know about this. Phil Shaw, Bill Cummins an auditor at Wexler & Santori, Phil Shaw's attorney, and me."

"Why are you involved in this Charlie?" Gina asked innocently, "why wouldn't this be a matter for the senior management of the company?"

"Normally it would be, Gina, but Phil Shaw has said that he does not plan to remain as CEO. Apparently, he values life too much. If he announces that he will step down or he delegates this job to the Executive or Finance Committee there will be a lot of infighting and most certainly some will try to gain personal advantage or power. Big bucks are involved here."

"Wow, that's news, no? I mean about Phillip stepping down."

"Yep, he will come back, pretend to be recovering so he can resume his normal duties, and in the meantime be preparing to unload the company. I, together with Wexler & Santori will be looking around for acquisition targets to use up the company's cash."

"Sounds like the kind of shopping I'd like to do – here take a few million and go out and buy something!" Gina laughed out loud.

"Well, that's the message behind my assignment but the shopping will be a little more complex than what you have just described. The companies I buy should not serve to reduce the value of the company and, if possible, they should increase it while absorbing the cash."

"It sounds like a lot of responsibility and not terribly easy to do."

"It is, but the hard part won't be making the acquisitions, it will be keeping the whole process a secret until Phillip is ready to announce the initial placement offer, what they call the IPO. I have up to about 9 months to get the whole thing set up. That's a long time to keep a secret like this one."

"When do you start, Charlie?"

"Well, actually right away. I told Phil Shaw's attorney that I wanted a week to evaluate the size of the challenge. I will have to review the company's financials. I'll probably go to the auditors' office tomorrow to talk to my contact there."

"Gina, we now have two big secrets to protect. No one, but absolutely no one can know about this plan. The slightest leak and the whole thing will become a mess. If the press gets on it, the price of everything we try to buy will go sky high. If we pay too much for acquisitions, the value of Shaw stock will go down. If the companies we acquire are part of a long-term growth strategy we will have more leverage with the shareholders and the stock market analysts."

"That really sounds exciting, Charlie, I didn't know business could be that fascinating. It's almost like negotiating a bunch of secret treaties!"

"I guess that's a fair comparison, sweets." Charlie laughed.

"There is just one problem though, I have to do all this in off hours and I've still got that ruse in Shoreville to watch over. I can't let our situation get exposed either. I have to think all this through very carefully. Now, to the important stuff, what's for dinner my dear?"

"You in the mood for a nice shrimp risotto? I sure hope so, because that's what I fixed."

"I'll open the wine!"

While Gina set the plates and heated the risotto, Charlie grabbed his pocket notebook and started planning his assignment. Over dinner he said to Gina, "Baby, I think I should talk to your uncle about this. Can you set up something for next Sunday? I want to draw on his business experience and experience with keeping things secret. I'm not used to that side of the assignment."

"I'll call him tomorrow Charlie."

They ate calmly and the delicious risotto allowed Charlie to temporarily forget about the assignment.

XXVIII

Charlie woke up at six-thirty on Tuesday morning and walked into the kitchen where Gina was busy fixing some breakfast. "What would you like, Charlie?"

"Something light, sweets, maybe I'll just have a bowl of granola."

"Gina poured him a cup of coffee. You sure? You're gonna need your strength, you've got a horny wife, and a lot of stuff to do."

"I think I can handle the horny wife part," she added.

"That's for sure, just make sure you keep up the good work."

Charlie ate his granola, showered and shaved, and took off for Wilmington. As soon as he arrived at work and settled into his office Charlie called Bill Cummins at Wexler & Santori.

"Bill, I met yesterday with Warren Carpenter. I need to talk to you. Are you available after work this evening? I can stop by your office and we can talk there or go somewhere else."

"Warren called me last night, Charlie. I was expecting you to call. Let's get together tonight. There's a lot of ground to cover. We can meet here. No one will be surprised to see you coming in and most people will be gone by five-thirty anyway."

"Thanks, Bill, see you tonight then."

Today would be easy for Charlie because he would have meetings all day with the operating department heads and Fred Perkins. Normally the meetings would be tense and disagreeable, but Perkins was so damned scared of offending anyone who might have power that he was being almost charming. He was rolling over on everything. Charlie could hardly keep a straight face during the meetings.

At five he left as usual and drove up to Philly on I-95 and crossed the Ben Franklin Bridge to Camden for his meeting with Bill Cummins. He pulled into the Wexler & Santori parking lot precisely at five-thirty. When he walked through the door, Phyllis Simpson was clearing her desk and getting ready to leave. "Hello, Mr. Mullins. Nice to see you again. Mr. Cummins told me you would be coming up. He is waiting for you in his office. I'm leaving now, is there anything I can get you before I go? Would you like me to order some coffee? It will only take a few seconds."

"Thanks, Phyllis. I appreciate that." Charlie took the elevator up to Bill Cummins' office. As he entered the elevator, he could hear Phyllis on the phone ordering some coffee from the company kitchen.

He knocked on the doorjamb of Cummins' spacious professional digs, "Hey Bill, how are you?"

"Come in, Charlie. Close the door and please have a seat."

A knock on the door kept them from initiating their conversation as the white jacketed company waiter brought in a pot of hot coffee. Bill Cummins said, "Thank you Maurice, you can just leave the coffee pot here. I'll return it to the kitchen myself after Mr. Mullins and I have our meeting. You don't need to stay around."

"Thank you, Mr. Cummins. I can stay if you wish."

"No, it won't be necessary, I think I still know the way to the kitchen", Cummins laughed amiably.

"OK, sir. Good night."

"Good night and thank you."

The waiter departed and closed the door behind him.

"I'm glad you said you will work with us on this project, Charlie. The thought of having to deal with Perkins would have given me nightmares. Phil Shaw does not want to have any of the senior executives working on this because he knows there would be all sorts of power plays, possibly even some malfeasance, and most certainly some leaks to the press to gain advantage and leverage."

"I understand Bill, it's a delicate issue. I told Warren Carpenter I first wanted to thoroughly review the company's financials and any possible hidden assets or liabilities. If anyone suspects anything, they will immediately go for the financials. The business press is no different from the regular press or even the banks. They smell blood in the water and they go into a frenzy."

"Been there and done that, Charlie, let's go through the figures. There are some things that have to be cleaned up and unfortunately they will increase rather than decrease the available cash. The company owns some residential properties that it leases to family members. The Shaws do it for tax purposes. They will have to buy those properties from the company at fair market prices. Some of the properties are quite expensive. The family members have the money, of course, but it will all go into the pot. We can do 'desk drawer' transactions and hold the contracts here rather than run the money into cash. That will not draw the attention of the analysts. At the right time we will consolidate. Since the properties are on the books as company assets, we are simply switching one asset for another. Where there are mortgages still being paid, we will have private contracts written up for those properties so the family can reimburse the company for the mortgage payments that will continue to be made through the company until we consolidate. I have it in mind to store the actual funds in an offshore account pending consolidation. It should work."

Charlie was taking notes. "OK, Bill then the first order of business is to remove any assets and liabilities the company has for the private benefit of the family. By the way, what are the chances that some family members won't have the money to cough up their share? Some of them live pretty high on the hog."

"Phil and his father have agreed to privately finance any family members if they don't have the cash. I expect that Old Phil's divorced daughter might have a problem. She goes through money like some people go through candy."

"Is there any chance that some family member will leak information about all this?"

"Not now, no. None of them wants to do anything that will cut off their share of the pie. Money has a way of encouraging people to keep mum, you know. They like their polo ponies and high life. Besides, most of them won't even know what the hell is going on. As long as they get their monthly stipends from the family trust fund, you can count on them to be in an alcoholic fog most of the time and talking nonsense with their hoity-toity crowd. That won't be a problem, at least for a good while. But Warren will keep us informed. Warren also handles the family's private affairs and that means fixing DUI charges, paternity suits, abortions, and the like. He knows how to deal with the Shaw family."

"I should add that Phil Shaw has asked me to discuss his return strategy with you. He knows that you have been working on next quarter's operating budget figures. His plan is as follows: When he returns to the company and everyone is convinced that the CEO is back, he is going to hold a press conference. He will thank all those people who sent letters and get well cards and the rest of that kind of stuff; say how glad he is to be back in command, and so on. Then he will say that while he was convalescing he had a chance to evaluate his own performance as CEO and concluded that since he took over the company from his father he might have been too timid in seeking to expand the Shaw Corporation. He will state that by the time he retires at what he hopes will be the ripe and mandatory retirement age of 65 the company will be twice its current size. He will make it clear that he has a long term strategy in mind and joke that if he could stay around after 65 he would love to do so to continue to manage the results of his efforts."

Cummins continued, "He's going to have to say something because we will have to involve the operating departments in the evaluation and selection of many of the acquisitions. You can't acquire companies on the sly. This can't *seem* to be secret. It has to look like it is a strategy and that Phillip remains firmly committed to staying in charge. He will say that he and he alone will coordinate and control the execution of his expansion strategy. You will not be mentioned. First of all that would send Fred right up the wall and he would wonder if you were next in his chair. Second, no one wants to draw attention to you because the press would be driving you nuts. Phil and the PR department will handle comments to the public."

"It sounds like a pretty logical strategy to me, Bill." Charlie replied, "We certainly would find it difficult to keep acquisitions secret. People would immediately assume that something like going public might be why everything is hush-hush."

"Right, so we agree. I will tell Warren that the strategy is approved."

"Let's get some sort of action plan put together now," Charlie said, "I want to have some idea of the sequence of events. As I see it our second step is to analyze the needs and opportunities of the operating departments. Before we can look at acquisition targets, we will need to figure out what kinds of businesses will be attractive and add value to the company. I know, for example, that the Chemical Division has been complaining that it needs a technology boost. New product formulations are needed as well as some new products. We would find ready acceptance of any project to address that need. Moreover, it would make tremendous sense to the market."

"I agree, that's precisely why Phillip wanted you involved in this project. He knows you are aware of the needs of the operating departments and can get their support for acquisitions without raising any red flags."

"What about Perkins?" Charlie asked.

"Phil Shaw will have a conversation with him and 'ask' his cooperation. He will tell Perkins that the ideas are his and he will keep Perkins informed. That will certainly neutralize any opposition from Fred. He'll be so anxious to please Phil he won't dare try to criticize any of the acquisitions."

"Boy, Phil has him down pat, doesn't he?"

"Never underestimate Phil Shaw, Charlie. He stays in his father's shadow because it is convenient for him to do so. Let the old man be the hero. Phil has a quick mind and a good nose for business. A lot of times when the son succeeds the father the company suffers. Phillip held his own, professionalized the company's management, quietly recruited good people, and stayed in the background to let them do their thing. But he has his finger on every project in this company and knows full well who is doing what and who his friends and enemies are. How do you think he knows about you?"

"I don't have the slightest idea, Bill."

"Phil's VPs talk to him about their investment plans. They don't just talk in committee meetings. They talk to him on the golf course or at the country club, too. They have told him how difficult Perkins can be and he has told them how important Perkins is to keeping things tight. None of them can stand Perkins but they respect his professionalism. They have made it clear to Phil that when you came on board they thought they might have a good interface. They were right and they all know that getting their projects through Perkins means working with you first. You think Phil Shaw doesn't know that? Why do you think you got promoted so quickly in the company? Phil Shaw would never undermine Perkins by calling you into his office to talk to you. That's not his style. Instead, he just mentions you to Fred once in a while. That's enough to remind Fred to say at least neutral, and sometimes even good things about you in performance evaluations. Phil can read Fred like a book and play him like a good musician plays a violin."

"I'd never figured Phil Shaw to be so Machiavellian, Bill."

"You don't run the Shaw Corporation by being a Boy Scout, Charlie. The old man was tough and straightforward. He called them like he saw them because that was what was needed in a start-up company. Phillip inherited a complex and enormous corporate bureaucracy. Being tough and straightforward would have left him vulnerable to a lot of very subtle sons of bitches that now work for the company. Old man Shaw was like a warrior-king. Phillip is a prince. Old man Shaw saw and conquered. Phillip sees and negotiates. Each has a mind like a steel trap but the old man had to make his known and feared. Phillip keeps his a secret until he needs it. He can make himself feared if need be, but he prefers 'corporate diplomacy'. But believe me, he is no stranger to the power game."

"Maybe it would be a good idea to tell you something about Phillip Shaw II before we go further, Charlie. Phillip would have his own mother whacked if she got in the way of his running the company. His father picked him over his other brothers and sisters because Phillip had the right amount of ruthlessness and polish at the same time. The old man knew that he would not be able to run the company he himself had built. He was an entrepreneur. He took chances. He beat his competitors to the punch. The same behavior that built the company would not serve to advance its interests today. He was wise enough to recognize that. He felt it as he went to meetings with 'Junior' going along at his side. At precisely the right moments, 'Junior' would call for a break and get his father's permission to intervene. When the break was over, 'Junior' would come back and close the deal or shut it down completely. You should know that he hates bankers – I mean really *hates* them. I've seen him verbally tear bankers to shreds without so much as raising his voice or saying a nasty word. Phil Shaw is a 'swordsman' to his father's 'boxer'. He would not tire of cutting you 40 times before dealing a final blow. If he thought you were underestimating him, he would cut you 60 times. He would not get angry or show any emotion whatsoever. He would just cut away at you to make sure you understood his tactical superiority. He's the kind of guy that Lyndon Johnson was referring to when he said he would rather have the guy inside his tent pissing out than outside the tent pissing in. However, Junior's loyalty can be fierce. He is as loyal to you as you are to him. He's the kind of guy you would like to have as a back up in any tough situation. But only if he knew that you would back him up the same way that you expect him to back you up. Otherwise, he would just put a bullet in your back."

"Many who know Phillip observed that they did not believe he had a heart attack because he does not have a heart. I know that does not match his public image, but it's pretty close to the real thing. Although I have never heard him say it, I am sure his motto is and always has been: Never get mad, always get even!"

"Wow! Who would have thought it? He always looks so relaxed, calm, and affable."

"Relaxed and calm he is, Charlie. I would stop before I said affable. Slick is a better word."

"So, Charlie, that's the guy you're working for. Don't cross him and do your best. He will appreciate it, I can assure you. He won't be unreasonable because he knows the limits in the business world. He is comfortable in that environment. I think one of the real reasons he wants out is because he might have political ambitions. I don't really know. Nobody really does with him. But I tend to think he is a bit bored by just sailing on an even keel. He will enthusiastically welcome being involved in an expansion, but once it's all over, he will get bored again. He is smart enough to know that, so I am sure he has some ace up his sleeve."

"It sounds even more challenging than before, Bill. I'm finding businesses for a guy who could easily find them himself if he wanted to. He's got a sharp pencil and I will have to find what I think he would find. I'll have to get inside his business mind."

"Well, I for one am confident that you can do it, Charlie. I've talked to a lot of guys in the company about you and I've worked with you in the finance area. You're as sharp as any I've met, so it won't be that tough."

"Well, thanks for that, Bill."

"Now", Charlie said, "let's get back to our action plan. Phil Shaw will create a plausible story for us to go shopping around. He will pretend he is doing it himself and we will send the targets to him for analysis. So, as I see it, once he has laid the groundwork we should have some companies at the ready. You agree?"

"Yes, we will lay out what we consider the weaknesses or needs of each operating area and then look around for companies that can fill the need. We give those to Phillip who will either tell us to go ahead or drop it."

"Should I prepare a written analysis of the various departments? It might be good for Phillip Shaw to know where we see weaknesses. Maybe he doesn't see the same thing we do."

"Good idea. A kind of 'white paper' would be a good place to start. Do you feel comfortable putting one together?"

"With your help, yes."

"OK, I've got a full financial report for you in this folder. It lists the assets and related liabilities that have to be taken off the books. They are the personal holdings of the family that have been held in the company's name. Take a look at those and see how we can move them and then let's pull together the 'white paper'. Should Phillip make any changes, we will adapt. If he makes none, then we move to developing a list of targets. When do you want to meet again?"

"Today is Tuesday, what do you say we meet again on Friday to discuss what's in the folders? We can set up another meeting then."

"Fine", said Bill Cummins, "how do you feel about meeting here?"

"We might have to be careful. If I start coming here too frequently people might wonder what is going on. Maybe we could meet sometimes in Warren Carpenter's office. We'll have to mix it up. We could also meet in a hotel in Philly once in a while. I could rent a meeting room. No one would know I was meeting you. I could claim it was to meet a banker. We can work something out. But we should avoid meeting always in the same place, I think."

"Agreed. Then I'll see you here on Friday, right? I will call and tell Warren that you are on board. You agree?"

"Yeah, I'm in, Bill!"

"You want a shot of scotch to seal this Charlie?"

"Why not? I might need a lot more before it's all over!" They both laughed.

Bill Cummins poured about a shot of scotch into each of two glasses, handed one to Charlie, held up his own and said, "To successfully hoodwinking the excessively curious!"

Charlie laughed inwardly at the irony of the toast, "I can relate to that, Bill. Cheers!" and they both swallowed their scotch in a single gulp.

Charlie grabbed the folders that Bill had given him, shook hands with him, and went down to the parking lot. He drove home thinking about the challenges that lay ahead.

* * * * *

When he arrived to the apartment Gina was waiting for him with a dry martini. "Hello, big guy. Like a drink? I've been waiting for you."

"Sorry, Gina, believe it or not I was working late. I had to go over to Camden to meet with Bill Cummins."

"That's what they all say, Mullins! You sure you weren't out with some floozy?" Gina feigned a serious look.

"Gina, you can't be serious after all we have talked about!"

"Just kidding, my Irish love, just kidding."

"Gina, you want to go out for dinner?"

"I have water ready to boil for some spaghetti, Charlie. I don't care that much if we go out but if you want to, let's go."

"No, I just wondered if you might not be tired of being at home so often."

Gina laughed, "I used to go out often because I didn't feel like sitting around an empty house. I don't belong to a bowling league and I don't play softball. So I would call my friends and we'd go somewhere like the *trattoria*. But now that you are in my life my house is not empty any more. I could stay inside forever. Well, nearly forever."

"OK, I just don't want you to think that we can't go out or that I don't want to."

"Charlie, how quickly men forget. Don't you remember that I invited you to dinner first? I have a mind of my own and if I feel like going out, you can rest assured that I will let you know and it won't be subtle. It will be Philly style like 'Hey you! Wanna eat out?'"

Charlie laughed, "Spaghetti it is, Gina. I'll open some wine."

Over dinner Charlie told Gina about his meeting with Bill Cummins and what Bill had told him about Phil Shaw. Gina was less impressed than was Charlie. "Charlie, I lived all my life with my uncle. Powerful men, truly powerful men, are like that. You never know what they are thinking and you don't feel their power until you challenge it. Phil Shaw can't possibly be a Boy Scout and run a huge organization like Shaw."

"I know that. I just never thought about what lay beyond his façade, know what I mean?"

"Exactly, but now you are going to have to know. You've got a big challenge ahead of you. By the way, I called my uncle and he said we could meet on Sunday. You game?"

"Yep, thanks baby."

After they had eaten they moved to the living room. Charlie asked, "Gina, could I ask a favor of you?"

"You want my body, big boy?"

"Well yes, but that's not what I was going to ask."

Gina feigned disappointment, "OK, what is it?"

"Could you pick up three large loose leaf binders for me at Office Depot or some place like that?"

"Sure, you want one with little teddy bears on the cover?"

"No smart aleck, I think just a plain white, blue, or black would be just fine. I'm going to have a lot of papers and I want to have them all in one place and secure. Do you have a safe or a place where I could lock the binders up?"

"Charlie, you really need to take ginko biloba. My uncle owns this building and the company that manages the property. You remember who my uncle is, don't you?"

"Of course....."

"Then Charlie, who do you think is going to have the balls, excuse my French, to break into this building much less this particular apartment? This is 'Don' Carlo's place and nobody with good sense is going to break in here! Take my word for it."

"Christ, I did forget. I just remember him as your uncle. Yeah, you're right. So I guess my papers are safe here."

"Safer than in a bank, Mr. Mullins, safer than in a bank", Gina smiled.

"Now, Mullins, I need to ask a favor of you."

"Sure, what?"

"I need to be sure you are wearing your navy blue silk boxers. You mind if I check?"

"Be my guest, Gina."

"To the bedroom!" Gina cried "I'm gonna pull your shorts down Mullins!"

They both laughed and retired to the bedroom to make love and go to sleep.

XXIX

Wednesday was league night and Charlie would again have to go to Shoreville. He advised Gina over breakfast that he would be home late but that he would return to Philly rather than stay in Shoreville. His day was taken up with budget review meetings with the operating guys and Fred Perkins. Charlie watched in amazement as Fred caved in on everything. He laughed to himself and thought, *"Why don't you just grab your ankles and take it, Fred? You're popping those antacid pills like jujubees!"*

Charlie decided that he would not stay for pizza and beer after bowling and he was trying to find a plausible explanation to give to his friends. Phillip Shaw was still out of the office and a lot of the guys would have questions. They were worried about their jobs and Charlie was their friend. But he had to go through the financial reports that Bill Cummins gave him.

The Wednesday afternoon Executive Committee bulletin on Phillip Shaw's medical condition informed company employees that Shaw had been released from the hospital and would begin his recovery program at home. Charlie decided that he would use Phillip Shaw's situation as justification for having to leave the bowling group before pizza and beer. He would say that Phillip's absence had made it necessary to bring some work home and he had to get back to work on pending matters. Under the circumstances that would be plausible and, in fact, it was the truth. He did have a lot to do and it was in response to Shaw's heart attack.

Charlie noticed that the guys in the bowling league all seemed to have been mollified by Wednesday's bulletin. The group indicated that they believed the worst was over and that Phillip Shaw would soon be returning to work and things would get back to normal. He made it a point to tell a few of his friends that with Shaw on sick leave, he had inherited a lot of work from the Executive and Finance Committees and that he would not be able to stay for pizza and beer. He was careful to make sure that Bill Gallagher and Bob Simms had been among the informed. He wanted both of them to tell their wives that Charlie was very busy with additional work. That might discourage them from trying to poke into his life, at least until Phillip Shaw returned to work. Just to make sure that circumstances at his house matched what he had told the group, Charlie went to his house after leaving the bowling alley and changed the timer on his bedroom light to burn a little longer than usual to suggest that he might be reading reports. He would leave the timers this way until Saturday when he would return for softball practice. After re-setting the bedroom timer, he went to his car, checked the street for surveillance, and then drove to Philadelphia to meet Gina.

* * * * *

Gina was waiting for him with a bottle of wine ready to be opened and some dinner heating in the oven. "Hey big boy, how was your day?"

"Busy. We had a handful of meetings with the heads of the operating departments. Fred Perkins was almost charming. He caved in on everything and barely criticized any of the final budget proposals. Then I had to head off to Shoreville for league night. I begged off the pizza and beer saying that Phil Shaw's absence had created a lot of additional work and I had to catch up. No one seemed to doubt my story. All those poor guys are sweating bullets because of their jobs. They all have families and Shaw is the most important employer in the area. I feel sorry for them."

"Any flack from the crazies?"

"No, I think they are quiet now because they don't want any problems while the situation at the company is so fluid. I didn't see anyone watching me or the house, and no one was following me around. I don't know how long that will last though."

"Probably for as long as Phillip Shaw is out. Once things return to normal or a semblance of normal they will forget their panic about job loss and start concentrating on you again, my dear."

"Wow, aren't you the optimistic one? Thanks, I needed that!"

Gina laughed, "I told you they will not back off easily. Right now they are scared for their husbands' jobs, the mortgages, and the kids' schools. The minute they are not, they will find something to keep them occupied and you are their best option, sweets."

"Well, I'll face that when it comes back around. Want some wine?"

"Good idea, open the bottle while I set up dinner. I hope you like Italian food!" Gina laughed.

Charlie was uncorking the wine as he said, "Still can't make Irish stew, huh?"

Gina set out their plates and silverware and then pulled a casserole out of the oven. As she put the food on the table she said, "I talked to Uncle Carlo today and he said to stop by his place for lunch on Sunday. Is that OK?"

"Perfect, Gina. I need his advice. It's nice to have someone I can talk to about this stuff. Dad was good for the stuff about life but he did not have executive experience. Even if he were alive, I doubt that he would have been able to give much counsel in the job I now face."

"Well, Uncle Carlo said he would be more than happy to talk to you. He likes you, I can tell. The fact that you make me happy means you can demand practically anything from him. I'm my 'daddy's girl' and if my world is in order, he is just fine. That's not a warning, by the way!" she laughed.

"Oh, I almost forgot ", Gina continued, "I picked up your binders today. I got navy blue to match your silk boxer shorts. I got three, is that OK?"

"At least for starters, I'm sure it's enough. Thanks."

"I also got you a three-hole punch so you can put your papers in the binders. You didn't mention that, but women are usually smarter than men when it comes to details."

"Oh my God", said Charlie, "who told you that?

"Did you remember the punch or didn't you?" Gina teased.

"Touché! Have some wine."

"So, Charlie, are you going to softball practice on Saturday?"

"I don't know yet, sweets, a lot will depend on my meeting with Bill Cummins on Friday. But I will try to make it simply to keep the rumor mill from buzzing. Why? Have you got something planned?"

"No, just wanted to know. Like I said before, I don't want some horny housewife in Shoreville to throw a net over you while you are there. I wouldn't mind stopping in at the *trattoria* for a glass of wine."

"If you are asking me for a date, you're on", Charlie laughed. "By the way, baby, how was your day?"

"Well, after going on my office supply run I stopped by the school for my tutoring sessions. You remember that architect I introduced you to?"

"Bob, right? The guy married to the artist."

"Yeah, well I talked to him today and his designs were approved by the city. They're going to use them in the next low-cost housing project."

"That should give his reputation a boost, no?"

"You betcha and it will improve his finances a lot so Emily will be able to relax a bit and paint some more. She needs to build up her collection for a show."

"It's nice to know that friends move ahead, no?"

Gina and Charlie talked for another half-hour about their now-mutual friends until Charlie said, "I've got to get to those financial statements, Gina."

"OK, I'll put the dishes in the dishwasher and watch some TV."

Charlie sat at the dining room table with his papers in front of him and began to file them away in one of the binders Gina had purchased. His first job was to identify the personal assets of the Shaw family that had been purchased by the company. He took copious notes and outlined a strategy for divesting the company properties without having to change the financial statements. No one could know that Phillip Shaw was even thinking about taking the company public. He decided that the best strategy would be to sell the properties to the family members who were using them with a "desk drawer contract" drawn up by Warren Carpenter. The cash payment and subsequent mortgage payments would be made to Warren who would put the money into an offshore account. The entries of the transactions would be officially booked when Phillip Shaw announced that the company would sell its shares on the market.

The next issue was to evaluate how much cash the company would need to invest to avoid being attractive for its cash value. That might mean reduced dividends to the family members. Charlie wondered if any of them would object to a short-term reduction in their quarterly dividend payments. They would have to ride out a short "dry spell" and he would have to check with Warren Carpenter to see if any of them would have cash flow problems if the dividends were cut back. The idea that any of the Shaw siblings would have cash flow problems amused Charlie but he knew that rich people tend to spend what they have, especially when they are the heirs to a veritable fortune and don't work for a living. He made a list of questions to be raised with Warren Carpenter and then put all of the papers in the binder.

"I hear somebody using a three-hole punch over there!" Gina laughed.

"Yeah, you were smart to buy it. What would I do without you?"

"Absolutely nothing, Mullins! Without me you would be lost!"

Charlie closed the binder and looked at Gina. "Chaaaarrlie, are you wearing those silk boxer shorts?" Gina asked teasingly.

"Yep."

"Well, I'm gonna yank 'em off. What say we head for the bedroom, or would you rather I pull them off here and now."

Charlie walked slowly to the sofa where Gina had been watching TV and she pulled him down on her. They made love right there, in front of a TV that neither bothered to watch. Exhausted, they both laughed and trodded off stark naked to the bedroom, threw themselves into bed and slept.

* * * * *

The next morning Charlie brought Gina a cup of coffee while she lay in bed. "I will never again look at that sofa the same way", said Charlie.

"Comfortable, no?"

"That's one way of looking at it!" he replied.

Charlie dressed for work while Gina put the breakfast dishes in the dishwasher. He kissed her fondly and left for Wilmington. "Give 'em hell, Mullins!" Gina said as he left the apartment.

Charlie sat through two morning meetings with the heads of the operating departments and watched, amused, as Perkins continued his lapdog routine. He kept copies of the budget figures for his pre-acquisition analysis of the requirements of each department.

The Thursday bulletin from the Executive Committee stated that Phillip Shaw had begun his recovery program and that if all went as expected, he would be back as CEO within a month. The bulletin also announced that daily bulletins would no longer be necessary and that the Executive Committee would resort to weekly reports on Phillip Shaw's health. Shaw's release from the hospital and the one month recovery time indicated that his heart attack was mild to moderate. The employees of the company were relieved at the news. Charlie presumed that he would not have to answer a lot of questions about the company at Saturday's softball practice.

For the rest of the afternoon, Charlie reviewed the approved budget figures in preparation for his white paper on the status of each division.

The Shaw Corporation had 5 operating divisions. It had an industrial chemicals division that was further subdivided into 3 units. One unit manufactured flavors and food additives. Another produced industrial cleaning solvents. The third subdivision manufactured cellulose capsules for the drug industry.

The company had a steel shot/abrasives division that manufactured inputs for blast cleaning of industrial machinery. The division also had a subsidiary unit that provided blast cleaning services for customers.

A third division, the oldest in the company, was a cutting tools manufacturing operation.

The remaining two divisions were, respectively, one to produce machinery for the paper industry and the other to produce food processing machinery.

Old man Shaw and his son had seen to it that the divisions were inter-related in terms of products and services to the market. The chemicals division sold flavors and additives to the food industry that purchased its machinery. Industrial cleaning solvents were sold to the machinery customers and sold internally to the blast cleaning division. The cutting tools, paper industry machinery, and food processing machinery divisions were "stand alone" operations serving three distinct industry segments while promoting the products of the chemicals and blast cleaning operations. The company emphasized customer relations in its marketing strategy. Sales personnel were expected to promote the products and services of the chemical and blast cleaning divisions. Customer feedback was vital to informing division heads of market needs across the full range of company products and services. The marketing "model" was based on that of the old Ethyl Gas Corporation whose sales personnel made it a point to know everyone in customer companies from the janitor who used cleaning solvents on the factory floor to the president and to the chief financial officer whose concern was for costs. A visit from a Shaw salesman to a client company could take up to half a day as the salesman moved up the customer company's hierarchy getting feedback on Shaw's products. By the time he reached the president's office for a brief visit, the salesman knew as much or more than the president himself knew about how Shaw Corporation's products were perceived. He might tell the president that he had spoken to the janitor and learned that a more powerful cleaning solvent was necessary or that he heard from operating personnel that there was a quality problem with the cellulose capsules. He would promise to look into the reported situation and get back to the customer and send a report to the president. This "in-depth" sales approach virtually assured that Shaw retained customer loyalty. Customer service reports were often detailed descriptions of the customer's observations and these were discussed up the chain of command at Shaw. Changes in products in response to customer observations were fed back to the sales personnel for follow-up with customers.

Each operating division reviewed the customer service reports to prepare its quarterly budget and capital requests to address customer issues. It was up to Fred Perkins to impose discipline on the budgeting process and make sure that the capital requests of each department were reasonable. If it was agreed that a capital allocation was necessary, Fred would so indicate and his department would then work with the operating divisions to finance the capital requests. Fred Perkins saw it as his almost-sacred duty to protect the company from what he considered the tendency toward profligate spending by the operating departments. It was his view that the people heading up operations always wanted the latest "technological toys" regardless of the effect such purchases might have on the company's finances. Since Shaw was flush with cash that meant maintaining close control over the transfer of cash to the operating division and following up on its use but first and foremost thoroughly questioning every request for additional funding. Over the ensuing quarters, the finance area would monitor the return on investment and provide feedback to the operating departments. It was a very tight system designed to provide the best possible service to customers while holding the line on unnecessary cost increases. The growth of the Shaw Corporation in its early years testified to the soundness of the system.

Charlie put the copies of the budgets, past and present, into his briefcase in preparation for the white paper. At five-o-clock Charlie left the office for Gina's place in Philly.

* * * * *

When he arrived, Gina was waiting with the fixings for a dry martini and a dry manhattan. Charlie was non-plussed. "Gina, how do you do it? Do you know when I will be home? Am I that predictable?"

"*Au contraire*, Mullins, I just know that you can't wait to see me and you can't keep your hands off me. Or am I wrong?"

"No, Ms. Ferrelli, you are not wrong. But don't get cocky."

After they had dinner, Charlie sat down to his papers. He was beginning to see a pattern that would enable him to write a well-documented briefing paper. The operating departments had all fallen behind the market in small increments, due largely to the badgering by Fred Perkins. Reluctant to make daring proposals, the operating department heads were very conservative in their demands. They were simply keeping up with the market and in some cases, falling gradually behind. The result was that the company gradually lost competitiveness in a number of areas. The loss was incremental and in no period was it felt with any great impact. It was just a gradual and almost imperceptible loss of clients to competitors.

In the context of his present assignment this situation was, in Charlie's view, an opportunity. Phillip Shaw could cite the gradual losses of competitive position as justification for a more aggressive approach to the growth possibilities of the company. Moreover, he could do so with impunity because the company is still in the hands of the family. There would be no shareholder complaints. A more aggressive growth strategy would also build employee morale while indicating that Phillip was back and in good form. Charlie could now see the general direction of his white paper.

Now comfortable with his planned approach, Charlie placed his papers in the binder and shut down his work for the evening. Gina who had been watching TV turned off the set, put a smooth jazz CD in the CD player and went to the kitchen to prepare two drinks. She came back with the drinks in her hand and said, "Let's listen to some music while we have a drink. You can come down from your work and we can both relax."

"Thanks, baby, here's to the patient fiancée." They clinked their glasses and sat on the sofa to relax.

XXX

Charlie was in a light mood as he drove to Wilmington Friday morning. He now had a rough outline of his white paper in mind. The pattern was clear but subtle. Charlie knew that in large companies bad news rarely came all at once. Usually there was a period of small imperceptible losses justified by what wound up being called "market conditions" and then frantic efforts to catch up once the changes were perceived on the bottom line. It was a rule of thumb that every dollar of lost market share usually costs five dollars to get back. But loss of market share did not occur overnight. He saw from the reports he had taken from the files that the operating department heads had been hedging their positions for more ambitious, and costly proposals to expand, largely in response to the opposition they expected to face from Perkins. No single report would have been sufficient to raise a red flag, but the pattern was clear.

When he arrived to his building he walked past Fred Perkins' office on his way to his own. Fred was sitting at his desk, a bottle of antacid pills in front of him, and staring off into space. He said, "Good morning Fred."

Perkins grudgingly acknowledged Charlie's greeting with a curt "Morning, Mullins". As he walked past Laura Metzer's desk he saw that she was smiling. "How ya' doin' Laura?"

She answered Charlie in an almost whisper, "I've never seen him so quiet, Charlie. He's almost human!"

Charlie chuckled as much to himself as in response to Laura's comment. He smiled at Laura and said, "Enjoy it while you can."

Walking to his office Charlie thought, *Fred must be in a real pickle. He doesn't know who he should badger.* With power dispersed among the members of the Executive Committee Perkins had decided that discretion was the better part of valor and to avoid trouble he would just keep mum until Phillip Shaw returned.

Once settled in his chair Charlie picked up his phone and dialed Bill Cummins' number. When Cummins came on the line he said, "Bill, good morning," Cummins returned the greeting and Charlie continued, "I've got a meeting today with Warren Carpenter. I think you should be there. I'm getting the white paper organized and I have noticed some things that could be important to our objective. Can you make it?"

"Sure, Charlie, I'll leave a little early and drive over to Wilmington. What time is your meeting?"

"Five-thirty, Bill, in Carpenter's office. See you there?"

"Right, five-thirty it is. See you then. Bye Charlie."

"Thanks. See you later." Charlie rang off.

Charlie spent the rest of his day gathering file copies of previous operating department budgets and customer service reports. He pored over them and his initial views were confirmed. Several customer service reports contained minor complaints from customers regarding product quality. Some had indicated that a few customers had purchased increasing amounts of product from competitors. In each case the sales personnel had told the customer that the complaint would be addressed. However, Charlie noted that in the budgets the underlying causes of the complaints had not been addressed. However, some of the draft budgets that he discussed with operating departments before submitting final budgets to Fred Perkins did have requests for capital equipment or investments that the department heads themselves removed, presumably to facilitate negotiations with Fred. He also noticed that the operating departments were reporting gradually increasing costs because of aging machinery that needed to be replaced or upgraded. Productivity was declining in small increments but the declines were narrowing profit margins.

He would have a lot to discuss with Bill Cummins and Warren Carpenter.

Charlie stuffed the file copies into his briefcase and at five-o-clock locked his desk. He would copy the documents at Warren Carpenter's office and return them to Central Files on Monday. He did not want to run the risk that someone might ask for some or any of the documents and be informed that he had checked them out. He wondered if he was not being excessive with his security concerns but concluded that if it was not necessary to run risks, why should he?

He waited for most of his department to clear out before he left. Fred Perkins had already gone. Charlie headed for the elevators and entered a nearly empty car to the street level. He said "have a nice weekend" as he departed the elevator and heard the expected "same to you" from the persons in the car with him. He walked out on to the street and looked for anyone who might see him heading away from the parking lot and toward the building where Warren Carpenter had his office. No one was paying attention. When he arrived to Carpenter's office, the front reception desk was vacant. Warren Carpenter was sitting on a sofa in the large reception area, reading a magazine. He looked up to see Charlie arriving and opened the glass door of the office.

"Hey Charlie, good to see you again, Bill Cummins told me you were on board and had already begun your white paper. He called to tell me he is on the way. Would you like a drink? It's after hours, you know."

"Maybe after our meeting, thanks", said Charlie.

"OK, that's fine", replied Carpenter, "Bill should be here shortly."

As he was finishing his sentence, Bill Cummins stepped from the elevator. Carpenter opened the glass door to the office to let Cummins enter then locked the door. He pointed both men toward his office and said, "Let's meet in my office. Nobody will bother us now."

The three men walked to Carpenter's office where they sat around a small conference table set off in a corner. Carpenter began, "Charlie, I'm glad you decided to take on this challenge. I'm sure Bill was as glad as I was to hear your decision. As you know from the Executive Committee bulletins, Phillip Shaw has begun his recovery program. He's working out on a treadmill and will move to more strenuous exercise in a week or two. He's well and curious to know what you have planned and what you have discovered so far."

Charlie began, "Bill and I met last week to go over the financials. There are some properties in the company's name that are used by family members for private purposes. They lease the properties from the company for vacations, claims of business activity, and so on. In fact, they are actually vacation residences or 'crash pads' for the rich. We identified all of those properties and recommend that the family members buy those properties from the company at fair market values. The transactions would be executed by contracts that Bill can keep at Wexler until just before the sale of the company is announced. Payment or payments from the family members to the company would be made to a temporary offshore company set up to hold the funds until such time as the IPO is practically set up. Likewise, any mortgage payments would continue to be made by the company in accordance with existing contracts and family members would reimburse the company via payments to the offshore company. At the right moment all the accounts would be settled and booked and the offshore company shut down.

The company books will be clean of any private family holdings before the IPO is announced."

"That should work just fine", said Carpenter, "I will draw up the contracts and collect the signatures of the family members. I don't see any legal problems but it is possible that Becky Shaw, Phillip's divorced sister, might have cash flow problems. She lives high on the hog and goes through money like shit through a goose – excuse my French! I will discuss her particular case with Phillip. He knows his sister well enough to be able to anticipate her reaction. Any advances to her will be documented and settled following the IPO."

Charlie continued, "In view of Phillip Shaw's plan to announce that he will be pursuing a more aggressive growth strategy after returning as CEO, I think I have found just the right information. I will, of course, report it in greater detail in my white paper on the status of the company. To make an otherwise long story short, the company has been suffering small but persistent losses of productivity and, consequently market share or reduced margins across the range of its products and services. The loss has been small in each quarter but when calculated over a one-year period it has turned out to be significant. When you figure that a 0.2% productivity loss in a given quarter can result in almost a 1% loss in a year – 0.804% to be exact and 1.6% over a two year period. In a company like Shaw, that can set you pretty far back if it doesn't get recognized and persists. I think the operating department heads were reluctant to take on Fred Perkins for more investment funding. You know that Fred is a bit difficult...."

Warren Carpenter interrupted, "A *bit* difficult?! He could scare Frankenstein himself with his attitudes."

Charlie laughed amiably, "Understood Warren, but let's remember that sometimes you have to fight for what you want if it's important enough. My impression is that during no single quarter the numbers were so out of synch that they justified a knock-down-drag-'em-out confrontation with Fred. So, to get their budgets approved with minimal resistance, the operating departments asked for only what they thought they could get rather than what they really needed. No one looked back far enough to see how far they had drifted away from the market. And they didn't fight for what they wanted or needed."

Used to the genteel sports of sailing and polo, Warren Carpenter said to Charlie, "I guess it's a bit like sailing. If you don't compensate for the lateral drift of your boat and look only at your forward progress through the water, you will soon be well off course."

Charlie smiled, "Sounds good to me. I only bowl and play softball", and then laughed.

Both Carpenter and Cummins laughed with Charlie, "Yeah, metaphors can be dangerous, Warren, not everyone has the same frame of reference."

"I think I have grasped the concept", Charlie said, "yes, there was some lateral drift that required course correction and it was not compensated as a result of internal politics. But the problem is not so great that it cannot be readily corrected and besides, it gives Phillip a plausible excuse for becoming more aggressive when he returns to office."

"Yeah, it's perfect", said Bill Cummins, "Phillip can say that he had sufficient time away from day-to-day matters to observe the company from a distance."

Charlie showed Warren Carpenter and Bill Cummins some of the figures and graphs he had put together to more visually grasp the amount of "lateral drift" that had affected the various operating divisions. He followed, "I don't want Phillip to see these yet, but you can see what has been happening. I intend to put these into the white paper and Phillip can show them to the press and to the Executive and Finance Committees as he sees fit."

Cummins and Carpenter reviewed Charlie's initial analysis and agreed that it provided a powerful argument for a series of "course corrections" that the market would accept and employees would welcome. "It's an excellent smoke screen", said Carpenter, "I'll discuss it with Phillip to show that we are moving ahead. He will feel good about this, I'm sure."

"Charlie", Carpenter asked, "how soon do you think you will have your final report ready?"

"I will probably need a week to two weeks to get it all together. There are 5 divisions to be looked at and each has a particular set of circumstances. But it is clear that overall the company needs a more aggressive posture in the market."

"OK, I will tell Phil that it will take about two weeks. That should give you some leeway and not pressure you. Phil will have plenty of time to review the report before his return press conference."

"Bill", Carpenter continued, "I presume that Wexler & Santori will endorse the report."

"By all means, Warren, we will sign off on the numbers Charlie puts together to strengthen Phil's statements and for Phil to know that we have reviewed Charlie's work. Meanwhile, I will work with Charlie to look for acquisitions that might resolve the productivity and quality problems while using up the company's excess cash."

"OK, agreed", Carpenter said, "I will see Phil tomorrow at his home and let him know where we stand so far. Good progress gentlemen, good progress. Now, let's seal this meeting with a drink!" Carpenter walked to the bar he had in a credenza in his office. He took out a bottle of expensive single malt scotch and poured a generous shot for each of them. "Here's to success!" and raised his glass in toast. "Here, here", said Charlie and Bill. They sipped their scotch and talked about the local sports teams for a brief while. Charlie was the first to rise, "OK, guys, I've still got a lot of work to do, so I'm going to head home. Warren, thanks for reviewing my figures and Bill, I'll call you first thing on Monday to go over what I put together over the weekend. Could I suggest that our next meeting be on Friday, a week from now, same time, at the Ritz-Carlton in Philly? I'll rent a meeting room for a couple of hours and pay cash. That OK?"

"Fine", said Warren Carpenter. "Ditto", said Bill Cummins.

* * * * *

Charlie took his leave and headed back to the parking lot near his office building. He picked up his car and headed for Gina's.

Gina was at home when Charlie arrived and met him with a warm kiss as he entered the apartment. "Oooo, how good it is to be able to wait at home for my man to arrive. Have a good day, Charlie?"

"Oh yeah, how about you?"

"I called Emily today, remember her? Bob's wife – you know, the architect."

"Of course I remember. I remember both of them. You told me that Bob got a contract to design some city housing projects."

"Yeah, well Emily is really excited about it. They will now have enough income for her to concentrate on her painting. She had been doing some substitute teaching to pick up extra money but with the contract Bob got, she can now spend more time doing what she loves most – painting."

"That's great", said Charlie, "will she be ready for a show soon?"

"Maybe in a month, maybe two", Gina replied, "but she's really on fire now."

"Will you organize the show?" Charlie asked.

"How could I do otherwise? They are such wonderful people. So committed to helping others and making the world a better place. I'm so glad to help!"

"Gina, I find you so amazing. You are such a fine, generous person, and so committed to bettering the world you live in who would have thought that your uncle..?"

A cloud crossed Gina's face. Charlie had never seen her so disturbed. "Hang on, Charlie. You know little about my uncle. He has helped a lot of people, especially poor people. I know what they say about him in the press but you don't know what they *don't* say about him. He has made donations to hospitals, schools, and orphanages. He has arranged jobs for people who needed to support their families. He has pressured politicians to help the poor. He has….."

"Oh, Gina, I'm sorry. I didn't mean…"

"I know what you meant, Charlie. I'm not angry at you. It's just that things are not so black and white in life. What if Carlo Rizzo had been born to a Mainline family? Would he be 'Don' Carlo Rizzo today? Maybe, but I doubt it. Maybe he would have gone to Wharton, earned an MBA and become a bank president or CEO, maybe even at a company like Shaw. Charlie, I want you to visualize a 5-year-old kid traumatized by war, a refugee – they called them 'displaced persons' – from a poor country that had known only exploitation and violence throughout its history. He spoke no English and had no money. He defended himself as best he could and he bent more than a few rules and broke many others to survive. Imagine his confusion as he was presented with the contradictions of this new society in which he lived. You remember the story of the construction engineer he told you over lunch? You think that engineer was right to rip off immigrant workers? Don't answer, because I know you don't. My uncle could have accepted the situation as his destiny. Instead, he challenged the bastard and improved his own situation and that of his friends. Wrong? How do I know? I just know that the man people call 'terrible' and they fear took me in when I was two years old, fed me when I was hungry, treated me when I was sick, sent me to the best schools, and loved me as only a father could. You need to talk more to my uncle to really understand this. I know it's not easy. Do you think I did not have a hard time getting my mind around the fact that I was as rich as any of the girls as Bryn Mawr but was somehow different? I was, in private conversation and in hushed tones of course, a 'wop'. You won't find my name on any sorority list, but you will find the names of the fathers of many sorority members in my father's coded notebooks!"

"Gina, I didn't mean…"

"I know that, Charlie. I know you love me and I love you. There are just some things that you don't and maybe can't understand. Talk to my Uncle

Carlo. You will understand what I mean. Only he can tell you. I was brought up in a 'hothouse", I know it. My uncle protected me from the meanness of poverty and the pettiness of others. But I was tainted by being born to a pair of Sicilian immigrants. My children will be born free of that 'taint' or 'original sin' but I could not avoid it. Luck of the draw but good luck from my own point of view. Had things been otherwise, I would never have met you, Charlie. Do you understand that?"

"I really do, Gina. It's just that it confuses me. This is a world with which I am not at all familiar. I was brought up in a small town to play softball and go bowling with my buddies. I chose to work at Shaw probably simply because that was what everybody else did in Shoreville. I never had any reason to question my life. I was supposed to marry a nice local girl, work hard, be successful within my limits, and have a couple of kids who would be in Little League or on a soccer team. I would go to PTA, see my kids graduate from high school, send them to college, see them come back to Shoreville, get married and have their own kids. Then I would retire and be a doting grandfather, and die. I never questioned that. My career wound up being more than I had expected largely as a result of circumstance, luck, and work. I think I just happened to be in the right place at the right time."

"Then I presume you can understand the situation of someone who just happened to be in the *wrong* place at the *wrong* time, Charlie."

"I never thought about it that way, but you are right. It's just nothing but luck of the draw. We don't get to choose where we are born nor to whom. We just show up and then deal with it. Because of you I began to question my life. I have to admit that I concluded that I had been complacent. I learned to love with you. I learned passion for you and for life and I would not trade that lesson for anything else in this world. It has opened a whole new world to me."

"Now, isn't it interesting Charlie, that that is exactly what has happened to me too? We come from such different circumstances, but both of us find love and passion that changes our lives? What does that tell you, Charlie?"

"It tells me, Gina that each person has a destiny to fulfill. It tells me that each of us must control that destiny. And it tells me that it is nobody else's damned business how we got here or where we are going. It tells me, Gina, that life is a creative process and that we must rise above our circumstances to be the best we can in both human and intellectual terms."

"Beautiful, Charlie, that's right, but don't dwell on it. You do what you have to do at the time you have to do it and the devil take the hindmost. If it offends the Church, the Senate, the Republican Party, the PTA, or any other man-made organization you choose to mention, then it's just too fucking bad. They don't pay your bills! And please excuse my French."

"Your French is excused. I like it when you talk dirty." Charlie laughed.

Gina laughed with him and then said seriously, "Just talk to my uncle. He will understand where you are coming from and will expect you to understand where he is coming from. He will offer no apologies nor will he bask in his accomplishments or reputation. He is a man who, as you say, puts his pants on one leg at a time."

"Look, Gina, I hope I did not offend you or your uncle…"

"No Charlie, I am not offended and you did not offend Uncle Carlo. I know this is a different world for you. Your world is different in a lot of ways for me, too. The normalcy of your life that you find so tedious would have been wonderful for me. You didn't have to worry about whether someone you just met would be terrified of your father or think that you might be able to do them some unusual favor like having someone killed. People think that, you know."

"Gina, the only thing I am really sure about at this point in my life is that I love you and want you with me for the rest of my life. Everything else pales by comparison to that goal."

"That's all we need, Charlie. Just that commitment to each other, as long as we have it, nothing can bring us down." She kissed him tenderly, "I love you Mullins and thanks for showing up when you did."

"Now, changing the subject, would you like some veal parmagiana? It's in the oven steeping in a delicious tomato sauce. I'll cook up some pasta and we can forget the world and have a delicious meal. Can I trust you to open the wine?"

"I'll do my best my Italian countess", Charlie headed for the wine rack.

As they ate their dinner, Charlie told Gina of his plans for Saturday. "Gina, I'm going to softball practice tomorrow. I want to hear what the guys are saying about the company and I am especially interested in what two of them might say about their wives. I have not seen anyone following me around so I presume my little trick with the timers worked."

"I hate to disappoint you Charlie. My feminine intuition and knowledge of the wiles of busybody women tell me that your little trick, as you call it, didn't fool them."

"What was I supposed to do? I couldn't just leave the house dark all the time. That would have set them off too."

"There's nothing you could have done, my dear. If you left the house dark they would have been curious. They are still curious and they are certain that you have your lights turned on and off for a reason that they are determined to discover. You did the only thing you could have done. But male logic is no competition for female determination. Take my word for it, they are as curious or more so today than they were before. They probably have some reason for lying low right now and I suspect it is the situation at the company."

"That's hardly encouraging!"

"I don't mean to encourage or discourage. It's just the way they are. Be prepared! Just go to your softball practice and see what you can find out. That's the only thing you can do."

* * * * *

Saturday morning Charlie brought Gina her coffee in bed and then left for Shoreville. He went first to his house to check the timers and to pick up his gear. The house seemed deserted and devoid of any life now that he was sharing Gina's apartment with her. It was eerily quiet and he looked at his furniture as if it really belonged to someone else. He had been there only a couple of days ago, on Wednesday night, but it seemed like it was long ago. It was amazing to him how Gina had so filled his life. He decided to take a few of his books with him when he returned to Philly. He looked for a number of business books, especially those that dealt with acquisitions, to use as references in his assignment. He threw the books into the trunk of his car and drove to the park for softball practice.

Charlie noticed that the mood of the group was light. Everyone had been relieved to know that Phillip Shaw had been released from the hospital and was initiating his recovery program. They were now convinced that things would, in short time, be as before. He made sure that he was close to Bill Gallagher and Bob Simms when he told several of his colleagues that he was extremely busy because of Phillip Shaw's absence. The Executive and Finance committees tended to pass down more work than Phillip did. He told them that the tendency to delegate had increased with management by committee. He hoped that Bill and Bob would pass on the information to their wives.

* * * * *

Charlie had no way of knowing that at this precise moment, Sharon Gallagher and Diane Simms were talking on the telephone. "Diane, do you believe me now? Charlie Mullins is not, I repeat, not at home when his lights are on. Even if we accept that he has more work to do, where is he doing it? It certainly is not at home, right?"

"Well, Sharon, to be honest, I had not checked on his comings and goings recently. Bob has been worried about whether he will have a job if Phillip does not return and I confess that I have been too worried to think about Charlie."

"You can forget that now, Diane. Phillip Shaw will be back on the job within a month and Charlie will still not be home. You can bet on it."

"Sharon, do you really want to continue with this stuff? I mean it's not really our business. Charlie has his own life. I kind of like the guy and I feel funny about prying…"

"Oh for heaven's sake, Diane," Sharon admonished "I like Charlie Mullins too. We all went to school together. I knew Mary Jo but didn't like her that much and I know a lot of women who could make Charlie happy. Has it occurred to you that I might not be prying but simply trying to help Charlie? But we can't help him if we don't know who that woman is that he is seeing. I mean what if she is some gold-digger or some floozy? Charlie made a mistake once with Mary Jo, how do we know he won't make another one?"

"It would be *Charlie's* mistake, wouldn't it?" Diane asked.

"Diane, if I were making a mistake, wouldn't you tell me as a friend? Wouldn't you let me know if I was running the risk of ruining my life?"

"Well, yes, Sharon…"

"How is this any different? Once we find out who the woman is, we can either back off or tell Charlie what we have learned if he is treading on thin ice."

"OK, Sharon, OK, but I really feel a lit bit uneasy about all this."

"Cool it, Diane! We are just trying to help a friend. That's all. Get that through your head and quit fretting. Now, once the dust settles on the company situation and Charlie is less burdened with extra work, we can get back to trying to help him. Bill has been a nervous wreck with Phil Shaw out and I have been making a point of staying quiet and at home."

"Yeah, Bob has been nervous too. He said people in the lab are all wondering what might happen. He seems to have calmed down a bit since the last announcement that Phillip Shaw is recovering and will be back on the job in about a month. He was even telling me to watch my spending and tighten up the household budget."

"Well, it will be over soon and no one will be happier than I to see it end. Even the kids are asking if Bill might lose his job. By the way, are you going to the beauty parlor today? I thought I would be a little extravagant and get my hair done for the first time in a couple of weeks."

"I hadn't planned on it, but yes, let's go. Now that it appears that Phillip Shaw will be coming back, I think I can afford to go back to familiar ways." Diane laughed.

"OK, I'll see you at Mabel's place in about an hour. Bye." Sharon rang off.

In view of the light mood of his teammates, Charlie decided to stay for a beer and a slice of pizza. He would keep it short, but he might get some information from Bill and Bob about what their wives were up to.

When they sat down to their beer Charlie heard Bill Gallagher say, "Well, I was nervous about the job situation with Phil Shaw being out, but I have to confess that his heart attack put the fear of God into Sharon. She's been treating me like a king! Even the sex has improved! Anything she can do to keep me from getting upset she does. Maybe Phil should stay out a little longer," he laughed.

"You guys are something else," Tony Mazza chimed in, "Charlie told us all that things were more or less normal in the company and that nothing was going to change."

"Yeah? Well how do we know if they are lying to Charlie, too?" Bob Simms asked, "I mean he's not on either the Executive Committee or the Finance Committee so he just knows what they tell him, too, right?"

"Well, yeah," answered Tony, "but he is smart enough to know if he is being conned. He gets a lot of information from the operations guys and they *do* sit on the Executive Committee and his boss, Perkins, sits on the Finance Committee. He's in a helluva lot better situation than we are to know what's going on, that's for sure."

"Tony's right," said Artie Samuels, "if Charlie thought something bad was coming down for his friends, he'd tell us."

"I guess you're right," said Bob Simms, "but I've been nervous as hell since Shaw went to the hospital."

Charlie entered the conversation, "Guys, come on, you can relax now. Phillip Shaw will soon be back on the job and things will return to normal. There's no need to worry." He knew that for the first time he was hedging his information to his friends. "Well guys, I'm gonna have to cut out a little early today. I've got a backlog of papers to work on. It seems those guys in the boardroom don't like to work so hard and we all know that shit rolls downhill."

The group laughed in unison and Tony Mazza said, "OK, Charlie, get your ass moving. Our jobs are in your hands," he laughed.

Charlie took his leave and headed home. He reset his timers, washed his uniform and put it in the dryer. While the uniform was spinning in the dryer he showered, changed, and then went through his bookshelf to see if he might not have skipped over a useful book or two. He picked out one more volume and set it aside to take back to Philly. When the dryer stopped spinning he removed his uniform and folded it carefully on top of the dryer. He checked around the house one more time, and then went to the garage, got into his car and drove to Philly. As usual he checked for surveillance along the way.

* * * * *

When he got back to Gina's apartment he went immediately to work on his assignment. Gina walked over to him and kissed the top of his head, "My, aren't we busy on a Saturday? How was softball practice?"

"Fine, sweets, the guys were in a much lighter mood after hearing that Phil Shaw would be returning to the company. They see him as steady and cool and they don't know the personalities of the members of the Executive Committee so they were all worried."

"And the wacky wives?"

"Well, Bill Gallagher and Bob Simms both said their wives were quiet and doing everything to keep peace in their respective households. Bill even said he hoped Phil Shaw would stay out a little longer!"

"Boy, his wife must be a piece of work!"

"She is. I've known Sharon since we were both kids in school. When she gets her mind fixed on something, she is relentless. She recognizes no limits and is as irritating and shrill as a dentist's drill when pursuing what she wants. Diane Simms is a little different. She has always been Sharon's alter ego but she gets scared if things get a bit rough. She doesn't like confrontation while Sharon welcomes it. Sharon always pushed Diane around when we were in school."

"She sounds like the kind of woman I would like to meet in a dark alley. I'd welcome the chance to scratch her eyes out!"

"You know something? I think you could do it!"

"Just let her mess with my man and I'll show her what a South Philly broad can really be like!"

"I hope it never comes to that, Gina, but if I need your help, I'll ask for it." Charlie laughed.

"Deal," Gina said firmly, "Now, would you like some lunch? I thought I would put together a light antipasto. Is that OK?"

"Great," said Charlie, "I want to get back to my papers so I can talk to your uncle tomorrow."

Charlie picked up his binders and moved to the dining room table while Gina went to the kitchen to fix their lunch. "Charlie," she cried from the kitchen "don't forget we are going to the *trattoria* tonight."

"How could I forget my date with a beautiful woman?"

"Ah, that Irish charm," Gina replied and set about putting the antipasto together.

Charlie decided that he would begin his report with a short executive summary that would lay out the overall situation of the company and cite the major challenges of each division. He would then follow with a section on each operating division that would provide a more detailed analysis of the gradual erosion of profitability and the reported needs of each. He would avoid any negative references to Fred Perkins even though it was Fred's abrasiveness that could be considered part of the problem. Phil Shaw was not looking for scapegoats, he wanted to bring positive news to the market and to Shaw employees.

Gina interrupted Charlie's work to tell him their lunch was ready. She opened a half bottle of wine to accompany the antipasto. "This looks delicious, Gina." Charlie said. They ate slowly and Charlie came down from his work.

After lunch Charlie went back to his papers while Gina put the dishes in the dishwasher and organized her kitchen. Charlie worked for the next several hours while Gina used the time to call friends and arrange meetings to discuss her volunteer work the following week.

When Charlie set aside his binders he was ready for a relaxing evening at the *trattoria*. "Gina," he called, "what time do you want to leave for the *trattoria*?"

"In about an hour, sweetheart, is that OK?"

"Fine," said Charlie. He wandered into the bedroom where Gina was dressing. He looked at her lithe body as she slipped into a light silk dress that clung to her curves almost like a second skin. "My God, you are beautiful," he said.

"Ah, you're just horny from all that exercise playing baseball!" Gina said.

Charlie pulled her to him and kissed her, "No, young lady, it's not the baseball, it's the 'Gina' in my life."

"You might be in for a long night, Charlie, if you keep that up!"

"That's the best news I've had this week," Charlie replied, "ever since I bought those navy blue silk boxer shorts I have been out of control," he laughed.

"Out of *your* control, Mullins, but you're in *mine*! I reserve the right to pull 'em off every time I have the urge!"

Charlie changed into a pair of khaki pants, and as he was reaching for a blue oxford cloth button down collar shirt Gina said "Whoa, Mullins, I bought you a silk shirt today – no collar. Think you can handle that?" She handed him a gift-wrapped package.

Charlie opened the package and pulled out a blue silk T-shirt. He said, "Gina, I have been wondering if I should try this kind of shirt some time. What do you think?"

"I think it's sexy as hell, Mullins. Put it on!"

Charlie put on the T-shirt and pulled his blue blazer on over it. He looked in the mirror and was a bit disconcerted but thought he looked pretty good. Gina thought he looked great and said so, "Mullins, you will be the sexiest male in the whole place tonight!"

"I have to admit, it looks pretty cool, but I will probably be grabbing all night to try to find the collar."

Gina laughed, "Enough of the button down world, Charlie. You're with an Italian broad now. Look the part."

"You think I should have a gold chain with this shirt?"

"Oh God, Charlie – less is more. You don't want to look like the producer of a pornographic movie, just like a dashing Italian bachelor walking around the streets of Rome!"

"Is that what I look like?"

"I can assure you, Mullins, if you showed up in Rome dressed like that the women would pinch your bottom," Gina laughed out loud, "OK Mr. Sexy, I'm going to call a cab."

Charlie and Gina took the elevator to street level and waited in the lobby of her building for the cab. When the car arrived, Charlie held the door for Gina then entered the taxi. He gave the driver the address of the *trattoria*. When they arrived, Charlie held the door for Gina. He didn't see the two "availables" from Shoreville that were on their way to the parking garage across from the *trattoria*. They were on the way home after some pizza in a local pizzeria. "Say, that's Charlie Mullins who just got out of that cab."

"Nah, Charlie doesn't dress like that. But it sure looks like him."

"No, it's Charlie, I know it. And that girl with him looks just like the one Sharon Gallagher described at the beauty parlor. I *know* it's him."

"Well the girl with him sure didn't buy that outfit in Macy's basement! Look at her. That purse and those shoes must have cost as much as my car!"

"Yeah, she's decked out all right. Do you think Charlie is paying for all that?"

"Well, he might be paying for it, but he is not picking it out. He wouldn't know how to buy that stuff!"

"I'll betcha it's not even Charlie Mullins. We've just been listening to Sharon and Diane too much!"

"It looks a lot like Charlie to me. And she looks an awful lot like the girl that Sharon and Diane described. I'm gonna call Sharon tomorrow and see what she says."

Charlie and Gina entered the *trattoria* where they spent a few relaxing hours with some good wine and dividing a delicious lasagna. Johnny the waiter took care of their table and made some conversation with them. He was glad to see them both and to tell Gina how grateful he was for her tutoring of his children. They left the *trattoria* at about 11 pm and Johnny hailed a cab for them, standing at his usual post until the cab had departed.

Tomorrow they would have lunch with Gina's Uncle Carlo.

XXXI

Sunday morning Gina and Charlie slept in until just after 9 am. Charlie got out of bed and went to the kitchen to make coffee for them both and brought back two steaming mugs for them to drink in bed.

"Good morning, beautiful. Does every Italian woman wake up looking as beautiful as you do in the morning?" Charlie asked.

"I don't know Charlie, I have never woken up with an Italian woman and I don't plan to," Gina laughed.

"Point made and taken," Charlie replied. "By the way, what time shall we head for your uncle's place?"

"I would suggest we go a bit earlier so you have plenty of time to talk. We should try to get there by about one-o-clock. Uncle Carlo likes to have lunch around two or three-o-clock on Sundays and, of course, we can stay for as long as you want. Don't forget that you will have to wear the same cap and sunglasses."

"What? No false beard?" Charlie laughed.

"Maybe next time wise guy!"

"Oh my God, she's serious!"

They finished their coffee and Charlie went to the front door to pick up the Sunday newspaper. He refilled both their coffee mugs and settled back into bed to read the news. Gina cuddled close to him and said, "I used to dream of Sundays like this, you know?"

Charlie kissed her forehead tenderly and said, "We'll have lots of them and they will all be as pleasant and relaxing as this one. I love you."

"If that's the case, then give me the funnies." Gina said.

They read the paper and then began dressing to leave for Carlo Rizzo's home. Charlie grabbed his disguise from the closet and then took the elevator to the garage to leave in Gina's Mercedes. When they arrived to Carlo Rizzo's home, the same group of agents was standing around and one of them dutifully photographed Gina's car as it entered the property and until the automatic gate closed.

As soon as Gina's car pulled up to the rear door of the house, the hefty Frankie was holding it open. "Hi Frankie, how's the family?" Gina asked. Gina and Charlie exited her Mercedes and went into the kitchen.

Frankie followed them into the house, "Everybody's fine, Miss Gina, thanks for asking. Your uncle is in the living room. It's good to see you again."

"Thanks Frankie, and give my regards to your wife and the kids."

"Will do, Miss Gina, thanks."

They entered the living room where Carlo Rizzo was waiting for them. He rose as they entered, "Look at my beautiful *bambina*!" he exclaimed, "This Irishman must be good for you! You look radiant."

Charlie flushed.

"And you, my New Jersey Irishman, you look like a man who is being well-treated. Are you gaining weight from Gina's cooking?"

"Not yet, Mr. Rizzo, but I have to watch out. She's dynamite in the kitchen."

"Eh, be careful she doesn't give you the Sicilian 'prosperity'!" Carlo laughed and patted Charlie's stomach.

"She told me about that, I'm being careful." Charlie laughed.

"Come in, come in. Have a seat. I've asked Paola to prepare her delicious *antipasti* for us. Let's have some wine! It's so good to see my *bambina* looking so beautiful!"

Charlie and Gina sat on the sofa and Carlo sat across from them in a chair. "So, Charlie, Gina told me you wanted to see me about something."

"Yes sir, I need your advice on some business matters." He told Carlo about Phillip Shaw's heart attack and his assignment to prepare the company to go public.

·When he finished Carlo said, "*Madonna mia*! That young Phillip is a sharp guy. He wants to get into politics. I knew he would eventually. He has bigger ambitions that just being the CEO of a company his father set up. I wouldn't be a bit surprised if the whole thing was not a set-up from the start. It sure doesn't sound like his heart attack was very serious."

"No sir, the story is that it was a mild one and that he will be back on the job in about a month or less."

"So, you're the guy in charge of the scam? You're the one who will do the background work to make an IPO possible?"

"Yes, sir, the company has a lot of excess cash that will have to be invested before the company goes public or the sharks will buy it up for the cash value and possibly spin off the divisions. That would break up the Shaw Corporation and that is not what Phillip wants."

"Of course not, he wants to go out like a hero. You can't run for office if you've put a lot of voters out of their jobs. He wants people to love him – and *vote* for him. He thinks like a Sicilian, that guy!"

Carlo continued, "So he wants you to find some good acquisitions for him, right? He wants to make sure he has the cash locked up in longer term investments so no one will buy his money, right?"

"Yes sir, that's about it."

"So, how does this change your life, Charlie?" Carlo asked. "I'm sure you know how much the information you have is worth. You could make a small fortune if you told the right people..."

"Yeah, except that I signed a confidentiality agreement. Besides perhaps going to jail, I would most certainly get sued by the Shaw family and whatever money I made would go to attorneys, fines, and paying back the Shaw's. It would not be a smart move on my part."

"Smart guy," Carlo answered, "just negotiating that information would not only be dumb, it would not be very subtle. It would make you into a 'bad guy'. There are smarter ways to turn a buck in such situations."

"I suppose." said Charlie, "But I have not seen how my situation has changed. I mean my plans are just as they were before. I want to marry Gina and I am going to. But I still have the same problem I had before except now I have a lot more on my plate."

"OK, that's good that you don't intend to negotiate the information. But before we continue, I want to raise some questions to you. There may be opportunity for you in this assignment Charlie, but I want to say some things first."

"Yes sir," Charlie said.

"First of all, stop calling me 'sir'. I'm Gina's uncle and father. You can call me Carlo, which I prefer, or if that bothers you, call me Mr. Rizzo. But let's drop the 'sir'', OK?"

"OK. I might call you Mr. Rizzo once in a while, but I will try to call you Carlo."

"Good, now listen. You and I come from different 'Americas'. Over there in Shoreville you live in a nice, quiet town that is like the ones in the Civics books that kids read in school and you see in the movies and on TV. You live in the Great American Democracy, at least the way it is sold to the public. I was raised in the American Plutocracy. In my world it was money that counted and it really didn't matter too much how you got it. I told you a bit about my past when an engineer was taking part of my pay for no reason other than I was, in his view, an 'illiterate guinea'. Whatever I got as a young man I *fought* for. Whatever you got, you *worked* for. Oh I worked, too, and I worked damned hard. But besides working, I had to fight. Many of those who came over here with me did nothing but work while the fat cats exploited them. They *hoped* for the next generation. They *worked* for the next generation. Some of them were lucky enough to get their kids through high school and college. Some weren't. I decided that I would get my share immediately. It's ironic I suppose that two different societies can exist so close to one another and yet be so different. I don't remember much from my native Sicily. But I do remember being hungry. I remember the American soldiers, chocolate bars and getting cigarettes to trade for food. I remember that I didn't have shoes. I remember the trip over here and the hardship. We had twenty-five dollars when we arrived. I couldn't say a word of English. The Church helped us get settled. We also got help from the 'Black Hand'. Of course, their help was always tied to something. They were the same people who exploited us in Sicily and they did the same thing here. I worked for them when I was just a little kid. I used to run numbers for them to pick up some extra money for the family. My father never knew it, but my mother did. I would give her my money to buy extra food. I'm willing to bet that kind of thing would have been unusual for you. You were out riding a bike, maybe even stealing some fruit from some small orchard, and I was running numbers at the same age. Your father had something we didn't have Charlie; he had *hope*. He believed that if he worked hard he would be able to educate his son, send him to college, and move ahead in life. That engineer taught me a valuable lesson. He taught me that I did not have and would not have the same hope that he had or your father had unless I took it for myself. He taught me that I could work hard and *he* would be the one who benefited. I didn't envy his hope. I just wanted some of the same for myself. Since I didn't get it, I *took* it. If I had been born into his family would I have done what he did? I don't know. That didn't matter to me. What mattered was that he was taking what was mine so I took it back. And I helped out my friends in the bargain. Are you with me, Charlie?"

"Yes, I think so. It's a different world for me."

"That's my point, Charlie. It *is* a different world. I wouldn't even expect you to understand my world. But I am willing to bet that your Irish ancestor would. He knew hunger. He knew rejection and discrimination. He knew violence."

"Now let's look at Phillip Shaw." Carlo continued, "He never knew any of that. I don't begrudge him his luck – and it was luck. He just happened to be born into the right family. He never knew hunger. He never knew what it was like to not know if you would have dinner the next evening. He was never blacklisted from a job. He takes what he wants as a birthright. I just did the same. The fact that we were born into different circumstances is just a matter of luck. But we both have the right to the so-called pursuit of happiness. We have the right to the fruits of our labor and if someone tries to use his birthright to take away ours, we have the right and the obligation to fight back. I fought back and I prospered."

Carlo went on, "But now, Charlie, simply because you have fallen in love you have been thrown into *my* world. You will suffer because you fell in love with the 'wrong person'. I know you have thought about that and you have made your decision with regard to Gina. The question is, are you ready to enter the 'other world' that awaits you? I know that you are emotionally committed to Gina. I know that you love her and I know that you will stop at nothing to be with her. My question is do you know what that means? Because, as far as I can see, it means you will be thrown into my world, like it or not. Do you really want to be in my world, Charlie?"

"I've already made that commitment, Carlo. I love Gina. There is nothing I would not do in this world to be with her for the rest of my life."

"I believe you, Charlie. I see it in my daughter's eyes. I see it in her face. You love each other and you would walk through fire, both of you, to be together. But you don't know how, am I right?"

"Yes, you are right. I had been thinking everything through when this new assignment fell into my lap. I still had not figured out what I was going to do when this whole new situation came up."

"Well, how does it change things, Charlie?"

"It doesn't, that's part of my problem."

"Well, maybe the new circumstances provide you with the opportunity to solve your problem."

"I'm not sure I understand…"

"Let me give you some more background, Charlie. Over the past 40 years I have been deliberately moving my operations into legitimate business areas. You know how I am perceived publicly. But there are things you don't know. Unlike a lot of my colleagues, I never got involved in some of the nastier parts of our business. I have always believed that honorable men did honorable things. I never saw anything honorable in prostitution. I never saw anything honorable in drugs. I stayed out of those businesses. I was involved in money lending, gambling, and what the sociologists call 'victimless' crime. I have been under a lot of pressure from my colleagues and the guys who work for me to expand into those other areas. When I started getting the pressure, I figured it was time for me to start legitimizing a lot of my money. The younger guys in my business want to get into drugs. It's profitable. It's quick and easy money. My guys running numbers always come back to tell me how the drug guys are doing and how we are missing opportunity. My colleagues in other parts of the country want me to protect Philly for us instead of letting others move in. I know enough about this business to know that sooner or later someone will make a move on me. There's too much money involved. The only reason no one has moved on me yet is because I am still very useful to a lot of people. My financial and political connections are good. But sooner or later I am going to have to relinquish my control over what have been my main lines of business over the years. Who's going to take a nickel bet on a number when he can sell ten dollars worth of dope? What bookie is going to take a ten dollar bet on a football game when he can sell a kilo of heroin? There's just too damned much at stake. Once I lose the loyalty of my people, I will be tossed out like a burned out candle. However, if I make the move before someone else does, I will be OK. I will have to let someone in my organization assume the reins of power and then I can bow out. I'm ready to do that now if I have to. I'm only hanging on because some of my friends still need me. But if I dropped everything now, I'd have no financial problems and I would get rid of a lot of other problems. Now, let's get back to you. What do you think Phillip Shaw will do after the IPO?"

"Well, like you said, maybe he will get into politics."

"No, I mean as regards *you*."

"I don't know, I hadn't really thought about it."

"I can tell you and you let me know if you think I am wrong. Phillip Shaw will thank you for a job well done once a few billion dollars have gone into his bank account. He will shake your hand, maybe even pour you a shot of expensive scotch and then move on."

"Yeah, I guess that's about it," said Charlie.

"Right, and you will still be at Shaw Corporation, right? And under new ownership, right?"

"Yes to both."

"And who do you figure those new owners will be?"

"Well, most probably a bunch of banks, hedge funds, and pension funds in today's economy."

"Right, Charlie, and will they continue to have contracts with the Defense Department?"

"Of course."

"And will Shaw senior managers and employees involved in sensitive projects still have to have security clearances?"

"Most certainly."

"And even if you survive in your current position, will you get a positive security clearance if you are engaged or married to Gina?"

"No."

"And if you have to leave the Shaw Corporation will you find another high level job somewhere else?"

"No."

"So, Charlie, as you yourself said at the outset. Nothing has really changed for you, right?"

"Correct."

"So, Charlie, what if we decided to help each other?"

"I don't think I understand, Carlo."

"Oh, I forgot, Machiavelli was an Italian!" Carlo laughed.

"Simple, Charlie. I have to get out of my current job and you have to get out of yours."

"Ahhh, Carlo, I think I understand where you are going, but that is very unfamiliar territory for me."

"I'm not so sure you really do understand, my Irish son-in-law-to-be, but you have the counsel of a wise old man to guide you. But think about one thing before you say another word. You might also wind up getting Fred Perkins' job and maybe even have a crack at becoming CEO when the company changes hands. The new owners will need you and, at least in my view, you have what it takes. The problem is Gina."

Gina, bored until now by the business conversation, suddenly looked apprehensive.

Charlie did not let her down. "No, Carlo, Gina is definitely *not* a problem. I love her and she loves me. I won't give that up, not now, not ever."

"It seems to me then, that your decision has been made and your path chosen. But before you say 'go' I want you to think for a week about what I am about to propose. I don't want an answer now. You think it all through very carefully. I admire you for your courage, Charlie. Listen carefully to what I am about to tell you." Carlo Rizzo explained his plan to Charlie.

When he finished Charlie looked perplexed. Carlo asked, "What is it Charlie. I'm sure you understood what I was saying. Is it the ethics that bother you?"

"Yeah, I think that is at least part of it, maybe it's the whole issue."

"I understand, Charlie, believe me I do. Even in my business, we have a sense of ethics. We call it 'honor' but fundamentally it is a question of ethics. Let me ask you just one thing. Just how 'ethical' is Phillip Shaw's attitude? Has he asked his senior management if they would like to buy out the company? Has he told the employees that their jobs might be at stake if he goes public?"

"No to both, Carlo."

"OK, Charlie, I want you to think about this conversation. Take a week and get back to me. I want Gina and you isolated from my kind of business and I want to see both of you happy. My game is one that is destined to end, Charlie. I saw that years ago and many of my friends did not. We are all a part of history. States are setting up lotteries. Casinos are popping up everywhere. There is even gambling on the Internet. I know one investment banker who has a one-hundred-thousand dollars a year cocaine habit. That's just one guy who is dumping a hundred grand of after-tax cash flow Charlie! That's a far cry from my weekly football or basketball bets from the same guy. And there are a lot more out there like him. Don't you think my bookies would rather sell those guys their 'fix' than to take a lousy hundred dollar bet on a ball game? And what about the 'ethics' of that banker? Do you think he is serving his clients properly with a head full of coke?"

Charlie looked at Gina. She had tears welling up in her eyes. She knew how difficult this would be for Charlie and she knew how much he must love her to even consider her uncle's proposition. Charlie smiled at her and she smiled weakly back.

"I want you kids to talk this over. It's your life. I see the love you have for each other and it makes me happy. But life has a way of playing with us and hurting us later. I wish I could do as I always did and just decide for Gina. But this is too serious. It's her life and her happiness that are at stake. Only she can decide that. And you, Charlie, only you can decide what you want from this life. I'm here to help the only way I can. Think about it! Now, let's eat some lunch!"

Paola had surpassed her last endeavor for Charlie and Gina with a filet of sole Florentine that was exquisitely light and absolutely delicious. Over lunch Charlie told Carlo about his findings so far and the loss of margin and competitiveness of the operating divisions. Carlo listened attentively.

When they finished lunch they retired to the living room for espresso and sambuca. Gina told her uncle about her recent activities, her tutoring at the school and the planned art show for Emily. Charlie was quiet and immersed in his own thoughts about what Carlo had said. He was wondering if he could really do what Carlo had proposed and he knew that it was really his only option. After a second round of espresso and liqueur Carlo said, "I think you kids have a lot to talk about. Why don't you come back for lunch next Sunday after you have had time to think about all we have discussed today?"

Gina looked relieved and Charlie could hardly wait to talk to her about the things Carlo had said.

"Thank you, Carlo. It was a marvelous lunch and you have been most helpful. I truly appreciate your time and your interest in our future. I will discuss all this with Gina and think things through very carefully. I will have an answer for you next week. Thanks," Charlie said.

Carlo gave Charlie a warm embrace and then turned to kiss Gina goodbye. "Until next week my beautiful child, never forget how much I love you."

"Thank you, Uncle Carlo. I love you too, and I want you to know that I am truly happy."

Charlie and Gina took their leave and Charlie grabbed his disguise as they headed for the kitchen. "So long, Frankie." Gina said, "Give my love to the missus and the children."

"Thank you, Miss Gina," Frankie replied as he opened the driver side door for her.

They left the house through the battery of agent/photographers and drove back to Gina's apartment.

Once in the apartment Charlie said, "Whew, Gina your uncle really messed with my head. He's right of course that getting this assignment changed nothing as regards our future. No matter what Phillip Shaw does or does not do, I will be out of a job once our relationship becomes known. In fact, I could be out even faster if the new owners bring in their own management team. And as for walking away from our relationship, that is not on the table. Definitely not!"

Gina had tears in her eyes and said, "Charlie, I know this has to be difficult for you. You are a man of high principles and ethics. You will have to betray some of those and it will be because of our relationship. Will you be able to live with that five years from now?"

"Look, Gina, until now I had not thought through the question the way I should. I have to admit that my high principles, as you call them, were largely a function of my own complacency. I didn't have to question anything because I was really going nowhere with my emotional life. I know it's a cliché, but you can't make an omelet without breaking some eggs. I have decided to take my own life into my hands and every major decision requires that we evaluate our principles and ethics. I have never taken a thing that did not belong to me and as I think about it that's probably because I never really *had* to. I had never come to a crossroads where that kind of choice presented itself. Even your uncle started out taking no more than was due him. Someone was taking what actually belonged to *him*. He simply took it back and used the only means available to him. It's nice and it's comfortable to see the world in black and white terms, but that is not the real world. Is it more evil to overcharge on a government contract than it is to fix a football game? I don't think there is an answer to that, at least not in terms of ethics. Is there anything evil about my loving you and wanting you for my wife? I think there is something evil about not being able to live my love for you because of an accident of birth. I am the same guy I was before I met you. I have the same principles I had before we met. But if those principles get in the way of my happiness, then what purpose have they served? I'm sure I can live with whatever I have to do to be happy with you. I will never look back. I'm sure of it."

Gina was now crying. "I love you so much, Charlie, and I know what you are going through. You have all my trust and my love and your happiness means more to me than even my own. I will support you no matter what you decide."

"The decision is already made, Gina."

Gina kissed him passionately. She had nothing more to say. Charlie had made his choice and she would support it for the rest of her life. Charlie returned her kiss with equal passion and they made their way to the bedroom where they made love and then fell asleep in each other's arms.

* * * * *

That same Sunday, Sharon Gallagher was on the phone with the woman who had seen Charlie and Gina in Philly. "Sharon, I could swear I saw Charlie Mullins entering a South Philly Italian restaurant with a woman."

"Describe the woman, Ethel, what did she look like?"

"Well, she looked like she had a lot of money, that's for sure. You don't buy the stuff she was wearing in a department store basement. And the shoes and the purse, holy cow!"

"Did she have shoulder-length wavy black hair?"

"Yeah, and she was attractive enough. I mean she looked like she had class, know what I mean?"

"It's the same girl that others have seen him with. I'm certain. Was he holding her hand or kissing her?"

"No, he was just holding the taxi door. I'm not even sure it was Charlie. The guy had on a blazer and a shirt with no collar. That's not Charlie Mullins' style. You know, he is always so preppie looking."

"Oh, it was Charlie all right. Maybe his girl friend has changed the way he dresses nowadays, but the description of her matches everything everyone has told me so far. Yeah, it was Charlie. Listen, thanks Ethel. I don't want to pry into Charlie's life," Sharon lied, "but I don't know what he finds wrong with hometown girls. I just wonder if he is not making another mistake like he made with Mary Jo."

"Well that was some time ago, Sharon. He's hardly on the rebound now."

"Who knows, Ethel? Who knows? You know men. A nice figure and a pretty face, and they don't look beyond. I've seen that girl and she is as pretty as everyone says she is. She probably has poor Charlie wrapped around her little finger. She's probably a gold digger. You can bet on it."

"Well, anyway I just thought I would let you know. I mean, you once did try to fix me up with Charlie before I got married. He is a really nice guy. I have to go Sharon, it was nice talking to you."

"Same here, Ethel, regards bye." Sharon rang off to call Diane Simms.

"Diane, Ethel just called me to say that she saw Charlie in South Philly. From her description of the girl with him, it was the same one."

"Sharon, don't you think we should drop this whole thing?"

"No way, Diane, the lights at Charlie's house keep going on and off like he was home and we know he is not. Why the big secret? He never talks about this girl. He has never brought her over here. There is some mystery here that I think we need to uncover."

"Jeez, Sharon, it's just a girl friend."

"My point exactly! If it's just a girl friend, why all the secrecy and subterfuge? Why does he need to give the impression that he is at home when he is not? I mean it's not like he is doing something wrong, or is he? I think we need to find out. Who is this mystery woman that she requires such elaborate efforts to hide their relationship? I think we need to start checking on Charlie again."

"I don't know Sharon…"

"Don't be such a wuss Diane, we will just check it out and see for ourselves. Come on, you know you can't resist."

"OK, Sharon, but just to see the girlfriend, OK? I don't want to get into trouble. Bob doesn't like this kind of stuff."

"Bob's not going to know, Diane. Let's just do it, OK?"

"All right, but just to see the girl, OK?"

"I'll call you later, Diane. We can work out a plan and start next week. All right?"

"I guess so. Talk to you tomorrow, all right?"

"Good, bye Diane. See you tomorrow." Sharon rang off.

XXXII

Charlie Mullins spent the next week working on his white paper. For the first time in his career he was grateful that Fred Perkins was such a sycophant. Fred did not venture from his office except to go to the toilet. He was keeping as far below the horizon as possible for as long as Phillip Shaw was out of the office. This allowed Charlie to work uninterrupted on his assignment.

He put together a series of graphs of return on investment, ROI, for each operating department. He then analyzed the graphs showing that ROI had been increasing in decreasing increments. The reason, he showed, was because investment was declining faster than revenues but both were suffering incremental reductions. If new investments were made, the ROI would decline in the short term until revenues caught up. But if the current situation were allowed to continue, revenues would eventually grow more slowly and ROI would decline. With excess cash in the till, a declining ROI would make the company even more attractive to the financial "sharks" who would want to buy the company for its cash.

He observed that the oldest division, cutting tools, had serious supply problems. The division was buying from US suppliers whose prices were no longer competitive when compared to foreign suppliers. It appeared that it would be financially attractive to begin purchasing from abroad for the high-carbon steel the division needed. This was now a commodity business and cost reduction was the single most important strategy the company could follow.

The steel shot and blast cleaning division had the same problem. Buying its shot locally was no longer a financially viable strategy. The company could either acquire a foreign supplier or outsource via purchasing contracts. This would allow the company to reduce the price of the blast cleaning service without compromising profitability.

Two other divisions, the paper industry machinery division and the food processing machinery division needed new equipment to remain competitive.

No acquisitions seemed to be necessary for either division to achieve an appropriate level of competitiveness.

Finally, the industrial chemicals division needed to upgrade its technology. The flavors and food additives business needed a better research arm and it would make sense to acquire a small research company or hire new researchers and expand current research facilities. The same was true of the industrial cleaning solvents business. The quality of product in this area was a subject of constant concern in the customer service reports that Charlie had reviewed. The cellulose capsule business needed new machinery. This was a high-volume, low-margin business that purchased raw material from the company's customers in the pulp and paper business. Higher output per revenue dollar was necessary to ensure that the company could afford to stay in this business.

Charlie put all of his findings into a draft report that he would discuss on Friday with Bill Cummins and Warren Carpenter. He would have to work with Bill to identify acquisition targets and flesh out the costs of new investments to upgrade the other divisions. He felt reasonably sure that he could employ the company's excess cash in the requisite investments while ensuring that the acquisitions and the new machinery and equipment would enhance profitability over the longer-term. Under those terms, the company would prove attractive to investors who would want to manage it as an on-going business and unattractive to anyone who wanted to buy it for its cash value.

* * * * *

While Charlie was developing his analysis of the company, Sharon Gallagher and Diane Simms were busily developing their analysis of Charlie's private life. The two met for lunch on Monday to plan the resumption of their surveillance. They decided that they would see where Charlie went after league night on Wednesday. "Diane, let's do the following. We will park near the bowling alley and see if Charlie leaves before the other guys. If he does we will follow him. He will either go home or he will not. If he goes home, we can just stop right there. But if he doesn't go home, we will follow him. OK?"

"OK, Sharon, but what if he doesn't leave before the guys? I don't want to be out for too long after Bob gets home."

"Then we'll just go home and try again on Saturday after softball practice. I don't want to be out when Bill gets home either."

"OK, that sounds good. But, what will we do if he goes to Philly? That's half-an-hour each way and we will get home late."

"No, if it looks like he is heading for Philly, we will follow him on Saturday. Bill and Bob cannot know that we are out together late at night. They might suspect that we are back on Charlie's case. We don't want that."

Charlie showed up for the regular bowling league night on Wednesday. He went first to his house to pick up his gear and change clothes. He turned off the timers so the lights would not go on while he was at the bowling alley. Alleging a backlog of work, he begged off the pizza and beer and left before the others. He didn't see Sharon and Diane parked nearby. While he drove home, they took another route to his street. When Charlie pulled into his garage, Diane Simms said, "OK, Sharon, we can go home. Charlie is in his house."

"No, Diane. We are going to wait to see if he stays in his house. Then we will see where he goes. If he heads for Philly we will come back and see if his lights are on and we will pick him up again on Saturday."

Charlie entered the house, turned on the lights and stowed his bowling gear. He then set the timers as usual and went back out to his car to drive to Philly. Sharon said, "Look Diane, he is leaving again. Let's see where he goes. I'm willing to bet he's going to go back over the bridge to go to Philly. Want to bet?"

As Charlie pulled out of his garage and closed the door with the automatic control he did not see Sharon and Diane just around the corner. He drove off calmly and Sharon followed from a safe distance. There was no need to follow closely because they only needed to know if he was going to drive back over the bridge to I-95. Charlie watched in his rear view mirror and saw a car in the distance that might be following him. He watched closely as he came to the approach to the bridge but the car continued on and he concluded that he was not being followed.

"See, Diane? He's going back toward Wilmington and I'm willing to bet he will pick up I-95 to Philly. Let's drive by his house now to see if his lights are on and then we'll go home." They drove by Charlie's house and the lights were on. "See? He's not home and the lights are on. We don't even have to hang around to see if he comes back. We know he won't. Didn't I tell you? I'm telling you, Charlie Mullins has a secret life. This is exciting."

"Do you think he might be going back to his office? Maybe he forgot something."

"Come on, Diane! Even if he was only going back to his office, why would he leave his lights on? Wake up! If you want to hang around to see if the lights go off even if he doesn't return you can do that. But I can tell you right now, he is not, read my lips, not coming back. So, if the lights go off, he has a ghost in his house or he is playing a game."

"Sharon, you think Charlie might be a spy or something? The company does have defense contracts, you know."

"Oh Jesus, Diane, come off it. Charlie's not a spy! He's going to that girl's place. For heaven's sake, Diane, wake up! Spy! How ridiculous. That's not Charlie Mullins. He doesn't need money and he's not the type. I'm telling you it is the girl. From what everybody said, she dresses well so she is probably some kind of professional – maybe an attorney or something like that. She's certainly got some money so she probably has her own apartment. Maybe she's divorced. Or maybe she is just a single career woman. But Charlie is living with her, of that much I am sure. I want to find out who she is."

They drove by Charlie's place on the way home and as Sharon had predicted, the lights were on as if Charlie was still at home. "Didn't I tell you, Diane? Now if you doubt my word, just hang around until the lights go off. Charlie won't be home and Casper the Friendly Ghost will turn off his lights."

"I'll take your word for it, Sharon, now let's get home before our husbands arrive and wonder what the hell we are doing."

"Right," said Sharon, "and Saturday we will follow Charlie if he leaves town. Make an excuse to Bob because we might have to drive to Philly and be out for most of the afternoon." Sharon pulled up to the curb in front of Diane's house. Bob Simms had not returned home and was probably still having beer and pizza at the bowling alley. Diane took a deep breath and said, "OK, Sharon, see ya. I'll tell Bob we are going to go shopping in Wilmington on Saturday. He won't suspect Philly."

* * * * *

Charlie arrived to Gina's place, parked in the garage, and took the elevator up to her apartment. Gina was waiting with dinner and an open bottle of wine. "Hey Mullins, did you knock those pins all over the place?"

"Oh yeah, I did OK. How was your day?"

"Same old, I worked with the kids at school and called Emily to see how her painting was coming along."

"And...?"

"And she is progressing. In about a month or two she should be ready for a show. How's your report coming along?"

"I've got a draft together. I'll revise it tomorrow and Friday and then present it to Bill Cummins and Warren Carpenter Friday evening. It looks pretty good and should be just what Phillip needs to justify an aggressive investment strategy. By the way, I guess I must be getting paranoid. I thought I was being followed out of Shoreville but the car behind me kept going after I turned off for the bridge."

"Just because you're paranoid doesn't mean someone is not really following you, Charlie," Gina laughed.

"I've heard that one before, but yeah, you might be right. But the car kept on going straight when I turned off toward the bridge. Besides, the car was pretty far behind me so maybe it was nothing. It was too dark to recognize the car."

"Well, just don't forget what I told you about those women Charlie. They'll be back so just be ready."

Charlie and Gina watched the evening news and a movie before Charlie said, "I'm bushed, Gina. You want to go to bed?"

"Only if you are wearing your silk boxers, tiger!"

"I am – anything else you need to know?"

"That's it – let's go!"

* * * * *

On the way to work Thursday morning Charlie stopped by the Ritz-Carlton hotel and reserved a small conference room for Friday evening. He spent Thursday and Friday revising his draft report. The Executive Committee had advised that Phillip Shaw's recovery was progressing satisfactorily and he could be expected to return to work within two to three weeks. Friday afternoon, Charlie left the office a little earlier and went to the Ritz-Carlton where he paid cash for the rented conference room. He called Bill Cummins and Warren Carpenter from a pay phone in the lobby to tell them the name of the meeting room. At five-thirty both Cummins and Carpenter arrived and went directly to the meeting room. Charlie had ordered a pot of coffee and some soft drinks. He had two copies of his draft report for the group to discuss. "Gentlemen, good afternoon, I've got copies of my draft report for us to review and there are soft drinks on the credenza together with a pot of coffee. Help yourself."

Warren Carpenter grabbed a diet soft drink while Bill Cummins and Charlie poured themselves some coffee. They sat down to the table and Charlie began. "The draft report shows clearly that even if the company was not going to go public, Phillip would probably have to pursue an aggressive investment strategy. The ROI figures are misleading because depreciation has reduced the value of the company's investments while revenue is declining more slowly. The result in the short term is a rising ROI but it is increasing in ever smaller increments. I've got a summary division by division where I look at what is causing problems and I've made some recommendations as to investment strategies for each division. If Phillip agrees on the strategies we can start looking for acquisition targets. It will take a while because we will have to review any companies we plan to acquire. I have also recommended that we seek out some off-shore suppliers for certain commodity inputs. We can't continue to rely on US-based suppliers that are losing their competitive edge while our competitors are buying abroad. That's going to hurt some of our US suppliers and some might even see it as a kiss of death. That could be a sensitive issue for some communities. Shaw would be seen as the executioner of smaller companies. On the other hand we are simply following a trend in our industry.

Warren Carpenter was the first to address Charlie's comments, "I'm sure Phillip will be sensitive to any community issues that arise as a result of his strategy."

"Yeah, especially if he has political ambitions," Charlie thought to himself.

Carpenter continued, "We might want to think about changing suppliers early in the game. It will give us time to evaluate the reactions to and results of the changes. I'm certain the market will react favorably to the strategy, but we would like to avoid pushing any companies into bankruptcy. Things are bad enough with all the layoffs occurring in other industries, we don't want to seem to be adding to the misery."

Charlie had to stifle a wry smile. Bill Cummins simply nodded his head in agreement. It was clear to Charlie that Warren Carpenter was fully aware of Phil Shaw's post-management political ambitions and was protecting his client from a reputation as a hard-nosed bastard. In fact, he was pretty sure that Carpenter was the architect of a post-CEO electoral strategy to project Phillip into national politics.

Bill Cummins said that he would verify the figures and sign off on them. Warren could then take the draft to Phil Shaw so he could see where the report was headed. He said he felt sure that Shaw would like the approach and the supporting documentation. Cummins said, "Warren, I will check these numbers against our audit figures and have a preliminary opinion for you by Wednesday. Is that OK?"

"Wednesday is fine, Bill. We can meet again next Friday when I will have any suggestions Phil wishes to make to the draft report and Charlie can put the final draft together. That will put us close to Phil's expected date of return to the company. Do you have anything to add Charlie?"

"No, I don't think so. I think the challenge to the company is clear and the nucleus of a growth strategy is there. What about you, Bill?"

"I'm fine. You've done a fine job Charlie. I'm willing to bet that most of the company's management has not looked at the figures the way you did. You might make a fine CEO of the new company!"

"Thanks, but no thanks, Bill. I'm not ready for those kinds of games yet."

Warren Carpenter laughed, "I'm not so sure about that Charlie, but why get ahead of ourselves here? I suspect that Phil will love this draft report."

"Well, we will soon know." Charlie said, "Now I think we should all leave separately just in case somebody in the lobby should recognize any of us and wonder why we are together."

"Charlie, if I didn't know better I would think you had done a stint in the CIA," Warren Carpenter laughed.

"Nah, Warren, just careful, that's all. We financial types not only relish secrecy, we are also detail-oriented."

"Whatever," Carpenter replied, "in any case, shall we meet next Friday at Bill's office or should we meet again here?"

"After hours at my office is fine," Bill Cummins said, "maybe we should meet around 6, is that all right?"

They all agreed. Warren Carpenter left first. Fifteen minutes later Bill Cummins left and Charlie locked up the conference room checking for any loose papers or notes that anyone might have forgotten. He took the key to the front desk and thanked the receptionist. He paid for the refreshments consumed and left.

* * * * *

While Carpenter, Cummins, and Charlie were working out their strategy Sharon Gallagher was doing the same with Diane Simms. "Sharon, can we use your car tomorrow or do we use mine?"

"We'll use mine. I'll tell Bill that we plan to go shopping in Wilmington and you suggest to Bob that he pick Bill up for softball practice."

"Will Bill agree to that?" Diane whined.

"Bill? Hell yes! He does what I tell him to do," Sharon laughed. "You just get Bob to pick him up!"

"Don't pull too hard on that leash, Sharon. You never know...."

"Don't worry, I can handle Bill Gallagher. As long as I leave lunch ready he could care less about the car. If he doesn't have to cook for the kids, he's perfectly satisfied."

"OK, then how do you want to work this?"

"We should drive by the softball field when the guys are about ready to break up. Charlie will most probably drop his gear off at his house. We just have to know if he will hang around for the beer and pizza. Once we see him leave, we know where he will have to go. We can take our time getting to his place. He'll probably wash his uniform and shower before leaving so I figure we have a good hour to get in place. Bill and Bob will be eating pizza and drinking beer so we don't risk being seen by our husbands. We'll just lay low until we see Charlie start to leave. We can then hustle down to the turnoff to the bridge and pick him up there. I'm willing to bet he has become complacent and won't be expecting to be followed."

"OK, Sharon. I'll be ready around 10 am. Just give me a call when you are leaving the house."

* * * * *

Charlie let himself into Gina's apartment. He could hear her moving around in the kitchen, "Hey is there a beautiful Italian girl here that might just be waiting for a handsome Irishman?"

"She was here but got tired of waiting, will I do?" Gina replied.

"Damn! Why are you so quick with the answers? Staying ahead of you is not easy!"

"Oh my God, a macho type! What makes you think you have to stay *ahead* of me?"

"See what I mean? I give up! I don't want to stay ahead of you sweets. I would be content just to be able to keep up with you."

"Oh, I think you hold your own pretty well. Now where's that handsome Irishman you were talking about?"

"Oh shit," Charlie said in exasperation, "what's for dinner?"

"Today's Friday, right?"

"Yeah, what's that got to do with dinner?"

"Well you asked what's for dinner. What does any self-respecting Bryn Mawr graduate make for dinner on a Friday?"

"I don't know; what?"

"Reservations, darling, reservations."

Charlie laughed, "OK, beautiful, we'll go out."

"I knew you would understand," Gina chuckled, "now get out of that buttoned down outfit. Get yourself into a turtleneck and a blazer."

"Gina, I don't have any turtlenecks."

"Now you do, I went shopping today. Check out the bedroom. The packages are on the bed. I also bought some very interesting lingerie but you will only see that later."

Charlie found the packages on the bed. Two new sport jackets were also hanging on the closet door. He walked toward the kitchen where Gina met him and kissed him. "You like?"

"The kiss or the clothes?"

"You'd better say 'both' Mr. Smartass or you won't get to see that lingerie I mentioned."

"Oh no, not the lingerie deprivation trick," Charlie exclaimed.

Gina laughed, "Get dressed Mullins. Wear whatever you want as long as it's something I bought!"

Charlie picked out an off-white turtleneck shirt to wear with a black blazer and grey slacks. He quickly showered and splashed on some Armani cologne. Gina slipped into a fantastic silk sheath that clung to her like skin. She would once again turn heads in a restaurant.

Gina had made reservations in a small family-owned French restaurant in the neighborhood. The food was fantastic.

When they got back to the apartment, Gina put some slow music on the CD player and started a slow strip tease. Charlie watched her dumbstruck. She had barely got out of her dress before Charlie was practically salivating. She began a slow bump and grind that drove Charlie crazy. All he could say was, "Gina, my God, Gina!" She danced right up to him as he sat on the sofa. He tried to stand up and she pushed him back, "Take it easy Mullins, this is meant to last."

Charlie could hardly contain himself. She had indeed bought some very sexy lingerie and Charlie was beside himself with excitement. When she reached to remove her bra, he could stand it no longer and he stood up and grabbed her. He picked her up and carried her to the bedroom. He tore off his clothes and pounced on her like an animal in heat. Gina corresponded to his passion and they made love. When they were both spent, Charlie said, "Gina, you have to be careful with that kind of stuff. You could drive a man crazy."

"That's what I meant to do, Mullins. How do you feel now?"

"Whew! I think I am exhausted!"

"Really? I don't think so!" She leaned over and kissed him hard. He began to respond immediately and they made love again. They slept as always, in each other's arms. Charlie had never known such happiness.

XXXIII

Saturday morning Charlie woke up early. Gina was still asleep and stark naked. The transparent baby doll she had planned to wear to bed the night before lay on the floor, unused. Charlie took a moment to appreciate her beautiful body and then put on his shorts and went to the kitchen to prepare some coffee. He had softball practice in Shoreville and he didn't want to miss it. The last thing he needed now was people asking why he was not around.

He came back to the bedroom with two steaming mugs of coffee and Gina woke up slowly, stretched like a cat, and said, "Sleep well last night, Mullins? I sure did. I dreamt a handsome Irishman made love to me several times."

"Ah, so that's what ye dreamed is it?" Charlie said with a mock-Irish brogue, "and where might your handsome Irishman be at this moment lassie?"

"He's getting ready to go off to play with his balls," Gina laughed heartily.

"It's too early for this," Charlie laughed, "here, have some coffee."

Gina smiled and took the steaming mug in both hands. It was warm and the coffee smelled delicious.

"Baby, I'm going off to softball practice. I should be back in a few hours." He bent over to kiss Gina.

"Don't be surprised if I am still in this bed when you get back. I'm turning into a wanton woman with you Mullins and I just want to lie here and think about what happened last night."

"Feel free to repeat the show any time you are in the mood," Charlie said.

"Off with you Mullins before I pull you back into this bed!"

Charlie kissed Gina again and left the apartment. He stopped at the bakery downstairs and purchased a Danish to eat on the way to Shoreville. Arriving to his home he followed the routine that had become almost automatic over the past months. He turned off the timers, changed into his softball uniform and grabbed his gear. He drove to the softball field where some of his buddies were already tossing a ball back and forth. "Hey guys."

"Mornin' Charlie, how's it goin'?"

They went through their drills, batting practice, and engaged in the usual infield chatter that made them all feel like kids again. This was their bonding moment that they had shared from childhood and was more important and more fun than the softball game itself. They burned off the frustrations of the previous week, told stale dirty jokes, spit, scratched their crotch, and behaved like young boys for a few hours.

While the softball team was going through its male bonding rituals, Diane Simms and Sharon Gallagher drove casually by. Sharon saw Charlie and said, "There he is, Diane. Now, all we have to do is wait for practice to end. If he goes off for pizza and beer with the guys, we have plenty of time but if he goes straight home we will probably have no more than an hour to position ourselves to follow him. It looks like they are about ready to finish practice so let's go around the block and come back to park where we can't be seen. We'll watch to see when Charlie leaves. If he doesn't head for Tony D'Amato's place then he won't be joining the guys for pizza."

Sharon drove around the block and pulled up short of the softball field where she and Diane could observe the cars parked nearby. They could see Charlie's car without being seen. After about 20 minutes some of the men started moving toward their cars. Bill Gallagher and Bob Simms got into Bob's car and they saw Charlie heading for his. Charlie had begged off the pizza saying that he had a lot of paperwork to catch up on and drove off toward his home. "There he goes, Diane," Sharon said, "he's going home. Let's drive around to his place and see where he goes after changing."

Charlie pulled up to his garage and did not see Sharon Gallagher's car pulling up around the corner. He pulled into the garage, closed the door with the automatic control, and went into the house to wash his uniform, shower, and change. Almost an hour later he came back out of the house, pulled his car out of the garage and started back to Philly. Sharon pulled out from her parking spot and took a different route to the entrance to the bridge to Wilmington. She was sure she would not lose Charlie because she was certain that he was headed to Philadelphia. She had been in position for only a few minutes when Diane Simms saw Charlie's car approaching the overpass that would give him access to the bridge. "Eureka," exclaimed Sharon, "we've got him now."

She pulled out behind Charlie's car as he approached the bridge. Charlie thought he saw a familiar car in his rear view mirror. He decided that before heading for Philly he would drive into downtown Wilmington. The area around the Shaw Corporation would be virtually deserted on a Saturday and if the car was following him, he would quickly know it. He drove at his usual pace and took no evasive maneuvers. When he reached the entrance to I-95 he headed for downtown Wilmington. As expected there was practically no vehicle traffic in the area around the Shaw Corporation. He saw the vehicle still following him and he recognized the car as Bill Gallagher's. *"Dammit,"* he thought, *"Gina was right. Those wackos are at it again! All right, Sharon, if you want to play, let's play."*

Charlie drove slowly around the center of Wilmington. Then he headed north toward the Pennsylvania border. He doubled back and headed back toward town again. Sharon had no choice but to continue following him. Diane Simms was starting to panic, "Sharon, he's on to us. He's just playing with us. I know it!"

"Shut up, Diane. I know he has seen us but so what? He saw us before. Let's just stay on him for a while."

"Sharon, the last time he saw us he talked to our husbands. I don't want to go through that again. Besides, he said that he would have us arrested for stalking. Let's get out of here! Come on, Sharon, let's go," Diane pleaded.

"God, Diane, you are such a wuss. If he's leading us on a wild goose chase it's proof that he is hiding something. If he has seen us he is probably off balance. Maybe his girl friend lives here in Wilmington. Let's just stay on his tail for a little more."

"Oh jeez, oh jeez," Diane whined, "I don't like this Sharon."

Charlie interrupted their conversation when he stopped at a service station and topped off his fuel tank. Sharon had to stop to wait and she knew that the chase was now over. As she started to turn around to head home she saw Charlie turning to follow her. Diane was now out of control. "Oh my God, Sharon, he's going to follow *us* now. This is not good, no indeed, it is not good."

"I'll show Charlie Mullins a thing or two," Sharon said as she pressed down on the accelerator. Charlie kept pace but at a reasonable distance. He let Sharon get well ahead. As Sharon headed out of Wilmington and back toward the bridge to Shoreville she accelerated through a red light. It was her bad luck that a Delaware state police officer saw her drive through the stop light and pulled her over. Charlie broke out laughing and turned off for the entrance to I-95. He could see the trooper in his rear view mirror as he asked for Sharon's driver's license and vehicle registration. *"Serves you right, bitch,"* Charlie thought, *"Bill will love to pay the ticket."*

When he arrived to Gina's apartment he was still chuckling in amusement at Sharon's distress and the traffic ticket. Gina was up and around, contrary to her forecast that she would still be in bed when he arrived. "Did you stay for pizza and beer, sweets?"

"No, Gina, I had to shake off some surveillance. The wackos are back!"

"Didn't I tell you?"

Charlie told her the story about how Sharon had to follow him into downtown Wilmington where her surveillance was obvious and how he turned the tables on her by suddenly starting to follow her. Gina laughed out loud when Charlie told her about the traffic violation. "I'll bet she is really pissed now, Charlie. Her little escapade is going to cost her a good bit of change. If she doesn't tell her husband, she'll have to eat a lot more beans and franks for a while to pay off the ticket from her grocery money."

Charlie laughed. "I guess it really blew her mind to see me turn around and start to follow her. I could see that it was Sharon and Diane Simms. Diane must have been in a nervous fit."

"Maybe you have bought yourself some time now Charlie. Sharon will certainly be a lot more careful and she is probably peeing her pants right now wondering if you will talk this over with her husband."

"You know, I think I'm going to let this incident slide, Gina. Sharon won't know what the hell to do. She'll be expecting me to tell Bill and raise a fuss. I'll just sit tight this time. Diane will be a wreck in a couple of days. Changing the subject, we are going to your uncle's place tomorrow, right?"

"Yes. He called to confirm while you were out. He sounded happy. He likes you and he is glad to have us come around to visit him. Do you know what you are going to tell him? We haven't exactly talked about anything, you know."

"That's because there is nothing to talk about, beautiful. I made my decision a long time ago. *You* are my life and my happiness. End of story. Telling Carlo that I accept his advice and counsel is a mere formality."

"Oh Charlie, I am so happy. I just hope we will always be this way."

"We will, baby, we will. Now I am going to work a bit on my report. Later we can go out for lunch if you want."

Charlie sat down to the dining room table to polish up his draft report while Gina set about cleaning the apartment. She put some easy listening music on the CD player and when she finished fussing around the apartment she sat down to read a book. Charlie was immersed in his report. They went out for a light lunch and returned so Charlie could continue to work on his report. Gina rented a DVD from the local Blockbuster and watched a movie while Charlie worked. Later she went to the kitchen to prepare dinner. They ate stuffed manicotti and shared half a bottle of wine. Charlie put his work aside and they took a cab to the *trattoria* just to get out of the house for a while. When they arrived home Charlie said, "Gina, I think we should go to your uncle's place a little earlier than usual. There might be a lot to talk about."

"No problem, Charlie. He wakes up early. I'll call and tell him to expect us about, what, an hour earlier?"

"That's fine."

They watched the late news on TV and then went to bed. Charlie was still amused at Sharon Gallagher's discomfort and the traffic ticket.

* * * * *

The next morning Charlie fixed coffee and picked up the newspaper from the front door. He and Gina sat in bed, read the paper, and enjoyed their coffee. Breakfast would be light in anticipation of the feast that Carlo usually put out for lunch.

They dressed for lunch and Charlie grabbed his baseball cap and dark glasses from the closet. They left for Carlo's house at about 12:30, passed through the phalanx of "suits" who took the regular pictures of the car, and drove around to the rear entrance where Frankie stood at his regular post by the kitchen door. Carlo received them in the living room and gave Gina a tender hug and Charlie a bear-like embrace. "Ah, it's so good to have you both over here. Have some wine and antipasto while we talk. How did each of you pass the week?"

"Oh, it was just fine, Uncle Carlo," Gina began, "I love being domestic. I used to go out so often and now I just love to sit around the house with Charlie."

"And you, Irish? How was your week?"

"Uncle Carlo! You promised," Gina protested.

"Ah, I'm just kidding. You mind, Charlie?"

"No, I've been called a lot worse in my time," he laughed.

"See, Gina, he's not upset."

"OK, OK, you guys win. It must be a kind of guy thing, this nickname stuff. Have it your way."

Charlie said, "Well Carlo, I spent most of the week working on my draft report. I've brought a copy for you to look at. I don't think it comes as a surprise that I agree with our conversation of last week and I will need your help and counsel. I can't afford to make a mistake."

"Take my word for it, Charlie, I am used to not being able to make a mistake," Carlo laughed, "let me see your report while we have some antipasto."

Charlie handed Carlo a copy of his draft report. Carlo read attentively while they all munched on the antipasto. "This looks good Charlie. I have no way of knowing how accurate the figures are, but the report is tight and seems logical in view of the numbers you present. I think I can help you. Let's talk."

Carlo Rizzo shared his thoughts with Charlie and offered some suggestions as to how to devise a strategy for accomplishing the objectives of the assignment. The strategy was a simple one and Charlie thought it might be deceptively so. But it seemed airtight from what Charlie could discern. He was certain he could make it work. "You understand, Charlie?" Carlo asked.

"Yes, actually it seems quite simple. I wonder if I am not missing something."

"I don't think so. Most of these kinds of things are extremely simple. Bankers, who are none too smart in my book, do it all the time. Some of them do it with a head full of cocaine, so it can't be that tough. But think it through carefully, Charlie. You have to be confident and you will need nerves of steel in the beginning – at least until you get comfortable with the plan. I suggest we talk it over as you move forward and we adjust as you go. I'll get started immediately on my side so we have appropriate lead time."

"Agreed," said Charlie, "I understand the basic mechanics of the plan and it looks seamless to me. But I will need your help if there are any glitches and I'm sure there will be some. When the whole thing has been done, Gina and I will announce our engagement."

"Wow," said Gina, "it looks like I have finally figured into the calculations."

Charlie kissed her, "You *are* the calculations baby. This is all designed so we can be together."

Carlo said, "OK, let's have lunch. Paola has prepared a linguine with red clam sauce that is unequaled anywhere in the world. We eat, have some good wine, and laugh at the world. How's that?"

"Sounds good to me," said Charlie. "Count me in," said Gina.

Carlo Rizzo was in an expansive mood over lunch. He talked about the future and how he had always wanted a "nice guy" for Gina. He laughed and said he hoped he would live long enough to have 300 grandchildren. Gina blushed several times as Carlo hinted that Charlie would certainly enjoy making that many babies. She interjected, "Uncle Carlo, this is my figure and my body you are talking about. I don't want 300 babies. I don't want to be one of the big Sicilian 'mamas' or one of those skinny hags dressed in black all the time. I'll settle for just one or two kids, thank you."

Carlo laughed, "Yeah, if your Irishman can keep his hands off you!"

Charlie noticed that Carlo always spoke of the future but never told any stories from the past. When they left Carlo's house he turned to Gina in the car and said, "It's interesting, Gina. Your uncle was really in a good mood but I noticed he never talks about the past or tells any stories."

Gina broke out in a loud laugh. "Charlie, my uncle could *never* talk about the past. Are you kidding me? If he wanted to discuss the past he would have to join a witness protection program! Don't forget that he is *Don Carlo Rizzo* to everybody in this town! You have to learn that Sicilians don't have memories. The only thing a memory is good for is a *vendetta*! Honestly, Charlie, sometimes you are so naïve it's actually funny."

Charlie laughed with Gina, "Yeah, sorry, I forgot. It's just that your uncle at home and with you has nothing to do with the Carlo Rizzo that people talk about."

"That's because he is not doing business, Charlie. At home he is dealing from the heart. You don't want to cross his path in business, believe me."

"Yeah, Bill Cummins told me the same thing about Phillip Shaw. He said that Phillip is a real hard-nosed son-of-a-bitch under his affable surface."

"Well, like I told you before, my uncle came up the hard way. He has his enemies and his loyal friends. But they are *business* friends. They come to the house through the front door and they are received formally. I used to have to leave the room whenever his associates came by. I learned early on that you never ask my uncle how was his day. He will always tell you it was OK. Never good, never bad. Just OK. If he told stories from his past a lot of people would be in jail and you would be surprised indeed as to who they are. I learned long ago never to see or hear anything and never to talk about things I heard at home. You also saw that he is 'old country'. You guys talked business and while you were doing so he said nothing at all to me. Women are not supposed to hear anything that is said and never to understand why things are done as they are. They know, of course, but the men pretend that they believe the women don't know and the women pretend they don't know. Everything works well that way. The world of the Sicilian is a man's world only, Charlie. And don't you even think of converting to Sicilian ways!"

"What would you do if I did, Gina?" Charlie asked laughing.

"That's easy. I would just pour boiling olive oil in your ear while you slept. How's that?"

"Oh my God, it hurts just to think about it."

"Good!" said Gina resolutely. Charlie was not sure if she was kidding.

"You want to stop by the *trattoria* for a glass of wine before we go home?" asked Charlie.

"You want an honest answer, Charlie?"

"Of course."

"Well, I would rather go home, put on some soft jazz and just cuddle on the sofa. It's been a great day and I'd like to just savor it. Is that OK?"

"It's better than my suggestion," Charlie responded.

While Charlie and Gina were sitting on the sofa listening to quiet jazz Charlie said, "Gina, I've got an idea for dealing with those wacko wives over in Shoreville. I'm going to go over there early on Wednesday. I'll mow the lawn and make myself seen around the neighborhood. I will make it a point to run into Sharon Gallagher and Diane Simms. I'm not going to mention anything. I'll just make them uncomfortable and let them think I might discuss the matter with their husbands again. In short, I'll let them think there is a different Charlie Mullins behind the one they have known over the years."

"Charlie, you're getting positively sadistic. I think you might have a hidden mean streak," she laughed.

"Maybe, but I think it is time to turn the tables. They knew I was chasing them as they left Wilmington on Saturday. Why not let them think I intend to persecute them a bit? It will certainly get them off balance."

"The hunted becomes the hunter, huh?"

"Yep"

"I like it Charlie. It might scare them, at least at the outset. They will be confused and afraid you might take the matter up with their husbands again. Good thinking."

"I'm going to tell Fred that I want to leave early on Wednesday because I have some things to do at home. He won't object because right now he is not objecting to *anything*."

Gina snuggled up against Charlie and they sat quietly listening to the music until they both were hungry. Charlie was the first to say something,

"Gina, you want to get something light down at the bakery? After that lunch I don't think I could handle a dinner, but a croissant and a cappuccino might go down well."

"Took the words right out of my mouth, Mullins! Let's take a walk and then get something light. Good idea." They left the apartment and walked for about an hour before returning to the bakery near Gina's building. They enjoyed croissants and cappuccinos and then went back to the apartment. After watching some TV, they went to bed. It had been a good day and Charlie now knew not only what he was going to do but also *how* he was going to do it.

* * * * *

On Monday Charlie told Fred Perkins he had some problems with his house and wanted to leave early on Wednesday. At Charlie's level of management telling Perkins was a mere formality but he wanted to make sure that Fred agreed and was informed. Perkins grunted his agreement in his usual manner for agreeing with anything. Charlie thanked him and went to his office to work on his assignment and clear his desk of pending work. On Wednesday he left the office at lunch time and drove to Shoreville. When he arrived to Shoreville he stopped by a local sandwich shop to purchase a take-out lunch and a soft drink He went home, took his time eating his lunch, then changed into some work clothes and went outside to mow the lawn. He took his time cutting the grass and then trimming along the sidewalk. He made sure some of his neighbors saw him and he waved to them. He checked his watch and noticed that it was time for the local school to let out and was betting that Sharon Gallagher would drive by his house after picking up her children at school. He was right. He saw Sharon's car coming down his street and he thought he saw surprise on Sharon's face when she saw him in the yard. He put on a wide smile and waved as she passed. "Hey Sharon, how are you?" he yelled. With the windows of her car closed Sharon could not hear him, but she clearly understood his greeting. Charlie laughed to himself as he saw Sharon's discomfort. She was not sure if she should wave back to Charlie and she almost lost control of the car in her confusion. *"What's the matter Sharon?"* Charlie thought, *"You look surprised. Gotcha!"*

He was certain that Sharon would call Diane Simms and they would both drive by the house again before he went off to the bowling alley. He put his yard tools in the garage, swept the grass trimmings from the sidewalk and edge of the driveway into a trash bag and went into the house for a beer.

Again he was right. Sharon was already on the phone to Diane. "My God, Diane, I drove by Charlie's house after picking up the kids and he was working in the yard. He must have left work early or something. You think something is up?"

"Jeez, Sharon, he was just working in the yard, right? I mean what's so special about that?"

"It's Wednesday, Diane. Why doesn't he do it on the weekend like everybody else?"

"Because he is not here on weekends, remember? That's why you want to follow him around."

"Well, anyway, he flashed this big smile and me and waved yelling something I couldn't hear."

"Well now, that might be a bit weird. He knows we followed him on Saturday. By all rights, he should be at least a little bit angry. In fact, he should be *very* angry. He sure was last time!"

"Let's drive by just before he should be leaving for league night. We can see if he is still at home or in the yard. You think he's up to something?"

"I don't know, Sharon. I wonder if he is going to tell our husbands about our following him on Saturday. He knows we got stopped by the police so he has some proof. I don't like this, I really don't."

"Well, it's a little late now to be worried, Diane. Let's just drive by his house. I'll pick you up in about 10 minutes. We have to try to figure out what's up."

Sharon drove by Diane's house and they headed toward Charlie's place. Charlie had pulled his car out of the garage and was washing it. He saw Sharon's car approaching and Diane was in the passenger seat. *"Just as I thought,"* he said to himself. As they drew near he flashed a large, friendly smile, and playfully pointed the hose in the direction of the car as if he meant to spray it as they passed. He laughed and then lowered the hose and waved to them.

"Oh Christ, Sharon, he's acting silly. He doesn't appear to be the least bit upset about Saturday. I think he is going to tell our husbands tonight. Oh my God! Bob will lock me in the basement. Oh, I am in deep trouble now. I don't even want to think about it!"

"Hang on, Diane. We need to have a story just in case he does tell them. Why don't we just say that he is imagining things? We saw him in Wilmington as we were driving around and he just *thought* we were following him. It's his word against ours after all. We're just going to have to tough it out. And the traffic ticket doesn't prove anything. So what if he saw us getting a ticket? That doesn't prove we were following him, does it?"

"No, I guess not, but I wonder if saying that Charlie is imagining things will work. I mean he is not one for being paranoid, you know."

"Well, suppose we just say it was probably the strain from the extra work he has been doing and his recollection of the last time we followed him. We just have to deny, Diane, just deny and keep denying. They'll believe us. I'm sure they will. Remember, you just have to say we *did* see him and he saw us. After all we were over there shopping. Our husbands knew that. It's not our fault if Charlie *thought* we were following him. Just stick to your story and deny, deny, deny. OK?"

Sharon dropped Diane off at her home and then went to her own. She had agreed with Diane that neither would be out of the house when their husbands returned from bowling and they would wait to see what Charlie had told them.

Charlie showered after his yard work and washing the car, and put his bowling gear in the trunk. He drove to the bowling alley and bowled with his team. Afterward they had their regular pizza and beer. The mood was light and some of the guys asked Charlie about Phil Shaw's return. Charlie told them that he understood that Shaw would be returning in another week or so and that it appeared that things were perfectly normal. Artie Samuels told his collection of stale and off-color jokes and the group teased Mildred about her sex life, or lack of it. When the group broke up, Charlie drove home, washed his uniform and put it in the dryer, stowed his gear and then drove off to Philly. He was certain that no one would be following him.

Bill Gallagher arrived home to find Sharon waiting for him in the living room. "Hi Bill, how was league night?"

"It was fine, Sharon. Why aren't you watching TV?"

"Just bored, I guess. Was everything all right at the bowling alley?"

"Huh, what do you mean everything all right? Of course everything was all right. It was just a regular league night."

"Was Charlie Mullins there?"

"Sharon! Of course Charlie was there. Where else would he be on league night? Bingo?"

"Did he say anything?"

"No Sharon," he replied sarcastically, "he sat in a corner and sucked his thumb! Of course he said something. You think Charlie can't talk?"

"Well, what did he say?"

"Sharon, what the hell is going on? What the hell do you care what Charlie said tonight? He just said Phil Shaw would be back in about a week or so. Is that what you wanted to know?"

"Well, of course, Bill. Everybody has been concerned about when things will get back to normal." Sharon lied.

"Well, OK, so now you know. Wanna stop the third degree now? I'm gonna shower up. Anything else you want to know? Want to hear some of Artie's jokes?"

"Heaven's no, Bill. Sorry," Sharon whined, "I was just asking if things were going to get back to normal at the company, that's all."

"Whatever," Bill said as he headed toward the bathroom to take his shower.

Bob Simms was going through the same sort of questioning at his home. Diane asked if Charlie had been to league night and if he had said anything. Bob's answers were much like Bill's. "Diane, what's this about Charlie? Of course he said something. You think he goes to league night and then sits there like a dummy? What the hell is this all about?"

"Well, sweetheart, I was just worried about the company. You know, Phil Shaw and all..."

"Oh, yeah, well Charlie said Shaw will soon be back on the job if that's what you want to know."

"Oh, thank heavens for that, Bob. I was worried. You know a heart attack and all...."

"OK, OK, Diane. Cool it. Now you know so how 'bout getting me a beer out of the fridge?"

Charlie laughed all the way back to Philly. *"I'll bet Bill and Bob are getting the third degree right now and don't have the slightest notion what's going on."* Charlie had said nothing at league night to either about being followed on Saturday. He gave the appearance of being totally relaxed and at ease with his pals. When he got to the apartment he told Gina what he had done. "You mean you let them see you, you pretended to be totally at peace with them, and said nothing at all to their husbands?" Gina laughed, "You are so terrible, Charlie. They must really be confused now. I bet neither of them sleeps tonight!"

The next morning after their husbands had left for work and the kids for school Sharon and Diane were on the phone to each other. "Diane, he didn't say a word to Bill about Saturday."

"To Bob either, Sharon, what do you think he is doing?"

"I don't know. It's completely out of character for Charlie. He usually says what is bothering him when it involves his privacy. He was even that way in school. You think maybe he is playing with us? You know, trying to shake us up?"

"Jeez, I don't know Sharon, but I agree with you that it is not like Charlie to let it pass. He was so mad last time, I really expected him to say something to Bob. And then that stuff with the garden hose as we drove past his house. He was smiling like nothing ever happened. What was that all about?"

"I think he is playing some kind of a game, Diane. He comes home early from work on a weekday, mows his lawn, makes sure everybody sees him, waves to us, goes bowling with the guys, and never says a word to our husbands about Saturday. He's mocking us, Diane. He's rubbing our noses in it, that's what he's doing. He's sending us a warning Diane, that's it. He's telling us to back off and gloating because he caught us trying to follow him. Well, two can play that game...."

"Whoa, Sharon....let's not go overboard here. Maybe Charlie is just giving us a chance to back off with grace. You know, without him having to talk to our husbands. They are his friends you know."

"Nonsense, Diane. He's telling us something. Maybe he's telling us that he is going to fight back and he was just daring us to take this whole thing to the next level."

"Sharon! I hope you don't intend to do that! Let's just drop this while we are ahead, OK? If we never follow Charlie again, I am sure he will never say anything. But if he sees us following him again...."

"Right, Diane, if he *sees* us. Suppose he doesn't know it's us? Suppose we don't drive your car or mine? Suppose we rent a car that he can't recognize? Suppose we wear wigs and sunglasses? It seems to me that Charlie Mullins is going to an awful lot of trouble to get us off his trail. There must be a reason for all this, and I am going to find out what it is! We're going to follow him next week and this time he won't recognize us."

"Are you sure you want to do this, Sharon?"

"Don't even think about backing out, Diane. You're in this as deep as I am and you're going to stick it out. Hear me?"

"OK, OK, Sharon, but I hope to God you know what you are doing!"

"Talk to you later, Diane, bye." Sharon hung up.

XXXIV

On Friday afternoon Charlie left work with his papers and drove over to Camden to the offices of Wexler & Santori. He arrived at 5:45 and the parking lot was practically empty. He entered the lobby and asked the security guard to call Bill Cummins' office. Cummins told the guard to send Charlie up and the guard used his badge to open the security door to the elevators. Charlie had barely arrived to Cummins' office when Warren Carpenter arrived to the lobby and after asking the security guard to call Cummins he, too, entered the building and took the elevator to Cummins' office.

"Gentlemen," Carpenter greeted them, "good to see you again."

"Have a seat guys." Bill Cummins gestured toward the sofa and matching chair and coffee table in the corner of his office.

Warren Carpenter began, "I showed the draft report to Phil Shaw and he was impressed and ecstatic. It fills the bill perfectly. He said he plans to return to the office a little over a week from now. He will schedule a press conference for his first day back. That gives you another week to finish the report, Charlie. Will it be ready?"

"For sure, Warren, unless Phil has recommended some changes, I just have to polish the report a bit and review the numbers. I will have it to Bill for sign off by early Wednesday and Phil will have it as soon as Bill signs. You agree, Bill?"

Warren Carpenter said, "Phil has not recommended any changes."

"In that case, I would prefer it by Tuesday, Charlie, if you can swing it. That will allow me to get it to Phil by Wednesday and he will have three weekdays plus the weekend to prepare his press conference."

"OK, Bill, Tuesday it is then."

Warren Carpenter interjected, "He has already begun working on the press conference so I am not too concerned about the time line. But if he has it by Wednesday, I am sure he will feel more comfortable."

"OK," Charlie said, "I'll have it to Bill by Tuesday. No problem. We should start looking around for the supply firms and acquisitions that we are going to recommend. I figure we can have some possible targets over the next quarter. What do you think, Bill?"

"I think that's OK. It will take us a while to vet the companies but we can have some under the microscope by then. How does Phil want to handle it?"

"As far as I know at this point," Carpenter said, "he will want to be able to say that he has identified a few targets. He will want to tease the press a bit but only after we have put together a short list and have already approached the owners. We don't want potential targets raising their prices because Shaw is on the prowl."

"How do we want to work this? Bill Cummins asked. "I can use some of my contacts to identify some targets."

Charlie said, "If you don't mind, I've got an old college buddy who works for a bank in Philly. He would be discreet and he could create the legend that he is looking around for some of the bank's customers. He has no connection to Shaw so he could pretty well inquire discreetly."

"Good idea, Charlie," Carpenter said "we want the buyer to be a secret until we have had a chance to value the company. When we sit down to talk turkey, then we can bring up Shaw's name. Everyone knows that I am Phil Shaw's attorney so the minute I open my mouth they know it is Shaw talking. Do you trust this guy?"

"Totally, Warren, we've been friends since college and I'm sure that helping us won't harm his prestige and career in the bank one bit."

"OK, Charlie." Carpenter agreed, "Talk to him and find out what the bank's fees would be to act as our scout in this deal."

"Done." Charlie said, "I'll meet him for lunch tomorrow and have an answer by early next week." The group agreed to meet again the following Friday at the Ritz-Carlton. Charlie would again rent a conference room and they would put the final touches on Phil Shaw's return and begin implementing the growth strategy for the company.

* * * * *

When Charlie arrived to Gina's apartment he kissed her and said, "Hello sweets, let me make one phone call and then we'll talk, OK?" He grabbed the phone and punched in Joey Esposito's number. "Joey? Charlie here, I'm fine thanks and you? Good. Listen Joey, are you free for a cheese steak sandwich tomorrow? I need to talk some business with you. OK, fine, I'll be at your place at about 2. See you tomorrow and thanks." Charlie rang off.

"Well hello, Mullins, how was your day?"

"It was good Gina, really good. How about you?"

"Same old, I tutored Johnny's kids and stopped by Emily's studio to see how she was doing with her painting. She'll be ready for a show soon."

"That's great Gina. I'll bet she is thrilled."

"Oh yeah, she can hardly wait and neither can I."

"Gina, you think we could visit your uncle again on Sunday? I have some things to discuss with him."

"I'm sure of it. I'll call him tomorrow morning and set it up. It sounds like things are moving now."

"They sure are. Phillip Shaw will be back on the job in just over a week from now. We might be able to wrap this whole thing up quickly. By the way, I'll have to go to softball practice tomorrow. I'll leave early."

"Gonna see the wackos, Charlie?"

"God, I hope not. I suspect my turning the tables on them might have upset their timing and their plans. At least I hope so."

* * * * *

The next morning Charlie made some coffee, served Gina in bed, and left for Shoreville. As usual he checked the house when he picked up his gear and changed into his uniform. He told his teammates that he heard that Phil Shaw would be returning within another 10 days and they were all relieved. They were in a light mood as they practiced. Again, Charlie begged off the pizza and beer after practice. He went home, set his timers, washed and dried his uniform and stowed his gear. Everything done, he went to his car and headed for I-95 to meet with Joey Esposito in Philly. He didn't pay attention to the car with two women in it that pulled out behind him on his street. The car was not a familiar one and the women were equally unfamiliar. Sharon Gallagher was a blonde and Diane Simms a brunette. Neither woman in the car resembled anyone he knew in Shoreville.

As he reached I-95 after crossing the bridge to Wilmington he saw that the car behind him appeared to be following him. He accelerated and so did the car behind. He slowed and the car did likewise. *"Damn,"* he thought, *"I wonder if those two were brazen enough to follow me again! I'll show them something this time."* Charlie pretended to ignore the chase car and continue his drive to Philly. Since he was going to Joey's place he figured he could really confuse his surveillance. *"Let them follow me. I'm going to blow their minds."*

He arrived to Joey Esposito's building and parked nearby. Sharon pulled up a distance behind Charlie and parked her car. "We've got him this time Diane. He didn't recognize us. This must be his girl friend's place. Let's wait and see if he comes out with her." They waited about 30 minutes when Charlie came out of the building with Joey and they walked toward the sandwich shop. Sharon was perplexed. "He's with a guy, for Christ's sake! Is that why he is keeping everything so secret? Do you think Charlie is gay?"

"Sharon," Diane replied, "I think you are going crazy with this stuff. Charlie is straight, for heaven's sake. It's probably just a friend of his."

"Well, I've never seen that guy before. We have to find out who he is. Let's see where they go."

They watched as Charlie and Joey walked down the street toward the sandwich shop. When they entered, Sharon and Diane got out of the car so they could see inside the shop. They crossed the street and then strolled by the shop so they could observe from the other side. They saw Charlie and Joey head for a booth.

"Sharon, let's get out of here," Diane pleaded, "God knows how long they might stay there. We just can't stand around on the street and we sure as hell can't go in the shop with these stupid wigs. Charlie will recognize us through these silly disguises."

"Cool it, Diane! We are here and we know now where Charlie goes when he comes up to Philly. Let's just hang around for a little longer."

"Oh jeez, Bob will crucify me if I get home too late. Come on, Sharon. Let's leave."

"No way, Diane, if you want to go home, get a taxi and go."

"A taxi? Get a taxi from Philly to Shoreville?! Are you crazy, Sharon? It would cost me an arm and a leg."

"Then just sit still, Diane. We can wait an hour or so. Let's see if there is some place we can go and still be able to watch this shop or at least watch Charlie's car. He's not going to spend the whole damned day in there!"

Sharon spied a coffee shop where they could sit and see both the entrance to the sandwich shop and Charlie's car just up the street near Joey's apartment. "There, look Diane, that little shop over there will give us a clear view. We can see when Charlie leaves." Sharon did not know that Charlie had observed her and Diane as they crossed the street and walked by the sandwich shop. He laughed to himself at the wigs and dark glasses they were both wearing. He decided he would raise the ante and make watching him an agonizing experience.

After he and Joey had ordered, Charlie explained his assignment at Shaw. He did not tell Joey about the IPO but he told him that Phil Shaw planned to make some investments to put the company on a growth trajectory. He explained how the company had been gradually losing competitiveness and margin and how Phil had had a chance to back away from his daily duties because of his heart attack and that viewing the company from a distance convinced him that he needed to lead it in a new direction. He swore Joey to secrecy and told him that he needed the services of a good bank to identify investment or acquisition targets without referring to Shaw Corporation. The company was prepared to hire the bank in a consulting role if the bank would agree to total confidentiality, which he presumed was normal practice anyway. "Gee Charlie, thanks for thinking of me on this deal. I'll have to talk to my boss about this, but we've done this sort of thing often and I'm sure it won't be a problem. I know the bank has been dying to develop a relationship with the Shaw Corporation. And it will be a hell of a feather in my cap!"

"Well that's what I thought, Joey. I figured if I have to spend the money to find some targets, why not help my friends? Besides, I know I can trust you. I will insist that you be my point man on this job. Will your boss have a problem with that?"

"No, I'm sure he won't, Charlie. He will be so anxious to bring in Shaw as a client, he would let Bozo the Clown be the point man if you asked for him!" Joey laughed.

"OK, good. I'll call you at the end of the day on Monday. You should probably set up a meeting between me and your boss. I'll get our legal people to draw up a draft contract and you can ask your guys to do the same. Don't let them stiff us on the fees, OK Joey?" Charlie laughed.

"You can count on me, Charlie. Boy, you don't know what a big deal this will be in the bank. They've been trying to enter the Shaw Corporation for a long time. You've really helped me out on this one. Thanks again, buddy. I won't let you down."

"I'm sure of that, Joey. But we have to move on this one as quickly and quietly as possible. No target company should know that the Shaw Corporation is looking at them until we get down to brass tacks."

"Not to worry, Charlie, our mergers and acquisitions people are good and they are discreet. They've done a lot of deals and have never had a problem. I'll look forward to hearing from you Monday afternoon."

They finished their meal and exited the sandwich shop. They had been there an hour-and-a-half. Sharon saw them coming out and said, "OK, Diane, they're leaving. Let's see where they go."

"Jeez, Sharon, I've had enough coffee to fill a bucket! I'll probably be peeing all day. And Bob is going to have my hide when I get home."

"Oh hell, Diane, tell him we took the bus to Philly. That will explain why we were so late. What's he going to do, ground you? You're an adult for Christ's sake! Bill won't dare give me any grief. I'll just tell him to drop dead and maybe stop talking to him for a few days. You've got to be more assertive, Diane."

"Yeah, yeah, Sharon, but Bob will still give me a hard time."

"Whatever," Sharon said, "now let's get moving!"

They followed Charlie and Joey at a reasonable distance as the two walked back to Joey's apartment building. Charlie saw them out of the corner of his eye and laughed to himself, *"Having fun, ladies? You ain't see nothing yet!"*

Sharon and Diane continued walking past Joey's building to their car while Charlie said goodbye to Joey. "OK, buddy, I'll call you Monday at the end of the day. Thanks for helping me out on this."

"I'm the one who's grateful, Charlie. I'll be a hero at the bank. Thanks a lot!" Joey and Charlie shook hands and Joey asked, "Want a beer before you leave?"

"No thanks, Joey, I have to get back to Shoreville. Talk to you Monday."

"Oh by the way, Charlie, I almost forgot. Are you still seeing Gina? The last time we talked you were a bit confused about her."

"Oh, yeah, Joey, I did like you said and just let things evolve. We have developed a good friendship and we go out once in a while. But it's nothing serious. Just good friends."

"I'm glad to hear it Charlie. Gina is a great gal. It's too bad I guess that you are just friends because she is a real looker besides being a great person. But who the hell knows, friendships can turn into romance."

"Well, I'm not pushing it, Joey. Your advice was good and I'm satisfied just to have Gina as a good friend," Charlie lied. He felt bad that he could not share his good news about Gina with his friend but Charlie was not about to make a mistake now. He was already trusting Joey with a big secret, no need to have to open the entire book. Charlie took his leave and headed for his car. He waved goodbye to Joey who was entering his apartment building. He looked down the street and could see Diane and Sharon in the car. *"Now for the fun,"* he thought.

Charlie got into his car and pulled away from the curb. He watched as Sharon pulled out behind him. He drove back to I-95 and headed toward Wilmington. "Sharon, he's going back to Wilmington!" Diane exclaimed.

"I can see that Diane, jeez. Maybe that's where his girlfriend lives. We just stay on him."

Charlie continued past Wilmington and headed toward the bridge to Shoreville. "Shit!" Sharon said. "It looks like he is heading back to Shoreville. Damn! Do you think he knows we are following him, Diane?"

"It sure looks like it, Sharon. If he does, we just wasted an entire Saturday chasing him."

Sharon was beside herself with frustration. "Dammit, I'm going to have to return this car before I go home and I'm sure Charlie is playing with us again. Damn, damn, damn!"

Charlie laughed out loud in his car as he watched the two women talking to each other animatedly while they followed him back toward Shoreville. He could almost feel their frustration. *"I hope you gals enjoyed watching me eat a sandwich with an old friend! I'll bet you feel like a couple of fools."* He was enjoying the moment.

He drove into Shoreville and headed toward his house. Sharon was furious. "That bastard just led us on a wild goose chase, Diane. Now I'm really mad. I'm going to catch him yet, that little bastard! I'm going to find out who that guy was and I'm going to find out who his girl friend is if it's the last thing I do. Who does he think he is? He thinks he is soooo smart! We'll see who is the smart one here."

Charlie was laughing out loud when he pulled into his garage and saw the car that had been following him speed past. He went into the house and called Gina to tell her what had happened. Gina was laughing so hard she had tears in her eyes. "Holy cow Charlie, you drove them crazy! They'll be mad as hornets and they are sure you were on to them and they don't know what you will do about it." She was laughing hysterically.

"I'll be home in a little while, Gina. I just want to wait to see if they come by here again."

But Sharon had dropped off Diane at her home and was busy returning the rental car so no one was going to check on Charlie Mullins again this Saturday. After waiting for about half-an-hour, Charlie backed out of the garage and headed back to Philly. He had used his meeting with Joey Esposito to frustrate and confound Sharon and Diane and he felt terrific. Tomorrow he would meet with Carlo Rizzo to discuss the events of the week.

* * * * *

Charlie and Gina followed what had become their regular Sunday morning ritual of breakfast in bed and reading the newspaper. They followed with showers and got ready for lunch with Carlo Rizzo. When they arrived to Carlo's home the "suits" were at their regular posts dutifully photographing Gina's vehicle. As usual, they entered through the back door. Over the antipasto Charlie briefed Carlo on the events at Shaw and his meeting with Warren Carpenter and Bill Cummins. He mentioned that Phillip Shaw would be returning to the company Monday morning and would be holding a press conference to reveal the expansion plan. He also told Carlo about his conversation with Joey Esposito. Carlo listened attentively. When Charlie finished his brief, Carlo told him how he would carry out his plan. Charlie was amazed at Carlo's business acumen and his range of contacts. When Carlo had finished telling Charlie how he intended to operate, Charlie felt sure that everything would work out just fine. They all enjoyed lunch in a light mood after which he and Gina took their leave.

On the way back to Gina's apartment, she said to Charlie, "My uncle really likes you, Charlie. I am so happy that you get along so well."

"He's a very smart guy, Gina. He should be teaching at Wharton or Harvard. I've met a lot of experienced guys in business who could not hold a candle to him."

Gina laughed out loud, "I wouldn't touch that comment with a ten-foot pole, Charlie! Imagine an accused Mafia boss teaching at a prestige business school!"

Charlie laughed, "Something tells me he would fit right in from some of the things I have seen."

Gina pulled her car into the garage of her building and parked in her spot. "Let's put on some music and relax, Charlie. That was some lunch and I need to just sit and relax."

"You're on," said Charlie.

XXXV

When Charlie arrived to the Shaw Corporation on Monday morning the entire building was abuzz with the news that Phillip Shaw was back in his office. Charlie made it a point to walk by Fred Perkins' office, "Good news that Phillip is back, huh Fred?" Perkins grunted an affirmative in his usual manner but Charlie could see that relief was written all over Perkins' face and his posture was relaxed for the first time in weeks. He smiled inwardly as he walked to his office. He greeted Laura Metzer as he passed her desk, "Hey Laura, good news that Phillip is back, no?"

"Don't know yet Charlie. It all depends on how *he* reacts," and she jerked her head toward Fred Perkins' door, "He might go back to his old ways now," she said in a low voice.

Charlie smiled sympathetically, "Yeah, let's hope for the best, Laura. You never can tell."

"Maybe you can't, Charlie, but I sure as hell can! But, at least it's the devil I know so what the hell. I'm just glad that Phillip is OK. By the way, Charlie, the conference room is all decked out. Some of the gals told me that Phillip has a press conference planned for 11-o-clock."

"Really? Well, I guess he wants to tell the world that he is back in the saddle," Charlie replied, "talk to you later Laura."

"See ya, Charlie."

After stopping at his office to drop off his papers, Charlie decided to check out the conference room on the 11th floor. The spacious room was already being set up. Soft drinks and small sandwiches were being set out for the reporters and camera crews. It was going to be a big deal from what Charlie could see. He saw Phillip Shaw walking to his office and he thought Phillip looked like he had just come from a week or two in Bermuda. He looked fit and was sporting a suntan. Charlie wandered back to his office. Not much would get done at the Shaw Corporation today. Every employee would be talking about Phillip's return and speculating on what would be said at the press conference.

At 10:30 the press started showing up. The PR department had done its work well. The majors were there – Bloomberg, the Wall Street Journal, Business Week, the New York Times, and several regional and local newspapers. The local TV stations and CNN had sent in camera crews as well as their reporters. Within minutes the conference room was strewn with cables and wires and reporters were jockeying for the best seats around the table.

At precisely 11-o-clock Phillip Shaw walked into the room. He had lost some weight and looked tremendously fit and healthy. He radiated the image of an aggressive executive. The cameras had started whirring as Phillip approached the lectern especially set up for the conference. He began.

"Good morning ladies and gentlemen. Thank you for coming. Before I begin my prepared statement, I want to thank all of those who wished me well during my convalescence. Your support was important to me and made me even more anxious to recover and get back to work. I'm back now and I've never felt better – thanks in no small measure to your support and good wishes."

"That said, I'd like to announce that not only am I back in command of the Shaw Corporation but I have returned with renewed energy. During my convalescence I had the opportunity to see the company and my tenure as its CEO in a much different light and from a distance. I concluded that while the company is in excellent financial shape, we have been far too complacent with regard to growth. We now face competitive pressures from abroad that require that we become more aggressive in the defense of our commercial interests."

The reporters all looked at each other. They had expected the normal corporate PR stuff about being glad to be back and comments about Phillip's convalescence period. They sat up in their chairs. This was news!

Phillip Shaw noticed the change in posture of the reporters and continued, "I had a chance to evaluate my tenure as CEO and confess that I concluded that I had been too timid in my approach to growth. At lot of my attention had been dedicated to the finances of the company and I think that was to the detriment of the operating divisions. The fact is, we need to grow and grow aggressively. Consequently, I will be meeting with my operating vice presidents over the next few days to devise an aggressive growth strategy that will keep the Shaw Corporation in the news for months to come. The company has plenty of cash as many of you know and I intend to use it to build a new base from which to expand our business. I intend to be less of a caretaker and more of a builder of value. It will be fun! You are all invited to watch our smoke!"

The excitement of the reporters was palpable in the conference room. This was unexpected. The staid Shaw Corporation was coming out of its corner swinging. Phillip Shaw was going to be a kick-ass CEO.

"I'll take your questions now," Phillip announced.

Reporters' hands popped up instantly like someone had pulled a lever. Phillip smiled inwardly as he recognized a young reporter from a local newspaper.

"Mr. Shaw, are you saying that the company has lost market share or competitiveness during your tenure?"

Phillip smiled, "No, on the contrary. I am saying that we do not *intend* to lose market share. All of you know that we are in excellent financial shape and we have accompanied market growth rates. What I am saying is that we are going to get tougher. It will be ever more difficult to take market share from us, if, of course, anyone out there would dare to try!"

The reporter was writing furiously.

Phillip fielded another question, "Mr. Shaw, how did you come to the conclusion that the company would have to be more aggressive?"

It was time to play the philosophical card, Phillip thought. "Look, I had a heart attack. Even though it was a mild one, a heart attack forces you to face your mortality and evaluate your life. My life is this company and I asked myself if I would be content to continue being just a caretaker of shareholder value or if I wanted to cut a wider swath for myself. You all know my father built this company from scratch. I saw no reason for me to just oversee the considerable work he had done. I thought it was time to put my own handprint on the Shaw Corporation's destiny. We have good people, we have excellent product lines, and we have marvelous customers. They all deserve the best leadership I can provide. I used my period of convalescence to step back and look at the company from a distance. We have the opportunity to excel and that's what we are going to do."

Another hand flew up, "Mr. Shaw, there has been a lot of speculation for some time that the Shaw family would take the company public. Does this new posture have anything to do with a possible IPO?"

Phillip laughed, "That question always comes up. I don't know why you guys insist on that issue." The reporters in the room laughed. "We have no plan to go public. Why should we mess with a winning team? Shaw is a company that has always been involved in the local community. I see no reason to turn it over to a faceless group of shareholders who don't live here and might be less concerned for the welfare of the employees. We already have a professional management team in place. I am the only family member working for the company. I simply see no advantage to going public."

Another reporter asked, "Mr. Shaw, how do you plan to execute this new strategy?"

Phillip gave the reporter his most charming smile, "Well, if I answered that question, I would be telling our competitors our plans, wouldn't I?" The group laughed. "Let me just say that I will be meeting with my operating personnel and they will tell me what they need and we will deal with those needs accordingly. You know that I have always delegated responsibility and power in this company. That will not change. Let me say however, that this initiative is my project and I will be directly involved in the interface with my operating department executives."

Phillip allowed for one more question, "Mr. Shaw does your strategy call for mergers or acquisitions? Will you be in the market for other companies?"

"Let me just say that we will do whatever is necessary to grow. We do not have a list of acquisition targets if that's what you mean. I will rely on my operating department heads to determine the best way to achieve our objectives. If that means acquisitions or mergers, then that's what we will do. If it means expanding from within, we will do that."

He answered some questions about his health status and his convalescence regime and then held up his hand to stop any further questions. "That's enough questions for the time being. We have sandwiches and soft drinks set aside for you. I want to thank all of you for coming. I will stay for a few more minutes but my 'on-the-record' comments have finished. Thanks again."

Phillip stepped down from the lectern and worked the room, shaking hands with reporters and engaging in small talk about his recovery, his exercise program, and the state of the economy. While he had said that his comments would now be "off-the-record", he knew that everything he said was subject to quotation. To aggressive reporters, "off-the-record" often meant, "this is really the hot stuff" and only the most experienced and well-known reporters would honor the request to refrain from publishing such comments. Phillip, however, was decidedly non-committal during this period of socializing. Once he had worked the room for a few minutes, he took his leave and again thanked the reporters for showing up.

A few reporters stayed around to munch some sandwiches in the hope of catching an employee for some inside comments. However, the company's security team made sure that no reporters could roam the halls and no employees were allowed to approach the conference room. The camera crews were putting their gear back into boxes while the reporters rushed back to their offices to edit the tapes for the evening news. No sooner had the reporters cleared out than the cleaning crew came in to restore the conference room to its pristine state.

Later that day Charlie called Joey Esposito. He told Joey about the press conference and asked if he had talked about the search assignment with his management. Joey was excited as he told Charlie that his boss had enthusiastically jumped at the opportunity to work with the Shaw Corporation and that he wanted to schedule a meeting to discuss the matter as soon as possible. Charlie said that either Bill Cummins or Warren Carpenter would contact Joey and that either would insist that Joey be the "point man" on the search.

* * * * *

No employee of the Shaw Corporation missed the evening news that night. Charlie watched from Gina's apartment. Gina watched attentively and turned to Charlie, "He looks like he just came back from a skiing holiday! Look at that suntan! Are you sure he had a heart attack?"

Charlie laughed, "That's the same thing I thought when I saw him in the hall today! I guess we will never know if he had an attack or not. The whole thing was so tightly buttoned down. But I confess that I've never seen Phillip Shaw looking so fit!"

"Wouldn't it be amazing if the whole thing was just a set-up?" Gina said.

"Well, Phillip is certainly clever enough to do something like that. I've learned a lot about him from Warren Carpenter and Bill Cummins over the past few weeks. He's a slick one, that's for sure."

"And what about that statement that he does not plan to take the company public?" Gina asked, "Won't that come back to haunt him when it happens?"

"I doubt it, Gina. Phillip needs to keep that card close to his vest so he had no choice but to deny any plans in that direction. Most probably his comment will either be forgotten or forgiven by the time it all happens. Everybody knows you don't go around announcing that sort of thing until the timing is right."

Phillip Shaw's press conference got a good chunk of air time. He actually got more than any national news item that was reported that evening. The talking heads dedicated ample time to the "instant analysis" and the "what-did-he-mean-by-that" commentary that characterizes the TV media. The emphasis was on the new aggressive profile of the Shaw Corporation and its CEO and nothing was said about whether an IPO was in the works. Phillip had got what he wanted.

After the evening news Charlie called Warren Carpenter at his home. "Warren? Charlie here, I just saw the evening news. It looks like Phillip came off pretty well."

"You bet, Charlie. He looked great and like he was ready to do battle. I thought he handled the questions superbly. The press was in a dither as they left the company."

"I talked to my friend at the bank today, and he told me that his boss literally jumped at the chance to work for Shaw on a search for acquisitions. I told him that someone would contact him soon to discuss terms. I also told him that we would insist that he be the 'point man' on the assignment."

"Good, Charlie. I think it best that Bill be the contact person with the bank. I am the family attorney and it might raise eyebrows if I were the one to do the contact work. Let the company's auditor do the footwork. I will review the documents and brief Phillip but no one should know that I am involved."

"OK Warren, I'll contact Bill and let him know. By the way, where do you want to meet on Friday?"

"Get a small meeting room at the Ritz again and let me know. We'll stagger our arrivals. I expect that the press might hound Bill a little bit to try to find out more about the company and Phillip's announced strategy but you and I will not have a problem."

"OK, I'll call Bill now and get back to you tomorrow. And when you talk to Phillip, congratulate him on his press conference. He looked great!"

"Will do, Charlie, talk to you tomorrow. Bye." They both rang off.

Charlie immediately called Bill Cummins on his home phone, "Bill, how are you? Did you see the news on the press conference?"

"See it? My God, I've been getting calls all afternoon from the press. Everybody wants an inside track to Phillip's announced expansion plan. Once the news hits the papers the calls will slow down or stop, but until everybody files I expect to be getting calls for the additional nugget of information."

"I thought it went well, Bill, what did you think?"

"Phillip is a smooth one all right. He put just enough out there to get front page in the business section of the majors. He also made sure that subsequent press coverage would be directed at him personally. He's smart."

"That's for sure. I talked with Warren a few minutes ago to tell him that my pal at the bank has accepted to represent Shaw's interests in an acquisition search. He said his boss was happy as hell. Warren thinks that you should call to set up a meeting to discuss terms. He doesn't want to show up given that he is the family's attorney. It might raise eyebrows."

"I agree. Normally this would be the bailiwick of the corporate legal office, not the family attorney's. It would not be a surprise however, if the company's auditor was doing the footwork."

"I told my pal that we would insist that he be the point man on the assignment."

"Agree again. We should keep our leverage and insist that we determine who will be our contact. That shouldn't do your friend's career any harm either."

"Yeah, he's really grateful and he's chomping at the bit to get started."

"Give me his contact details, and I will call him first thing tomorrow. I'll get all the necessary documents and contracts from him and we will review them with Warren. Your friend should have everything locked down by early next week."

Charlie gave Cummins Joey Esposito's office number. "By the way Bill, Warren suggested the Ritz for our Friday meeting. Is that OK for you?"

"Sure, but I'll have to leave my office a bit early to escape the possible collection of reporters looking for more dope on the company."

"Yeah, sorry about that, I'll call you tomorrow with the name of the meeting room. Good luck with the press hounds!"

"Thanks, Charlie. Talk to you tomorrow, bye." Cummins hung up.

* * * * *

The next day Bill Cummins called Joey Esposito and arranged a meeting with Joey and Joey's boss for the following day. Charlie arranged the meeting room at the Ritz-Carlton for Friday afternoon and called Cummins and Carpenter to provide the name of the room.

The day's newspapers all made front-page references to Phillip Shaw's press conference and provided ample detail and commentary on the front-page of the business and economics sections. The headlines proclaimed the expansion plan of the Shaw Corporation. "Phillip Shaw Announces Aggressive Growth Plan" was the lead in one newspaper. "Shaw Goes for Growth" was the lead in another. All emphasized the new posture of the company. Only one speculated that an IPO might be in the offing but it was one of the minor publications and the article was written by a junior reporter. It would not attract much attention or enjoy much credibility in the market. All of the articles informed that Phillip Shaw himself would lead the effort together with his "capable management team". This was what Phillip needed to ensure that he would be in the press often over the next several months. He wanted maximum press exposure of his management, political, and negotiating skills before the IPO took place.

Phillip reviewed the press coverage in his office with Warren Carpenter who had stopped by to brief Phillip on the latest developments in the search assignment. "What do you think, Warren? Did the press conference go well?"

"I think you knocked them all for a loop Phillip. Everyone was expecting you to come out and thank people for their support and assure the market that the conservative, staid Shaw Corporation would soon be back to business as usual."

"Yeah, I picked up on the surprise when I saw all those reporters suddenly pop up in their seats and start taking notes. They were expecting some of the same old PR bullshit and I think I caught them by surprise. How do you think I fielded that question about an IPO?"

"You deflected the issue nicely, I thought. It was good that you mentioned that it is always a question that gets asked so no one gave it much currency. Besides, the guy that asked it is a very junior reporter on a small publication. I saw that he mentioned it in his article but to the market I think it will sound like the kind of question someone who is not familiar with the Shaw Corporation would ask so no one will give it much attention."

"Dad called me last night to say he thought it was a successful press conference. He especially liked my reference to the 'considerable work' he had done to build the company. What an ego!"

"Well, it's nice to know your father is going strong as ever. I would have been worried if he had not made reference to the comment about him. At least he was pleased!"

Phillip laughed, "You got that right, Warren!" He continued, "By the way, Charlie Mullins did a bang-up job on his analysis of the company. He's a smart guy. You think I should bring him on to the campaign team when I run for office?"

"It's early yet, Phillip. Let's see how he follows through on the acquisitions. I like him. He has maturity and street smarts. Moreover, he is discreet and loyal. He's managed to keep the search compartmentalized so it can't be linked to us. He's got a friend at a bank that doesn't deal with Shaw so the search won't look as if it's Shaw that is shopping around. The banker will be reporting to Bill Cummins just in case something leaks. We still want to keep Mullins out of the spotlight mainly because of Fred Perkins."

"Glad you mentioned that. I have to talk to Fred. I want him to know that he will be included in the discussions but that Bill Cummins is leading the search effort. I don't want his nose out of joint and I sure don't want him to know that his subordinate is doing the footwork for me on this plan. There's no telling what he would do if he thought I was going around him. For sure, he'd be scared as hell." Phillip made a note to himself in a leather notebook he always carried with him. He would talk to Perkins first thing Wednesday morning. "Keep your eye on this Mullins guy, Warren. He could be useful. Loyalty is hard to come by."

* * * * *

Charlie went to Shoreville for his regular Wednesday bowling league night. His friends were anxious to hear his take on Phillip Shaw's return and the plans to expand the company. They all wanted to know what it meant for their jobs. Charlie was careful to emphasize that he did not have direct contact with Phillip Shaw but that from his contacts with the operating department heads he thought that the new posture of the company was good news for all. He said that growth and job security usually went hand-in-hand and that the Shaw Corporation had always been a good corporate citizen and could be counted on to look to employee welfare. He added that he did not think the company had it in mind to start moving production offshore or start cutting back on personnel.

He knew that the comments and questions of this group of friends were highly representative of what the rank-and-file of Shaw employees would be thinking about. He would pass on their concerns to Warren Carpenter so Phillip Shaw would know and could make sure to address such issues in press and employee conferences.

He stayed around for the customary pizza and beer after league night. Come Friday he would tell Warren Carpenter what he had heard from Shaw employees in Shoreville.

He was careful to make sure he was not being followed back to Philadelphia after washing and drying his bowling shirt and storing his gear. He suspected, correctly, that Sharon Gallagher was at least temporarily stymied by his last set of evasive maneuvers and that she was probably confused. But he knew that Sharon was obstinate and would not give up easily.

Gina was listening to some soft jazz when Charlie arrived to the apartment. She rushed up to kiss him as he entered the apartment. "Hello, handsome. I've missed you. How are things in Shoreville?"

"All abuzz, Gina, everybody was talking about Phillip's press conference and the expansion plan. There was some concern that the company might start doing what a lot of others have done by moving production offshore and leaving employees in the lurch. I told them that as far as I knew that was not in Phillip's plans. I hope for their sakes I am right. But I have to wonder what a bunch of new owners, especially if they are institutional investors, will do when they own the company."

"You think the new owners would shut down operations in places like Shoreville, Charlie?"

"I don't know, Gina. Company loyalty to employees is not what it used to be – if it ever really existed in the first place. You see what is happening in other companies. Thirty-thousand laid off in one company, another company moves its manufacturing to China, whole communities are suddenly without jobs. The only thing that might keep it from happening at Shaw is the possibility that Phillip will eventually go into politics. He would not want to leave that kind of misery in his wake if he wants to get elected to public office. But you just never know. Once he is no longer in control, anything could happen. I think a lot will depend on what Bill, Warren, and I come up with as acquisitions."

"Shoreville would collapse if Shaw were to shut down or move operations offshore, Charlie. Practically everyone there works for the company. And all those events that the company sponsors…the whole town would simply die."

"Well, I'll do what I can to keep it from happening, but times have changed sweetheart. Job security is a thing of the past in America."

"What about the wacky wives, Charlie? Did they follow you this time?"

Charlie laughed, "No, Gina, I think Sharon Gallagher is trying to figure out what to do next. She really looked mad as a hornet when I led her back to Shoreville. But I suppose she will be back as soon as she works out some new scheme."

Charlie pulled Gina to him and kissed her. "How'd you like to pull off my navy blue silk boxer shorts, you sexy creature?"

"Thought you'd never ask. Let's go!"

Charlie and Gina moved to the bedroom, made love, and fell asleep.

* * * * *

The following Friday afternoon Charlie, Warren, and Bill made their way to the Ritz-Carlton for their now-regular meeting. Charlie was the first to arrive and Warren Carpenter was close behind. They had to wait a bit for Bill Cummins who arrived looking harried.

"Whew," Cummins said when he walked into the meeting room, "I had to dodge reporters as I came out of the office. Those guys think that something is already happening and nobody wants to miss a story. I'm not used to that kind of stuff!"

Charlie laughed, "Yeah, I guess auditors are used to the background. Phillip has turned you into a rock star, Bill!"

"Well, at least the business reporters are a somewhat more staid bunch," Bill said, "but they can still be a pain in the butt. Anyway, I shook them off and told them I have other clients to worry about too, so I couldn't tell them anything right now. Let me fill you in on the meeting I had with Joey Esposito. I brought the contract the bank uses with me for your review, Warren. It looks OK. There will be a success fee for any deals we close with a company the bank introduces but it is a reasonable one. The bank wants Shaw to be a customer when this whole thing is over so they are soft-pedaling on the fees. I told them that we want Joey to be the point man on the search and they agreed." He handed the contract to Warren.

"Good work, Bill," Carpenter replied, "I'll run this by Phil over the weekend and get it back to you first thing next week. The sooner they get started, the better. Did you get a favorable impression of the guys who will be working on this?"

"Joey Esposito impressed me as a smart guy. He shows maturity and he understands our needs. Charlie did a good job briefing him and he is loyal to Charlie. He is also smart enough to know that this is a big break for him. His boss is so anxious to bring Shaw into the bank that he can be counted on to do the job right. I'm sure they will beat the bushes for some good acquisition targets."

"Good, so we are ready to start. What did you guys think of Phillip's press conference and the press coverage?"

Bill Cummins said, "Well if the reporters who keep calling me and the ones hanging out in front of our office are any indication, he has sure drawn attention to the Shaw Corporation and to himself."

Charlie told Warren and Bill about the reaction over in Shoreville and some of the questions his friends raised. Carpenter responded, "Phillip is not about to create a situation that will result in massive layoffs or shutdowns of manufacturing facilities. You can tell your friends that their jobs are secure, maybe even more secure than before. You should stay in touch with those friends of yours Charlie. They are an important source of intelligence to Phillip as we move forward with this project."

"I will, Warren, they're the ones who will be most affected by a change of ownership even though they have no idea that that is in the cards. I'll be sure to keep my ears tuned to the scuttlebutt from the factory floor."

"Good," Warren replied, "what's our next step now, Charlie?"

"Well, I thought I would start talking to the operating department heads. Will Phillip talk to Fred Perkins?"

"I'll find out over the weekend. I think he has already had a conversation with Fred. His plan is to have Fred working with him as a key financial advisor on the expansion project. That will keep him plenty busy and feed his ego. He won't be watching you closely if he is reviewing proposals for Phil. You know Fred. If Phil told him to jump off the bridge, he would do it. He'll be so wrapped up in keeping Phil happy that he won't have time for anything else!"

Charlie laughed.

Bill Cummins said, "I'll take the contract over to Joey Esposito as soon as you have it reviewed and signed by Phillip. I'll arrange to have bi-weekly meetings with Joey until things heat up and then maybe we will go to weekly. You guys agree?"

Warren and Charlie nodded in agreement.

"OK, so we are running now," Warren Carpenter said, "let's meet again next week. I suggest we use my office next time. I don't think we should schedule any more meetings at Bill's office in view of the press coverage. If anything urgent should come up, we will communicate by telephone. Do we all have secure lines?"

"We do," said Bill Cummins, "and I have a secure line at home too, because of my auditing work."

"Both my office and my home are covered," said Carpenter, "you OK, Charlie?"

"I'll get an accommodation line here in Philly that will forward calls to my home" Charlie lied. "I'll take care of it." He smiled inwardly because he knew that Gina's phone was secure for other reasons. Carlo Rizzo made sure of that and Carlo could get him just what he needed in a flash.

"OK guys, next week at my office? Same time?"

"Agreed," Charlie and Bill said in unison. They left the hotel separately.

Charlie arrived to Gina's apartment to find her dressed to go out. "Trattoria, Mullins? How about some happy hour and a light meal. It's been a while."

"Great idea, beautiful. Let's go out."

* * * * *

The next morning Charlie drove over to Shoreville for softball practice. He went through his regular routine of securing his house. The team was in a light mood. Charlie noticed that Bill Gallagher showed up with Bob Simms. That meant that Sharon had the car. Charlie noticed that at least twice during practice he saw Sharon drive by the practice field. After practice he went off with his teammates for pizza and beer where he fielded the same questions that had been posed on Wednesday. He assured his friends that Phillip Shaw was serious about the expansion and that no one should worry about job security.

When he drove back to his house, Charlie did a tour around the block before pulling into his garage. He saw Sharon Gallagher's car parked around the corner from his house where she thought she would not been seen. After Charlie drove past her car, he noticed in his rear view mirror that she pulled away from the curb and quickly left. He entered the house, went through the usual routine of setting his timers and washing and drying his uniform. When he was finished he got into his car and headed back to Philly and Gina. His drive-by had shaken Sharon who had not expected to be seen, and he did not see anyone following him as he drove up I-95.

He got back to the apartment without incident. "Gina, I'm back!" he called as he entered the front door. Gina ran from the kitchen to meet him. She was beautiful in a sweatshirt and jeans and Charlie just looked at her for a moment.

"What is it, Mullins? Spinach on my teeth, or something?"

"No, baby, I'm just amazed at how beautiful you are. I can't stop staring at you."

"Wow! What a great way to start a weekend!" Gina exclaimed, "you sure know how to charm a lady, you silver-tongued devil." She laughed.

Charlie smiled. Gina always had an answer for everything and he loved it. "OK, OK," he said, "I was just being honest. Now, I need to speak to your uncle. Will he be at home?"

Gina laughed out loud, "Where else would he be? If he goes out he always has some entourage of suits with him. He prefers that people come to him rather then going out. I'm sure he is home. You want to go over there?"

"No, I think it is too risky to be going over there on a regular basis. Sooner or later something could go wrong. I'd like to talk to him over the phone."

"OK, but there is a ritual to be followed, Charlie."

"A ritual? What do you mean?"

"I mean I will call and leave a message for him to call. Even though he makes sure his phone is not tapped, he is still very careful about telephone conversations. Try to keep your conversation general if possible."

Gotcha," Charlie replied.

Gina picked up the phone and dialed. She did not identify herself and she left a message with someone to have her uncle call. Ten minutes later her phone rang. Charlie heard her say that someone wanted to talk to Mr. French and she handed the phone to Charlie. "Be quick," she whispered.

Charlie spoke into the phone, "I just wanted you to know that all the formalities have been arranged. The search will begin next week. We'll talk again over lunch."

Carlo Rizzo said only "Good!" and then hung up. Charlie remained holding the phone unit for a brief moment.

Gina laughed, "Not used to those quick conversations, Mullins? My uncle doesn't like telephones. He says that telephones should only be used to arrange a lunch meeting, and even then, without saying where."

Charlie smiled, "I have a lot to learn," he said.

XXXVI

Warren Carpenter sat down opposite Phillip Shaw in front of a coffee table in Phillip's spacious living room where a silver coffee set had been put out for them. They served themselves coffee. Warren started the conversation, "Phillip, I have the contract from the bank with me. It looks OK. They will charge a small success fee for any deals we close with companies they introduce to us. I feel good about the people doing the scouting for us. They are mature and discreet. Bill Cummins will be the point of contact with the bank's representative assigned to the project. I'll deliver the contract to them through Bill on Monday."

Phillip Shaw took the contract and read it carefully. "This looks OK, Warren. It's pretty much boilerplate as I read it. Is there anything that could trip me up in there?"

"No, I've been through it several times. It's really a pretty good deal. The fees are more than reasonable because the bank is salivating at the prospect of working with Shaw."

"Good, that's the way I like it."

"By the way, that Mullins fellow still hangs around with his friends from over in Shoreville. He filled me in on the questions they were asking about the expansion project. A lot of them were worried that the company would be offshoring jobs. I asked him to continue with his activities with his friends because they can offer important feedback on how the rank-and-file in the company are viewing events."

"Good idea, Warren, we need that kind of feedback. It wouldn't do to have workers showing up in front of the company with placards and picketing to keep their jobs. That would be political suicide."

"That reminds me, Phillip, I've also brought the outline of a campaign strategy for you to review. The IPO will be the first step and we have to make sure it doesn't look like you are selling out your employees for a political career. It has to look like you are responding to a higher calling as you leave the business world for public service."

"Can we lock in the buyers of the company for long enough to get me elected?"

"I'm pretty sure of that. In the first place, the IPO limits them from "flipping" the stock immediately. Second the acquisitions will lock them in for a while at least. Third, I think we can stack the membership of the Boards of Directors of the acquired companies to ensure that we have inside information regarding the new owners' plans and can block any initiatives we consider to not be in our interest."

"OK, I'm counting on you Warren. I don't want to be going into a campaign with the opposition being able to say I sold out my employees."

"No problem, Phillip. I've covered some of that in the outline. Obviously, this is only a first run at a strategy. We have time to review and refine as we move forward with the acquisitions."

"Who knows about my plans to run for office, Warren?"

"So far, just you and me, Phillip; unless you have told somebody. Neither Bill Cummins nor Charlie Mullins knows anything about it nor do they need to."

"Good. I don't want this to get out, even as speculation, if it can be avoided. I want everyone to think the rest of my life will be with the company until I announce that I have been *asked* to run for office."

"Understood," Warren Carpenter replied, "we want you running for political office by 'popular demand'" Carpenter smiled. "By the way, are you going to the Eagles' game tomorrow?"

"Yeah, I will be in the owners' box. I'm hoping the TV cameras will pick me up. Ideally, the game commentators will make some comment about my heart attack and the expansion plans for the company. I have to keep that iron hot."

* * * * *

When Charlie Mullins arrived to the office on Monday morning he noticed that Fred Perkins was not at his desk. As he walked by Laura Metzer's desk she looked up and whispered conspiratorially, "He's with Phillip Shaw, Charlie. Phillip called down here as soon Fred arrived and called him to his office. Do you know what's going on?"

"I suppose it has to do with the expansion plans, Laura. Fred is the company treasurer. Phillip would certainly want his advice and counsel. He always has before."

"Oh God, I hope so. If Fred loses his job, whoever steps in will bring his own team and I could be out of a job. Unless of course, *you* were to be his successor, Charlie."

"I'm pretty sure he is not about to lose his job, Laura. Don't worry." Charlie patted her on the shoulder and walked to his office. He smiled to himself and made a mental note to walk by Fred's office a little later just to see the man's reaction.

Charlie would have a full day setting up meetings with the heads of the operating departments. He would have to swear them to secrecy regarding his role in the expansion project. He did not anticipate any problems because all of the department heads had a vested interest in getting more investment funds and reviewing acquisition targets. None of them would be talking to Fred Perkins about Charlie's work. In the first place they didn't like Perkins and in the second, talking to him would probably only serve to squelch their projects. They would cooperate with Charlie, especially if they knew they could circumvent Perkins by doing so. Moreover, they would be able to save themselves a lot of work if Charlie screened acquisition targets or uncovered some for them. Finally, they would also be off the hook if any acquisitions turned out to be lemons. They could blame Charlie, and it was an unwritten rule that in corporate politics you took credit for the successes and blamed others for the failures. So, Charlie felt secure that his role would not be unmasked.

After setting up a full week of meetings, Charlie headed out to lunch. As he walked by Fred Perkins' office and he noticed that Perkins was sitting upright in his chair, his chest puffed out. Phillip had made him his financial "deputy" in the expansion project. When Perkins saw Charlie walking by he barked, "Mullins! Step into my office for a minute."

Charlie entered Perkins' space, "What is it Fred?"

"I suppose I should not tell you this, it's highly confidential, but I am going to have to rely on you to keep this department in order for the next several months."

Charlie smiled inwardly. Fred was about to tell him how important he was to Phillip Shaw's new strategy, "Phillip Shaw called me into his office this morning. He wants me to work closely with him on the execution of his strategy to expand the company," Perkins' face revealed a smug self-satisfaction, "He has commissioned Bill Cummins to identify expansion opportunities and he will need me to evaluate them. I will have to work closely with Phillip and clearly won't have time for the mundane tasks of keeping the office on an even keel. Can you do that, Mullins?"

"I'm flattered and honored that you have asked me, Fred. And congratulations on being asked to help Phillip in this important task. You can count on me to do my best."

Perkins puffed up even more, "You can start this week. I've got meetings set up with Phillip starting tomorrow. If you do a good job, I'll make sure Phillip knows about it. Just remember, this is all highly confidential. That's all Mullins."

"OK, Fred, and thanks for your confidence in me."

"No problem, Mullins."

Charlie left Perkins's office to catch an elevator to street level. He could hardly keep a straight face as he listened to Perkins' pompous declarations. When he got to street level and outside the building he broke out laughing. *"What an ass,"* he thought, *"I hope I can keep up this farce without cracking up in front of the idiot!"* He had to hand it to Phillip Shaw, he knew how to manipulate Perkins. Perkins would think he was the one who would be instrumental in making the growth project a reality. He would strut and posture around the company making sure everyone knew that he had Phillip's absolute confidence. Well, at least maybe he would treat Laura better – *noblesse oblige*, and all that.

When he returned from lunch he walked by Fred's office again. Perkins gave him a smug look and a nod that implied that they were now co-conspirators. He walked by Laura Metzer's desk. "How goes it Laura?"

"He's a lamb, Charlie. After his meeting with Phillip Shaw he looked like he would actually smile. He didn't say anything but he walked out of here to the meeting stooped over and looking like he was heading for the scaffold and came back all puffed up and with a spring in his step. What's going on?"

"I don't know Laura, but remember, Fred has always been Phillip's s-o-b. Every CEO needs one. Maybe he was told to whack somebody," Charlie laughed.

Laura smiled, "You're terrible, Charlie. I just hope it stays this way for a while. What a relief from the past couple of months!"

"Maybe he's just mellowing Laura, just mellowing," Charlie said jokingly.

"Yeah, right, and the Pope is my uncle, Charlie!" Laura laughed.

Charlie left Laura still giggling about her own comment. He laughed inwardly as he walked to his office. He couldn't wait to tell Gina about this day.

* * * * *

The rest of Charlie's week was occupied with meetings with the heads of the operating departments. Some of them had expansion plans filed away for the day that Fred Perkins would die of a stroke or otherwise be out of the way. They were more than pleased to show the plans to Charlie. Some of the plans even identified possible acquisition targets. Charlie wondered if some of the companies cited might still be viable targets. He would have Joey Esposito discreetly check them out. As he had expected, he had no trouble at all convincing the department heads to keep their meetings quiet. He assured them that Fred Perkins would only see their plans after the companies had been well vetted by Charlie and the company's auditors. He told them that Phillip Shaw would soon announce that Fred Perkins would be nominated as Phillip's deputy for the expansion project. They all knew that this meant Fred would do whatever Phillip said to do. They were quick to recognize that Fred had been effectively neutralized. Charlie, however, was equally quick to say that Fred's role was an important one. He didn't want it getting back to Fred that he had said anything bad about him or in any way had seemed to diminish his importance to the project.

* * * * *

He went to his weekly bowling league night and softball practice on Saturday. He noticed that Sharon Gallagher and Diane Simms were still hanging around his house and driving past the softball practice field whenever he was in Shoreville. They were stalking him in Shoreville but unable to devise a strategy that would allow them to follow him to Philly. He made a mental note to stay vigilant. Sooner or later they would try something again and he had to be prepared.

Charlie's relationship with Gina had evolved into a comfortable quasi-marriage and both of them were anxious to make things official. They did not go out as often as they would have liked to because they wanted to avoid the chance encounter with someone from Shoreville or to cause a lot of speculation among those who knew Gina. To the outside world they were best of friends. They were both happy but anxious to get on with their life together as man and wife. Gina was perhaps more patient than Charlie. She had lived all her life in the infamous shadow of her uncle and she knew the importance of discretion. Charlie, on the other hand, had lived a totally open life. Even the fact that he liked his privacy was a matter of public knowledge.

In spite of his insistence on keeping his private life totally private, he really had nothing to hide. It was just his way. Gina *did* have something to hide. She had to protect not just herself but also her uncle. Those who knew her did not talk about her Uncle Carlo and she never commented to anyone about his life.

So, Charlie was often more impatient with their situation than was Gina and he often talked to her about it. "Geez, Gina, I would really love to just walk away from all this bullshit and announce to the whole damned world that you are mine."

"Take it easy, Charlie. You have a lot to lose being publicly engaged to Carlo Rizzo's daughter. I can wait. I've been waiting all my life. My uncle used to say to me that a big meal has to be eaten in small bites. You wouldn't be happy if you lost everything and had to run a pizzeria to make a living. You could do it, I'm sure of that and I'm sure you *would* if it came to that. But you would not be happy. You might one day come to regret having made the sacrifice and we both would suffer."

"You're right, Gina. It's just that I would love for the whole world to know that we are together."

"Everybody will know soon enough Charlie and you might find that you wish they didn't!" Gina laughed, "Do you have any idea what the press will do with our engagement and wedding? Do you have any idea how many 'suits' will show up. There'll be more photographers than guests! I can see the headlines in the tabloids 'Mafia Princess Weds'! There will be a big spread on my uncle and speculation that you are his heir apparent. So, just be patient Mullins. Your fifteen minutes of fame will come soon enough and you will wish it hadn't. You've never had to live with this, Charlie. People can be mean and nasty when they set their mind to it. The announcement of our relationship will allow a lot of people to get their own fifteen minutes of fame at our expense and the expense of my uncle."

"I know you're right Gina. This is a new kind of situation for me. I spent all of my life seeking privacy without really needing it. Now that I need it, I realize just how tough it is to actually have it. It's like that old saying that you have to be careful what you wish for, you might just get it."

Gina laughed, "Exactly, Charlie. Why do you think I understand those wacky wives that are pestering you? I know what it's like for people to want to shoehorn their way into your life so they can upset it. People feel threatened by what is different. They want to get inside you to assure themselves that you really are just like them. When they finally break into your privacy and find out that you are just like they are, they refuse to believe it so they look even harder. They ask stupid questions. They want to know if my uncle is really the way the press says he is. I've even had people ask me if I could have somebody killed if I wanted to. I have no illusions about my uncle, but he doesn't walk around the house dragging his knuckles on the floor, but you would be surprised at the number of people who seem to think that he does."

"Well, beautiful, things are moving ahead. It won't be too long before we can be together and our love a matter of public knowledge."

"It'll happen, Charlie, it'll happen. Just be patient and, of course, careful."

XXXVII

Charlie followed his routine through the week. On Thursday he called Joey Esposito, "Joey, how ya' doin'?"

"Hey Charlie, what's new?"

"Listen, are you in the mood for a cheese steak lunch on Saturday? I have to go to softball practice and then I thought I would drive up to Philly so we can have lunch and see how things are going."

"Sure Charlie, you want to come by around two or thereabouts?"

"OK, thanks Joey. I'll see you then."

At softball practice Charlie noticed that Sharon and Diane were still stalking him. They drove by the practice field at least twice. He made a mental note to play close attention as he drove to Philly. But since he was going to Joey's place he could repeat the routine he used the last time they followed him and head back to Shoreville.

When softball practice was finished he begged off the pizza and beer telling the group he had another meeting with an old friend. He drove back to his house and went through his regular routine of setting the timers and washing and drying his uniform and then headed off for Philly. He drove once around the block and saw Sharon's car again. However, Sharon did not follow him and simply drove away quickly.

He arrived to Joey's building at two-fifteen . The doorman let him into the vestibule. Charlie took the elevator up to Joey's apartment. Joey had opened the door and Charlie walked in, closing the door behind him. "Hey Charles, want a beer?" Joey tossed him a can.

"Thanks, Joey. How was your week?"

"Busy as hell now that I am trying to find acquisitions for you guys," he laughed.

"Just make sure you get some good ones, OK?"

"Hey Charlie, changing the subject for a minute, are you screwing some guy's wife or something?"

"What? What the hell are you talking about Joey? Where did you get an idea like that?"

"My doorman, Charlie."

"Your *doorman*? What the hell does he know about my sex life?"

"Nothing I suppose. But two broads came by here last week asking him if he knew you. They asked him if you ever came by here with a girlfriend. They even described some woman that sounded a bit like a description of Gina. He told them he'd never seen you come here with a woman and that if they wanted to know anything else they should talk to you directly. He told me about it the other day."

Charlie did not know what to do. He never expected that Sharon and Diane would have the guts to show up at Joey's building. "Did the women give their names?" Charlie asked.

"No, the doorman said one was a blonde the other a brunette. He said the blonde did all the talking and she was even pretty aggressive. He said he thought you might have been screwing the blonde and she was trying to check up on you or something."

"Christ, Joey! This is ridiculous. Those are two busybodies from Shoreville who are, God knows why, sticking their nose into my private life. Man, I'm sorry they bothered you."

"Well, they didn't bother *me*, but the doorman was sure as hell confused. Are you leveling with me, Charlie? You're not screwing some guy's wife are you?"

"Hell no, Joey! I don't even screw the single women in Shoreville. It's such a small town, the whole place would know about it in a New York minute. Man, what a fucking drag!"

"Well, you got some blonde broad pissed at you for some reason, Charlie. And according to the doorman she was not even much of a looker," Joey laughed, "You chasing ugly pussy, Charlie?"

"C'mon, Joey, you know me better than that."

"Yeah, I'm just giving you a hard time. But it was really weird, Charlie. And the description of the woman they said you were going out with sounded like it was Gina they were talking about. Are you serious about Gina, Charlie? It would be good if you were. She's really top notch."

"No, I already told you that we have a strong friendship. I like Gina but I'm not looking for a relationship right now. We are good friends and we have gone out once in a while. Maybe that's where the whole thing got started. Maybe they saw me somewhere with her or something."

"Well they're sure going to a helluva lot of trouble to poke into your life Charlie. I mean asking my doorman if you ever came here with a woman…Are you sure they're not a bit nuts? Did you ever screw one of them? I mean what reason would they have to be poking around like that?"

"You know Shoreville, Joey. It's a small place and I'm an eligible bachelor with a good job and a good income. Those two women have tried to fix me up with friends and I've refused to go along. But, hell, this kind of stuff is really over the top. I'll check it out when I get home. Jesus, I'm sorry this wound up literally at your front door, Joey. I'm embarrassed."

"Nah, Charlie. I'm your buddy. I just wanted to know if you were gonna get shot by some jealous husband any time soon. I figured maybe you just got horny and decked some guy's wife, you know."

"Well, thanks Joey but I'm not into messing around in my own backyard. You know how I operate. If I want pussy I go down to Atlantic City. I don't shit where I eat, you know that."

"OK, well forget about it. I just wanted to give you a heads up. The doorman said they were a weird couple of broads. Seems to me you're being stalked, Charlie. Watch your ass, OK?"

"Thanks, Joey. Now what about some lunch?" Charlie really didn't have much appetite after hearing about Sharon's most recent escapade, but he couldn't afford to let Joey in on his relationship with Gina. He was mad as hell and even more concerned but he couldn't show it.

Charlie and Joey went down to their favorite sandwich shop and talked about the acquisition search. Joey said he had alerted his M&A people at the bank and that they were already beating the bushes for targets. He commented that he liked Bill Cummins and thought they could work well together. He thanked Charlie again for making sure he was on the search team and would be the point of contact for Cummins. He said his management treats him a little differently now.

Charlie was pleased that Joey was benefiting from the assignment and he regretted having to lie to his friend about his situation with Gina but the stakes were too high for even the slightest risk.

Charlie took his leave and drove to Gina's. He checked along the way to make sure he was not being followed. He was hopping mad about Sharon's behavior and wondered if he should confront her. He would have to talk this over with Gina.

* * * * *

By the time he reached Gina's place Charlie was fuming. When he came through the door his expression told Gina that something was wrong. "Charlie, what's the matter? Did something happen over in Shoreville?"

"No, baby, I'm ready to blow up. I just came from lunch with Joey Esposito…"

"Something go wrong on the project, Charlie?"

"No, Gina, the project's moving along just fine. Joey told me that those two crazy broads from Shoreville went to his building and asked his doorman if I had ever shown up at Joey's place with a woman. They described a woman they thought I would show up with and Joey said the description matched *you* pretty closely. I am so goddamned mad I can't even think straight. Who the fuck does that bitch think she is going around like that? I'd like to wring her goddamned neck!"

"Whoa, Charlie, calm down. What did you tell Joey about the description?"

"Oh, I told him that they might have seen me in Philly at one time or another when I was with you. I told him what I had said before, that you and I were very good friends and we had gone out on a few occasions just to talk. You know – the same stuff I said before. I'm pretty sure he believed me."

"OK, so now let's think about what the wacky ladies are doing. Charlie, Sharon Gallagher is baiting you. She *wants* you to get pissed. I'm sure she thought you would find out that she was asking about you. You said she and that other nut have been stalking you in Shoreville – showing up at the softball practice field and hiding around the corner from your house, right?"

"Yeah, right, Gina. I've got a good mind to just confront her once and for all!"

"No, Charlie, think with me on this. Why did she go to Joey's place?"

"Because she's a nosy damned bitch, that's why!"

"No, no, she is a nosy damned bitch that's for sure. But that's not why she went to Joey's place. She went there because she doesn't know where else to go. That's why. She wants you to know that she can find things out about you no matter what you do. Because you are wise to the surveillance and frustrated her last attempts to follow you, she's got to do something to get you off balance. You see that?"

Charlie started to calm down, "Yeah, I guess so, but I am really pissed."

"That's exactly what she wants, Charlie. Suppose you confront her. She will just deny that it was her. You would have to get the doorman to look her straight in the eye and say 'yeah, that's her'. Otherwise, she will just say you're crazy. She wants to create a scene. She wants you to get angry enough to make a mistake. Maybe you will take it up with her husband again. Then she'll deny, deny, and deny. What if the doorman had told her that you had been to Joey's with me? What do you think would happen next? I can tell you. She would then try to approach Joey. The fact is, Charlie, she doesn't know a damned thing more now than she knew before. Before she talked to the doorman she knew about me. She saw us together at least once, right?"

"Yeah, right."

"OK, she described the girl she saw you with to the doorman. What did he tell her?"

"Well, Joey said that the doorman said he had never seen me enter the building with a woman and that she should take up the matter with me if she wanted to know more."

"Good! So the only information she got was that you never went to Joey's place with me. Now tell me truthfully, Charlie, how much more does she know now?"

"I guess you're right, Gina."

"Of course I am. What you are really worried about is that she raised a question in Joey's mind."

"Yeah! You're right, Gina. I was afraid she had made our relationship public. Joey has no idea that you and I are in love with each other."

"Exactly! And what did you tell Joey?"

"I told him that we were friends, good friends."

"Does he believe you?"

"I'm pretty sure he does."

"So as far as Joey is concerned this is some personal matter of yours that does not concern him, right?"

"Right, he even asked me if I was screwing Sharon and she was jealously chasing after me."

"So, see Charlie? Sharon got nothing. She's just as frustrated as she was before. Her gamble didn't work and now *she* is the one who is exposed. Do you think the doorman gives a shit if you are screwing her? I seriously doubt it. He probably thinks she is just a nut case."

Charlie was calmer, "Well, that's what Joey said."

"Sure, because that's how she came across. As far as he is concerned you just laid some woman and then left her for someone younger. That's not exactly something new in this world. She came across as some desperate broad who is trying to get information on a two-timing lover. A week from now he won't even remember the incident."

"I hope you're right, Gina. I'd love to give that bitch a punch in the face!"

"She knows that, Charlie. That's exactly what she wants you to feel and maybe even try. That would give her a lot to talk about and maybe even get the entire town on her side. She would make herself a victim. She would claim she never did a thing to upset you. She would say you were stressed on your job. She would say you are delusional and the worst part is that a lot of people would believe it. Confront her and she will provoke you further to make herself a victim."

Charlie heaved a deep sigh, "You're right, Gina. If I make an issue of this, she will say I am imagining things and obsessed with her. So what do I do?"

"To start with, you should ignore the incident. Make sure you keep your eyes open to see if she tries to follow you. If she does, do what you did last time. Go back to Shoreville. She has a family and a home to take care of. She can't be on you 24/7. There's just no way she can do that. She is expecting you to do something, so surprise her – do nothing! She has no idea that I am Carlo Rizzo's adopted daughter. She didn't know it before and she doesn't know it now. Remember that your only vulnerability is my name. If my name was Betty Smith you could have taken me to Shoreville, introduced me to your friends, announced our engagement and told Sharon Gallagher to fuck off. But that's not the way it is. I am Gina Ferelli, Mafia Princess. Being engaged to me or maybe even just dating me could bring your career to an abrupt end. You now have something to hide, Charlie Mullins. So you can't afford to make a mistake. You have to be careful who you challenge. And because that woman has no idea what is at stake she is more dangerous than someone who does know. She's just trying to find out who is the mysterious woman in your life. She has no idea what the stakes are so she is like a bull in a china shop. Don't challenge her. Lead her astray. Keep her away from what counts. In short, put up with it!"

"Holy cow, Gina, you're right of course, but how did you learn all that stuff? You're a real strategist."

"Charlie, remember who I am. I'm not just Gina Ferelli, daughter of a Sicilian couple who died many years ago. I am the adopted daughter of Carlo Rizzo, alleged Mafia 'don'. My uncle taught me well. Don't you think the 'suits' tried to approach me when I was a child? When I got my first job after Bryn Mawr my income tax was audited three years in a row. That's when my uncle convinced me to accept his financial help. It took the 'suits' five years to figure out that I was just a young woman and not some kind of 'moll' working for my uncle, picking up numbers slips, or privy to his secrets. For years I had people asking about me, poking into my personal life, provoking me to see if I would say something that could be used against my uncle. What you are dealing with is small change, Charlie. They finally left me alone after having tapped my phone, investigated my finances, checked out my personal life, trying to get agents to date me, and so on. That woman is just a nut case. Dealing with her is easy compared to what I have been through."

"Like I said Gina, I guess I have a lot to learn. I'm calm now, but I was really out of it for a while there."

"I understand Charlie, I really do. You have to look behind the incident to see what really happened. In this case, that woman got nothing – n-o-t-h-i-n-g! Zilch! She still doesn't know who I am so nothing has changed."

"Thanks, sweetheart, I would have challenged her and probably have blown it."

Gina kissed Charlie, "You're a good man, Charlie. You know what's right and you stand up for it. But the world I lived in is not as black-and-white as yours. What's 'right' often gets lost in the shuffle. That woman thinks she has a right to find out what you are up to. She thinks you might be doing something wrong. You think you have a right to privacy. As far as each of you is concerned, you are doing the 'right thing'. You are not going to change her. You've got only to neutralize her, and even so for a limited period of time. Don't waste time on her. Just keep her where she is right now – still in the dark. The Feds will show you what invasion of privacy is really about."

Charlie stepped over to the bar, grabbed a bottle of scotch and poured himself a drink.

"There you go, Mullins! Have a drink and forget about it. Mind if I join you?"

"Oh jeez, sorry Gina, let me pour you a drink." Charlie poured her a measure of scotch and they clinked their glasses together, "To us!"

"Yes, to us!"

XXXVIII

The next three business quarters were marked by a flurry of meetings with operating department heads, preparing proposals for acquisitions and listing new suppliers submitted by Joey Esposito's bank, due diligence investigations of the target companies and suppliers, and writing reports to be submitted to Phillip Shaw. Charlie met weekly with Warren Carpenter and Bill Cummins. They reviewed the financials of all the companies that Joey Esposito brought to them and checked out the management and owners of all of them. Phillip Shaw's strategy to expand the company while locking it in to long-term relationships and using up Shaw's excess cash was beginning to take shape.

Phillip Shaw made sure that Fred Perkins was brought in to deliberate on the potential acquisitions and supply relationships. Fred proudly strutted around the company making sure that everyone was aware of his "special relationship" with the CEO. Charlie watched Fred doing his cock of the walk routine with mild amusement. The operating department heads humored Perkins and pretended to defer to his judgment and his ego knowing full well that Phillip and Charlie, the latter behind the scenes, were running the entire show.

From the companies targeted for acquisition, Charlie made up a "short list" of the most attractive candidates. He did the same for new suppliers and Warren Carpenter drew up long-term supply contracts that included heavy penalties for cancellation by either party. The acquisitions would also be locked in with contracts that prohibited Shaw from "flipping" the companies for a quick profit. Charlie and Bill Cummins provided their recommendations as to the best companies to acquire and Phillip Shaw accepted their recommendations and approved the deals.

Warren Carpenter set up an offshore holding company that would negotiate the sale of the real estate holdings that were on the company's books but used exclusively by the family and hold the funds until just before the IPO was to take place. The properties would be taken off the company's books and the company reimbursed for all mortgage payments made on behalf of the Shaw family members. The new owners would get a clean balance sheet and a re-vamped and highly lucrative supply chain.

Sales personnel submitted customer reports indicating that Shaw's customers were very pleased with Phillip's announced strategy. Customers swore fidelity and praised the company for its aggressive posture. The sales personnel did not know which companies would eventually be acquired but they knew acquisitions were on the table and informed customers accordingly.

Charlie continued his twice weekly trips to Shoreville for bowling and softball and kept up the innocuous ruse of having his lights and TV turn on and off. He really didn't care if it worked or not because he now had a method for dealing with Sharon Gallagher and Diane Simms. Gina had been right. There was no way the two women could watch Charlie on a continuous basis. They had families that kept them busy. Whenever they tried to follow Charlie he had only to double back and head for Shoreville again. Because of his busy schedule he and Gina did not go out as often as before so the risk of being seen in Philly by someone from Shoreville was reduced. He would occasionally stay overnight in Shoreville at random intervals so anyone watching the house would not know if the lights were on because he was there or because of the timers. Sharon was consumed with frustration and remained obsessed with discovering the identity of Charlie's girlfriend. She was just waiting for an opportunity. Diane, however, was beginning to tire of the game. Her attempts to back out of the surveillance of Charlie Mullins were unsuccessful as Sharon bullied her into staying the course.

* * * * *

Charlie and Gina were also busy planning their future as the expansion drive of the Shaw Corporation approached the final stretch. They met with Carlo Rizzo every Sunday when Charlie would provide Carlo with a briefing of progress on the expansion project and copies of his reports to Phillip Shaw. Carlo said nothing but "thanks" and would put the documents aside for later review. Gina had cut back on her volunteer activities. She continued with her tutoring at the local Catholic school and sponsored her friend Emily's art show. But she sharply reduced her other activities and stayed home more often. With Charlie busy with the expansion project, they went out less often. Gina kept in contact with her friends by telephone, advising them that she was simply taking a long-needed rest from her frantic schedule.

No one seemed to disbelieve her given her previous level of activity. Unlike Charlie's Shoreville "friends", Gina's friends did not pry into her private life.

* * * * *

Following selection of the companies he decided to acquire, Phillip Shaw instructed Bill Cummins to move forward on the acquisition contracts with Warren Carpenter. Simultaneously, Phillip would plan his announcement of the acquisitions and supply chain contracts. Later he would announce the IPO and his answer to a "higher calling" to enter public service as an elected official. He met with Warren Carpenter at home where they discussed Phillip's strategy.

"Warren, we are almost ready now to announce the end of the expansion project followed later by the announcement of the IPO. We will most certainly catch the market by surprise. The announcement of the expansion plan received excellent press coverage and I've kept that issue up front with a few comments to the business press. I will soon want to release the news of the acquisitions. I think it best to do it with a press release rather than a press conference. There's such a thing as overexposure and I want the IPO announcement to be more than just an anti-climax. Are you ready?"

"Yes, Phillip, we have vetted the companies thoroughly and Bill Cummins has negotiated some very interesting and profitable long-term supply contracts. The company will be in excellent shape for a sale. The acquisitions have been locked in with guarantees that Shaw will not "flip" the companies for short-term gain. The supply contracts are locked in with heavy indemnities for cancellation. The new shareholders will get a well-structured supply chain and some very interesting acquisitions plus severe penalties for backing out or selling off. You've seen the reports so you know the income and cost projections are positive and solid. Moreover, we have made a point of acquiring only US-based companies and signing up US-based suppliers. You will be able to say that you have guaranteed that the Shaw Corporation will continue to 'buy American' and we will use that in your campaign."

"When do you think we can announce the IPO, Warren?"

"Probably in about a month, maybe two. We have been negotiating with the acquisition targets and the suppliers through the bank that has referred them without identifying Shaw. We will tell them that Shaw is the buyer this week. The contracts have all been negotiated and confidentiality statements signed. It remains only to fill in the company's name on the contracts, get them signed, and everything is ready to go. Since they have agreed to the relationships and the sale prices no one is going to back out or try to change terms once Shaw has been identified. In fact, I suspect that some of them probably know at the intuitive level that the buyer is Shaw given your announcement of the expansion plan and the nature of their businesses. I feel confident that we can push the paperwork through the SEC without major delays. You can announce the acquisitions and new supply arrangements roughly a week from now."

"Good, let's look to the statement I will make to the public about the IPO. I plan to justify it by saying that many of my friends have suggested that now that the Shaw Corporation is on a long-term stable growth trajectory, it is time for me to think about how I can contribute more. I will say that I have given careful thought to entreaties that I run for public office and I have decided that to fail to respond to this 'public service calling' would be selfish on my part. Do we have sufficient support for a candidacy? I will be facing a fairly strong incumbent you know. He will have ample time to adopt a defense strategy to ensure his re-election."

"I agree, Phillip. I have talked to several organizers and some Political Action Committees have been set up. With the IPO, money won't necessarily be a problem, but we will have to break down loyalties to the incumbent and build up your image. The incumbent has some chinks in his armor and we will exploit them. One, for example, is his position on globalization. He can be accused of supporting the export of US jobs while you, with the acquisitions you made, have guaranteed that jobs stay in the USA, at least in the Shaw Corporation. It might help to add that you intend to try to protect American jobs in the Senate now that you have done it as an executive."

"I like that! Do we have any significant weaknesses?"

"Well, the company has Defense Department contracts, so in theory you are familiar with national security matters albeit in limited areas. But you can at least speak knowledgeably on the issues or so the voters will think anyway. Shaw is also a global corporation so you are familiar with international economic issues but we may have a weakness in the area of foreign affairs. However, most voters don't give a shit about that anyway, at least not for a legislative post. I've got a handful of public relations firms lined up for some image development and we can talk about that at a later date and after we have conducted some discreet polls to find out how you are perceived by the voting public."

"OK, so it sounds like we are ready to go. Let's do it!"

They shook hands and Warren Carpenter took his leave. After Carpenter left, Phillip sat down on his sofa to muse over his statements to the public.

* * * * *

The following week Phillip instructed his PR director to put together a press release on the acquisitions. Again, to ensure the kind of coverage Phillip wanted, the release would be communicated to editors and limited to members of the local press and selected business media. Following the exclusive releases, the company would then advise PR Newswire for national distribution. The first media release would give privileged access to the announcement and that would ensure the loyalty of senior journalists. Journalists hated the widespread releases where every Tom, Dick, and Harry got the information at the same time. They didn't like being treated on an equal basis with their juniors.

Within the week the press release had been sent as planned, first to senior editors and journalists and then a few days later to PR Newswire. The market reacted favorably to the news and the names of the acquired firms. The reports that Shaw had made some highly intelligent acquisitions were unanimous and Wexler & Santori estimated that the value of the company's shares would rise sharply.

Phillip Shaw was beaming.

* * * * *

Charlie Mullins was also beaming. The ordeal of selecting firms, analyzing their numbers, following the negotiations through Wexler & Santori had required a lot of work. He was tired but elated. The deals had gone through and he was now free to concentrate on his life with Gina. They were on countdown now. Once the IPO took place, everything else would click into place and they could begin their life together without concern for who knew about it.

Charlie would still meet with Warren Carpenter and Bill Cummins at least once per week over the next two months. There were filings to be prepared and final details cleaning up the company's balance sheets and making sure all was prepared for a successful IPO. There would be one last flurry of activity and then it would be over. Shaw Corporation would change ownership.

He continued his trips to Shoreville for bowling and softball. He noticed Sharon Gallagher hanging around the softball practice field once in a while and he saw her shopping at the Acme Supermarket once. She made it a point to avoid him. Sharon was beside herself with frustration ever since Charlie had turned the tables on her by doubling back to Shoreville every time she tried to follow him. However, Charlie had made sure that both Bill Gallagher and Bob Simms were informed of his enormous work load with the acquisition projects. He told them that sometimes he had to hole up in a Wilmington hotel so he could meet with the auditors and attorneys working with him. He was sure that the information would reach Sharon and Diane. But he knew they were just biding their time and waiting for a good opportunity to catch him unawares.

* * * * *

Within a month-and-a-half everything had been prepared for the IPO and it was time for Phillip Shaw to announce it to the press.

When Charlie arrived to the Shaw Corporation parking lot on a sunny Tuesday morning he could see the press vehicles and the camera crews unloading their equipment for a press conference. He smiled inwardly, "*It's started, we're on countdown now,*" he thought. He took the elevator up to the floor where the conference room was located and saw the preparations of the camera crews and the buzz of the company's kitchen staff putting out coffee, soft drinks, and sandwiches for the reporters and their crews. He entered the stairwell to go down to his own floor. He walked by Fred Perkins' office to see Fred sitting straight up in his chair in a navy blue suit and a light blue plain tie over a white shirt. Today Fred has eschewed his traditional brown suits. "*Looks like Fred will be in on the press conference,*" he said to himself. He saw Laura Metzer looking at him, "Spiffy, no, Charlie? I've never seen him looking so starched. Phillip invited him to be at the press conference. He even put on aftershave instead of his usual Witch Hazel. Like the TV is going to transmit the smell," she laughed.

Charlie smiled, "As far as I know Laura, this will be the first time he has ever been on TV. He's really decked out like a peacock – a discreet peacock of course, but a peacock nonetheless."

Laura laughed, "You're too much, Charlie! Imagine a discreet peacock!"

"Something tells me you're going to have an easy day today, Laura."

"I sure as hell deserve one, no?"

"Right on, Laura, see you later."

Charlie moved to his office. The whole floor was abuzz with speculation as to what the press conference would be about. A couple of subordinates approached him, "What's happening, Charlie? It looks like we're gonna have another press conference."

"Looks that way, doesn't it? I guess Phillip Shaw has something he wants to say. We'll just have to wait to see what it is so go on back to your work. Nobody's told me anything."

At precisely 11-o-clock Phillip Shaw made his entrance to the conference room. Fred Perkins followed at what he hoped was an appropriate distance. Phillip moved directly to the lectern and Fred took the seat that had been reserved for him at the conference table.

He began, "Ladies and gentlemen, many thanks for coming. I hope you won't be disappointed in what I have to say." He smiled. "Today I want to make a very special announcement. You will remember that 9 months ago I said that we were going to grow this company and do so aggressively. You were all informed of the acquisitions we made to put the company on a growth trajectory", the reporters were still waiting for the meat and had not yet turned on their tape recorders or picked up their pens. Phillip continued, "I am certain that the company is now poised to grow and grow aggressively and..." Phillip paused for a moment, "can do so without my help or leadership."

Suddenly, the tape recorders were turned on and pens started moving quickly on notepads. This comment was not expected.

"Following the acquisitions I was approached by a number of people who felt that my leadership at Shaw Corporation could be put to good use in leading this country forward to a new level of competitiveness in the global economy. They asked me to consider running for public office where I could have a greater impact than as president and CEO of Shaw Corporation." Reporters glanced around the room at each other.

"Obviously, I would not be able to hold public office and remain as an officer of a corporation with contracts with the government so I would have to step down as CEO. Consequently,..." again he paused for effect, "I have decided that the Shaw Corporation will go public."

Now the room was abuzz with commentary, reporters checking to make sure their tape recorders were running, glancing around at each other, shifting in their seats as if to hear better, and frantically taking notes.

"Within a couple of weeks we will launch an IPO to sell Shaw's shares to the public."

Hands flew up throughout the room as reporters tried to pose questions.

"Give me just another minute and I will address your questions," Phillip said to the group, "Following the IPO I will begin working on my campaign to run for the US Senate. Now I will take your questions."

Every reporter in the room had his or her hand up.

Phillip recognized first a female senior reporter from a major financial publication, "Mr. Shaw, less than a year ago you said that going public was not in your plans and that you would retire from a larger and more powerful Shaw Corporation. What happened?"

Phillip smiled graciously, "I am fully aware of what I said. Over the past several months I was approached by a lot of people who felt that I had something to contribute to this great country besides running this company. I confess that I listened to their entreaties and arguments with great care. This company has been my entire life and I told them I was reluctant to leave it. However, public service is a high calling and our economy has been assaulted by the effects of globalization. Jobs have moved abroad and whole communities have been prejudiced by factory closings and massive layoffs. My insistence on buying American and my efforts at keeping our company strong in the face of foreign competition were presented to me as a contribution I could make at a much higher level and influence the lives of more people."

The hands flew up again. Phillip acknowledged a reporter from a local publication. "Mr. Shaw, your company has always prided itself on its role in the local community. Won't going public have an effect on the company's local presence? Won't new owners cut back on the various community programs Shaw has carried out over the years?"

"I don't think so," Phillip responded, "a close relationship with the local community is one of the strengths of Shaw's business. A new owner will not want to change that. Obviously, I can't speak for the new owners, whoever they might turn out to be, but it is important to remember that one of the principal reasons for the high worker productivity at Shaw has been the company's dedication to the overall welfare of its work force. No intelligent investor would want to remove one of the supporting pillars of the company's success."

Hands rose again as Phillip recognized another reporter, "Mr. Shaw, a lot of acquisitions and IPOs are followed by layoffs and force reductions. Aren't you concerned that the new owners might do the same thing?"

"I'm glad you asked that question. The answer is clearly 'no'. Had we decided to go public before making the acquisitions that were announced, that might have been the case. We had been losing market share, albeit gradually, and cutting back on our labor force might have been an option at that time. However, with the new acquisitions, the new owners will need every man and woman working for this company and may even have to hire more. I should add that we have locked in the supply arrangements and acquisitions with long-term contracts that include heavy cancellation costs to ensure that the new owners treat this company as an on-going business and not a speculative acquisition. They will have no incentive to cut back anywhere in the company and will have an enormous incentive to pour more resources into a much stronger organization. You should also remember that we have a highly qualified professional management team in the company so I don't even expect many changes in the senior levels of the company. In fact, one of those capable managers is with me today, Mr. Fred Perkins, our principal financial executive who helped me with the selection of the acquired companies."

Fred Perkins lit up and sat even straighter in his chair. All eyes focused on him and he was temporarily blinded by the flashes of the multitude of cameras in the room. He offered a somewhat flustered acknowledgement of the reporters and Phillip's comment by nodding his head to the group. He was at a loss for words. Phillip smiled inwardly. He knew that Fred was articulate as a rock unless he was yelling at someone. He hoped that no one would ask him a question. No one did.

Again, hands went up. Phillip pointed to a reporter from a national news service, "Mr. Shaw, would you comment on your decision to run for the Senate? What made you decide to do it? Won't the Shaw Corporation suffer from your departure?"

"Well, I would like to believe I will be missed, but I hope that it is as a personality and not simply as a CEO. As I mentioned previously, I am confident of the professional capabilities of the management team I have assembled. I am sure that any new owners will be hard-pressed to find more capable management elsewhere, so the policies and procedures that are in place at the Shaw Corporation are not simply the result of *my* leadership. A lot of very capable people were behind that leadership. In that regard, I am sure I won't be missed and the company will not suffer by my departure. As for my decision to run for public office, I truly believe that public service is one of the highest callings an individual can answer. I listened to the people who approached me and I carefully weighed their comments. As you all know, I had a mild heart attack not too long ago and as I said when returning to my job, incidents like that tend to make you look more carefully at your life and what you have contributed. I was perfectly content to remain as CEO of Shaw until others convinced me that I could do much more for my country as a Senator. I would not be a responsible citizen and a leader if I did not respond to that call."

"Mr. Shaw," one of the reporters interrupted, "you must be aware that you will be taking on one or another of two very strong incumbents for a Senate seat. Are you prepared for a campaign?"

"To be perfectly honest," Phillip lied, "I had not even thought about a campaign yet. I have been extremely busy with the acquisitions and I was caught by surprise by the suggestions that I run for office. The only thing I have decided so far is to respond to the call. I am convinced that I can be a good Senator and contribute to the well-being of this great country. I have no illusions about the qualifications of those already holding office. Once the IPO has taken place, I will spend some time analyzing issues and preparing myself for a campaign. But I am not ready at this point to discuss specifics. I hope you understand."

As soon as Phillip finished his sentence hands flew up again. "I think I have said enough now. You all know what everyone has been asking for years, that is, will the Shaw Corporation ever go public? For years the answer has been 'no' and had it not been for a number of my friends and colleagues, it might have continued that way. I am stepping down as CEO and putting the company up for public ownership to avoid any conflicts of interest should I be elected to public office. Let me say in closing that I am sure than many of you will be far more critical of me as a candidate to public office than you have been of my performance as CEO." Phillip laughed and the room laughed with him. Stepping from behind the lectern, Phillip worked the room, shaking hands with reporters and thanking them for coming to what would be his last press conference as CEO of the Shaw Corporation. Several reporters tried to get some off-the-record comments about Phillip's political views and the kind of campaign he intended to wage. Phillip dodged the questions by repeating that he had not yet had time to think about his campaign. After rubbing elbows with the reporters, Phillip took his leave and the reporters all rushed back to their offices to write their stories, edit their videos, and speculate on the future of the Shaw Corporation and Phillip's chances to get elected to the Senate.

When Phillip returned to his office, Warren Carpenter was waiting for him. "I watched the conference from the back of the room, Phillip. You were terrific! It was nice to know that you have not yet given any thought to your campaign," Warren laughed. "Boy did you handle that one well!" They both laughed heartily.

"You want a scotch, Warren? I think I need a drink after that conference. It's not too early is it? I mean hell, I've just quit my job as CEO of the Shaw Corporation!"

"Let's have one, Phillip. That conference deserves a toast!"

Phillip went to a liquor cabinet and took out a bottle of single malt scotch and poured a couple of fingers of the expensive stuff for each of them. They clinked their glasses together and Phillip said "To a helluva campaign."

"Here, here," Warren Carpenter replied and they both emptied their glasses in a single bolt. "By the way, Phillip, that was a masterful touch having Fred Perkins at the conference. It showed continuity and teamwork are valued and recognized."

Phillip laughed, "Poor Fred, he didn't have the slightest idea what to say or do. He just nodded to everyone in the room and sat ramrod straight in his chair. He looked almost like a statue! That was his fifteen minutes of fame and I suppose he will treasure the moment until the day he dies. I know he is difficult, but he is loyal, if inarticulate except when berating someone and I hope he stays on with the new management. He's competent but damned difficult and hardly a political animal. He's about as political as a Doberman!" They both laughed heartily. "Now, let's start talking about that campaign, Warren. Let's go back to the house. Nobody's going to work today after that press conference. They won't even know I'm gone."

* * * * *

Laura Metzer burst into Charlie's office, "My God, Charlie, did you hear the news? Phillip Shaw is going to sell the company! The whole building is buzzing with rumors. Everybody is scared to death that they will lose their jobs. Jesus, Charlie, what's going on?"

"Take it easy, Laura. This is news to me too," Charlie lied, "but I am certain that Phillip Shaw is not going to throw this company to the sharks. Maybe he is just tired of running it. He did have a heart attack you know!"

"You know what somebody told me? He's going to run for the Senate in the next elections. Can you believe it?!"

"Well, think about that Laura, would he be able to run for public office if he had thrown his company to a bunch of sharks? He wouldn't get many votes from people who had lost their jobs, would he?"

"No, I guess you're right Charlie. But, it's still scary. I mean what if the new owners do what a lot of others have done and go through the company with a hatchet?"

"Laura, look at the acquisitions Phillip made. You can be sure that Phillip has locked in any new investors to long term relationships with the acquired companies. The Shaw Corporation has been repositioned in the market. The new owners are buying into what is practically a new company. They won't be inclined to put people on the street."

"Yeah, but what about people like you and me who are linked to executives of the company? If Fred loses his job, his successor will want to bring in his own team. Have you thought about that, Charlie?"

"Of course, Laura. In the first place, I don't think Fred will get the ax. He's well regarded in financial circles and he knows where the rocks are here. It's possible of course, but I don't think it is probable. Didn't Phillip invite him to be at the press conference? I'm sure he had a reason for that. Phillip Shaw doesn't do *anything* without thinking about what it means and how it will be interpreted, believe me."

"God, I hope you are right Charlie. Billy is still in college and I would hate to have to look for another job before he finishes."

"Relax Laura, even in a worst case scenario it will take the new owners a long time to evaluate the company and the personnel. They're not going to walk in the day after buying the company and start kicking people out. If I remember correctly, Billy should graduate this summer so that won't be an issue in short order. Besides, I just don't see you getting fired anyway. Take it easy. I know people are on edge, but if I know this company and Phillip Shaw, there won't be any upheaval. Maybe a few waves, but no upheaval."

"Thanks Charlie. I feel better, not good mind you, but better than before. I'll leave you alone now. Thanks for the ear."

"No problem, Laura. See ya later." Charlie felt bad that he could not tell Laura everything. She was scared, just as everyone else would be now that Shaw was going to change hands. He knew he would get a lot of questions from his buddies in Shoreville and they would all reflect the same fears that Laura discussed with him. He drew some comfort from knowing that both Sharon Gallagher and Diane Simms would be worried and not thinking much about him for the next couple of weeks. In fact, since he was an important source of information about what was happening in the company, they would make it a point to not antagonize him. But, in spite of his anger at Sharon and Diane's behavior, he could not help but feel sorry for them. They had kids in school, mortgages on their homes, and their husbands had good jobs. Their lives would be disrupted by the IPO and they would be on edge for a long time wondering if and when the ax would fall.

Phillip Shaw was right. Nobody in the company did any work that day. As the news of his press conference was passed along the "water-cooler-telegraph" people either stood around speculating about what would happen or walked quietly back to their desks to worry.

Charlie had seen this kind of reaction in individuals who were afraid of being fired but he had never seen it take over an entire company. He decided that he would call a staff meeting of his own personnel to try to put them a little more at ease. He summoned a meeting for 3 pm and was surprised to see everyone standing around his office at two-forty-five. No one was talking or telling jokes. The mood was somber. He led the group to the meeting room just down the corridor and everyone sat down in absolute silence. Charlie could not tell his staff everything he knew but he could assure them that their jobs were less in danger than they all seemed to think. He explained that he had known about the acquisitions from Fred, of course, and from what he could see, the acquisitions virtually ensured that no one would be given walking papers after the IPO. A couple of employees asked why he thought this would apply to the staff people whose jobs involved processing papers rather than producing things. Charlie told the group that first of all he was sure that Fred Perkins would still be around when the dust settled. This led to a couple of good natured groans from some of his staff. Charlie smiled and continued to explain that there was no real reason to fire any of the financial staff. When he finished the meeting the employees appeared a little more relaxed. He could not in good conscience make any promises but he could also not bear to see his loyal staff go home before trying to help them stay calm and be a little more confident about the future. He knew that this staff meeting was just a small prelude to what he would hear at bowling league night tomorrow.

Charlie and all the employees in his department left the office promptly at 5-o-clock. Within 5 minutes not a single person was around. Charlie went directly to the parking lot, got into his car, and drove to Philly. Within 20 minutes he was pulling into the garage at Gina's building.

* * * * *

Gina was waiting for Charlie with a vodka martini in her hand. She handed it to him and grabbed her own manhattan and accompanied him to the couch. "I had the TV on when a reporter came out with the breaking news that the Shaw Corporation was going to be sold. I figured you would leave the office precisely at 5 and that you would need a drink."

Charlie kissed her, "Boy was that a good call! What a day, Gina. Yeah, I do need a drink. Thanks." He took a deep gulp of his drink before sitting down with Gina. He clinked his glass to hers and said, "Here's to us now, sweets. It's been a long, hard slog but we made it."

"Here's to our life, Charlie. I know this has been very tough for you. I'm with you for whatever lies ahead. I love you."

"Gina, I've never seen so many terrified people at one time. Everyone in the company is wondering who will be the new owners and whether they will have a job when the dust settles. It's really sad to see it, even knowing that not much will change. The anxiety is palpable and, probably to large degree, not justified but they don't know what I know. They are suffering."

"Those poor people, Charlie. They all have responsibilities, kids in school, mortgages, car payments, bank loans, and God knows what else. Each and every one of them must be a nervous wreck. Shaw is by far the biggest and best paying employer in the whole region. Isn't there anything the company can do to assure them?"

"I think Phillip Shaw did as much as he could. He doesn't have much control over what the new owners will do. He has to trust his business acumen and believe that he has structured the company in such a way that no buyer would want to mess too much with it for fear of messing up a good thing. He's a sharp businessman and has done what he could but no one is really going to feel good until the dust settles on this thing. The Shaw Corporation was for many of those who worked for it a bit like the Catholic Church; priests, bishops, cardinals, and popes come and go, but the Church is still the same. Everyone just took it for granted that the Shaw family would stay in charge forever. People get settled in their lives and see the company as a rock. It's always there and it is solid. Now they fear the rock could be moved and they are disoriented. Besides, they've seen it happen all over America. Companies move entire facilities to China. Jobs are exported to India, or Brazil, or Mexico. Whole communities get wiped out. The Shaws are sure to make a lot of money on the IPO and a lot of people will resent the fact that their lives have been disrupted while the Shaw family makes a bundle. They will feel betrayed until things settle down. I truly believe that Phillip has done a good job of making sure the disruption will be minimal, if only because he plans to run for office and it wouldn't do to have destroyed whole communities through the sale. But, I don't know of any way to make people feel safe under the circumstances."

"Charlie, you sound a lot like my uncle!" Gina said. "Things are as they are and we have to live with the situation. I guess you're right but I really feel sorry for the families who will have to worry their way through the situation."

"Me too, Gina, but I am powerless to help in this case."

"Well, at least you can try to help your friends in Shoreville."

"Yeah, tomorrow is league night and I am sure I will be barraged with questions. I'll do what I can, but it's not going to be easy for anyone right now. There will be some anger and a lot of fear. I'm sure of that. I saw it in the past whenever the economy turned south. This is much more dramatic and more widespread. I'll do what I can, but it won't be enough, I'm sure of that."

"Are you hungry Charlie, I can fix something or we can go out. It's up to you."

"No, sweets, I think I would just like to order a pizza a little later. I want to watch the 7-o-clock news to see what's reported on the press conference. Maybe we could open a bottle of wine and have some pizza. I'm really not in the mood for a fancy dinner or making you work. I'd like to just have you beside me. Is that OK?"

"Sure, Charlie, I know what you must be going through. But don't feel responsible for this. Phillip Shaw was going to sell the company anyway. He wants his political career and you can feel comfortable knowing that you did your best to protect the jobs of your friends and colleagues."

They sat down to watch the evening news. The local stations ran the story of the IPO and Phillip's announcement of a calling to public service as the first item on the agenda. There were film clips of Phillip's presentation followed by analysis of what the whole thing meant for the Delaware Valley communities. The national networks covered the press conference in the business news segments. The emphasis was on the expectations for the IPO and for Phillip Shaw's bid for the Senate. A few pundits had been brought in to comment on both. The consensus was that Phillip had done a masterful job of preparing the company for long-term growth. There were comments on the quality of the management team and the likelihood that there would be no major upheavals inside the company. The comments on Phillip's planned political career were also positive but emphasized that he would have to face a difficult campaign to unseat an incumbent, especially the one who had been a Senator for several terms.

Charlie took some comfort in the national news reports and hoped that his friends in Shoreville had seen both the local and national coverage. Tomorrow night would be a little easier if he could refer to the rather positive outlook of the pundits.

When the news was over, Gina turned off the TV and put some relaxing jazz on the CD player. She called and ordered a pizza and asked Charlie to open a bottle of wine. She could see that Charlie felt better but was still worried for his friends. She walked over to him and embraced him tightly. "It'll all work out OK, Charlie. I know it. I'm here for you. Your friends will be all right."

"I believe that Gina, I really do. They will suffer because of their fear, but I'm pretty sure they won't lose their jobs. It's just that I know what they are going through. I saw my parents go through it a few times. Nobody likes to really know that life is uncertain. Faith and hope far outweigh objective reason in people's lives. I've felt that way myself a lot of times."

"Do you want to talk to Uncle Carlo, Charlie?"

"No, Gina, we will see him on Sunday anyway and I'm comfortable that things have been done with as much care and concern for the fate of others as could possibly be the case." Charlie ate a couple of slices of pizza slowly and drank a little more wine than usual. Gina, too, ate slowly but drank little wine. She was worried about Charlie. After listening to some music for a couple of hours and sitting in silence on the sofa with Charlie's arm around Gina, they went to bed. Tomorrow would be a tough day for Charlie Mullins.

* * * * *

Wednesday was not a typical work day at the Shaw Corporation. People walked around hugging the walls with hangdog expressions on their faces. They seemed to be moving in slow motion while thinking about something else. Charlie took comfort in seeing that his team seemed at least a little more relaxed than many of the other employees. He was glad he had held the staff meeting. During the day he made it a point to walk around the office and encourage those who seemed to be the most worried. He stopped by Laura's desk and noticed that Fred Perkins was again wearing his blue suit. *"What a bastard!"* Charlie thought. *"The least he could do would be to provide some support for his people!"* But he knew that empathy was not in Fred Perkins' emotional lexicon. He was basking in his 15 minutes of fame and could not care less if everyone else was scared shitless. Laura was a little more composed than she had been yesterday and said, "Thanks for your words yesterday, Charlie. I think you are right. Some things will change, but there's not going to be any mass executions. I feel better."

"That's good, Laura. Try to take an objective approach. Phillip did his homework and he has no interest in selling out the employees. In fact, he will need their votes, so he wants 'em happy. Stick with it."

"Thanks, Charlie. Did anyone ever tell you that you are just one helluva nice guy?"

"Maybe once or twice, Laura, but I try not to believe them," Charlie laughed, "see ya' later." Charlie headed back to his office. He had to prepare himself for the questions of his friends that night.

Charlie left the office precisely at 5-o-clock and drove directly to Shoreville. He would take a few minutes at his house to collect his thoughts before heading off to the bowling alley. Tonight he would definitely stay for the pizza and beer. He advised Gina that morning that he might stay in Shoreville if he wound up drinking too much beer or if the questions dragged on into the late hours.

When he got to Shoreville, he went through the regular ritual of checking his timers. He found a bottle of scotch and poured himself a small shot and sat down to think through his encounter with his friends. When he finished his drink he picked up his gear and drove to the bowling alley. No sooner had he entered than Artie Samuels called out, "Hey Charlie, how about that son of a bitch selling us out? What the fuck is going on over there in Wilmington?"

"Good evening Artie", Charlie said.

"Good evening my ass, Charlie. Those rich bastards are gonna sell the company and if we don't move to China, we're all fucked."

By the time Artie finished his diatribe, the others had gathered around, "Yeah, what's goin' on Charlie?" Tony Mazza asked.

"Did you know about this, Charlie?" Bill Gallagher asked in a slightly accusatory tone.

"Whoa, guys! Hang on." Charlie said, "I know what you are going through, this is Charlie, remember? My father went through this same sort of thing when layoffs were planned. I lived through it myself so I know what you are feeling."

"Yeah, but when your old man worried about layoffs, they weren't selling the company!" Artie Samuels chimed in.

"Look, guys, I'll tell you what I know. I don't have access to everything but I hear stuff around the halls. If you saw the news broadcasts, you saw Fred Perkins sitting there so what I have to say comes from someone close to the decision to go public. OK? Now, let's calm down and talk about it, all right?"

"OK, Charlie," Tony Mazza said, "sorry but you know that everybody in Shoreville is shitting their pants. Shaw is the biggest and best employer and nobody wants to leave this town. We're scared and nobody's ashamed to admit it."

"I know, Tony, and as far as I can tell, nobody is going to have to leave. Let me tell you what I know about Phillip Shaw's strategy and the acquisitions he made. He's put the company on a growth track, locked in the acquisitions, and provided the new owners, whoever they might be, with enormous incentives to leave things alone and let the company do its work. Obviously, he can't guarantee anything but at least he has stopped the loss of market share which *would* have cost a few jobs eventually. If things had continued as they were going, some of you would have lost jobs."

Artie Samuels interrupted him, "Yeah, but did he have to sell the fucking company too?"

"No, Artie, but you can't expect that he would be around forever either. The guy did have a heart attack and if he stuck around he might have had a fatal one. You think the family would have held on to the company if the only one qualified to run it had croaked?"

"Yeah, I know, Charlie but my wife is hysterical. She's driving me nuts and I ain't feelin' too good myself, if you get my drift."

"I do, Artie. I really do. Like I said, I've been there and all of you know that. We went to school together and all of our families worried at one time or another about layoffs. But I'm confident that when it is all said and done, you will still have your jobs and maybe working a little harder to move the company forward."

"Just so long as I'm working Charlie," Artie said.

"Look, I'm giving you guys everything I know. More than that is impossible. I'm not going to speculate and I'm not going to ask that you take my word for everything, but you all know I would not bullshit you. The acquisitions have been tightly wound up and it is highly unlikely that layoffs are in the cards."

Tony Mazza was the first to speak after a moment or two of silence, "Thanks, Charlie. We all know you have been there yourself. You are one of us and your folks went through a lot. Things are tough everywhere. Auto companies are shutting down. A lot of what you buy at Wal-Mart now has 'Made in China' on the label, it's not easy to stay calm in that kind of environment."

"I know Tony, I could lose my job too, you know. I just don't see it in the cards. I watched the whole thing being set up and the acquisitions all came across my desk for analysis as you all know. I ran the numbers and I am confident that Phillip Shaw knew what he was doing. Besides, the guy announced that he is running for the Senate. You think he wants to leave a trail of disaster behind? He wouldn't get many votes that way! But like I said, we don't have any guarantees but then, we never did anyway, right?"

"Yeah, you're right Charlie," Bob Simms said. "We are all just uptight. We've seen a lot of people lose their jobs over the past few years. It's hard not to be scared."

The group murmured its agreement.

"Look," Charlie said, "let's bowl a few games and forget about things for a little while. We can all calm down and then talk some more. That OK with everybody?"

"Shit yeah!" said Artie, "Maybe if I knock a few pins around I'll work off my anger. What the hell, this is a matter for the big shots. Let's just knock the shit out of those pins!"

The group walked to the lanes and did just as Artie suggested. By the end of the evening, everyone was more relaxed. They went off for pizza and beer and Charlie joined the group. When they got to the pizzeria and had ordered a few pitchers of beer and a few pizzas, Charlie opened the conversation. "Look, you guys are all my friends. We've all known each other since grammar school I've never left Shoreville even after getting one of the big shot jobs in the company. I don't want to see my home town disappear. I know your wives. I knew your parents. I know your kids. I go to the high school football and basketball games. I watch your kids play Babe Ruth baseball. I also know that times are uncertain everywhere, not just in Shoreville. We all thought the Shaw Corporation was like a safe harbor, isolated from all of the storms going on around it. It's not true. Shaw is a company that had begun to slide. Phillip Shaw recognized it and did something about it. He has decided to run for the Senate to try to make sure that the US continues to be competitive in the world economy. He can't be in the Senate and own a company at the same time. Personally, I would rather have him in the Senate than getting the shit beat out of him by the Chinese and not be able to do anything about it."

Charlie thought to himself, *"Shit, Phillip Shaw owes me one! I sure as hell hope I am right about this!"*

Everyone listened in silence to Charlie's statement. They all knew it to be true. The old days of employer-employee loyalty were gone. Phillip Shaw had done what he could to protect his employees and he would do his best in the Senate to reverse the economic tide against America's manufacturing companies. He was better than a lot of other CEOs that the group had heard or read about.

Bill Gallagher was the first to speak, "We know, Charlie and thanks for your comments and information. It's not Phillip Shaw's fault. It's just that we all know that he'll get a few billion to his credit and we have mortgages. He didn't bring this down on us, but that's small comfort when you think you might be out of a job at 40 and not find another one. Sorry if we seemed to be attacking you. We know you are with us and that you are a friend. Because you are a well-informed friend, you wind up bearing the brunt of our anxiety. I just hope you are right."

"Me too, Bill, me too."

The group was more relaxed when Charlie took his leave. He decided to go back to Philly because he did not want to be alone in his old house. He wanted to be near Gina.

When he arrived to Gina's apartment, she was sitting on the sofa with her legs curled under her. She had a glass of wine in her hand and she rose to kiss Charlie. "Well, Mullins, how did it go?"

"It was tough, Gina. I was raised with those guys. We played football and sandlot baseball together. I went to their weddings. In some cases, I listened to their problems as they courted the girlfriends who later became their wives. I know how hard they worked and still work. It's not just Shaw, it's the whole damned situation. The same thing they fear is what is happening in Detroit, Sandusky, Akron, Milwaukee, and other industrial cities. I did what I could to calm them down, but it's a far bigger problem than I can solve. In the end, I think they were all calmer knowing that no one is planning to eliminate their jobs."

"You did what you could do, Charlie. Nobody can ask more."

"Yeah, I know Gina. It's just tough when it happens to good people who are your friends. They feel betrayed and they need to strike out at someone or something. They see their way of life and everything they know being taken from them and they are powerless to do anything about it. I was always a kind of security blanket for my friends because of my contacts with the top levels of the company. Now I am the guy who set up the IPO that has them all scared shitless. I feel like a traitor."

"Charlie! You can't say that about yourself. You know as well as I do that Phillip Shaw could have taken that company public, shut it down, or sold it to Romania whenever he damned well felt like! If you did anything, it was to try to make sure the sale kept your friends in their jobs. We both know that Phillip Shaw doesn't give a shit – excuse my French – about those people.

His concern is that he does not put them out on the street because it will fuck up – excuse my French again – his chances to get elected. Go easy on yourself Mullins. You can't save the world or even your small circle of friends, at least not as an executive of Shaw Corporation. You're just a cipher, Charlie – an expendable part of Shaw. Kill the illusion, Charlie, kill it or it will kill you!"

"You're right, Gina. It's arrogance on my part. I just have to learn to accept my limitations. I have to move beyond Shoreville and the fact that I placed myself as 'savior'. I did what was in my power to do."

"Right, my dear, and it was a lot more than many others could or would do. No matter what happens, you know you gave it your best shot. That's all you can do."

"I love you, Gina. It's the one thing I am certain about in this whole situation. We are going to have our life together."

"Well said, Mullins. I can deal with that!" Gina kissed him and held him tightly. He relaxed.

XXXIX

The IPO was highly successful. It was over-subscribed and the strike price of $16.50 per share was exceeded by just over $7.00 and the deal closed at $23.76 per share – 20% over the strike price. Phillip Shaw and his family came out with a few billion dollars of windfall. The new owners, a consortium of pension funds and insurance companies announced quickly afterward that they would make no changes in the current management of the company. This was a portfolio investment as far as they were concerned and they had no interest in getting involved in day-to-day management unless returns turned south. They were content with the management team Phillip Shaw had put in place and said so publicly and enthusiastically.

Phillip Shaw and his family were extremely satisfied. They picked up a few billion dollars more than they had expected when the strike price had been exceeded. There was visible relief on the faces of Shaw employees when they heard that the new owners were content to let the current management team continue to run the company.

Fred Perkins was strutting around the company like he was the new owner. He was no longer wearing his brown suits. He had purchased some grays, blues, pin stripes and muted plaids. He was still his normal unpleasant self and continued to bully everyone beneath him and suck up to everyone above. But he now had a full head of steam. He was a survivor, or so he thought.

It was in the aftermath of the IPO that Charlie Mullins mysteriously disappeared. He did not show up for work the day after the IPO. Fred Perkins dispatched Laura Metzer to check his office. Laura noticed that all of the desk drawers were empty and none of Charlie's personal effects were to be seen. Calls to Charlie's home met only with his answering machine and the calls were not returned. Laura told Fred what she had seen and Fred was perplexed. Was Charlie taking an unauthorized vacation? Fred's new bosses would not like that. Neither did Fred. Charlie had always checked with him before taking time off. This was highly unusual behavior and Fred was concerned – not for Charlie per se but for what Charlie's behavior would mean for him. Charlie was a high level subordinate who did not normally behave that way.

Laura suggested that perhaps it might be a good idea to call the police. She said that perhaps Charlie had had an accident and was in a hospital unable to identify himself. Perkins went ballistic. The last thing he needed was to have to report a missing person. He could see the headlines in the local papers: "Local Shaw Executive Goes Missing". No, he would not call the police, at least not yet. Before he did anything, he would check with his bosses, the new owners represented by a new Board of Directors.

Charlie also did not show up in Shoreville for bowling league night or softball practice. His friends were concerned but did not know who to call. Charlie had always been so private that no one in Shoreville knew any of his friends or contacts outside his home town.

Bill Gallagher commented to Sharon that Charlie had not showed up for either bowling or softball practice and he was worried. Sharon volunteered that he was probably just shacked up with that "hussy" from Philly and that he would soon show up. "C'mon Sharon, I'm really worried. I called his office and they told me he was not in. They wouldn't say if he had been in during the past few days, but I suspect from the way they talked to me, he has not."

"Oh, Bill, quit being so damned dramatic. People like Charlie don't just disappear. Maybe he is just chilling out but I am willing to bet it's that woman. He'll show up once he's screwed his brains out. He was acting kind of strange in recent months anyway. Maybe he wants to get fired."

Fred Perkins decided to call Bill Cummins at Wexler & Santori to see if he had talked to Charlie recently. "Bill? Fred Perkins here. I've got a bit of a problem here. It seems that Charlie Mullins has not been into the office since the IPO. Have you talked to him recently?"

"No, Fred, the last time I talked to Charlie was just before the IPO. He called to congratulate me on the work we did and said that you were the point of contact in the new company. I thought that was strange since you had said nothing to me and Charlie had always been our contact at Shaw. But I figured the new management team might have made some changes and we would hear about them soon enough."

In spite of his concern, Perkins could not avoid puffing up. "Well, Charlie was right that I am the new point of contact, but I'm calling because I can't seem to find him anywhere. He's not at home and he hasn't been to the office. Do you think he might have snapped or something? I mean he had been under a lot of pressure."

"No, Fred, Charlie is not the 'snapping' kind. There must be some explanation. If I learn anything I'll get back to you."

"Good, Bill." Perkins rang off. He was not the type to say "thank you".

Bill Cummins put the phone in the cradle and sat for a few minutes trying to figure what might have happened to Charlie. He was a private person for sure, but he was never irresponsible. There must be a reason for his disappearance. He picked up the phone and dialed Warren Carpenter. "Warren? This is Bill, I'm fine and you? Listen, I just got a strange call from Fred Perkins over at Shaw. He asked me if I had seen Charlie since the IPO. It seems the guy has not showed up for work for several days now. I've known Charlie for years and this is completely out of character for him. Did he say anything to you after the IPO?"

"No, Bill, on the contrary. He called me on the day of the IPO and congratulated me on the sale. He sounded perfectly normal. We talked about the overprice and I told him that Phillip was highly satisfied and would certainly speak to the new Board of Directors about him. He thanked me for that and said goodbye. I haven't heard from him since."

"OK, Warren, thanks. If you do hear from him, will you give me a call? I tried his house but I only got the answering machine."

Warren Carpenter was sly. He had to be to have been the Shaw family's personal attorney for so many years. He decided that Charlie's disappearance might be significant and that he would take it upon himself to hire some private investigators to try to determine Charlie's whereabouts. He suspected that Charlie's disappearance would have to be related to the IPO. There was no other explanation other than the fact that Charlie had snapped from the pressure and he did not believe that for a minute. Charlie was not the type to snap easily. There was something else behind his disappearance and Warren Carpenter did not feel comfortable about it. He instructed the investigators to interview all of the companies that had been acquired There might be some leads from the months leading up to the IPO that might prove worth following.

He called back Bill Cummins. "Bill? Warren. I tried calling Charlie's house and only got the answering machine. I called the accommodation number he got in Philly and it has been disconnected. Do you remember the name of that friend of Charlie's at the bank? You know the one who was coordinating the search for the companies to acquire?"

"Sure, Warren, his name was Joey Esposito. Nice kid! Why?"

"Nothing right now, but I'd appreciate it if you would go back over the records of the companies we bought. Check out the shareholders again. I'll get back to you."

"You think Charlie's done something crazy, Warren? I never figured him for the type, but I'll check anyway."

"Thanks, Bill. Keep your eyes peeled for anything unusual about the companies. Something we might have missed when going over the numbers."

The next day Warren called Joey Esposito at his bank. "Mr. Esposito, my name is Warren Carpenter. I am the family attorney for the Shaw family. Can you talk for a few minutes?"

"Sure," said Joey, "is this related to the IPO?"

"Well, I don't know yet. I am trying to find Charlie Mullins. It seems he has just disappeared. He has not been to his office and he doesn't answer his home phone. Bill Cummins told me you are a friend of his. Have you heard from him recently?"

"No sir, I talked to Charlie over the phone the day before the IPO. He didn't say anything about taking time off or anything like that. He just congratulated me on the companies we referred to Shaw. Charlie was a classmate of mine at LaSalle and we have been good friends since college. Do you think something might have happened to him?"

"It's a little early to entertain those kinds of hypotheses Mr. Esposito. Tell me, did Charlie ever propose anything unethical to you?"

"Charlie? What do mean unethical? Charlie is straight as an arrow, Mr. Carpenter. I don't think he would even know *how* to propose something unethical. In college he would rather fail an exam than cheat. Unless he went nuts or something, I would say that Charlie would never make an unethical proposal to anyone."

"Well, suppose it was something that did not *seem* to be unethical, say a kickback from your bank for buying firms you recommended?"

"Oh God no, Mr. Carpenter, in the first place the bank would refuse to accept such a proposal. We've never done business that way and we certainly would not have done that with the Shaw Corporation. Our only expectation was to be able to work with Shaw after the IPO. Charlie would know better than to even suggest that sort of thing to me and I don't think it would occur to him anyway."

"Come now, Mr. Esposito, yours would not be the first bank to double dip on the fees. I'm not making any accusations. I am just trying to find out why Mr. Mullins has apparently disappeared."

"Well, if Charlie calls or contacts me, I'll tell him you are looking for him. But, like I said, I have not talked to Charlie since just before the IPO."

"OK, thanks for your time Mr. Esposito. Sorry to bother you."

"Ah, Mr. Carpenter…"

"Yes?"

"If you find Charlie, would you be good enough to let me know? We have been friends a long time and now I am worried."

"Not to worry, Mr. Esposito, you will be hearing from me again. Thanks for your time and goodbye." Carpenter rang off before Joey could answer.

Carpenter made a note on a pad next his phone to have the investigators get Joey's home address and put surveillance on his apartment and a tap on his phone.

* * * * *

The next day, immediately after the investigators had left Shoreville following contacts with some of Charlie's neighbors, a woman showed up to put a "For Sale" sign in front of Charlie's house. Sharon Gallagher saw the sign as she drove to school to pick up her children. She stopped and challenged the woman. "What is this? That's Charlie Mullins' house. Nobody told me it's for sale and I'm sure it's not. You'd better remove that sign and get out of here before I call the police."

The woman looked Sharon straight in the eye and said, "Call anybody you like sweetheart. I have a signed statement from Mr. Mullins instructing me to sell his house and everything in it. Feel free to call the cops, but be informed that if you interrupt my legitimate business I'll slap a lawsuit on you so fast your apparently empty head will spin. Is that clear?"

Sharon was tempted to challenge the woman further but thought better of it when she saw the woman's firm gaze. She had not been intimidated and Sharon knew that meant she must be covered. Sharon stomped off to her car and drove off to pick up her children at school. When she got home she immediately called Diane Simms. "Diane? What the hell is going on here? Some woman showed up at Charlie's house and put a 'for sale' sign in front of it. I told her that it was Charlie's house and it was not for sale and she told me to bug off. She said she had written instructions from Charlie to sell the house and everything in it. Now, if he's really telling people to sell his house, he's not disappeared, right? He's around some place."

"Christ, Sharon, he could be anywhere. He could have signed that paper a long time ago or yesterday. Did you see the paper? Was there a date?"

"No, Diane. I was so shook, I didn't think to ask for proof. I'm not sure she would have shown it to me anyway. She was a tough bitch. You know what I'm going to do? I'm going down to the police station. She will have to come back and show the paper to the police and then we will know when it was signed." Sharon left the house and drove down to the police station. Tom Coffee was on duty. "Hey Sharon, what brings you into this place?"

"Tom, are you aware of any authorization by Charlie Mullins to a real estate agent to sell his house and everything in it?"

"Sure am, Sharon. Some woman came in here a few hours ago with a notarized authorization signed by Charlie. The paper authorized her to sell his place, settle all his accounts and bills, and lock it up until somebody bought it."

"Was there a date on the document, Tom? Yeah, I'm pretty sure it was the day the Shaw Corporation got sold. I can't be certain because I was more interested in checking the notary's seal and Charlie's signature than the date."

"Shit!" Sharon exclaimed, "That's the day before he is reported to have disappeared. It doesn't help."

"Help what, Sharon?" Tom Coffee asked.

"Oh never mind, Tom, forget it!" Sharon stomped from the police station back to her car. She drove home and called Diane Simms. "Diane? I went down to the police station to see what could be done about that 'for sale' sign in front of Charlie's place. You know what, that woman had already cleared everything with the police. Tom Coffee was there and he told me that she came in and showed him papers signed by Charlie and notarized. Tom said he thought they had been signed on the day that the company was put up for sale but he wasn't sure. What do you think is going on?"

"Jeez Sharon, I don't have the slightest idea. This is way above both of us. It doesn't seem to me that anything has happened to Charlie, otherwise why would he have sent someone to sell his house? I think we just ought to leave it. It's too weird for me!"

"Bullshit, bullshit, bullshit, Diane! We are not going to leave anything. Charlie has been acting strangely for a long time now. Maybe he has just gone off his rocker. Or maybe it's that Philadelphia hussy that is taking him for a ride. We have to *do* something!"

"Do *what* exactly, Sharon? We don't know where Charlie is. It's like he got picked up by aliens or something. What do we do? I say we just forget about it. We'll know sooner or later what's going on. Chill out Sharon."

"Look Diane, I'm going to find out what's going on. Maybe I should file a missing person report or something. You know, get the police involved."

"Whatever Sharon, I just know that Charlie is missing. Maybe he has good reason, maybe he has taken another job, hell I don't know and I've got my own problems to deal with."

"I'll get back to you Diane. See ya'" and Sharon hung up.

* * * * *

Warren Carpenter thought it might be time to talk to Phillip Shaw about Charlie's disappearance. He was concerned that something might be wrong with the IPO and if that was the case, Phillip's plans for a future in politics could come unraveled. He called Phillip and set up a meeting at the Shaw home.

"Phillip, you remember that Mullins fellow, the one who worked with Bill Cummins and me on the acquisitions?"

"Yeah. What about him?"

"Well, he simply disappeared immediately after the IPO. He never came back to work and nobody seems to know where he is. He's not at home in Shoreville and I just learned that his house has been put up for sale. I called the realtor that announced the sale and they told me that they were handling the entire matter and that Mr. Mullins had left the appropriate powers of attorney for them to handle everything including receipt of payment."

"That's strange Warren, what do you make of it?"

"Well, I don't know yet. I've put some private investigators on the case and I've asked Bill Cummins to go over the companies we bought. I told him to check everything he could think of."

"Do you think something might be amiss with the IPO, something that could prove embarrassing to me?"

"I just don't know yet Phillip. Everybody says that Mullins' disappearance is out of character and I can't think of any reason other than some kind of malfeasance that would cause him to simply vanish. I also called that friend of his at the bank, the one who presented the companies to us. He told me that he and Mullins had been friends since college. I put a team watching his home and I've had a tap put on his phone. The way I figure it, if there is something fishy, he might be in the middle of it and Mullins will contact him at some point."

"OK Warren, it sounds like that's all you can do for the time being. Keep me informed, especially about what Bill Cummins finds out. If there is something wrong with the IPO that would invalidate it, we have a big fucking problem on our hands."

"Yeah, that's my concern, Phillip. If this whole thing goes haywire, every newspaper in the country will cover it."

"OK Warren, stay on top of it and keep me informed."

Warren Carpenter took his leave and went back to his office.

* * * * *

Two days later Bill Cummins called Warren Carpenter. "Warren? Good morning. I think I might have something. I was going over the companies that we acquired and I noticed that each of them had hired management consulting firms during the period we had them on our short list. Each of the contracts called for rather large indemnities if the contracts were cancelled before the work was terminated. The consulting companies are all different but they have one thing in common, they are owned by offshore companies. When I tried to reach the consulting companies I only got attorneys' offices."

"Oh shit, Bill, this smells like yesterday's fish to me. Did you check on the offshores?"

"I went as far as I could Warren. They are owned by other offshore companies that are registered as bearer share corporations."

"Christ! Do you have any idea how much was paid out in contract cancellation fees?"

"It's all here in the work papers – sixteen million dollars."

"You mean we saw it? It was right under our noses?"

"Yeah, it was there all the time and was included in the acquisition price. It was all above board Warren. Nothing hidden from us, from Shaw, or from the buyers."

"Well that's a relief at least. There was nothing hidden in the IPO that would invalidate it or create problems for Phillip. Is that your opinion?"

"Absolutely, everything was transparent. All the costs of acquisition were fully reported and signed off. Fred Perkins reviewed the data and approved the deals."

"What about the bank that presented the companies? Was there anything there?"

"I couldn't see anything. It doesn't look like the bank snookered us. There doesn't seem to be any connection between the offshore companies and the bank, but you really can't tell from the paperwork. I called the companies that we acquired and asked about the contracts. All of them were having management problems, which is why the owners chose to sell. Well before they had talked to the bank they had been approached by the consulting companies that offered to put their respective houses in order either for eventual sale or to reverse their fortunes. When the bank approached them, they decided they would rather sell than continue to try to stay afloat. They told the bank about the contracts, and the bank told us. Nothing had been hidden. We absorbed the cancellation fees and reported the payments in the acquisition documents."

"Well," Warren said, "my first suspect would be that kid at the bank, but he hasn't disappeared. Mullins has. What do you think about the possibility that Mullins is behind this and has pocketed sixteen million for his own account?"

"Well, it doesn't sound like Charlie but it sure doesn't pass the smell test either. And he is gone, so I guess we have to assume that he has done *something.*"

"You think we should report his disappearance to the police or the feds?"

"No way Bill, first of all we have no indication of a crime. Everything was duly recorded and reported. There was no fraud involved in the IPO. Second, we have no proof that Charlie Mullins did anything other than not show up for work. The very best we could do would be to file a missing person report and that would be all over the news in a matter of minutes. It would draw attention to the IPO and there would be an investigation that would go nowhere but would be embarrassing. We will have to handle this ourselves. I'm sure Phillip or the new owners are not interested in filing a criminal complaint against Mullins at this time and there is no evidence for one anyway."

"You're right Warren. We'll have to check this out ourselves. What do you suggest?"

"I've done all I can for the time being. I hired detectives to try to find Mullins and I've put surveillance on that banker's place and a tap on his phone. If he is involved with Mullins in a scam, they will eventually talk to each other."

After talking to Bill Cummins, Warren called Phillip Shaw. "Phillip, Warren here, I think we need to meet again. I have some more information."

Warren Carpenter drove over to Phillip Shaw's home and told him what Bill Cummins had told him. "Well, I'll be damned!" Phillip said, "Do you think that guy scammed me for sixteen million? That takes balls and brains. And you say it was right under our noses all the time? We saw and approved the contract cancellation fees?"

"That's right, Phillip. The IPO was transparent as hell. The new owners got a complete audit report with everything in it. They knew exactly what they were buying so they have no legal grounds for complaint."

"Who signed off on the acquisitions?"

"Fred Perkins did and he looked through the figures with a damned magnifying glass. He saw nothing unusual. Interestingly, he looked at each company as it was presented and not at the whole bunch of them together so he did not notice the pattern of consulting contracts. Even if he did catch them, the contracts were all with different companies so he would not be inclined to suspect anything or recognize a pattern."

"And the kid at the bank, did he have anything to do with the scam?"

"It doesn't look like it at this point. His team found the companies. The bank put out the word that they were searching and the companies approached his team members. Bill Cummins told me that he talked to the companies and none of them said anything about any indecent proposals from the bank or its management. The management contracts were in place before the bank had even talked to them."

"It seems to me Warren that we have to find this Mullins character and talk to him. I'd like my sixteen million back and if he's got it we might be able to make him cough it up. Do you think the police will be involved?"

"I don't see why. So far there does not seem to be any crime. Everything was reported and approved. The consulting contracts are all perfectly legal. The cancellation fees were paid in accordance with the contracts and the beneficiaries of the payments were duly recorded. It's just that we can't identify the ultimate beneficial owners. All we have is a missing person which, in theory at least, is none of our business."

"Except that it is our business, right Warren? It would appear that somebody got sixteen million dollars of my money. I'd like it back."

"Well, my detectives are pretty good. Unless Mullins has departed this planet, they will find him."

"Good, see to it Warren."

* * * * *

Carlo Rizzo had ordered a sumptuous banquet prepared by his cook/housekeeper. Charlie and Gina were about to get married in his home by a judge. Carlo had known the judge for years and was assured that the registration of the marriage would be held until everything regarding Charlie's "disappearance" settled down. He was beaming as Gina entered the room in a white silk sheath dress. He walked her to Charlie, kissed her and delivered her to her husband-to-be. The ceremony was simple and quick and Gina never looked happier. Carlo was beaming and Charlie was clearly the happiest man in the world.

When the ceremony was over Gina turned to her uncle and said, "Thank you Uncle Carlo, this is the happiest moment of my life." She had tears in her eyes. Charlie gave Carlo an enormous bear hug and said "Carlo, besides being an absolute genius, you are the most generous man I have ever met. I am honored to be your son-in-law."

Carlo Rizzo was choked up with emotion. He looked at Charlie and said "You have made my little girl very happy. I want you both to have a wonderful life together and don't forget my grandchildren. I want as many as you can produce!" He laughed and gave Charlie another bear hug. "You're a good man, Charlie and you will have no more cares in this world. I'm glad you met my baby."

They sat down to lunch with the judge as honored guest. Carlo said, "Frank, can you leave the papers with me? I'll get them to you when things have calmed down and you can make the proper registries."

"Not a problem Don Carlo, I'll have a marriage license issued as soon as you give me the word."

They enjoyed the best lunch that Carlo Rizzo had ever had on his table.

* * * * *

Sharon Gallagher walked into the Shoreville police station. "Tom? I'm here to file a missing person report."

"What is this, Sharon?" Tom Coffee asked, "Someone in your family disappear?"

"You know what I am talking about, Tom! I'm referring to Charlie Mullins. Nobody has seen hide nor hair of him for over a month now and nothing is happening."

"Well, Sharon, what does that have to do with you? Nobody else has complained and I have no indications that Charlie's disappearance was involuntary. There were no signs that he was incapable of knowing what he was doing, that he had gone nuts, or committed any crime. He is a grown man who for all intents and purposes just walked off his job. His bills are paid and he has no relatives. Seems to me he is free to disappear if he wants to. What basis do you have for filing a report?"

"The fact that he is fucking missing, Tom, that's the basis!" Sharon shouted.

"Sharon, cool it, you are nothing but a concerned citizen sticking your nose into a matter that doesn't concern you. Charlie Mullins is not related to you, he's not married to you, as far as I know he doesn't owe you any money, and his employers don't seem to be concerned that he has disappeared. So why in the hell should you be filing a missing person report? Go on home, Sharon. Mind your own damned business and don't come back here!"

Sharon stormed out of the police station and went straight to the local newspaper office. She sat down at the desk of May Brown, a local society reporter who covered what little of note ever happened in Shoreville. "May, do you know that Charlie Mullins has disappeared?"

"Well, I had heard some things, but it's not exactly news when a bachelor leaves town. I mean what's the angle here? Charlie Mullins quit his job? That's not exactly the kind of thing that I would bother to report."

"May, he put up his house for sale with an authorization to some real estate company. He has not been seen for over a month. He has not showed up for work and nobody is saying a word. Isn't that weird?"

"Kinda, Sharon, but maybe he served notice to his boss and has taken a job in Seattle. Did you ever think about that?"

"C'mon May, you know Charlie. That's not his style. I know for a fact that he has been seeing some hussy in Philly. Maybe he is in trouble. Maybe he's been shot by some boyfriend of hers or her pimp!"

"Well, if he was shot, why would he be selling his house, Sharon? C'mon, give me a break! What's news about a bachelor dating a hussy? Jesus!"

"Will you check it out or not?" Sharon challenged.

"OK, I'll tell you what, I'll drive over to Wilmington and talk to his boss. If everything seems normal, I'll forget about it and you won't come back here with some half-baked theory, OK?"

"Well, I guess that is as good as I am going to get from you." Sharon said with no small amount of frustration and anger.

"All right, Sharon. I'll check it out and if there is a story, I'll write something. But I think you're delusional. The guy can do whatever he wants with his life."

"OK, just get on it, will ya'?"

"Tomorrow, I promise," May said.

Sharon left the newspaper office with a small amount of satisfaction. At least somebody would check on Charlie.

* * * * *

May Brown showed up to the Shaw Corporation offices at precisely 9-o-clock the next morning. She called Fred Perkins' office and asked Laura if she could meet with Fred for about 15 minutes. She could hear Laura asking Fred if he would talk to May. When she came back to the phone, Laura said, "He said he can see you for a few minutes but with the promise that you will not quote him in anything you write."

"Yeah, sure," May replied, "that's OK."

May took the elevator to Fred's office, identified herself to Laura, and introduced herself to Fred Perkins. "Mr. Perkins, I understand you are Charlie Mullins boss, is that correct?"

"Yes."

"I was informed that Charlie has simply disappeared. After the sale of the Shaw Corporation he just never showed up for work. Is that correct?"

"Well, in part, yes. However, I have been informed by my superiors that Charlie is simply working on some confidential matters related to the IPO. You know there are a lot of filings that have to be done and new strategies worked out for the companies we acquired. I don't think disappeared is really the right word. I understand that Charlie is simply on assignment on a matter of utmost confidentiality and importance to the company. I expect his return when the assignment is finished."

"Are you aware that his house was put up for sale?"

"No, and there is no reason I should be. That strikes me as a personal matter. Why should I be involved in Charlie Mullins' personal business?"

"Understood Mr. Perkins, do you know if Mr. Mullins is alive and well?"

Perkins laughed for perhaps the first time in his life, "Ms. Brown, how many dead people do you know who put their house up for sale?"

"Point taken, well I guess that settles things from my side. No story here. While I am here can you tell me something about the sale of the company? A lot of people in Shoreville would like to know their jobs are secure. At least I won't have driven over here for nothing."

Fred perked up. "You can quote me on this one if you wish, no one has any reason to fear layoffs in this company. We are on a growth trajectory. The new owners have made it clear that this is a portfolio investment for them. They won't get involved in the day-to-day management of Shaw. They have made some new appointments to the Board of Directors and that's it. Everything else is as it was before."

"Thank you, Mr. Perkins. I'll send you the draft of my article. The readers in Shoreville will be happy to hear that news."

Fred Perkins beamed with self-satisfaction.

May Brown took her leave and drove back to Shoreville. At least she had a story for her effort.

She was hardly back to her office when Sharon Gallagher called. "Well, May, what did you find out?"

"I found out that Charlie Mullins is on a confidential assignment for the new owners of Shaw. He is alive and well and working."

"That's a load of crap, May!" Sharon screamed into the telephone. "They're hiding something. What the hell kind of reporter are you? Can't you tell they are hiding something from you?"

"That's enough Sharon, I'm not going to listen to your ranting. The story is that Charlie is working on a confidential matter for his employer. That's not news and it ain't a story so cool it!" May slammed the telephone receiver into its cradle.

Sharon just sat and fumed. She was stymied again and mad as a hornet.

* * * * *

Warren Carpenter called Phillip Shaw. "Phillip, there is nothing at all out there on Charlie Mullins. It's like he just disappeared into thin air. My investigators have come up with nothing. I told them to sit tight until I could talk to you to see what to do next. I still have the surveillance on the bank kid but he just comes and goes normally. The phone tap has revealed nothing except a fairly active love life. No Charlie!"

"Warren, I think I know how to handle this. I talked to my father yesterday and he suggested something. I won't discuss it with you now but have your investigators sit tight until we talk again. I think I know how to find this guy. Meanwhile, keep the surveillance on his friend just to be safe and stay on his phone until we can talk again."

"I'm your attorney Phillip, please don't do anything that could cause you trouble."

"Not to worry, Warren. I will just talk to someone who I am sure can find this guy Mullins. I'll keep you in the loop."

* * * * *

Phillip Shaw parked in the South Philly garage, across the street from a *trattoria* as he had been instructed to do. He was told to go into the *trattoria* and order a glass of Chianti and wait for someone to contact him.

He did as instructed and was sipping his Chianti when a waiter named Johnny approached him, "Mr. Shaw, there is car waiting outside for you. The Chianti is on the house."

Phillip got up and walked outside to see a black Mercedes with deeply tinted windows. A driver was holding open a rear door. "Good afternoon, Mr. Shaw, please get in." The driver's gentle demeanor was totally incongruous with his beefy appearance and what appeared to be a bulge on the left side of his suit jacket.

Phillip Shaw entered the Mercedes. The driver gently closed the door and they left the site of the *trattoria*. The gate to Carlo Rizzo's home opened before they had to stop and they drove straight through. A number of men in suits were busy photographing the Mercedes. "Who are those people?" he asked with anxiety in his voice.

"Probably just tourists," the driver responded. *"Tourists don't wear suits!"* thought Phillip Shaw.

"Not to worry, Mr. Shaw, they can't photograph the interior of this car."

Phillip Shaw relaxed a bit. The last thing he needed was to be seen entering the home of Carlo Rizzo, reputed head of the Philly mafia.

The driver pulled the Mercedes around to the back door of the residence and Phillip Shaw was quickly escorted into the house. He was ushered through the kitchen and into a study off the living room where Carlo Rizzo was seated behind a large and very expensive-looking desk.

Carlo rose to meet Phillip, "Mr. Shaw, I apologize for your having to enter through the rear of my home, but I thought it would not do to have you seen. After all, both of us are well-known to the public for quite different reasons and I would not want to prejudice your bid for the Senate by having it known you visited me."

"Don Carlo, I am honored that you receive me in your home." He reached for Carlo's extended hand and touched it to his forehead. "Thank you. I know you are a busy man."

"Have a seat Mr. Shaw." Carlo pointed to a comfortable chair in front of his desk and Phillip sat down. "What brings you to me, Mr. Shaw? Surely you have not come to ask my business advice, not a man of your caliber and experience."

"No, Don Carlo, it is about another matter. My father suggested I talk to you."

"Ah yes, your father, I have been privileged to help him in the past. He has accomplished a great deal and deserves his retirement. He was always a hard working man and has a good head for business. We never socialized much for reasons I am sure you know, but I have always held your father in great esteem. Please give him my regards."

"Thank you, Don Carlo. I will. He will be glad to know you remember him fondly."

"Now, Mr. Shaw, what's on your mind?"

"I have to find somebody, Don Carlo, somebody who apparently does not want to be found. My father indicated that you might be able to help in such matters."

"It's possible, Mr. Shaw. I have contacts that few others have and we are usually able to find missing persons, especially those who might not want to be found. Why do you want to find this person, if I might ask?"

"I have reason to believe he has embezzled sixteen million dollars of my money."

"Embezzlement is a crime, Mr. Shaw, why don't you just go to the police?"

"Well, in the first place I don't have sufficient proof to file a complaint. Second..."

"You mean you are not sure that he is the one who did it, or you are not sure if the money was stolen?" interrupted Carlo.

"Well, it's a bit of both Don Carlo. I know that sixteen million dollars of contract indemnities were paid by the companies we acquired prior to the IPO and they were paid to offshore companies that have a rather suspicious ownership pattern. We think the money was, ah, skimmed, as it were, from the deals."

"You mean no one knew about the indemnities, Mr. Shaw?"

"Oh no, they were duly paid and recorded in the acquisition documentation. The contracts were legal and the payment of the indemnities was duly noted."

"So there was no embezzlement then? At least not in any legal sense as I understand it. You, I mean the Shaw Corporation, paid the indemnity fees when you acquired the companies. You reported all the costs of acquisition properly, and the investors knew what they were buying. Is that right?"

"That's correct, Don Carlo."

"Then why do you want to find this person?"

"Well, I suspect that he was the one who received the money from the indemnities. You see, the day after the IPO this man just never showed up again at work. No one can find him at his home and now his telephone has been disconnected."

"In other words, an employee has walked off the job without so much as a by your leave, is that it? Is this the first time an employee has simply walked off his job at the Shaw Corporation?"

"No, it's happened before but the conditions in this case…"

"The conditions in this case indicate that the employee might have made a lot of money while working for you, is that it?"

"Well, it's actually my money. You see my company paid those fees."

"But weren't those fees paid for breaking legal contracts? And didn't you recover those in the sale price?"

Phillip Shaw was getting exasperated but he dared not show impatience with Don Carlo Rizzo. "Well yes, but it just looks to me like the contracts were set up to ensure the payments when we acquired the companies."

"And you have proof of that?"

"Well, no. But I have been in business for long enough to know that this whole thing smells funny."

"Well, so who is this person you want to find?"

"He's a former financial executive with the company. He worked on the IPO. His name is Charlie Mullins and he lives, or lived, in Shoreville, New Jersey."

"Irish, huh? What you described as embezzlement sounds like the kind of thing that only a Sicilian could cook up." Carlo let a wry smile cross his face.

Phillip continued, "I want to find this guy and get my sixteen million dollars back."

"What if you are wrong, Mr. Shaw? Suppose this fellow never took the money in the first place? Maybe he just got tired of working for a living and went off to the backwoods of Montana."

"With all due respect, Don Carlo, I've been in business a long time. I can tell when a deal smells bad and this one really stinks. Mullins was the guy who did all the due diligence on the deals. He reviewed all the numbers. He was in a position to benefit if he was so inclined. And his disappearance indicates to me that he was, in fact, so inclined. He's got sixteen million dollars of my money and I would like to get it back. Can you help me, Don Carlo?" Phillip added the plea at the end of his statement because he realized he was becoming a little forceful and one did not do that with Don Carlo Rizzo.

"Mr. Shaw, would you indulge an old man with some brief comments before I answer your question?"

"Of course, Don Carlo."

"When I came to this country I was just a dumb, poor 'wop' kid. Other kids made fun of my accent and my lack of knowledge of English. I learned. I studied. A Sicilian priest took me under his wing and helped me learn to speak English properly. I pursued the American Dream and took a job when I finished high school. It was in construction. The engineer in charge of the project was stealing from me by shorting my wages. It was nothing like what you say Mr. Mullins did. He simply signed for one thing and paid another. I solved that problem and it's of no interest to either of us now how I did it. But the one thing I learned from that experience is that people, especially those in power, have a sense of entitlement that somehow does not seem to be justified. You say the sixteen million dollars is yours. However, the papers show that the money was paid out for the cancellation of duly constituted contracts with the companies that you bought. You believe that this fellow Mullins received that money and you say that you are entitled to it." Don Carlo had a menacing look on his face that caused Phillip Shaw to feel real fear. "You want me to find this Mullins person so you can take from him what might not even be yours to take. You come to me because you don't have enough proof to file a complaint with the police. You have accused him because you feel that he has violated your sense of entitlement. You are a rich man, Mr. Shaw, you made a few billion more than you even expected to on the sale of your family's company, and you begrudge a lousy sixteen million dollars to a man that you are not even sure took the money in the first place. Do you think you are being reasonable Mr. Shaw?"

Phillip Shaw was ashen. He was both angry and frightened.

"Let me continue, Mr. Shaw. You have come to me because you think I am just some dumb guinea who will punch the money out of this fellow Mullins. You obviously do not have a legal right to the money or you wouldn't be talking to me at all. The fellow Mullins has stepped out of line in your mind. He has violated your sense of entitlement because he is Mullins and you are Shaw. Who the hell does he think he is, right? Moreover, it is entirely possible that he simply hustled you and that leaves you mad as hell, doesn't it? Imagine some dumb mick from Shoreville putting one over on Phillip Shaw. Who does he think he is? Am I right, Mr. Shaw, is that what this is all about?"

"No, Don Carlo, it's not that at all it's just...."

Don Carlo's voice grew cold and Phillip Shaw was scared out of his wits. He had not expected a lecture from this man. He saw the cold in Carlo's eyes and it sent a chill through his body.

"Relax, Mr. Shaw, I'll find this Mullins for you. You look like you could use a drink, would you like a glass of wine?"

"Thank you, Don Carlo, yes that would be nice." Shaw wanted only to be out of Carlo's steely gaze.

"Frankie, get a couple of glasses of wine for me and Mr. Shaw, please."

Carlo's beefy bodyguard disappeared into the kitchen and returned with a fine red Tuscan wine and two glasses. Phillip Shaw's hand was shaking as Frankie filled his glass with a wry smile on his face. Carlo took his glass and said, "Salute, Mr. Shaw we will find Mr. Mullins for you."

Phillip Shaw relaxed a bit and said, "I thank you Don Carlo, thank you. I will pay whatever you require."

"Oh no, Mr. Shaw, I would not think of charging you a cent to find Mr. Mullins. It so happens that he is in this house right now so there is no work involved."

Phillip Shaw turned white. "What?" his voice cracked. His hand started to shake uncontrollably and Frankie walked over and took the wine glass from him before he shook its contents all over the floor. "He's here? What do you mean he's here, Don Carlo? I don't understand!"

"Mr. Shaw, please calm down. Charlie Mullins is my son-in-law. He married my adopted daughter just a few days ago. He is staying here in the house and I think when you hear the rest of what I have to say, you will not share the information with anyone. Am I right?"

"Ah, uh, yes, you're right Don Carlo. Of course you are right. But I don't understand. You said he is your *son-in-law*?"

"Surely you know that Italians have kids, Mr. Shaw. In fact we are known to have lots of them. Unfortunately, I only had one – my sister's daughter. She is beautiful and she fell in love with Mr. Mullins. Now tell me something Mr. Shaw, how long do you think Mr. Mullins would have worked for your company once he married the daughter of the alleged head of the Philadelphia mafia? Would the Shaw Corporation keep him on its payroll? Would the FBI give him a security clearance to work on Defense Department contracts? I would think that if his connection to me was known and he was still working for the Shaw Corporation he would be given his walking papers. No one would say it was because of his wife, but he would be on the street, am I right?"

"I suppose that is what would happen, yes."

"You know Mr. Mullins and I am sure you saw him as an honorable fellow, hard-working and loyal. But you would not have been loyal to him, Mr. Shaw. For reasons related to your business, you would have to put him on the street. Nothing personal, just business. But for Mr. Mullins it would be a highly personal matter. His chances would be zero of ever working in finance for a large company. His career would go to hell, and all because he fell in love with the wrong woman. We Italians are romantic, Mr. Shaw. Mr. Mullins fell in love and it was with my daughter. I had to see to his welfare."

"You mean you...."

"Let's just say I gave Mr. Mullins the benefit of my experience."

"Now, as to your plans for Mr. Mullins...."

"No, Don Carlo, I didn't know he is your son-in-law, I mean I never...."

"Relax Mr. Shaw, I'm not the thug you think I am. I have a proposal to make. You plan to run for the US Senate. It would not do for people to know that the son-in-law of a mob boss, which is what the papers call me, was involved in the choice of your acquisitions. Your IPO was an enormous success and your reputation is excellent. Frankly, I think you will make a fine Senator. You are certainly not going to really miss sixteen million dollars. That's the kind of luxury you can afford and for which you should be thankful. But Mr. Mullins is a working stiff. He can certainly use the money, assuming of course that he has it. My proposal is that we simply forget the matter. No one knows it happened. Nothing illegal took place. Mr. Mullins should be allowed to resign from the Shaw Corporation and get on with his life. In exchange, I will see to it that you have as much discreet support from me as you need to win your seat in the US Senate."

Phillip Shaw knew when he had come across a better negotiator than he was and he knew when he had been outfoxed. He also knew that everything that had just been said would never leave the room. His face visibly relaxed. "Don Carlo, I can accept your proposal and I hope you will forgive me for the accusation against your son-in-law. This has all been an unfortunate misunderstanding and I agree that we should forget about it. No one has been hurt."

"I thought we could come to an agreement." Don Carlo's face turned soft again. "We should seal this bargain with a toast. Frankie, bring us another two glasses of wine, please."

Phillip Shaw's hand did not shake this time. He smiled at Carlo Rizzo and held up his glass, "I salute you sir, congratulations. It was a master stroke."

Don Carlo merely said, "Thank you, Mr. Shaw, *salute*".

When they finished their wine Don Carlo said, "My driver will take you back to your car, Mr. Shaw. Please give my best regards to your father. He is a good man."

"I will do that, Don Carlo, and please tell Mr. Mullins that I will arrange for him to submit his resignation dated for the day immediately after the IPO. He merely has to prepare a letter and have it delivered to me. I'll discuss it with the new owners."

"Thank you, Mr. Shaw and good luck to you in the elections."

Phillip Shaw was escorted through the kitchen to the black Mercedes waiting for him. Frankie drove him straight to his car in the parking garage. Phillip Shaw got into his car and thought, *"What the hell, sixteen million is not so much compared to being a US Senator!"* He smiled and started his car and left the garage.

* * * * *

Carlo Rizzo walked back to the guest room where Charlie and Gina had been staying. He entered smiling and said, "OK Charlie, you need to write a letter of resignation today. It's all been worked out. Phillip Shaw will handle the formalities and your severance package. Date the letter for the day after the IPO. You can use whatever reason you want for resigning. Just make it positive. This is all being done in a highly professional way and you are simply going off to pursue other career options. That sound OK?"

"Wow, Carlo, it's that simple? Phillip Shaw rolled over on the sixteen million? How did you convince him to do that?"

Carlo's eyes twinkled and he said with a mock mafia accent, "As Don Corleone would say, 'I made him an offer he couldn't refuse'" and broke out laughing. When he stopped laughing at his own joke, he turned to Charlie and Gina and said, "You kids can go public now, too. It doesn't matter now who knows that you love each other. As soon as the transaction is finished and your resignation accepted, I will have the judge record your marriage and issue a certificate. It's done!" Carlo Rizzo smiled and hugged Gina and Charlie. "I think I'm gonna retire next year, you know that? I want to play with my grandchildren so get busy!"

* * * * *

Charlie's letter of resignation was accepted by Fred Perkins without Fred understanding anything that was going on. He received a call from Phillip Shaw followed by a call from a new member of the Board of Directors instructing him to prepare an answer to Charlie's letter expressing the company's regret at his departure and wishing him luck in his new career.

Fred had better sense than to ask what it was all about so he just did what he was told. Laura typed the letter for Fred, smiling the whole time. Charlie had broken out. She didn't know how but he broke loose and that was enough for her.

Warren Carpenter received a call from Phillip Shaw telling him to call off the investigation and the surveillance and phone tap on Joey Esposito. Carpenter knew enough to not ask why. If Phillip wanted to tell him he would. His job now was to get Phillip elected to the Senate and if nothing more was to be said about Charlie Mullins, that was it. Warren called Bill Cummins who was also wise enough to know what he did not need to know. He filed the work papers of the acquisitions and did not bother to discuss the matter further. He poured himself a scotch and silently toasted Charlie and wished him luck. He knew they would eventually get together once everything had been forgotten.

Charlie had one thing left to do and he dialed Joey Esposito's number. "Joey?"

"Holy Christ, Charlie, where the hell have you been? The whole goddamned town has been looking for you."

"I know Joey; I have to talk to you. I think you are the guy who might wind up getting the short end of the stick when everything is settled."

"What are you talking about Charlie?"

"Meet me at the *trattoria* tonight. I'll fill you in. I've got some news for you. Be there around 8-o-clock."

"Sounds mysterious, Charlie, would you like to give me some more information?"

"I'll tell you everything tonight." Charlie rang off.

XL

Charlie and Gina arrived at the *trattoria* at 8:15. They walked in holding hands. Johnny the waiter had a huge smile on his face as he pointed them to Joey's table. Joey's shock was visible as he saw Charlie and Gina walking toward him. They sat down and Johnny quickly showed up with a bottle of wine and two additional glasses.

Joey was flustered, "Charlie? Gina? Wha…"

"Easy Joey, you started this whole thing, you know."

"What are you talking about, Charlie? Are you and Gina going together?"

"No, Joey, we're *married*."

"Charlie, this is a lot for me to put together. What the hell is going on? You two are *married*?"

"Yeah, and to each other, if you can believe it," Gina laughed.

"Joey," Charlie began, "did you know who Gina was when you introduced us?"

"Of course, I'm from Philly. I know who Gina Ferelli is – ah Mullins now I guess."

"Why didn't you tell me, Joey?"

"You remember what I told you Charlie when you asked about Gina? I told you that she would tell you about herself if she felt like it and when she was good and ready. It's not up to me to be talking about other people. I've known Gina for years and she is a great gal, but I'm not gonna run around telling everybody I know who her uncle is. Everybody knows that anyway – except maybe some micks from Shoreville!" Joey laughed.

"Well, Joey, as you can see, I owe you a big favor. We both do. You may have heard that I resigned from the Shaw Corporation after the IPO."

"Yeah, I heard something to that effect." Joey said.

"What else did you hear, Joey?"

"Knock it off Charlie. We go way back, remember? Yeah I heard some comments. They were not really about you. They were more about our friendship and my being picked to find some acquisition targets."

"That's more or less what I figured, Joey."

"Yeah, well it's nothin' I can't handle Charlie. You know me."

"Joey, you introduced me to the woman I married. It was the best thing you ever did for me. I put you in the middle of something that has not done justice to the favor you did me. Am I right?"

"C'mon Charlie, we're friends. I don't hold anything against you. You didn't mess anything up."

"Maybe not Joey, but you will sooner or later hear some things that will make you think I used you. I didn't. I wanted to help your career. But I realize now that I probably did not. No one will ever tell you that your career might be stunted because of our friendship and your work on the acquisitions, but it will, believe me."

"So, I'll quit and get a job somewhere else. Fuck 'em!"

"That's my Joey! South Philly tough! Well since you plan to quit anyway maybe you might want to come and work with me."

"What are you talking about, Charlie? My understanding is that you are now gainfully unemployed."

"Joey, I've got some money to invest and I plan to set up an asset management company here in Philly. It won't be a big bank. I plan to make it a private asset management firm. Obviously, my marriage to Gina will draw the attention of the feds so I don't think I should be running the operation."

"Yeah, well I can appreciate that. You might be marked for the occasional harassment." Joey chuckled.

"Would you like to run the company, Joey?"

"No one will know that I am the investor. I have a structure that will protect the ownership of the firm from becoming known. You'll be your own boss and share in the profits. What do you say?"

"Joey Esposito front for Charlie Mullins? You bet your ass! I'm in. I hate that goddamned bank anyway. Shake on it!" Joey offered his hand to Charlie.

"Done," said Charlie, "I'll get the paper work drawn up and have an attorney take care of the registries. It will take a couple of months, and then you can quit the bank."

"Thanks Charlie. I don't know what else to say. You won't be disappointed. And man, am I ever glad you two guys found each other. As my old Sicilian grandfather would say, 'It's the thunderbolt.' I'm happy for both of you. Now let's eat something, I'm starved!"

* * * * *

The following week Charlie drove over to Shoreville for league night. He walked into the bowling alley like he had always done and his buddies froze in their tracks. Artie Samuels was the first to speak, "Look what the wind just blew in! Holy shit, the mystery man returns. You mind tellin' your friends where the fuck you been, asshole?"

Charlie laughed, "Not at all, Artie. After the IPO I quit my job at Shaw and the next day I got married. I've been on my honeymoon!"

Bill Gallagher piped in, "You quit your job and then got married, Charlie? Isn't that kind of assbackwards? You're not supposed to get married if you're out of a job!"

Charlie laughed, "Yeah Bill, it's usually the other way around. You get a job and then you get married. But if you recall that's what I did the first time and it didn't work!" The group broke out in laughter.

"Good old Charlie!" Tony Mazza exclaimed, "You always have to do it your way!"

"So, c'mon Charlie," Artie Samuels said, "tell us who is the unfortunate broad that married an unemployed executive."

"It's a girl from Philly," Charlie said, "I'll bring her over here one day soon. You'll like her."

"She's got a name, right?" asked Artie.

"Of course, it's Mullins."

"Oh bullshit, Charlie, I mean her goddamned maiden name. You know the one she had before she had the bad luck to run into you."

"It's Ferelli – Gina Ferelli."

"Wait a minute," Bill Gallagher said, "isn't she....I mean that name sounds famil..."

"Yeah, Bob, that's her. Carlo Rizzo's adopted daughter."

"Holy shit," said Artie, "you don't do anything by half measures do ya'?"

Charlie laughed but noticed that the group had now gone serious. They were now with the son-in-law of a very powerful man. "C'mon guys, this is the same Charlie you always knew. Relax."

Charlie could sense the tension dissolve and Tony Mazza said, "OK, a round of beer for everybody. Charlie Mullins got married again!"

"Listen guys, I'm not gonna hang around to bowl tonight. I just came by to tell all of you the news. You're my buddies and always will be. I'm happy and I hope you are all happy for me. Now I'm going home to my bride if you don't mind."

"Oh my God, pussy whipped already!" Artie Samuels cried out. "I guess we'll never see you again Charlie Mullins!"

"I'll be around, Artie. Not to worry."

Charlie pulled Tony Mazza aside as he was leaving and said, "Tony, thanks for being a buddy. You were right that there is nothing like making love to the woman you really love. Tell Marie hello for me."

"Will do, Charlie, and best of luck to you."

Charlie drove back to Philly to what was now his and Gina's apartment.

* * * * *

Bill Gallagher could hardly wait to get home to tell Sharon the news. She had been so obsessed with Charlie's disappearance, she would be glad to know he showed up. Sharon had been in a foul mood the past few days. Bill burst into the living room where Sharon was glumly staring at a TV screen. "Sharon, guess who showed up for league night?"

"I give up Bill, who? Peter Pan?" she answered with sarcasm.

"Nope, Charlie."

Sharon almost jumped from the sofa. "Did you say Charlie? Charlie Mullins? He just walked into the bowling alley, just like that?"

"Yeah, can you believe it? He quit his job at Shaw the day after the buyout, got married and has been on his honeymoon. He came in to tell us all. What a story, huh? I guess that explains why he put a for sale sign on his house and hired an agent to sell it. He was off on his honeymoon!"

"Right, Bill, and you believe in the tooth fairy too, yeah?"

"C'mon Sharon, aren't you happy for the guy?"

"How should I know? Who did he marry?"

"He married a girl from South Philly, and get this, her maiden name was Ferelli – Gina Ferelli."

"So, who is Gina Ferelli, Bill, some South Philly wop broad?"

"Careful Sharon, she's the adopted daughter of Carlo Rizzo."

"Carlo Rizzo, Carlo Rizz…holy shit, Bill, that's the name of the mob boss in Philly."

"The same, Sharon. She was the girl we saw Charlie with in Philly that time. Now I recognize her. She has not been in the papers often, but the one picture I saw of her was beautiful. She is one looker, that's for sure."

Sharon slumped back on the sofa. Her desperate and obsessive hunt for Charlie's girlfriend was over. Worse yet, everyone in Shoreville will know by tonight who is Charlie's girlfriend when the husbands tell their wives that Charlie showed up. No sooner had she finished her thought than the phone rang. It was Diane Simms. "Sharon, my God, did you year the news? Charlie…"

"Diane?" Sharon interrupted, "go fuck yourself!" and slammed the phone on its cradle.

* * * * *

A week later as Charlie Mullins was passing a news kiosk he saw the headline of a local tabloid publication: MAFIA PRINCESS WEDS IN SECRET CEREMONY. He bought a copy of the paper and sat down on a park bench to read the article. It began:

Philadelphia….According to anonymous sources interviewed by this reporter, Mafia princess Gina Ferelli, adopted daughter of Carlo Rizzo, alleged head of the Philadelphia mafia was secretly married to a former financial executive of a major Delaware Valley corporation….

The article provided the date of the marriage as the one on the marriage certificate prepared and filed by the judge who married Charlie and Gina. The article went on to say that they had been married at an undisclosed location. It also said that the couple had been on their honeymoon, also at an undisclosed location. Finally the reporter wrote that the couple was unavailable for comment. Charlie knew immediately that Sharon Gallagher was the "anonymous source" cited in the article. At first he was angry as hell. Then he just broke out laughing. Sharon always had to have the last word and seem to be the person who was "on the inside". She must have been so frustrated that she simply had to tell someone.

Charlie folded the paper and tucked it under his arm. He walked home to Gina. She was going to make her lasagna tonight.